# BRAD SHACK
# GOING HOME

Published under licence by Brown Dog Books and
The Self-Publishing Partnership Ltd, 10b Greenway Farm, Bath Rd,
Wick, nr. Bath BS30 5RL

www.selfpublishingpartnership.co.uk

ISBN printed book: 978-1-83952-683-1

Cover design by Kevin Rylands
Internal design by Andrew Easton

Printed and bound in the UK

This book is printed on FSC® certified paper

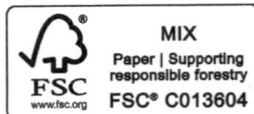

FSC
www.fsc.org

MIX
Paper | Supporting
responsible forestry
FSC® C013604

# BRAD SHACK GOING HOME

## Wagons roll

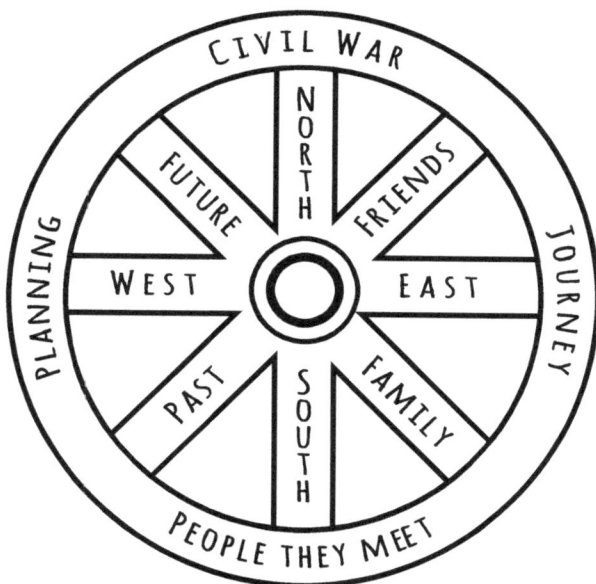

# BRANDON SHACKELL

BROWN
DOG
BOOKS

# Acknowledgements

All the names mentioned in this book are either family members or friends of mine.

Every night before I went to sleep this recurring dream kept coming to me, every night its characters and people on a journey, their lives, their predicaments, their changes, their futures and destinies. It was as though I was living their lives with them, a story that needed to be told. I wrote page after page without stopping, no writer's block for me, the words just rolled off my pen word after word.

I hope you enjoy this story as much as I enjoyed writing it.

Thank you, Cassy, Julie and Suzie for helping me getting it to the next stage.

I would love this to be turned into a TV series, bringing these people alive!

# Contents

# Part One

## The Start of the Journey

### PROFILE: BRAD SHACK

In his thirties, dark hair, slim, 6' 1", fit, can speak a little Spanish. Very handsome with chiselled features. Sergeant in the US Army (Union). A gentle, kind and thoughtful man. Worked on the ranch since leaving school. Jack of all trades. Loves to go fishing, camping in the woods and reading.

### PROFILE: STEVE WRIGHT

Late twenties, sunburnt blond hair, handsome, muscular, 6' plus. Bit of a drifter in life, no plans or commitments, left home at young age. His dad was a dentist and taught his son the trade. Steve was an excellent student, but his concentration wavered. Easily distracted, a daydreamer.

### PROFILE: ARCHIBALD CERIL (JACK) SHACK
### DAD

A big, strong, robust man, arms like a weight lifter, kind and considerate, loves his family and wife, would help anybody at any time.

Enjoys making apple cider, very successful construction business. Best friend Ching-Ching. Well read, laid-back.

### PROFILE: VIRGINIA ANN MARY SHACK
### MUM

Loves her family and husband. Loves to cook, plant, harvest, make apple pies. Worries about Alan's asthma, gets on well with his wife Dianna. Wishes she could see more of her daughter Molly. Hopes Brad settles down, finds a wife and has kids, so she can have grandchildren. Loves Ching-Ching. He's like a brother to her.

## PROFILE: ALAN SHACK
## BRAD'S BROTHER

Youngest of the three children, bad asthma attacks since childhood, married Dianna, no kids, kept ranch going while Brad was away, misses his brother and sister. Fond memories of them all growing up on ranch and playing, will probably stay on the ranch for the rest of his days.

## PROFILE: DIANNA SHACK
## ALAN'S WIFE

Met Alan when they were young, fell in love and got married, loves working with MA, pottering in garden, picking apples, general helping around house, washing ironing, cleaning, very reliable good hearted person.

## PROFILE: CHING-CHING

Chinese ethnicity, but born in the USA. Had trouble fitting in with school mates, trained in kung-fu, loves working and living at the ranch, with Ma and Pa.

Happiest days of his life, now has family, friends, jobs he loves, a roof over his head, regular meals. So happy in life, finds laughter in all situations. A lovely character with a good heart and soul.

## PROFILE: HELEN

Blond, petite, beautiful smile. Widow with two children, James and Ellis, now homeless and jobless moving her family to California for a new start in life. She is so thankful that Brad and Steve have come into her life, and given her hope and confidence that things will turn out ok.

## PROFILE: JAMES

All he ever wanted to do in life was to join the army like his dad. Those dreams have been shattered now, he's lost in life, no direction, doesn't talk much, depressed and feeling low, hopes move to California will be a new challenge in life.

## PROFILE: ELLIS

Cute, pretty girl, with ringlets. Warm hearted, will talk to anybody and bring a smile to their face.

Loves all animals, insects, birds, all creatures, great and small, wants to be a nurse like her mum when she grows up.

## PROFILE: MR GEORGE BLACKSMITH

Considering his upbringing George was a hunk of a man, 6' plus. Broad shoulders huge arms and legs, muscular body, amazing teeth, with a huge broad smile, not much education, but could hold a conversation with anyone, his favourite subject to talk about was the Lord God. He was so happy just to be a freeman, good things lay ahead for George, he could feel it in his bones and soul, the start of a new life. Hallelujah! Praise the Lord.

# Chapter 1

## The Start

**Brad asked**

'Well, buddy, what are you going to do now?'

**Steve said**

'Mmmm!' He thinks. 'I'm going to head for California, probably to lie on a beach, catch some waves, party, and probably get drunk!'

**Brad asked**

'Then what will you do?'

**Steve said**

'Mmmm,' he thinks, 'don't know. I have no plans. Anyway enough about me and questions, what about you?'

**Brad said**

'I'm going home, back to our ranch in California.'

**Steve asked**

'What's it like there?'

**Brad said**

'Like nowhere else on earth. We have a beautiful five-bedroom house, a barn, a cowshed, an orchard, our own woodland, a lake, a stream, a river and a pond, all have fish in of many species, with acres of wide open fields, crops, gardens of fruit and veg.'

**Steve said**

'It sounds amazing, how do you keep it all ticking over?'

**Brad said**

'Mum and Dad are always tinkering with things planting, harvesting. Dad can fix anything, Mum bakes these amazing apple pies. You can smell them from miles away, on a good wind. My brother Alan and his wife Diana do a lot of the work, sometimes he has to take a break as he has bad asthma attacks. Oh also a long-time family friend Ching-Ching, he does a lot of the heavy work, helps Mum with cooking and cleaning, he lives at the back of the house. He's a real character, always joking about, playing tricks on people, you can hear his laughter throughout the house.'

**Steve asked**

'The place sounds amazing. How did your family come about the place?'

**Brad said**

'Dad has been supplying the railways with nuts and bolts for railway lines to be laid in years to come, from east to west and north to south. Steve, after your beach trip, you must come and visit and stay as long as you like. We'll do a bit of fishing.'

Steve buts in, 'Yeah it won't be long before you having me working to pay for my keep.'

**Brad said**

'Yeah but just think of Ma's apple pie.'

**Steve said**

'Yeah sounds good maybe I will visit.'

**Brad said**

'Well Steve we've got our own wagons we'll get some supplies. We might as well travel together. We're heading in the same direction.'

**Steve said**

'Yep, safety in numbers. Ye-hah! California here we come.'

**Brad said**

'Yeah you'd better lock up your daughters because here we come.'

**Steve said**

'I'll drink to that.' With a lash of the whip they set off. They travelled the rest of the day. They stopped next to a stream and decided to make camp for the night, after eating.

**Steve asked**

'Do you have any other members in your family?'

'Yes, we have a sister named Molly.'

**Steve said**

'Now you're talking – carry on.'

**Brad said**

'Forget that. She's married to a very wealthier man, and she lives in Chicago, she's spoiled. Tries to be posh and a bit of a snob.'

**Steve said**

'What about any pretty nieces or cousins even a rich auntie?'

Brad gave him a look.

'OK-OK-OK. Tell me more about the house and grounds.'

'Mum and Dad had been saving up for years. The business was doing well and expanding. When Dad saw the ranch, he knew it would be a wonderful place to bring his children up. The fresh air would help Alan with his asthma, the open fields, and woods to play in. The lake and waters, he could teach his kids to fish and sail a boat, climb trees, build a tree house. Ma could plant flowers, vegetables. The orchard. Mmm. Ma's apple pie, Yum-mee!

'Ma got onboard quickly she could see the potential of the property, they could have their own livestock, pigs, sheep, cattle, chickens. The children would grow up quickly and help with the chores. She decided she would home school them, teach them how to read and write, cook, respect the land and animals on it including the birds, insects, and to appreciate the circle of life and death.

'Not far away was a small town, it had a few amenities, a hardware store, a saloon. It was a growing community in progress. Ching-Ching was the funniest person she had ever met, he found humour in everything you could hear his laughter all over the house. If he dropped a plate of food on the floor he would explode with laughter, with his broken English, he would say many a word wrongly, no point in correcting him. He would just instantly forget what you had said.

'Ching-Ching worked for Dad. As soon as we purchased the ranch, he moved in. He's been a godsend, never moans or complains. Gets stuck into any job that needs doing, works from sunrise to sunset. We couldn't cope without him, he picks apples from the orchard, peels them for Ma. He'll help with the cooking, cleaning, when asked why he works so hard, he replied "I'm free. No more worrying about a roof over my head, where's my next meal coming from, I love my work, I love the people around me, I'm respected, not bullied, I am part of a family."

**'Ma said**

'"Yes, Ching-Ching, you will always be part of this family."

'After the conflict of North and South broke out, Ma and Pa, were visited by high-ranking senior officials of the government. They wanted to use their land to train officers. A map had already been drawn up. They wanted to build huts, so officers and their families could train, and be taught military plans and actions.

'The proposal was to:-

(1)     Build fourteen self-contained huts/shacks.
(2)     With generators to supply electricity to each shack.
(3)     Running water and sewage.
(4)     The wood would come from the woodlands, therefore a giant wood saw would be constructed inside its own barn.

(5)     A boat would be used on the lake and river to teach sailing and landing skills.

(6)     All crops would be planted, and vegetables, so that the officers and families could be fed.

(7)     A corral would be constructed to hold the horses, and a large barn to keep the hay.

(8)     Along with a blacksmith's furnace and anvil.

(9)     A flour mill would be built on the river to provide flour.

(10)    A cowshed erected with milking facilities.

(11)    A chicken shed, to collect eggs, and a slaughterhouse.

(12)    After the conflict was over, anything Ma and Pa wanted to keep would be left on the land FOC anything they did not want would be removed.

'Plus a large settlement fee.

'Soldiers that were to undertake the work would sleep in tents at the back of the property with their own shower block and canteen. Wherever possible local tradesmen would be used, along with any commodities needed.

'Dad could see the potential of local men getting paid work, companies starting up, all could be good for the local area and people. After all, everybody had to do their bit for the war effort.

'Documents had already been drawn up to allow access to all land and properties, except the main house. This would be out of bounds to all personnel, even the major, unless invited in.

'Ma and Pa signed the paperwork. Within days, the whole land was swamped by people, wagons coming and going, tents going up, wood saw churning day and night, people working in the fields. A boat was delivered, horses arrived, cattle, chickens; the locals came and went, deliveries, noise, but in a very short period of time the soldiers left, the tents disappeared.

You'd see the officers ride out in the mornings and return later in the day, the families kept themselves to themselves. Occasionally you'd see a family walkabout but no one ever came to the house, so life pretty well carried on as normal.'

Brad drew into the sand roughly what it looked like:

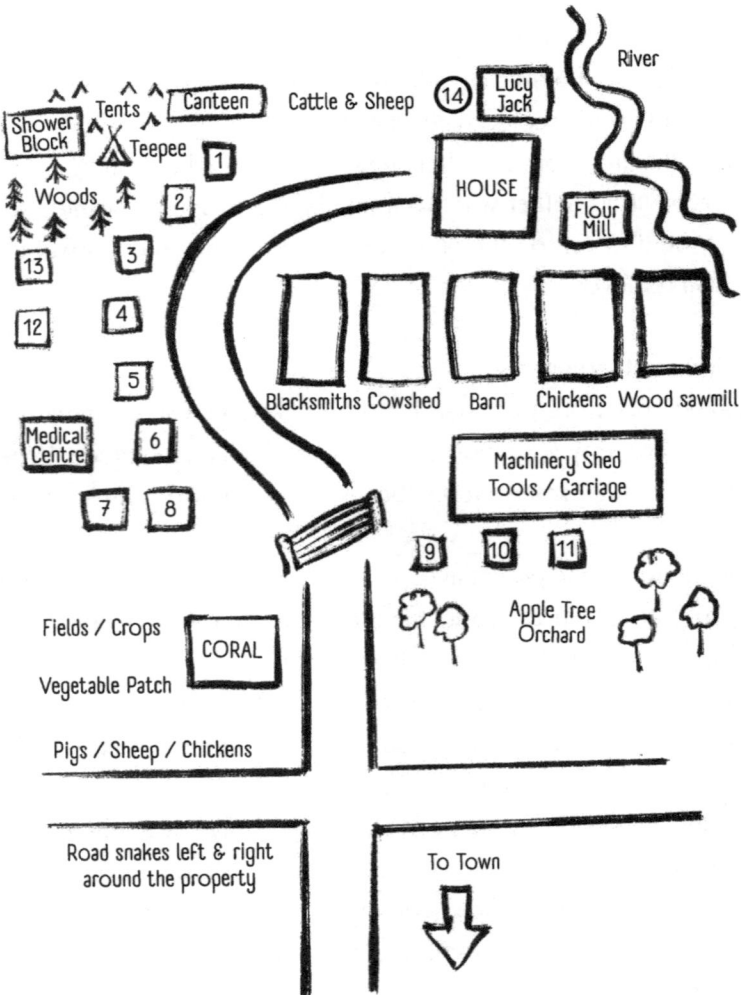

Shower Block | Tents | Canteen | Cattle & Sheep | 14 | Lucy Jack | River

Teepee | 1

Woods | 2 | HOUSE | Flour Mill

13 | 3

12 | 4

5

Blacksmiths Cowshed | Barn | Chickens | Wood sawmill

Medical Centre | 6

7 | 8 | Machinery Shed Tools / Carriage

9 | 10 | 11

Fields / Crops | CORAL | Apple Tree Orchard

Vegetable Patch

Pigs / Sheep / Chickens

Road snakes left & right around the property | To Town

**Brad said**

'It's very difficult to explain you'll just have to come and see it for yourself.'

**Steve said**

'I will, I will, is there any nice ladies that live in the town?' Brad gives him that look again.

**Brad said**

'Just before we turn in for the night I think we should offer up a prayer. (Steve agrees)

Lord hear our prayer. We give thanks for sparing our lives, many good men lost their lives on both sides. God bless our families and keep them safe, and guide us on our travel homeward to help and to care for people along the way, amen (Amen says Steve). PS Lord, if along the way you want to send pretty ladies into our lives that would be OK by us. (Amen.)'

Brad gives one of his stares at Steve, they say goodnight to each other, rollover and go to sleep. Next morning they get up nice and early, pack up their bits and pieces, water and feed horses, and set off on their next leg of the journey.

They'd been travelling a while, when they heard a commotion around the next bend. They sped the horses up.. Around the bend they saw a wagon stuck in a pool of muddy water, with a woman frantically trying to pull the horses forward, with two children up to their knees in muddy water, trying to push the wagon out. Brad and Steve pulled up, jumped out, introduced themselves and offered to help. The woman broke down in tears, mumbling she said, 'I'm Helen, these are my children, James and Ellis.' The kids just grunted.

**Steve said**

'Hi, calm down, calm down we'll have you out of here in a jiffy.' So they attached their horses to the wagon, Steve took charge of the horses. Brad/Helen/James/Ellis started pushing from the back. After a while the horses began to pull the wagon forward, then it lurched forward, all those at the back faceplanted themselves into the muddy water. When Steve went to the back of the wagon they were all standing up dripping with muddy water. You could just see their eyes through all the muck on their faces, Steve roared with laughter, which did not amuse the rest of them.

**Steve said**

'Apparently mud is very good for your complexion.' They all splashed water in his direction and roared with laughter. Steve waded in, picked up Helen and walked her out of the muddy pool, then went back in for Ellis while Brad helped James out.

**Brad said**

'Well I think we should get a fire going. There's access to the river through the bushes, so we can have a swim, get clean, wash our clothes and get them dry.'

**Steve said**

'Yeah and get a brew on. I'm hungry I'll do a stew!' They all went swimming, splashed around, laughed, dunked each other and had a good time.

**Helen said**

'Thank you, guys, one for helping us out of the muddy pool, and secondly my children have laughed for the first time since their father was killed in the conflict.'

**Brad said**

'Right let's get a brew on, start the stew. Later when the kids are asleep we can talk more.'

The meal was an astounding success. Steve and Helen went to wash the dishes together, Brad James, Ellis washed the horses down and fed them.

They all sat around the fire, telling stories talking about school and friends. Steve got his harmonica out and played a few tunes and sung a bit.

The kids were ready for bed, James said goodnight to Brad and Steve and kissed Mum. She said, 'Everything's going to be OK, James. Love you.'

'Love you too, Mum.'

Ellis hugged Brad and Steve, which choked them up. Mum gave her a special hug. 'I'll be in in a minute to tuck you in.' Once the children had settled, and fallen asleep Helen returned to the fire where Brad and Steve were sitting. Steve had made a pot of coffee, which Helen took willingly. Cup in her hands she looked thoughtful. After a few seconds Brad said, 'Helen, what are your plans?'

Helen took a deep breath in, and said, 'I guess I'd better start at the beginning

'I was happily married to Wayne for twelve years. We were childhood sweethearts, we got married, had two wonderful children, rented a little farm house, put a well in, grew some crops. Then Wayne got called up into the army, and our whole world changed overnight. We were getting by, I was a fully trained nurse, and helped and worked for Doctor Curtis.

'What with getting the kids ready for school and picking them up, washing, cooking, cleaning and my job, time flew by. The evenings were always the hardest. Once the children went to bed, sitting alone, wondering where Wayne was, what was he doing right now, time passed quickly as I made children's clothes, cutting stitching material. By ten o'clock I was ready for my bed. I always mentioned Wayne and the children in my prays, and hoped Wayne would return home safe.

'Then that awful day arrived a telegram was sent to us. I'll never forget those words written on it. We are sorry to inform you Wayne Curtis is presumed killed in action. No body found.

'I fell to the floor, was he dead or not? What am I going to tell the children and how? I felt as though the room was spinning I felt sick, and couldn't stop crying. No goodbyes, not to be able to tell him I love him, surely he knows I love him, that last night together I made sure he knew I loved him and so did the children. No body, no funeral, no grave, no father to watch his kids grow, and nurture, teach them and keep them keep safe. No goodbyes, no hugs, no kisses.

'When the children returned home, I just had rivers of tears. I couldn't say a single word I just handed them the telegram, then listened to their shrieks of pain and sorrow. We just all sat together huddled up, nobody talking, just huddled together like a ball of wool. Eventually we went to bed, as I held them, one in each arm, and they cried themselves to sleep, I stayed awake all night just thinking and crying.

'Then Doctor Curtis got sick, I was trying to sort his patients out, with their pills and creams, nurse the doctor the best I could. Then suddenly he passed away. I had to close the doctor's surgery, arrange the funeral, contact family members. If that was not bad enough, while we were at his funeral our house caught fire. We lost everything, furniture, clothes, ornaments, pictures, Wayne's letters, the kids' toys, beds, pots, pans, everything. The only one piece of good news, the wagon and horse were away from the house, so here we are today. Me, two kids, a wagon a horse, and our neighbour made us some sandwiches, a pork pie and some cake. What we wear is all that we own.'

**Steve said**

'So where you heading for, when we came across you in the muddy pool?'

**Helen said**

'First of all I didn't just drive straight into the muddy pool. Something spooked the horse in the bushes, he just took off. I couldn't control him, he roamed straight into the muddy-pole where he stopped dead. There was just too many memories back home. I'd lost my husband I'd lost my home, I'd lost my job, I'd lost my employer. I felt as though we all needed a new start, a new beginning, a change of scenery, to leave the old life behind. So here we are.'

**Steve said**

'But where are you heading for?'

**Helen said**

'California, I hear there are new jobs, housing, land, beautiful scenery, mountains, lakes and rivers and all year round sunshine.'

**Brad said**

'We're both heading to California, would you like to join us on our wagon train?'

**Steve said**

'Yep there's safety in numbers.'

Brad took Helen's hands and cupped them in his own. He told her all about the ranch, the shacks, and that she could stay there as long as she wanted to help her get back on her feet, make some clothes, get some good food inside of them, some of Ma's apple pie, that not to worry things would work out alright for them. She thanked Brad for all that he and Steve had done for them up to now, to give them a new start in life was all she could hope for in this moment of life, and kindly told Brad that she would love to take him up on his offer. 'But at this moment in time I have little money to offer, but in time I will pay you back in full.'

Brad assured her not to worry about that, it was a pleasure to be able to help. Here Helen said, 'Shall we pray,' all three held hands as Helen said, 'Dear Lord, hear our prayers. Thank you for our food today. Thank you for sending Brad and Steve into our lives, for giving us hope, to see my children laugh and smile again. God bless us all.' Amen, they all said. Brad and Steve both gave Helen a hug, kissed her on her forehead, and told her not to worry about anything. Everything will turn out OK.

Goodnight, they said to each other and went to their beds.


That morning they ate breakfast, packed camp, loaded the wagons, hitched up the horses and got onto the road, Brad leading the wagon, Helen and family in the middle followed by Steve at the rear.

They travelled all morning, stopping to rest horses, have drinks and

Helen's pie and sandwich and cake. It was late afternoon when in the distance they could see a man strapped to a tree.

As they approached they saw it was a Black man. His shirt had been ripped off, he just had his pants on that were saturated in blood. He had been bull whipped on his back many times. The blood trickling down his body had attracted flies. He was semi-conscious, drifting in and out of consciousness, the pain and agony clearly clearly visible on his face. Brad and Steve approached him with caution, not knowing if he had committed a crime. Was this his punishment? Was he an innocent man but punished anyway?

**Brad said**

'Steve bring some water, dab it on his lips, don't let him drink straight away it could make him very ill.' Once they'd dabbed his lips, Brad and Steve took the man's weight and cut the ropes binding him to the tree and laid him face down on the ground. By now Helen was already there. As a trained nurse she knew exactly how to treat his wounds, with every touch and dab of his wounds, he gave a yelp or a moan or simply cried out.

**Brad said**

'Let's get him into the wagon and out of the sun.' The sweat with salt in stinging his every wound.

**Helen said**

'Put him in my wagon, I can tend his wounds as we move along. James can steer the wagon, his dad taught him how years ago.' They put him gently into the wagon face down.

**Brad said**

'We need to get out of here as soon as possible. The people who did this to him may come back and there might be trouble.'

## PROFILE: VIRGINIA

Was approximately twenty-two. She'd had an hard upbringing, forever moving around. Her dad left when she was young. Her mum was a singer and moved around a lot, sometimes she was left with grandma to be brought up, her whole life she'd not had any grounding or stability, moving from pillar to post. Restless, not putting down any roots, she wasn't sure what to do with her life, where she was going, or what she wanted to do, but she'd always get her faith in God, attended church regularly, sometimes to ask forgiveness for her sins, or hoping for a sign that things would turn out OK for her.

## PROFILE: FATHER MICK O'FLANAGAN

Father Mick O'Flanagan, born of Irish parents. Mick knew from an early age that he would follow the Lord and do his work if he could. It was like a calling to him. Never interested in material things or savings, buying a house settling down, he always felt he would be a wanderer.
Going where he could do the most possible good, he would give you the clothes off his back if he thought it would help you. Sometimes he believed God spoke to him through his prayers and was guided in life. He would love to have his own parish. A school, a library, just to teach, especially the word of the Lord.

# Chapter 2

## The Pick Ups

The three wagons travelled as far as they could the rest of the afternoon and into the early part of the evening, finally parking up in a triangle shape in case anybody approached them.

Helen needed to stretch her legs and to cool down. It was very hot in the back of the wagon. She managed to get the man to drink some water. She treated his wounds, and bandaged him the best she could.

**Brad asked**

'How's he doing?'

Helen says, 'Better than when we first found him. I think they left him out there to die. Good job we came alone when we did. He's sleeping now, when he wakes up we'll get some food into him and as much water as possible so that he doesn't dehydrate. He may also have sun stroke so I keep dabbing his head with water, to bring his temperature down.'

**Brad said**

'We need to keep a close eye on him, until he can talk and tell us what's been happening. Caution is the word.'

The group sat around the fire and ate a soup of vegetables and the last of the bread, a bowl of soup and a chunk of bread was saved for the mystery man to wake up to.

A few hours had passed, they were thinking of going to bed. Steve said Helen and the kids could sleep in his wagon, he would keep an eye on the man. Brad said good idea, James and Ellis, Steve and Brad went off to arrange the bedding.

As Helen sat by the fire, she became aware of someone behind her, a shadow flicked over the fire. She became scared, but thought Brad and Steve were not far away. If she screamed they would be there in seconds.

Just then she heard this deep, southern voice, it said, 'Excuse me, Mam, but are you responsible for treating my wounds and taking care of me?' She turned slowly to see her patient, the bandages lit up by the moonlight.

She answered, 'Yes I am, how do you feel now?'

'Mam I am so grateful for your kindness and attention. I feel a bit weak, but very happy to be alive. Thank you from the bottom of my heart.'

**Helen said**

'Please sit down we have saved you some soup and a chunk of bread.'

'Glory be to the Lord,' he said, 'my prayers were answered.'

He gingerly sat down on the log by the fire. Helen passed him the soup and chunk of bread. He bowed his head as in prayer, then tucked into his soup, dipping the bread in.

Brad and Steve reappeared, asking Helen straightaway if was everything OK. 'Yes,' she murmured, 'everything's fine, let him get food then we can talk.'

The Black man looked over his soup bowl, terrified of Brad and Steve as though they were going to hurt him.

He soon finished his soup and bread, putting the dish down. He looked at Helen and said. 'Thank you very much, that was delicious. I haven't eaten in days.' Turning to Brad and Steve, he said, 'I would imagine you have many questions. First of all I'd like to thank you for saving my life, you came along just at the right time. I don't think I would have lasted much longer.'

Steve jumped in quickly, 'Have you committed a crime? Why were you tied to a tree, whipped and left to die?'

'Oh brother,' he said, 'the only crime I've committed is the colour of my skin, I'm a hard-working, law-abiding citizen. I don't start any trouble, I'm a peaceful man, and believe in the Lord God. Amen.'

**Brad said**

'Tell us about yourself, your name, where you've come from and where you're going to.'

**Steve said**

'I'll stick some coffee on. I want to hear this.' Helen got up to go see the children.

**Helen said**

'Don't start without me, until I get back.' She soon returned, they all took their cups of coffee and looked at their mystery man. He looked around the group, felt comfortable, no threat here and said, 'My name is Smith, given to me by my boss, my owner. He thought it would be funny to call me Black-Smith so trained me to be a blacksmith, shoeing horses, cleaning out stables, washing and brushing the horses down, I was never allowed to ride one, had to walk the horses everywhere. We were all treated badly not much food to eat, no bed to sleep on long hours, sometimes twenty hours a day, from early morning to late in the evenings.

'When the conflict got nearer to the plantation one night I took my opportunity to escape. I ran like the wind, never stopping to look backwards, by morning I was miles away, as capture would lead to certain death, I learned how to hide during daylight and travel by moonlight, avoiding all troops along the way. I lived off berries and nuts. Once I even found a beehive, got a handful of honey then got chased away by the bees.

'I kept on moving, getting further and further away from the plantation, the further I got away the more I felt like a freeman for the first time in my life. No boss, no rules, freedom to roam and explore. I felt human for the first time in my life, but how long could I wander, where would I go? What will happen to me? I don't care as I'm free, the best feeling in the world, a freeman.'

**Steve said**

'So what name would you like? What would you like us to call you.'
*He thinks, says, 'Any name, I can choose any name I like.'*

**Brad said**

'Yeah, if you've never been given a name since birth I guess you can choose any name you like.'

'I only really know one name and that's George Washington. I heard people talking about him, that he was going to change the world for the better. I'd like to change the world for the better, so I'd like to be called George from now on.'

**Steve said**

'Just George? You can choose a last name as well.'

George thinks, 'I think I'd like to keep Blacksmith. It will always remind of my roots, from where I come from and what's made me the man I am today.'

**Brad said**

'Mr George Blacksmith welcome to our camp.'

**George said**

'That sounds good man.' They all raise their coffee cups and say, 'Cheers George, welcome.'

**George said**

'Yeah man, Hallelujah, praise the Lord.'

**Brad said**

'So George where were you heading for?'

**George**

'I was just taking God's path wherever he wanted me to go, unfortunately I ran into those wicked men who whipped me for no good reason. I guess I was just in the wrong place at the wrong time, but then the good Lord sent you people along to save me. It was not my time to join him yet! He still has plans for me yet.'

Brad tells George why they are on the road and where they are going, he tells him about the ranch, and that they are looking for a blacksmith.

**George said**

'I'm not looking for any charity, man.'

**Brad said**

'No it will be your own business, you'll have your own home, running water, lights,'

George buts in, 'My own bed.'

'Yeah, all the food you can eat.'

**George said**

'Hallelujah, the Lord has delivered, praise the Lord.'

**Brad said**

'And of course you would still be a freeman, with time off, to go walking, fishing anything you'd like to do.'

**George said**

'I'd like to pick some flowers, swim in a lake, but I can't swim.'

Steve says, I'll teach you

'Yeah man,' George says, 'to sleep in my own bed, shower when I want to, choose what food I want to eat, yeah man, pinch me, am I dreaming?'

'No, George, anything is possible.

'Yeah man.'

**George said**

'Good people will you join me in prayer?'

The group say yes, stand up and from a small circle, holding hands.

**George said**

'Oh Lord, hear our prayers, thank you for this day, and for our tomorrows. Thank you for my freedom, and new friends. Hallelujah! Praise the Lord, and God bless us all.'

They retire to the wagons for sleep. 'Goodnight all,' they say

Next morning they are woken by George singing 'That old man river he just keeps rolling along'. Brad is in the leading wagon, followed by Helen and kids. George sits up front with Steve, George, with the biggest grin on his face, says to Steve, 'Don't go over to many bumps, my back is still sore.'

**George said**

'Oh boy I'm so happy to be alive.' Off they go.

They travelled most of the day, stopping occasionally to stretch their legs. Helen attended to George's wounds, which he continually thanked her for, as the light was starting to fade and they were thinking of striking camp. They saw up ahead a lone person sitting under a tree, he was wearing a black gown and some sort of hat on his head. As they approached they could clearly see this was a priest, with his silver cross clearly on display.

**Brad said**

'Good evening.'

The reply comes, 'Good evening to you all, I've been waiting for you.'

**Brad said**

'You have, how did you know we were coming?'

**Priest said**

'God works in mysterious ways.'

**Brad said**

'Would you like to join us for a meal? We are about to stop for a meal, and camp up for the night.'

The priest says, 'Pull up over there, I've prepared a fire and caught some fish for us all.'

**Steve said to George**

'It's as though he knew we were coming. Amen.'

Sure as anything the fire was ready made, the fish were gutted in frying pans, waiting to be lit waiting to be cooked, and a fresh pot of coffee was boiled waiting to be poured.

**Steve said**

'How strange, how could he have known we were coming? And how many were coming. Look, seven fish waiting to be cooked. Interesting, let's get cooking. I'm starving, pour the coffee, George.'

Before they could eat the priest blessed the food, and thanked God for the food they were about to eat, amen, and all tucked in.

Sitting around after the meal Brad said, 'Father by what name do we call you?'

'Father Michael O'Flanagan, a priest for a very long time.'

**Steve said**

'What are you doing in the middle of nowhere, and how did you know we were coming?'

**Father said**

'All in good time, everything will become clear, I was going nowhere in particular, just waiting for God's calling and guidance and you all come along pure coincidence.' He winked at James and Ellis, he said, 'Well you'd better all introduce yourself.

'I'm Brad.'

'Ah,' Father says, 'you must be the leader.'

'Well not really. I'm just on my way home.'

**Father said**

'Ah! You're a good man I can tell.'

**Steve said**

'I'm Steve.'

**Father said**

'I can see you're a little lost in life, you need a little direction, a bit of guidance, I can help with that.'

Steve said, 'I'm fine,' but then thought to himself maybe the father is right.

'I'm Helen these are my children, James and Ellis.'

**Father said**

'Ah! I can see you need some healing and understanding, and explaining, I can help with that.'

'I'm George Blacksmith, very pleased to meet you.

'I'm so glad you survived your ordeal I see only good things happening for you a start of a new life.'

George said amen to that.

'Do you mind if I pray?' said Father. They all stood up and held hands together

'Thank you, Lord God, for bringing us all together, for feeding us, and preparing us for our journey through life, we give thanks and ask for your guidance.' Amen they say. 'Now,' Father says 'I'll be sleeping under the stars tonight, who wants to join me? Stick another log on the fire,' he says.

Next morning after they'd packed their things, Father said, 'So which wagon am I travelling in?'

Brad said, 'So you are coming with us?'

'Yes, yes, yes,' said Father, 'it's my destiny, my calling, after all he said you all need me and laughed.'

Father got in next to Brad, 'I like to guide from the front, you'll be needing a town soon to top up your supplies, there's a town a few miles ahead.'

**Brad said**

'Did you know we were going to be going to this town?' Brad said 'I'm not a fortune teller it's just common sense,' he said with a smirk. They pulled up into the park up.

Father said to James and Ellis, 'Right, you two come with me were going to get some cakes.'

Brad and Steve went to the grocery store, Helen and George went for a wander around the shops. George noticed how friendly people were to him saying good morning. Imagine for him, for the first time in his life, strangers said hello to him. He noticed the colour and shapes of things in the window, for sale, this was a brand new world for him. He'd never shopped for anything, ever in his life.

Helen spotted an old clothes shop, 'Come on, George,' she said. 'We're going in.'

'Yes, Mam,' said George.

There was a pick of old donated clothes in the corner. 'Come here,' said Helen to George holding a chequered shirt up to his body. 'That will fit nicely,' said Helen, and these pair of pants were ideal. George noticed a shiny buckled belt, made from leather.

It reminded him of the old days, and how many times he'd been whipped with one.

Helen said, 'George, take these to the lady at the counter, ask how much they are here's my purse and pay for them.'

George was traumatised, he said 'Go to the counter, ask how much and pay for them.'

'Don't worry,' said Helen, 'I'll be right behind you, if you need any help.'

George stumbled over to the counter shaking, he put the clothes on the counter and said to the lady, 'How much please?'

The kind little old lady replied, 'Don't worry, no charge, they are donated clothes. All we asks for are a few cents, which goes toward feeding the children at the orphanage.'

'Go on, George open the purse and give the kind lady some coins.'

George opened the purse. There was a mixture of different coloured metals he'd never seen money before and certainly never purchased anything. His big clumsy fingers went into the purse. He pulled out a coin, looked at Helen for approval, she nodded yes. George gave the coin, to the lady.

She said, 'Would you like them wrapped?'

George looked at Helen who nodded, in his big deep voice he said yes please. The lady took out some brown paper, neatly folded the two items, placed them on the paper, folded the paper around the clothes, produced some string with the flick of the wrist. The string went right around the package, and left a little hoop at the top, which the lady passed to George.

'Thank you,' said George, he turned to Helen, 'Thank you, Helen,' George said, 'I don't know how, or I don't know when, but one day I will repay.'

'Don't worry, George, wherever I go in life, you will come with me.'

'Thank you, Mam,' said George.

Just as they were about to turn and leave, the lady said, 'Would you like a free lollipop. Everybody who shops with me gets a free lollipop.' She produced a jar with all the colours of the rainbow on with little white sticks sticking out of them.

George looked at Helen, she nodded go on George pick one. George offered the jar to Helen first, who took one. He then offered the jar to the lady, and she took one. George looked in the jar seeing the one he wanted, pulled it out.

Watching Helen and the lady pop it into their mouths, George followed suit, he was hit with this zinging feeling in his mouth, he swallowed and got this sweet sugary feeling. It reminded him of the first time he tasted honey. 'Mmmmm!' George said, with another thank you they left the shop. As they walked out of the shop, George with his little parcel, taking the lollipop out of his mouth he turned to Helen and said, 'This is the best day of my life.'

**Helen said**

'Don't worry, George, you're going to have lots and lots of best days to come.'

'Hallelujah praise the Lord,' said George.

Over at the cake store, Father, James and Ellis were deciding which cakes to choose. 'Now don't forget,' said Father, 'we need to choose a cake for each member of our family.'

James heard what Father had said, but did not respond, Ellis was too excited to even speak.

**Ellis said**

'Mummy would like the strawberry tart, she likes strawberries, and Daddy would have picked the chocolate roll with cream in.' She stopped and paused. 'But I would like that chocolate cookie.'

James hesitated, he wanted Father to pick first, so he could copy him, so he'd look more grown up, although he really wanted the ice cream cone not fresh cream, but sweet-tasting cream. Father pointed at the sugary donuts, saw that James had a frown on his face then pointed to the ice cream cone.

**Father said**

'Maybe us men should have the cone.' James's face lit up.

Father said to the assistant, 'My dear we would like the strawberry tart for your mother, three chocolate cookies for Ellis and five whipped cream cones for us men folk.' They were all put into little white bags.

**Ellis said**

'I'll carry Mummy's and mine, James you can carry the men's.' James liked the sound of that.

Father said, 'We can't eat them now we will wait until the family is together.' By the time Father, James and Ellis caught up with Brad and Steve the wagons were all ready.'

**Steve said**

'That should see us through a few days, we purchased half the store, plus a few surprises.' He winked at Ellis, just then they saw Helen and George walking along, and all waved to each other. Ellis went running up to Mum.

'Guess what we've got, Mummy.'

'Uum cakes,' said Helen looking at the little white bags.

'Yes Mummy can you guess what cake I choose for you?'

'Uumm let me see would it be a lovely strawberry tart, as the little white bag had a strawberry juice oozing through it.'

'Yes Mummy, well done a good choice my favourite.'

'And I got a chocolate cookie.'

'Well don't eat it all at once.'

'I won't, Mummy. Father said we couldn't eat any until our family was together.'

Helen liked that statement, but wondered if Ellis meant her own daddy!

**Brad said**

'You look mighty happy, George.'

**George said**

'Yes sir I am, Helen got me clothes, and a kind lady gave me a lollipop, my first ever, I'm having a wonderful day.'

**Helen said**

'I know you've got bits and pieces for us. How much do we owe you? I want to pay for our share and you, Father.'

**Steve said**

'You need not worry, Helen, it's all been paid for from the war office.' He laughs, gives Helen a smile and a wink. She blushed and lowered her head.

**Father said**

'Mine's been blessed from above, the only payment you owe him, is to believe in him, and say your prayers.'

'We will Father.'

They got into the wagons, Brad was just about to say 'wagon's roll' when Father touched his hand and said, 'Just wait a few seconds.'

## PROFILE: JIMMY

Most people who met Jimmy thought he was a bit of a character. He loved his music, he could play nearly every instrument you gave him, he could even get a sound out of a kettle, or spoons or anything that moved. He loved his violin, the piano he'd play at weddings or funerals.

And he loved to sing the old songs. He had a beautiful voice, and would quite often write his own songs, but most of all, he loved to teach others how to play instruments, or how to sing.

*Jimmy was happy go lucky but dreamed of one day having a family of his own.*

## PROFILE: JACK AND LUCY

Lucy is such a loving and kind person, so caring and thoughtful. Jack is quite quiet and shy.

They always did everything together. Lucy would lead, Jack would follow. Their favourite pastime was fishing, Jack excelled at this. He'd even won trophies for his spectacular fish in weight and size.

Lucy would knit and sew, enjoyed cooking, and was very domesticated. She would sing her heart, much to Jack's annoyance.

Their parents were suddenly struck down with a mystery illness and died within a day of each other. Lucy nursed them to their last hours then she broke and cried for days. Jack to this day has never shed a tear.

## PROFILE: ANDY

He might be down and out now, with no prospects, home or money, but there was a time when Andy was very popular, worked hard as a carpenter very skilled, built hospitals, schools. He could design things in hours, then would work day and night to get them put up.

He lost his way in life when his childhood sweetheart, wife and love of his life was shot dead in an armed robbery at a bank. If only he hadn't asked her to deposit some money that fateful day, she would still be alive to this day, he believed it was all his fault, and carried with him all this guilt. Drink was his only relief.

## PROFILE: KEN

A massive man, built like a lumberjack, heart of gold but misunderstood. He had learning difficulties, some due to his lack of education, working on the farm with his dad was the happiest time of life. He could carry two bales of hay, one in each hand, and toss them up to the top of the barn, he doesn't remember much about his mum, as she left home when he was quite young. Dad looked after him, but died of a heart attack. Ken tried to keep the farm going but got into debt, eventually the bank, and money lenders took the farm away from Ken. Ken use to slip back in at nights to sleep in the barn.

## PROFILE: RUNNING BEAR

Running Bear had also been pushed from pillar to post. Never being allowed to settle anywhere permanently, reservations, high mountain ranges, short supply of crops, he hoped and dreamed of settling down, a place of his own where he could bring his family up, grow, crops, hunt and fish.

Maybe an education for his children in this ever-changing world.

His partner died recently and wondered how he would cope with a small child when he needed to hunt, but he looked forward to his son growing up, so he could teach him to fish and hunt, make fire and to dance, ride horses.

## PROFILE: MR MATSUDA

Of Japanese origin. His whole life he'd been spat at, verbally abused, refused admission to many a dwelling, kicked, punched in the street. He combated this by learning martial arts, not to attack people but could defend himself. He loved to cook but was a bit of a loner, but could open up to people that would accept him for who he was.

He wanted to make a success of his life to leave a legacy, so that in years to come, people would say, 'Do you remember Mr Matsuda? He was a lovely man, very clever, made a fortune and left it all for charity, also very handsome and debonair.'

## PROFILE: PAULINE AND BILL

Pauline and Bill had been together since childhood. They lived next door to each other. It was inevitable they would marry.

Both wanted children so badly, but Pauline couldn't conceive. Bill always blamed himself, the one thing that Pauline really wanted, Bill couldn't give her

They thought of adopting, but money was always tight. Both were chefs. When Bill could he'd get jobs in hotels. Pauline loved to cook, her specialty cakes, fancy, little ones, big ones, any shape and colour, when they lost their house, both feared the worst for the future. Surely they were too old to start all over again? Where will they go, what will they do? Bill was so grateful that Pauline made him buy the wagon and horse when they had a little savings. At least they owned something.

## PROFILE: CLIFF

Always a loner. Mum and Dad's farm was so out in the countryside, that he never had friends to play with, and rarely attended school.

Cliff's hero was his dad. He taught him how to lasso cattle, pull them to the floor, brand them, herd them. Once there was a stampede. Cliff was terrified, but thanks to Dad he knew exactly what to do.

When he was given his first horse it was love at first sight, he would constantly groom it, talk to it like a friend. He was confident rider. He could even break in a wild horse. The only problem he had, was he'd never actually been a real cowboy, never had a job, never had a herd. His dress sense was way over the top, bright shiny boots and clothes. He looked more like a movie star cowboy

## PROFILE: JUAN AND TOO

Mexican travellers. They'd crossed the border hoping to find work and places to live. He wanted to bring his daughter up right, with opportunities and prospects for her future. After the death of her mother, she'd been very supportive of her dad, never complaining of her living quarters, going hungry for days at a time, nowhere to wash, no friends, no toys, no future. She never complained once, knowing her dad was doing his best to provide

Juan took the worst jobs available. Jobs nobody else wanted to do, anything that paid a bit of money so his daughter could eat. He never worried about food for himself.

# Chapter 3

## Down but Not Out

All of a sudden there was a loud commotion up ahead, shouting, screaming, then a lady came tumbling down the steps, shouting and cursing, followed by a bag of clothes. 'Get out,' the man said, 'And don't come back.'

'Good riddance,' she said, and started to put her bits of clothing in her bag that had fallen out.

Brad turned to Father, 'You want me to go over there don't you?'

'Only if you want to,' said Father. He went on to say, 'Her name is Virginia, she has a good heart and soul, but is one of those sheep that have left the flock.'

Brad jumped down and gingerly approached the woman.

She saw him coming and shouted at him, 'I'm not working any more, I've been sacked, left homeless, no money, no food, no job, no hope.' She burst into tears and sat down on the ground sobbing.

Brad said, 'Virginia would you like to talk to a priest?' She half glanced upwards, wondering how he knew her name, she thought to herself, he's handsome, what harm can it do? Brad helped her up and carried her bag over to the wagon.

'Hello Virginia, do you remember me?'

'Yes Father I do, I remember you from the church services.

'Would you like a lift anywhere?'

**Virginia said**

'I don't know where I'm going, but to get out of here would be a start. I would like to take you up on your kind offer.'

Father said, 'You can ride along with Helen, James and Ellis, her children, girls together if that's alright with you, Brad.'

'Sure Father whatever you say.'

**Brad said**

'Can I go, Father.'

'Yes just pull a little way down the street and stop, you never know who you might meet!'

Brad shouted, 'Wagons roll.' Everybody else except Virginia shouted back 'Wagons roll' and laughed.

Father said, 'Just about here will do, Brad, just wait a while you never know what might happen.'

Just then the music started up, these beautiful sounds of a violin and a deep Irish accent singing, they all listened and tapped their feet to the music,

Father said, 'We all need a bit of singing in our lives, it's good for the soul, and it can up lift you in time of crisis or pleasure.'

**Brad said**

'So do I need to go in?'

**Father**

'Let's wait a while and see what happens.'

All of sudden a man came out backwards with another man grabbing hold of his jacket. Whack, he sent the little man flying, crashing to the ground, still holding his violin he made a quick exit. As he walked pass the wagon on the side of the Father, Father said, 'Hello Jimmy, how you doing?'

'Well hello, Father, fine thank you very much.'

**Brad said**

'What was that all about?'

**Jimmy said,**

'How was I supposed to know she was married to the biggest man in town? By the way Father where you be going?'

**Father**

'Wherever the Lord wants us to.'

**Jimmy**

'Er that would be fine by me, can I grade a lift?'

Brad said, 'Jump in, third wagon down, as he walked past Helen's wagon, he said 'Top of the morning to ya, Virginia.' She just smiled back.

'Good day, I'm Jimmy, Steve and George, jump in. Can we go Father now?'

'Yes, wagon's roll.'

'Wagons roll' came back.


They travelled most of the day, stopping for refreshments and things to eat. They all had their cakes. Ellis said, 'We don't have any cake for Virginia or Jimmy.'

Father said, 'Didn't we buy two extra chocolate cookies?'

'Yes we did,' said Ellis,

'Oh that was lucky then,' said Father.

Helen P Virginia chatted all day about their past lives. They bonded very quickly, each liking each other very much, especially when Virginia asked how they all met and where were they going.

Helen didn't have all the answers. She told Virginia about Brad and Steve, and that she felt so comfortable in the group, Virginia said, 'A bit like a family.'

'Yes,' Helen said, a bit like a family. Helen thought about those words, and wished that Wayne was with them on this new adventure.

Jimmy was in the back on the wagon and slept most of the day, he was used to sleeping day times, as he quite used to working late evenings.

They camped for the first night together. Some slept outside, some in the wagons, Jimmy after dinner got his violin out, and played lots of melodies, a few songs. People got up and danced around the fire, the music and Jimmy cheered everybody up. Jimmy was last to go asleep after talking to George, before he realised George was fast asleep. Jimmy thought what a lovely group of people. I usually charge to perform but tonight was pure pleasure.

Next morning they packed their bits and pieces up, got into the wagons, Brad shouted 'wagons roll,' back came 'wagon's roll'. Brad was sure that was getting louder and certainly more people shouting it. It was round about mid-day, very hot, Brad was thinking of stopping to get everybody into the shade for a few hours, when up ahead they saw a wagon parked up off the main road.

Brad pulled the wagon behind the wagon and stopped. They all stopped and most jumped down.

Brad called out 'Anybody there?' A little female voice answered back, 'In here we're in the back of the wagon.' Brad pulled the flap back to discover two teenagers, a boy and a girl.

'Please can you help us? My brother's dislocated his knee, he's in front, he jumped down from the wagon and his knee just seemed to jump out of his socket.'

Brad called for Helen. Helen knew exactly what to do. She told the lad this was going to hurt a bit at the start, but he will feel a lot better in a moment. She laid the lad flat, grabbed hold of his ankle and pulling slowly pulled on his leg, the lad gave a yelp that would have woken the dead, there was a massive clunk, as the knee joint seemed to go back into place. Helen said 'I'll just wrap that up for you, to give the knee a bit of support, it will be a bit sore and tender for a couple of days, then you'll be fit as a fiddle.'

'Thank you. My name's Jack and this is my twin sister, Lucy.'

'Hello and thank you, I didn't know what to do, especially as where in the middle of nowhere.'

**Helen said**

'Hello, my name's Helen, and this is Brad.'

'What are you doing out here?'

'It's a long story, but basically our parents both passed away, we were heading to California hoping to find our Mum's sister.'

Helen said, 'Do you know where she lives?'

'No,' said Lucy. 'But we didn't know what else to do.' Then she started crying.

'Now now,' said Helen, hugging Lucy. 'Everything will be alright, not to worry. You can join us were heading for California too. That will be alright, Brad?'

'Sure no problem,' said Brad.

Lucy got out of the wagon. Jack gingerly was lowered down. Lucy couldn't believe how many people were gathered around. 'Hello,' she said, 'I'm Lucy and this is my twin brother, Jack.'

'Hello,' said Jack, still a little pained from his knee. Lucy went round the group and hugged everybody.

**Steve said**

'Right let's get a fire going I'm hungry.'

**Helen said**

'You're always hungry, Steve.' Gave him a nod and wink, which made him grin.

'I'll help you,' said George.

'Me too,' said Jimmy.

Helen led the way in preparing lunch. Virginia asked if she could help.

'Yes,' said Helen, 'you're in charge of the potatoes for the mash.'

Ellis and Lucy both said they'd help. The boys sat around laughing and joking. Jack was a bit quiet. He could still feel the pain in his knee. George got up and disappeared, but returned with two pieces of wood, which he gave to Jack.

'This will help you get about.'

Jack thanked George, stood up and tried them out, he was much more mobile with the sticks. The lads all gave a cheer, the girls all turned around to see Jack on sticks. They all clapped, which embarrassed Jack so much. With a red face he sat down. The girls took the dishes of food to the boys, and the girls sat down to eat theirs. Father said, 'I think we should pray to thank the Lord for the food he had provided.'

**Virginia said**

'Father do you mind if I grab the prayers?'

'Not at all, Virginia, please go ahead.'

She started by saying, 'Lord thank you for this day, for the new friends we all have made.'

'I am so happy,' George cheered out loud, and they all said amen.

After lunch Brad went over to Jack and Lucy, explained about the range and said they could stay there as a base while they enquired about their auntie. Lucy cried again, Brad hugged them both.

They all got on board the wagons. 'Wagons roll,' said Brad. 'Wagons roll,' came back. Then a little voice said, 'Wagons roll.' It was Lucy, which made everybody laugh.

Again it was getting late in the day, Brad was looking for a place to camp up. A torrential thunderstorm struck, rain poured down, most stayed in their wagons, Steve went from wagon to wagon with sandwiches, they all had an early night, sleeping when the thunder or lightning stopped.

They woke up the next morning to find the strangest thing ever. Erected near the wagons was a teepee, and a long wagon with no covering on. Brad saw it first, as he was looking at it curiously, he heard a baby crying, then the flap was thrown back, and a Indian man appeared, bare chested with colourful markings on his arms and body, and a sole feather in his head band around his head. Brad spoke to him in English and Spanish. He could speak a little English and understood a bit of Spanish, Father approached and spoke to him in Navajo of words that he knew. The Indian man also spoke a bit of Navajo.

As the group stood around watching, Father approached them, he said, 'His name's Running Bear.'

Steve sniggered, thinking he meant running naked with no clothes, then soon realised he meant a wild bear.

Father carried on, 'He has recently lost his wife. (The women sighed) He has a young daughter, who is hungry, and wondered if we had anything to feed her.'

Helen said, 'We have powdered milk and eggs, maybe do an omelette.' Off she went with Ellis in tow to help. She warmed the milk, made the omelette, approached teepee. Running Bear beckoned her to go in, she went in and spoon fed the baby, and noticed she'd had an accident. She sent Ellis for some tissue paper and pants, asked if Virginia could wash the pants.

The baby seemed quiet content as it was handed around from girl to girl. Brad said to Father should we ask him if he'd like to join us. It won't do any harm by trying, after all he might need some help bringing up baby.

They both approached Running Bear, and each said what they could to each other, it ended by Running Bear nodding his head yes in agreement.

They broke the teepee down and helped Running Bear attach it to his long open-top Wagon

Virginia offered to hold the baby as the wagons were a bit bumpy, so the baby would need to be held.

Helen said to Brad, 'If we could stop at the next town, we could get baby a few bits.'

Father said to Brad, 'There's a town a few milks ahead.' Brad looked at him and wondered how he knew all these things. Wagon's roll sure enough 'wagons roll' came back, this time Lucy got her timing right, Running Bear just looked confused, but followed anyway.

Sure enough the town didn't take too long to get to: Father said to Brad 'now I wonder if anybody here needs our help.'

Brad said, 'I'm sure you know any case,' with that they both chuckled and got off the wagon. Everybody went different ways the ladies went off to find bits and pieces for baby, the boys just hung around the wagons, Brad went to get a few bits and pieces.

Telling the boys, 'We should hit California very soon, last change to top up.'

As the boys were talking an old alcoholic tramp was sitting on the steps, 'Excuse me gentlemen,' he said, 'could you spare me a bit of change.'

Father said, 'Hello Andy, what are you doing here?'

'Honest Father, minding my own business.'

'I see you're still drinking.'

'Oh yes Father, but only when my mouth feels a bit dry, like it does now.'

Father said, 'Andy, I'm not taking no for an answer. Get in the back of that wagon and sleep it off.'

'Thank you, Father very kind of you,' said Andy. As he was climbing up the wagon he fell off.

'Sorry Father,' he said, 'but I've just fallen off the wagon.' Giggling away he fell into the wagon, and crashed out to sleep almost immediately.

The rest of the gang turned up with bits and pieces, Helen had food and clothes for the baby, Virginia set about feeding and burping her, and changing her.

Brad jumped on board, Father said, 'Brad Andy, Andy Brad.'

Brad just said, 'Hi Andy,' bemused.

Father said, 'Don't ask.'

Brad said, 'I wasn't going to.'

'I'll explain as we go along.'

'Wagon's roll.' Wagons roll came back, except Bear Running.

At the edge of town stood this beautiful Mexican girl about ten years old, perfectly white trousers and top, plaited deeply black hair, with a white hat on top. She looked so cute, but so lost, then her father appeared from inside a building, shouting at a man, 'You owe me money for washing up.'

'Get lost,' the man said, 'you broke so many dishes, you owe me money.'

The Mexican said something rude in his language, turned, grabbed his daughter's hand and walked away.

Brad pulled up alongside them. 'Can we offer you a lift?' Brad said.

'Where you going?' came the sharp reply.

'Where you going?' Brad said. 'If you want a lift fourth wagon down, Jack and Lucy have room.'

As they approached Lucy said, 'Climb aboard there's plenty of room in the back.' They got in. Wagon's roll. Wagon's roll, except Running Bear the Mexicans and Andy.

Brad just looked at Father and shook his head.

'You're a good man Brad,' Father said. 'Just a bit further to go.'

Brad wasn't puzzled any more.

They were just pulling away when out on the street, they saw a ruck, five men were pushing this one man around, egging him onto fight.

'I don't want to fight,' he kept saying, 'I don't want to fight anybody.'

'Come on, come on,' they kept goading him. 'Yeah,' said one man, 'we've got money on this.'

'Fight, fight, fight,' they called.

Father said to Brad. 'That's one man who does need our help and now.' Father and Brad jumped down and ran over to the men.

Father said, 'Stop this, this man doesn't want to fight.'

'Well's he's got to,' said one man.

'Yeah and what's it got to do with you?' said another.

Brad said, 'He doesn't want to fight anybody.'

'Yeah well,' said one man 'perhaps you'll take his place.'

They all laughed out loud. Just then Steve arrived, followed by Jimmy and George, when Running Bear turned up, the men dispersed quickly, shouting back, 'Get out of town, Ken we don't want you here, this is not over.'

Steve put his arm around Ken, and said, 'Come with me there's room in my wagon for you.'

They all got back in their wagons. Wagons roll. Wagon's roll, came back. They all laughed especially when Running Bear said it, louder than anyone else.

As they pulled away Father started singing, 'Gathering in the sheep, gathering in the sheep, we are all rejoining, gathering in the sheep.' Brad couldn't help joining in, gathering in the sheep, when he heard the other wagons singing it as well he couldn't help but laugh!

Father said, 'Have you noticed our addition?'

'What addition?'

'Have a look behind.'

Brad poked his head out of the wagon and couldn't believe his eyes. Attached to the back of the wagon train was a buggy. Sitting upright in the buggy, was a waistcoated man.

Mr Matsuda, as he liked to be called, he never liked to use his first name which he always found embarrassing, so he rarely told anyone. He always dressed so smartly, clean shaven. Pristine clothes topped with a bowler hat, riding alone so proudly.

He'd watched the incident in the street, and thought to himself what a lovely group of people, standing up for the underdog. He felt like an underdog and felt he wouldn't be judged by them, he thought he'd follow them, and when they stopped he'd ask where they were heading for.

Just on the outskirts of town, they saw an elderly couple being evicted from their property. Luckily they had their own wagon, and were putting their last bits and pieces into the wagon. The lady looked very upset and distraught.

Shaking and sobbing, her husband was doing his best to load some furniture into the wagon.

Brad said to Father, 'It looks like they may need our help.'

'Yes,' said Father, 'it sure does.'

Getting out of the wagon Brad and Father approached the couple, 'Would you like some help?'

Father said, 'Yes please.'

The lady said, 'we're being evicted from our home.' Crying she added, 'We couldn't keep up with the payments, after Bill's accident.'

Steve jumped down, Brad and Steve loaded the last of the items into the wagon. Father said, 'Why don't you follow us. Down the road, we'll stop for something to eat and drink, and explain what we are all doing, introduce our selves, and explain where we are all going.'

**Brad said**

'Good luck with that, Father I'm not even myself sure.'

The lady said they'd like to do that, as she could really do with a cup of tea.

Bill said, 'Do you have any biscuits, I like a biscuit with a cup of tea.'

'I think so,' said Brad.

Once again they all piled into their wagons. 'Wagons roll' and 'wagons roll' came back, Brad was sure that was getting louder.

Off they all rumbled, only stopping when they saw a man with a lame horse. Pulling over, Brad shouted for George to join them. Straight away George picked up his back leg, and noticed a tiny piece of stone, sticking into his foot. 'That's the problem,' said George.

Brad produced a pen knife and George flicked the stone out, 'Let him rest tonight. He'll be as right as rain tomorrow.'

'Thank you,' he said, 'my name's Cliff. I'm a cowboy.'

'I'm Brad and this is George.'

Brad said

'We are about to rest up for the night do you know anywhere suitable around here?'

'Yeah,' said Cliff, 'just up there on the left is a picnic spot, with a running stream and drinking water, shaded picnic tables and seats.'

**Brad said**

'Would you like to join us for a meal?'

**Cliff said**

'Do you have any beans? I like cowboy beans.'

'I think so,' said Brad.

Cliff said, 'I'll see you up there as I'm going to walk my horse up there.'

Brad said 'what's his name'?

'Trigger.' Cliff said.

They got back into the wagons. 'Wagon's roll.'

'Wagon's roll,' came back.

They pulled off the road, which looked like a beauty spot, plenty of room for all the wagons, and buggy. Everybody jumped out. By now they had a routine going. Men sorting out the wood and fire, ladies sorting out the food. Pauline asked to join. 'Of course,' said Helen, then Pauline took over, barking out orders to everyone.

The meal was superb, soft meat melting in their mouths, with a stew base, with mash added and a chunk of bread.

Father stood up and said, 'Before we eat let us pray.' He said the Lord's prayer. 'Oh Father which art in heaven, hear our prayers.' Those that knew the words joined in but most said amen at the end.

**Father said**

'And stood up now I would like to introduce our wagon leader, Brad.' A thunderous applause rang out and seem to carry on for ages, even Running Bear clapped.

'Thank you, thank you,' said Brad. Just then he realised just how quiet it had gone. He cleared his throat with a ha-hum. 'Well first of all we should all introduce ourselves, and maybe tell us a bit about yourselves.'

**Brad said**

'Steve would you like to go first?'

'Yeah why not,' said Steve. 'Well hi, I'm Steve, I've known Brad for over three years, we fought together in the North and South civil war. The reason I'm here, originally I was heading to California's sunny beaches to take some time off, but I must admit this journey has been an adventure of a lifetime. I'm not sure I can leave you all, you're like family to me, I'm not such what lays ahead, but I feel I want to be part of it! Thank you.' As he went to sit down, an amazing applause could be heard as it went around the whole group.

**Brad shouted**

'Helen would you like to go next?' she stood up took Ellis's and Jack's hand.

'Hello everybody,' she said.

'Hello Helen,' came back.

'This is my wonderful daughter Ellis and son James.'

'Hello Ellis and James,' came back.

'My husband Wayne was killed in the civil conflict.' She began to cry, fighting back the tears, she carried on. 'Our house caught fire, the wagon and what's inside is all we have, we don't really know where we are going. Our wagon got stuck in the mud. That's how we met Brad and Steve, they rescued us from the mud, and have been helping us ever since, with food, company and general support, we feel safe and protected in their company.'

Virginia stepped forward and hugged Helen and called the kids in for a hug, a loud clap started and a few tears were shed by most.

**Brad said**

'Virginia whilst you're up perhaps you could be next.'

Helen and the kids left to another applause.

'Hi,' she said, 'I'm Virginia.'

'Hello Virginia,' came back.

'I'm young and beautiful (the lads all cheered) I'm homeless, jobless thrown out on the street penniless. Brad and Steve offered me a ride, to where I don't know, I love Helen and the kids, they've been so kind to me, shared everything, I love her like a sister.' Helen blushed and smiled, a large applause sounded around.

**Brad said**

'Jimmy.'

'Yes yes to be sure to be sure. I also know Virginia, and she is beautiful, but not just in looks, she's kind and loving and cute.'

**Virginia said**

'Enough about me talk about yourself.'

'Well I'm Jimmy.'

'Hello Jimmy,' came back.

'I love music, any type, anything I can get a tune out of, I also was thrown out on the streets. When offered a ride, it was mainly to get out of town, I also have no plans or direction.' The applause came but not as loud for Virginia.

**Brad said**

'Lucy, Jack.' Lucy came out and Jack hobbled behind her.

Jack thought, I'll let Lucy do all the talking.

'Hello everybody I'm Lucy and this my twin brother Jack.'

'Hello Lucy, hello Jack,' came the reply.

'Jack has damaged his knee, but Helen has helped him, and he's getting better every day. When Jack had his accident we were stranded in the middle of nowhere, Brad, Steve, Helen and the others came along and helped us. Our mother and father passed away quite recently and were heading to California hopefully to find our auntie, although we don't even know if she is alive. Brad offered us a base at his ranch, so we could make some enquiries about our auntie and so that is why we are here, thank you.' Applause.

**Brad said**

'George, would you mind coming up?'

**George said**

'Yes sir,' said George, he looked right around the circle. 'I'm George,' he said in his deep loud voice.

'Hi George,' came back.

He loved the fact at last in life, people knew his name, he continued, 'I'm so lucky to be alive. Hallelujah, praise the Lord. I was left for dead, strapped to a tree and had been whipped, if Brad and Steve and the others had not come along when they did, well I just don't know. I would personally like to thank Helen, who has nurtured me back to good health, been so kind and gentle.' George started clapping everybody joined in. 'She also brought me some clothes and I got my first lollipop ever.' George clapped, again, the rest joined in. 'Helen also said that wherever she goes in life, I can go with her.' George started clapping again, the rest joined in. George finally sat down. Helen thought now she knew why she wanted to be a nurse, it's so rewarding when people need help the most in life, hopefully you can ease their pain. Steve thought what a special woman Helen was, not just beautiful, but loving and caring with great kids.

**Brad said**

'Andy.'

**Andy said**

Andy gets up. 'You'll have to excuse me, but I've got a banging head, and I don't drink no more.'

People stood up and cheered they started shouting, 'Andy, Andy, Andy.'

'Thank you,' he said, 'but if you keep the noise down a bit, I'd appreciate it. (They all laughed.) Basically my problems are self-inflicted. When my wife was shot and died in a bank robbery, I blamed myself, so I turned to drink and lost everything, I don't know why I'm here I don't even know where we are.' Big laugh, clap. Andy sat down.

**Brad said**

'Juan too.'

Steve still grinned, he found that funny.

'Hola!' said Juan.

'Hola,' said the group, even Running Bear said 'hola' and he'd been clapping others and saying their names the best he could.

'This is my beautiful daughter too!

'Hola Too,' the group shouted. She held onto Daddy's trousers and occasionally poked her head out, but she did wave a little when she heard her name.

'My wife, her mother passed away, I tried to work and provide for her, but it's been very difficult. She never moans or complained, I just want the best for her, I also don't know where we are going, but we are so glad to be amongst such lovely people. Thank you, gracias.'

'Thank you, gracias back,' the group shouted and they sat down.

**Brad said**

'Ken, Ken.'

Ken didn't really want to get up but knew he had to, he didn't want to let anybody down. Ken got up twirling his hat around nervously he said quietly, 'Hi, I'm Ken.'

'Hi Ken,' they said.

'Umm! I'm a little slow in my thinking, I'm not stupid just a bit slow in my speech. Mum said something happened when I was born. These men in town wanted me to fight for money, I told them I didn't want to fight anybody, then you people turned up and stopped them, thank you.'

A round of applause went up. 'When Dad died, and I lost the farm, I used to sneak back and sleep in the barn on the hay, everybody here has been so kind to me, I also don't know where I'm going, thank you.' Large applause.

**Brad**

'Ah! Our new friend, would you like to tell us your name, and maybe why you are here?' Mr Matsuda

'Hui!' He bowed, took his hat off and said, 'My name is Mr Matsuda.'

'Hello Mr Matsuda,' they all said.

'I have not been invited to join your group, but I would very much like to join, when I was in town, how you stood up to those horrible men bullying Ken I thought these are nice people they do not judge you. I need some stability in life, I need a new life with purpose and responsibility, and I need new friends. If you would have me, I'd like to join your group on this new adventure, even though nobody knows where we are going.' Mr Matsuda laughed and the group laughed too!

Brad approached Mr Matsuda, shook his hand and said, 'Mr Matsuda welcome to our group.' He shook his hand and said 'Thank you' and bowed.

Everybody stood up and said, 'Welcome, Mr Matsuda,' then clapped him. He went around the whole circle, shaking everybody's hand and bowing at the same time.

**Brad said**

'Pauline and Bill.'

'Hello everybody, we are Pauline and Bill.'

'Hello Pauline and Bill,' the group said.

'We have been married forever, it seems like forever,' said Bill, and he got a laugh.

Pauline elbowed him for interrupting her, 'As I was saying, many of you might have seen us getting evicted from our home.' Pauline welled up, Bill put his arm around her and took over speaking.

'Pauline is the love of my life, I only hope I can make things right for her again.'

Pauline then took back-over, saying, 'Although he can be annoying, he is also the love of my life.'

Bill kissed her, the group all sighed, many thought that's the kind of love they were looking for.

Pauline said to Bill, 'Stop going on, I want to sit down.'

Bill just surrendered his shoulders and said, 'Yes dear whatever you say.' More laughter.

'We also don't know where we are going in life but we also don't have many options, thank you.' Clap, sits down.

Brad looked around the group. He said, 'Ah, Cliff we haven't heard from you.'

Cliff gets his whip out cracks it loudly, the group looked stunned. 'Howdy, I'm Cliff and I'm a cowboy.' He gives another crack of his whip.

Gingerly the group says, 'Howdy Cliff.'

'Yeah I'm not sure if I'm part of this group, you see I'm looking for some cattle to herd, you see I'm a cowboy, and I need to live a cowboy's way of life free, roaming the wilds, eating beans.'

There were a few sniggers in the group, Cliff cracked his whip for a third time. That got their attention he thought.

Just then Brad approached him and said, 'I've got a herd of cattle that need a cowboy to sort them out, brand them, breed them and sell them, are you in?'

'Ah hell yes I'm in,' said Cliff lead the way, with a yee ha Cliff stood by his horse, to an raptures applause.

Brad said, 'I've saved the best to last, Father and Running Bear.'

They got an applause as soon as they got up, 'Well,' said Father, 'you've all introduced yourselves and told us a little about yourselves.

Well Running Bear and I talk as one.'

'Hola,' said Running Bear.

'Hola,' Running Bear said the group.

Father says, 'Running Bear has a small child named …'

Running Bear hesitates, then says, 'Virginia' pointing at Virginia holding his baby. Virginia is shocked but pleasantly surprised. From the first meeting Virginia had attached herself to the baby, and couldn't put it down.

**Father said**

'Running Bear wants to thank you personally.' He took over a necklace, and put it over Virginia's head, he then had an identical necklace but smaller and put over his daughter's head. He then kissed Virginia and daughter on the forehead, returned to Father, then he flung himself around in a dance formation, standing on one foot then the other, twisting, turning in a circle, chanting, then flung himself on his knees, raised his arms, tilted head backwards and shouted, 'Virginia.'

Jimmy thought, cor blimey has Running Bear just married Virginia, and she doesn't know it? He laughed.

'By now you must all be wondering what's actually going on here, there's only one way to explain it, please put your hands together for Brad.'

They all stood up and hooted, 'Brad, Brad, Brad.' He strolled into the centre as Running Bear left. 'Thank you, thank you, please be seated I've got a lot of explaining to do. My family owns a massive ranch in California, Mum and Dad live there, along with my brother Alan and his wife Dianne, and a family friend Ching-Ching.

'The US Army took the whole place over as a training camp for US officers so that they could live on the land and train, at the same time they built thirteen shacks, with electricity for lights, running water, beds, mattresses, furniture toilet, bath, sewage, a home from home.

'If you look around and count the numbers there's exactly the right number of you, for one shack each, your own self-contained home.' A whoop went up, people stood, cheered and clapped, hugged each other, even those who didn't know what was going on like Running Bear hugged, and danced around, hollered, and jumped for joy.

Brad said, 'Please, please there's more.'

They all sat quickly, wondering what was coming next. How could he top that? Pauline turned to Bill, and said 'A place to live, Bill.'

'I know,' he said. Both with streaming eyes they kissed.

Brad said, 'I've listened to your pasts, and what you've been doing in life, your skills, your passions, pastimes, and with Father's help have come up with some ideas I want to run past you! On the ranch we have our own woodland running. Bear could do what he needs to do there, live free off the land, hunt, whatever his needs. It has its own river, lake, stream, I know Lucy and Jack love to fish, they could supply our needs, and we could open up a fishmongers and you could make a profit, save it up to possibly visit your auntie.' Lucy and Jack nodded, smiling.

'Just off the main house we have our own flour mill. Mr Matsuda would be in charge. From time to time, he will need help. Ching-Ching will show you the ropes.'

Mr Matsuda stood up and bowed. 'Hui.'

'We also have our own blacksmiths, furnace anvil, tools, George to run this. I don't think the smile on George's face could get any broader.'

'Hallelujah! Praise the Lord,' he shouted at the top of his voice. 'Yes sir, yes sir,' he said.

'Andy we have our own wood-sawing machine, built inside its own shed, saws, clamps, nails everything you would need to run a carpentry business.'

Andy shouted, 'I'll drink to that.'

'Oh no you won't,' shouted Jimmy.

'We have chickens to look after and eggs.'

James just put his thumb up and nodded.

'Ken, you're in charge of the crops, harvesting planting, brother Alan can do vegetables, planting, wife Dianna can help, Alan can take it more easily what with his asthma attacks. Mum and Dad will take care of the orchard and cooking of the apple pies.'

'Yippee,' said Steve.

'Cliff will take care of the cattle, branding herding, milking, breeding.'

'Yeeha,' shouted Cliff.

Virginia, you're in charge of clothing us all. We have a massive sewing machine, press, we will also produce clothes for sale, oh, which you will design and manufacture, we'll also get a business going for you, so you can sell to the locals and make a profit. Helen you will have the best medical centre around for miles, to look after everyone, and anyone that needs your help. Ellis we are going to give you full training, working with Mum and following in her footsteps.'

Helen and Ellis hugged and danced around, James joined in. 'Thank you, Brad,' said Helen and Ellis.

'Pauline and Bill, do you think you could cope cooking for all this lot? We have our canteen fully fitted with all the latest mod-cons, great big cooking pots, stoves, ovens, an outdoor fire pit, barbecue, benches, seats, plates, dishes,' Brad stopped. By then Pauline and Bill were not listening, just dancing around, kissing and crying at the same time.

'Thank you, Brad,' they shouted at the same time.

'Juan and Too, next to the canteen is a shower block. We will convert it into a launderette for washing clothes, ironing, we will take in local items, and turn this into business for Juan and Too.

'Olé,' shouted Juan, Too just gently clapped. Running Bear shouted out 'Olé,' but didn't know why.

'Which leaves Jimmy. You will be hired every night to play for us, to keep us all happy during the daytime we will open up a music school, and you teach anybody that wants to learn music, we will get you all the instruments you need.' Jimmy gave a quick tune on his violin.

**Brad said**

'Which only leaves Father Mick.' Everybody started clapping. 'Father, we're going to build you your own church, you already have your own congregation (a cheer went up), which will be attached to a school for you to teach in, and a library in the school stocked with as many books as we can find, plus children's books.'

Father for the first time in his life was speechless. It was his lifetime dream coming true he went to shake Brad's hand, but hugged him instead, then bowed his head and prayed.

**Brad said**

'Now Steve, my best buddy, you might not want to be part of this, but if you do you will live in the house with us, as there is much planning and organising to do.' Brad said, 'Can we have a show of hands of all those who want Steve to be the site manager?' All the hands went up cheering and clapping, even Running Bear, but he still didn't really know what was going on. Father sat with him, and did his best to explain. Juan joined in, Running Bear got the gist of it.

Steve was swamped by everyone around him saying please, please.

'OK, OK, OK,' he said. 'I'll put the beach on hold for now and help out as much as possible to get this project started.' He got mobbed, then Brad also got mobbed.

'One more thing, we will become a community sharing the workload, sharing the rewards, and building future business. To guarantee our futures and celebrate our successes Mr Matsuda will be our banker, he understands money, banking, investments, and interest rates.'

Then pandemonium broke out with Jimmy playing his violin, everybody dancing, hugging, tears, laughter, every human emotion was shown.

Brad and Steve walked away to talk.

Steve said to Brad, 'What have we done?'

**Brad replied,**

'We've given a lot of good people, some hope, some joy, some happiness maybe a future to look forward to.'

Steve said, 'I'm not going to leave you.'

'Good,' Brad said. 'I need you. I can't do all of this by myself.' They shook hands. 'By the way,' Brad said, 'I've seen the way you've been looking at Helen.'

**Steve said**

'Don't know what you mean, but I must admit she's a fine woman, beautiful, a lovely family.'

'Careful,' said Brad, 'sounds like you're falling in love.'

'Get out of here,' Steve said.

Father joined them. 'How do you feel, Brad?' he asked.

'Amazing, we've got a group of people with a bright future ahead of them.'

'Father, could you explain to Running Bear the woodland is his to do with what he likes. He can put a teepee up, or if it gets cold he can move into his shack. He can help fell the trees and use his long wagon to transfer the logs to the sawmill.'

'I'll go tell him now,' Father said.

**Steve said**

'How do you think your mum and dad will feel, with all these people coming onto their land?'

**Brad said**

'They'll love it, the land is too big for them to cope with, especially as they're getting older. Alan and Dianna could do with some help and so could Ching-Ching, he's no spring chicken any more. It will be like bringing new life to the ranch. Instead of crops dying, or the flour mill, or sawmill not being used and rusting we'll have the blacksmith's open, hay in the barn. New people to meet, to get to know, dancing music, entertainment for them to go to. The whole place will come alive again, it will have new life, and a new future, I can't wait for my family to meet our new family.'

Just then Helen and Virginia ran over, 'Come on you two, you're needed for the dancing,' said Virginia. Everybody stayed up late singing and dancing, chatting, hugging, most slept outside that night under the stars, just before they settled down Father said, 'Let us pray, oh Lord hear our prayers, thank you for our past, present and future, and your guidance amen.' Next morning amongst all of the excitement, sometime that day, they would arrive at the ranch, meet Brad's family, get to walk around see their shacks. Excitement was in the air.

Maybe for the last time, after they packed their bits and pieces up, and got into the wagons Brad said, 'Wagons roll.' Everybody shouted back, 'Wagons roll,' loudly. Even Running Bear joined in, he'd already learned some new words.

They travelled most of the day again stopping for refreshments and nibbles.

They arrived mid-afternoon at the ranch, Brad said it looked just as he had left: the crossroads leading to the main gate, which was open, the apple tree orchard to the right, with the crops in the field to the left, with the vegetable patch, to the left the military shacks. 'Thank God,' Brad said, 'they're still there.'

Father said, 'I knew they would be, son, I knew they would be,' patting his leg with a smile.

A bit further up was the corral with horses in and the machinery shed, then past the blacksmith's, cowshed, barn, the wood saw mill and chicken hatches, and pulled up outside the house, Ma was out front, hoeing some weeds, which she dropped when she saw the wagons coming. 'Father Father, you'd better come quickly. Alan, Diana, Ching-Ching come quickly,' she shouted.

Then she saw Brad jump down from the wagon, she ran towards him.

He picked her up and spun her around, saying, 'It's good to see you, Ma.'

'It's good to see you, son,' she said.

By now the rest of the family arrived, all hugging and kissing. 'You've lost weight,' she said to Brad. 'Apple pie for you tonight,' she looked across the all the wagons and said to Brad, 'What do we have here then? Looks like you've brought your own army home.'

# Chapter 4

## Coming Home

As the family stood around in a small group, one by one they dismounted from the wagons, dis-shelved, dirty, hungry, but all with a smile on their faces. Father led. He said, 'Form a line, it would be easier to introduce yourselves that way.' The family also formed a line, Brad at the front stepped out to introduce everybody, starting with Father.

**Brad said**

'Everybody this is Father Mick.'

'Hello Father,' said the family.

As he went along the family line, kissing Ma and Diana, shaking hands with Pa and Ching-Ching, Alan, you could hear, 'Pleased to meet you,' and 'I've heard so much about you,' all sorts of chitter chatter. For Ma, the line never seemed to end. Helen, James, Ellis, Steve Virginia, Baby Virginia, which Ma couldn't help but take and give a little cuddle to. She loved babies and hoped one day to be a grandma. Jimmy, Lucy and Jack, George, Andy, Juan and little too Ken, Mr Matsuda, Pauline and Bill, Cliff, and last was Running Bear, he didn't kiss the ladies or shake the man's hands, he had folded arms, and nodded to everybody in the family line.

Ma said, 'It's lovely to meet you all, let's just do a head count. Would everybody like a nice cold drink of apple juice?'

'Yes,' came a resounding reply.

'OK,' she said, 'everybody go and sit at the long benches and we will get the drinks, Pa, Alan, Diana, Ching-Ching let's get busy.' Virginia asked Ma could she fix baby a drink and some food.

'Yes,' said Ma, 'come with me, I'll show you the kitchen. Would you like me to carry the baby?

'Yes,' said Virginia, grateful of the rest.

While the group settled around the tables their eyes wandered around the surroundings. All agreed it was a massive place, so beautiful so clean and organised. The drinks soon arrived. Cheers everybody was the shout, cheers they all said, raising their glasses up into the air.

As they drank their apple juice, Pa stood up and said, 'We'd like to welcome you all to our humble abode. No doubt our son, Brad, has a plan. It's just at this moment in time we don't actually know what it is.'

Brad stood up. 'Thank you, Pa, and thank you for welcoming my friends. I should say family,' at which he got a big cheer from the group, 'to our home.'

'May I suggest, we do a head count. Ma, Pa, Alan, Diana and Ching-Ching, get dinner going.'

'Yeah,' shouted out Steve. 'I'm starving.'

'You're always starving,' shouted out some of the group

'Ma, Pa, if it's OK with you I'd like to walk my family (big cheer) around the grounds and familiarise themselves with the layout.'

'Does the shower block still have running water?' Pa said.

'We will turn the water on and get the heating going,' Ma said. 'We will get towels, soap, shampoo, combs et cetera and put them in the shower block.'

'Thank you, Ma,' said Brad.

Brad said, 'I'm sure some of you need a wash. If you're not sure, I'm sure. Ladies first of course, men last.'

'Right let's going,' Ma said to the family. 'We'll pick fresh vegetables from the garden peel some potatoes, cook some bread, we'll have a nice stew, with mash, followed by apple pie.'

'Right chop, chop, let's get going,' Alan said. 'I made it twenty-five plus baby. OK son, you turn the water and heating on in the shower house. Diana could you collect towels et cetera?'

As Brad led the group around the grounds, he thought of the time he'd been away from the ranch and how wonderful things looked, and how well his family had kept things going, flowers were in bloom he could see a few jobs that needed doing, but he had the manpower and womanpower to do it, he had so many ideas and plans whirling around his head.

'Right,' said Brad, 'this is the house, at a later time I will give you all a tour.'

'Let's walk on round to the lake, stream and river.' They all poured around the corner, what a beautiful sight, the lake was glistering with the sun shining off it, the reeds around the edges. A pontoon strutted out into water, tied up to that was a fishing boat, before they knew it Steve, Jimmy, jumped into the water, followed by Running Bear. 'It's freezing,' shouted Steve, 'but so exhilarating!'

**Brad said**

'Let's leave them to it, follow me. Lucy, Jack, this is your cabin.' They went into a large kitchen area and dining space with a table, stove cooker, sink, cupboards, two bedrooms, a shower room curtains, doors, pictures hung on the walls. It was too much for Lucy to take in, she just sat on a chair hands over her face and sobbed her heart out. The ladies put their arms around her and sobbed too.

'Jack, come with me,' said Brad. They went outside next door to the lodge was a large shed, Brad opened the door, there was a rowing boat, fishing nets, fishing rods, pots, flies, reels, all sorts of fishing gear.

Brad said to Jack, 'All yours, Jack, to do with whatever you want.'

Jack dropped his sticks and flew into Brad's arms, nearly knocking Brad over, Jack just couldn't stop saying, 'Thank you, Brad, thank you.'

'Lucy and I are going to be so happy here.'

'I know,' said Brad. 'Me, Alan, and our sister were so happy here, Molly. Lucy, Jack, you get settled in. See you a bit later outside the house for dinner, we'll show you the rest of the grounds later.'

Brad left Lucy and Jack hugging and crying together in the kitchen and shut the door.

'Right, next,' said Brad, 'follow me'.

He led them across to the canteen. Opening the doors he said, 'Pauline, Bill this will be your domain.' It was huge, with a big work bench, chopping boards, three sinks, a cooler cupboard, four cooking stoves, a fire with a spit, pots, pans stoves, rolling pin, cutting knives, jars, glasses plates, cutlery, it just went on and on.

'Could you cope with this?' Brad asked, Pauling nearly fainted and had to be held up by Bill.

'Oh Brad, oh Brad,' was all she kept saying.

Bill said, 'Thank you, Brad, you've made my wife and me very happy, thank you.'

'You're welcome,' said Brad, 'after all, you've got to do all the work not me.'

'No problem at all,' said Pauline, 'it will be a pleasure not a chore.'

They each hugged Brad.

'Follow me,' he said, 'there's more to come.'

As they walked they could see discoloured patches of grass where the soldiers had pitched their tents. Outside the canteen was a massive seating area with tables, beaches, chairs, a large fire pit and grate, barbecue, what looked like a pizza oven, out-buildings for food storage, a toilet block.

'Over there,' Brad said, 'was the shower block. You'll get to see that later.'

BRAD SHACK GOING HOME

Alan appeared from behind the shower block. He shouted to Brad, 'All good to go.'

'Thanks, Alan.'

'Good to see you, bruv.'

'Good to see you, bruv, too.'

'We'll have a catch up soon.'

'Can't wait,' said Alan.

Brad said, 'Alan, is the water and electricity supply on?'

'Just about to do it, bruv,' he said.

'Great to have you home, bruv,' said Alan.

'Great to be home,' said Brad.

Everybody could see the massive wooded area surrounding the back of the property, it reminded Brad of when he and Alan and Molly would play in the woods. Somewhere in there they built a den, Dad helped build a tree house with a rope swing, and a little hut, where Molly played with her dolls.

'Father, Running Bear,' Brad said, 'Father explain to Running Bear this is where he can put his wigwam, and number thirteen shack will be his home. If and when it gets too cold for him and Virginia.'

'George if you can help Running Bear bring his wagon up, and help erect his wigwam.'

'Yes sir,' said George.

'And rejoin us when it's done,' said Brad.

'Father, you'll be living next door to Running Bear to help him understand things.'

**Father said**

'We'll have to call him Chief, as he will be chief of his new tribe,' everybody laughed. Father talked to Chief, and he and George left to get his wagon.

**Brad said**

'Father, do you want to go inside your shack?'

71

'No, no,' he said, 'I'm staying with the group, I don't want to miss anything I'll see it later.'

'Right let's move on,' said Brad. 'Shack number one will be Pauline and Bill's, nice and near to the canteen and the house if you need anything.' Pauline and Bill stepped forward. 'Go on,' said Brad, 'go and see your new home.'

Pauline was shaking, Bill held her tight as he reached forward and opened the door, pushing it wide open.

It was amazing, cosy, clean, comfortable. 'Oh Brad, oh Brad,' Pauline kept saying, 'we can't believe it, it's beautiful, wonderful, lovely.'

'That's enough for now,' said Bill, 'but I have to agree it's amazing, amazing, amazing. Our new lovely home,' and he planted a big kiss on Pauline.

'Get off,' she said, 'People are watching.'

'OK, maybe later,' Bill said and winked at her.

Brad said, 'We've got to move on, lots still to do. Pauline, Bill settle in, we'll see you outside the house say about an hour's time.'

One by one he showed the group their allocated shacks. All the shacks were identical. Number two would be Helen, Ellis and James could have the backroom, Helen in the smaller room. Number three would be Virginia, who still was holding Baby Virginia. Virginia was getting very attached to Baby Virginia. Brad noted to make two cots.

'Number four, Steve, but you can have a room in the house if you want to, but if you need some space you can crash out or relax here. Number five, Juan and Too, see you for dinner soon. Number six, Mr Matsuda. Number seven, Jimmy. Number eight, Cliff, right near the corral and horses, the cattle and sheep.'

Just then George came running up. 'Good timing,' said Brad.

'All done, boss,' he said.

Brad said, 'Just call me Brad.'

'Yes sir, I mean yes, Brad.'

They crossed the road. 'George.'

'Yes Brad,' said George.

'You're number nine, go in get washed up, see you outside the house for dinner, say half-an-hour.'

'Yes Brad.'

'How will I know when it's half-an-hour?'

'Just come when you're ready.'

'Yes boss, I mean yes Brad-sir.'

They both laughed.

Number ten, Andy

Number eleven, Ken

'Right I've got to go I need a wash and a shave before dinner, I'll see you all soon for dinner.'

As he rushed back towards the house he felt so good inside. Good people, their faces when they opened the door to their new homes, a new start in life. Brad thought, 'They haven't seen anything yet, wait to I tell them of all the surprises yet to come.'

As he went into the house and through to the kitchen, everybody was working away hard and fast. 'Ma,' Brad shouted, and ran across and gave her a big kiss. They hugged for ages, 'I've missed you, son.'

'And I've missed you, Ma and all of you.'

'Love you.'

'Love you too, Ma.'

'Now we need to get on with things. Ching-Ching get on mashing that potato.'

'Ma I'm going to have a quick wash and shave, I'll be back as soon as possible.'

'Don't be too long, son, it's nearly ready.'

'I won't, Ma, I promise. Sorry to put this on all of you at short notice.'

Ma cut him short, 'get out of here and hurry back, you need to help serving this all up'

'Yes, Ma love you.'

'Go, go, go, love you too, son.'

Brad disappeared upstairs, his room had been left just how he'd left it. Ma kept it clean and spotless, dusted, there was his old bed, with clean crisp sheets on, his childhood memorabilia scattered around the room, his baseball bat and glove, all sorts.

'Right,' he said, 'I haven't got time for all this, must get ready. Can't wait for a bath later, and get into my old bed, for the first time in ages, a comfortable bed.'

Outside people were arriving, all the time jostling for seats, trying to sit somewhere near to people they knew, then a massive cheer went up as the family brought plates, dishes, knives, forks, spoons, big boiling pans with stew in, mash potatoes, pots, plates with chunks of bread on.

The noise of chatter amongst the guests brought a tear to her eye. Pa hugged her.

He too felt a tremendous amount of joy. Most of his family was back together plus whole new neighbours to get to know. 'Budge up, Ching-Ching,' said Mr Matsuda, 'room for a little one?'

What with all the noise, and clunking of plates and crockery, Father stood up, clinked his water glass with a spoon, and said, 'Let us pray.'

Everybody stood up, closed their eyes, held their hands together to all pray together.

**Father said**

'Lord hear our pray, thank you for the food we are to eat, thank you to the lovely people who have prepared food and served it. Thank you for bringing us all together. Amen.'

'Amen,' they all said. 'Now tuck in.'

Ma turned to Pa. 'That was nice,' she said, 'we should go to church more often, and give thanks for what we have, and our son home from the war safe and sound.'

'We will, Ma,' said Pa.

Dinner was a resounding success, there wasn't a scrap left over. Everybody had plenty to eat.

'Help me, Pa,' said Ma. They disappeared and returned with four piping hot apple pies. You could smell them in the air. She plonked one down near Steve.

He said, 'Is this all for me? I've been dreaming of this moment for ages.'

They all laughed, 'there's plenty more if we need it,' Ma said. They all tucked in, laughing and chatting.

Then Brad stood. He got a round of applause. 'Thank you, thank you, I would also like to thank Ma, Pa, Alan, Diana and Ching-Ching for supplying this wonderful meal at short notice.'

A big cheer went up. Clapping they bit by bit stood up. The clapping went on for quite a while.

Brad raised his hands. 'Thank you, thank you, we must get on before it gets dark. Steve will explain what is going to happen next.'

**Steve said**

'What?' choking on his breath. 'I don't know,' he said.

**Brad said**

'Ah, that is why my friend you might have the looks, but I've got the brains,' everybody roared with laughter and clapped. 'No, on a serious note let's get down to business. There's lots to do and lots to organise, we will all have plenty of time for leisure, but some things need taking care of straight away. First on my list, Andy, could you make a crib or cradle, something for Baby Virginia to sleep in. Two needed, one for shack number three, and one for shack number thirteen.

'On the wall in the entrance to the house will be a map of the whole area, shacks numbered and who occupies them, the lake, woodlands barn, blacksmith's, chickens, cowshed et cetera.'

'And don't forget the canteen,' shouted Pauline.

'Good point, there will always be snacks, drinks sandwiches available, and we will meet each evening when you hear the gong strike for dinner. Pauline, Bill I need a list of all food items you need, dishes, cups whatever you need, if anyone can't read or write, just draw what you need or tell Steve. Steve will draw up the map of the ranch.'

Steve put his thumb up for alright, Bill was thinking, 'I can't wait to clang that gong.'

'Anybody needing repairs to clothes, or new ones made, go to Virginia, she will measure you up, help you design your clothing and make it. Virginia there's massive room in the house, with dummies in, cutting scissors, rolls and rolls of fabric, sewing machines, pressing machines, dyes, string, lace et cetera. Make a list of anything you need and pass to Mr Matsuda.' Mr Matsuda, bowed and nodded

'Mr Matsuda will have a cash flow, you don't need anyone's permission to get what you need, give Mr Matsuda your lists, then we will organise shopping runs to get the required items. Juan and Too, collect everybody's dirty washing. You can use the shower block, it has soap powders, washing lines, pegs, a press, all sorts of things you may need, anything else tell Mr Matsuda.'

'Olé,' said Juan.

'Olé,' shouted the group.

'Mr Matsuda will hold all the purse strings, whatever you need, Mr Matsuda will get arranged. We would appreciate any receipts you can supply. This is not to check up on your spending, it will help us to work out our outgoings against our incomes. We can set budgets where we need to invest, when to save for a big project, when to splash out on luxuries, when to stockpile for the winter months, water, electric, oil, bills, when to buy tubs of ice cream, there is nothing for anybody to worry about, we will always have a roof over our heads, our fields and gardens are full of crops, we'll have chickens eggs, cows, milk, meat, fish and beautiful flowers to look at. We also want to turn a profit. At the end of each month, we will have a profit-sharing scheme, once costs are taken out the profit will be equally shared amongst everyone.

'Any questions so far?' Not a murmur came back. 'James you'll be our chicken man, collecting eggs clearing out, new straw, breeding programme. Lucy, Jack you will be our fish people sorting out stocks, catching fish, breeding pens, feeding, et cetera. Jimmy and Cliff, if you can take care of the cattle, sheep, horses, pigs, cleaning out, feeding, branding, and breeding programme. George, we're going to fire up the blacksmiths. Andy, can you make me a big sign saying "Mr George the blacksmith"? George, tell Mr Matsuda what you need, we can shoe horses, make iron gates, fire grills, we may even get some work from the railways.

'Andy there's already a load of planks cut in the wood sawmill, Chief will supply you with as much wood as you need. We will also cut firewood for ourselves and the local town folk. Ken, you've been a farmer. You will be in charge of our crops, planting, harvesting, ploughing. Which only leaves us with Helen and Ellis there's one building we haven't had a chance to show anybody yet, it's between Mr Matsuda's shack and Jimmy's shack, it's a medical centre. It has beds in, all sorts of pills, bandages, medical items tools and dentistry equipment.

'I would like you to care for our wellbeing, help us if we get sick, treat our wounds, patch us, prescribe medicines and stitch us up if we need it, there are loads of books of treatments, ailments, therapies. Ellis, if you could work alongside Mum, and train to be a nurse and follow in your mum's footsteps, we will build it up so that other local people will come here for treatments.'

Mr Matsuda shouted, 'Yes and buy some of our products on the way out. Make profit!'

Everybody cheered, clapped and hooted.

'Now, some of you may think how are you going to cope with such a large workload? Ma and Pa will carry on looking after the vegetable patch, with Ching-Ching's help, Ching-Ching will also be running the flour mill. He'll pass the flour over to Pauline and Bill and we will have hot bread every day.'

Up went a cheer.

Pauline said. 'Also cakes and buns.' Up want another cheer.

Ma shouted, 'but you can't make apple pies, that's my speciality.' Up want a cheer.

Steve shouted, 'Good, I'd like to put an order in for tomorrow for my very own apple pie.'

'I'll see what I can do,' said Ma. 'If you think Pa's been quite quiet it's because he's been writing all of this down. I'm just going to quickly read this to you so you can try and take some of this in.'

Pa hands his scrambled notes to Brad. 'Well done, son, I'm proud of you.'

Brad looks at the list, and begins to read:

'Lucy, Jack – fishing, with a plan to have a fishmonger stall and sell to public. Pauline and Bill to cook and feed us all (hooray, shouted Steve) in time to sell cakes, bread, buns et cetera. Sarah and Ellis will run the medical centre. In time we can generate revenue for treatments medicines, tooth extraction, et cetera. Virginia, you are responsible for clothing us all. Day uniforms, evening wear, Baby Virginia's clothes, in time to build up a clothes shop to sell to the public for a profit.

'Juan and Too, you are to keep us clean, smart and tidy, washing clothes like a launderette, we will take in local people's clothes, wash them for them and make a profit. Mr Matsuda, you will be responsible for all money invoices, receipts, ordering, each month we will produce a profit and loss sheet, a sharing scheme, in time we will open a bank and get people to invest in us. You will also be in charge of our advertising programme. We will paint up posters, post them all around the town, advertise what we do and bring the people to us to buy our wares and services.

'Running Bear, or Chief as Ma likes to call him, you will have the run of the woodlands, chopping down trees, replanting trees, getting the wood to Andy's in your long wagon, we will build up a log pile for our use, also sell to the locals.

'James you will be responsible for the chicken pies, collecting eggs, supplying the house, canteen, and anybody else who needs eggs. We will have a breading programme to increase our stock, we will sell chickens and eggs to the public. Jimmy and Cliff will work together, looking after the horses and cattle and sheep. Branding them, breeding them, to increase our stock and milking. We will always have meat to eat. Jimmy our long-term plan is to build you a music centre. Where you can have all the instruments you need. You can teach music to whoever wants to learn. Wouldn't it be amazing if we had our own singing group? Singing and playing instruments.'

Father shouted, 'We could have our own choir.'

'Good idea,' said Brad.

'Cliff, our cowboy, you will have your own cattle herd, to round up, brand, breed, same with the horses. We can create a riding school, shooting range.'

'Whip lash lessons,' said Cliff.

'Good idea,' said Brad. 'George is in charge of the blacksmith's, horse shoeing, metal gates, chains, you will be very popular and busy around here. Every horse needs a George the blacksmith. Andy we've got lots of wood and carpentry projects for you. Already in the wood sawmill are many planks left over from the army, we will add to that, Chief will supply the wood. Our first project two cribs. A partition wall or extension for Ellis and James, so they can have their own rooms and space. We need a fishmonger stall and cake bread shop, clothes shop, a music room and some wood instruments.

'Then we have a major project. We are going to build Father his own church (the people gasped, but not as loud as Father Mick). It will have benches in, an altar, pews, et cetera. That's not all, alongside this building will be a school room, with a built in library, for all our children to attend and the local children.'

Everybody stood and applauded for ages. Father just bowed his head, speechless, it was all he ever wanted the whole of his life to have his own personnel parish. A miracle, he thought, an absolute miracle. Thank you, Lord, God bless.

'Like I said before, some of you might be panicking, wondering how you are going to cope with this workload, don't worry, we are all one team. We survive together or sink together. Floating all the time is Steve. He's your first point of call if you need any help. He can pull people off jobs, add people to jobs, lifting, hauling, hammering, washing. Whatever you need go to Steve. He'll be our organiser, a bit like a ranch manager. He can call on me, Alan, Diana, Ma, Pa, anybody who has a spare moment. Now Ching-Ching will be running the flour mill.'

Ching-Ching stood up. 'You say you want me to work flour mill, help in gardens, clean house, cook. You want me to do work in dark?'

Brad said, 'You've always had it too easy for years it's about time you pulled your weight.'

**Ching-Ching said**

'You cheeky monkey. You always was problem child. You're not too big to clip around the ear, Brad,' Ching-Ching laughed and everybody joined in.

'Ken you probably know more about groups than any of us, but any help you need just ask. Now I don't know about you but I'm exhausted. It's been a long day, I suggest we get some sleep, meet up for pancakes in the morning outside the canteen when you hear the gong. Diana and Ma will give all the ingredients to Pauline and Bill, and help you. Thank you all for listening but I need some time with my family. Steve please join us.'

Everybody agreed, them hugged and kissed each other saying goodnight, shook Brad's hand, slapped him on the back, hugged him, kissed him and thanked him. Then they all disappeared, the family and Steve all held hands and walked back to the house in silence.

# Chapter 5

# A New Beginning

The family talked well into the night, swapping stories of what's been going on over the years, what it was like for Brad and Steve, how the family had coped, then got around to Brad's plan. Everybody gave their opinions, but in general they were all supportive, and were excited about the future.

Life had come to the ranch, it had a future, a purpose, it could help the local community build new lives for the group. The future looked promising, they all looked forward to new buildings, a church, the medical centre opening, little huts to sell produce, the cattle wouldn't be neglected, the fish would be used, the pigs, sheep, chickens would be looked after, along with the horses, crops, getting the flour mill going again, having all the wood chopped up, their own blacksmith's, straw, hay in the barn, music and entertainment, listening to the wood saw humming away again. Everybody felt a buzz of excitement and could not wait for tomorrow to get started, Ma and Diana had the pancake mix sorted, and would give it to Pauline and Bill first thing tomorrow morning.

**Brad said**

'Folks, I'm beat, so I'm going to have a long soak in the bath, and get into bed. Steve there's a bath and a bed free for you if you want it.'

Steve said, 'As long as I don't have to share a bath or a bed with you,' and chuckled.

**Brad said**

'I'm too tired to laugh. Goodnight everybody, love you all, see you all in the morning for pancakes over at the canteen.'

They all hugged, and kissed and said goodnight.

Steve felt part of the family already. He just knew he was going to be so happy here along with all the challenges, but with his best buddy Brad.

During the night some slept straight away, some bathed, the women had a chance to clean themselves up, do hair etc., hand wash a few items, talk, clean, whatever they fancied done. Excitement was in the air.

Before you knew it, the gong was clanging away. Bill was giving it a good bash, thinking it's got to be loud for Ken to hear it, as he was the furthest away. To his surprise Ken was already outside waiting for its pancakes and so were quite a few others. Pauline and Bill, Diana, Ma were bringing out plates of pancakes, with homemade honey from the bees next to the woodland, homemade apple jam. Pauline said, 'Eat up there's more to come for the stragglers.'

Bit by bit everybody arrived, said good morning and tucked into pancakes. Last to arrive was George. He'd washed himself, shaved and put on the clothes that Helen had got for him. He arrived whistling away, he had to be the happiest man in the whole wide world today, his walk had a swagger, he had confidence in every stride.

Everybody shouted, 'Good morning, George.'

He said, 'Yes it is. Good morning, everybody, do you have room for a hungry guy?'

Helen felt so good, George looked great, clean, happy, his wounds were healing well, so happy for him.

After lots of chatting and pancakes, hot tea and coffee, Brad finally stood up. 'Good morning, everybody,' he said.

'Good morning, Brad,' boomed back.

'Right, are we all fighting fit and ready to get stuck in?'

'Yeah, you bet,' came the response.

'Steve would you like to start?' he said.

'I'll just have one more pancake before I start.' Everybody laughed. Steve stood up, 'Good morning everybody,' he said.

'Good morning, Steve,' came back.

'Right,' he said, 'we should all have a day off and eat apple pie all day.'

'Boo, Boo,' they all shouted.

'I'm only kidding,' he said. 'First things first, food.' They all laughed. 'Lucy, Jack catch us some fish, take it over to Pauline and Bill, they will show you how to cut it up. We will need vegetables, potatoes and salad bits. Pauline, Bill make up a menu of food for the week. Tonight we're going to celebrate.

'James, take care of the chickens, they might need cleaning out, collect all the eggs, check if Ma needs any, get the rest over to Pauline and Bill. We will have egg sandwiches for lunch when you hear the gong. Those that are too busy to stop for lunch, James will deliver to your workplace along with a drink of your choice. Chief we need a big fire for party tonight. Collect lots of wood, put in a fire pit next to canteen.' Father told Chief, he understood straight away. 'Virginia you've got Baby Virginia, get a plan of action. Those who need clothes more urgently than others, start taking measurements.

'Juan and Too, start collecting dirty washing, get it washed and out on the lines. It's a beautiful drying day. Mr Matsuda, Father and I will be in my cabin number four. This will be known as the office, or as I like to call it, "the brain centre, the hub".'

'Bet they'll be food somewhere in there,' shouted Brad. Little snigger.

'We will be drawing up the plans for the church advertising posters, balance sheets, plans of sites for the buildings, which projects to start first, sorting out the money and getting all the lists of things you need. Helen and Ellis will open up the medical centre, blitz clean it, familiarise themselves with instruments, tools, books, et cetera. And let us know what else you need. Jimmy if you could help Cliff, there's a lot to sort out with the cattle, sheep and horses feeding, cleaning, milking, talk to Ma about storage. Anybody who hasn't got anything to do, or has a bit of spare time on their hands help out. So that's cow dung for you, Brad. Tonight, Jimmy, could you supply the music and singing. Ching-Ching, get the flour mill going. Shout if you need any help. Ma, Pa, Alan, Diana on vegetable and salad gardens, plus apple picking for the apple pie tonight.'

'You'll get fat,' shouted Brad.

'Not with all this work I won't. George, fire up the furnace, start making shoes, chains, tie up with Cliff what he may need. Andy you're going to be busy. First job get the cots and crib made, I noticed some paint and varnish in there. Ma's probably got old baby clothes and bedding somewhere stored in the house.'

'I have,' said Ma, 'I've even got Brad's first baby suit I knitted.'

'Oh Ma, nobody wants to see that.'

'Yes we do,' shouted the women.

'Ken have a look at the crops, see what needs doing, take to Ching-Ching what he may need from you. Right folks, have a good day. Get stuck in, if you need any help shout. Chop-chop, go, go, go, see you for lunch, when you hear the gong.'

Brad thought to himself what a good man Steve was, a good friend, a good buddy, they'd been through a lot together. He was so glad that their lives didn't go in different directions, that he was here by his side building a new life together with lots of new challenges. Everybody loved him, he was organised, got things sorted, asked people in a certain way that never rubbed them up the wrong way, always had a smile, banter, a joke, he was always great company, nothing much got him down, positive. Definitely the right man for the job in hand, but, he thought, always hungry, probably making up for all the years he went without.

**Steve said**

'Come on, Brad, you've got muck to shovel,' he said laughing.

The morning zoomed by, some came for sandwiches, some had them delivered. The furnace got lit up, the mill got grinding, Chief got a fire built, milking was done, Andy finished cot and crib and was just waiting for them to dry, Jack and Lucy caught amazing fish, Juan and Too got washing on the line, Mr Matsuda, Father, Steve got all their bits of work done, Cliff was riding around on his horse, Ken was cutting, weeding, tying up, the vegetable salad and apples were picked, Virginia had made Too a little dress, now all they had to do was get dressed up for tonight's party. When they heard the gong, they went over.

There was laughter and chatting, the food came.

'Well done Lucy and Jack for catching fish (big cheer), well done Pauline and Bill for cooking it, well done Ma and Pa, Alan, Diana, for the veg, pots and salad.'

**Steve said**

'Well done everybody for pulling together and getting things done. Pauline, Bill what's for breakfast tomorrow morning?'

**Pauline said**

'Fresh boiled eggs and toast, thanks to James.'

**Steve said**

'Well done, James. Now let's party.'

Jimmy came out playing his violin, singing, people joined in, singing dancing, chatting, laughing, Chief lit the fire, it was roaring, so hot they had to stand back a bit. Eventually Steve asked Helen to dance. She said yes. Brad danced with Ma, Dianna, Virginia, Helen, Ellis, Lucy, little Too, Ching-Ching danced with Mr Matsuda, which was hilarious, Chief did some sort of rain dance. What a night, bit by bit people disappeared to their beds, bidding everybody a goodnight, see you in the morning, God bless.

The last two left were Brad and Steve.

'Well, buddy,' said Steve, 'what are you thinking?'

*'Don't tell anybody yet, but I'm going to build these good people a town.'*

'What?' said Steve.

'Just the other side of the crossroads, it's still part of our land unused.'

He went and got some charcoal and on the bench in front of him he drew:

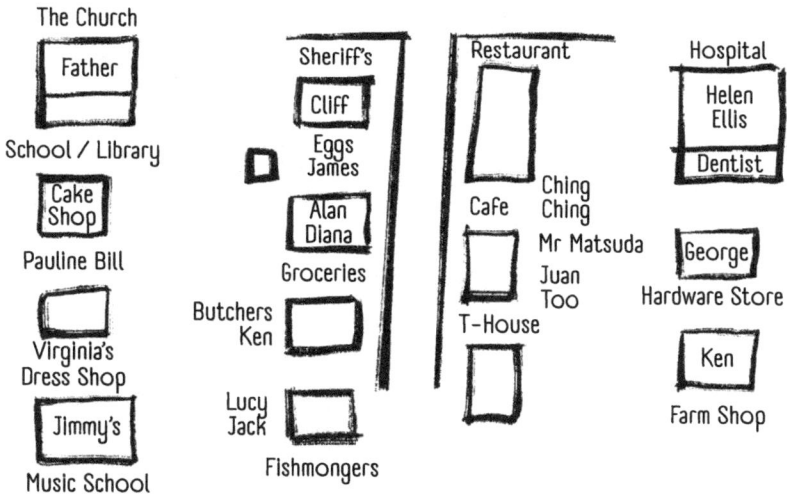

'Well,' Steve said, 'here's the finished map of the ranch.'

Brad said to Steve, 'Well drawn,' and he put two crosses on it, 'and this will be our town.'

'I don't think we need a work schedule. Everybody seems to know what they are doing,' Brad said to Steve. 'Let's make the church and the school our top priority. Everybody can pitch in when they've finished their morning chores.'

'Great idea,' said Steve, 'I'm off to bed. You coming?'

'No not for a minute. I just need some thinking time.'

'Need company?'

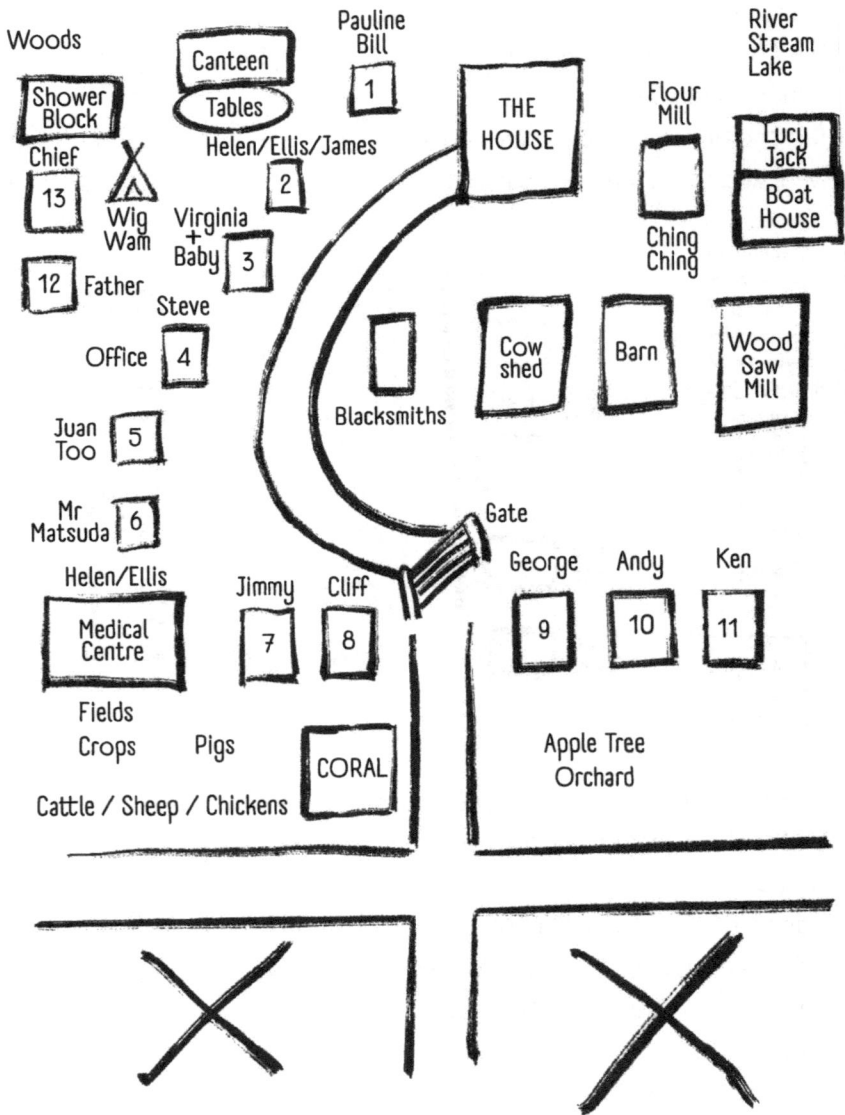

Woods

Pauline
Bill

River
Stream
Lake

Canteen

Tables

1

THE
HOUSE

Flour
Mill

Lucy
Jack

Shower
Block

Helen/Ellis/James

Chief

13

Wig
Wam

2

Virginia
+
Baby

3

Boat
House

Ching
Ching

12  Father

Steve

Office  4

Cow
shed

Barn

Wood
Saw
Mill

Juan
Too  5

Blacksmiths

Mr
Matsuda  6

Gate

George    Andy    Ken

Helen/Ellis

Jimmy    Cliff

9    10    11

Medical
Centre

7    8

Fields

Crops    Pigs

CORAL

Apple Tree
Orchard

Cattle / Sheep / Chickens

'No I'm OK. Goodnight, see you in the morning.'

'Yeah goodnight, buddy. See you in the morning.'

Brad went through in his mind the people he had met and things they had achieved already.

First Lucy and Jack, how Helen had helped him with his knee, two youngsters that now had a home, and had never mentioned their aunty once. They could do all the sailing and fishing they wanted to, they had a ready-made family around them. Ellis was becoming a good friend to Lucy, they each loved Virginia's and Helen's company, and little Too, and they had Ma and Pa, Pauline, Dianna's little Baby Virginia to swoon over.'

His mind turned to Helen, James and Ellis, Helen who lost her husband, her home, now settling in, the medical centre to occupy her mind, teaching her daughter nursing, giving her a future to look forward to, so proud that James was coming out of himself, maturing. It was a good idea of Steve's to give him the chicken and egg job. Responsibility, interacting with people, Ma and Pa, Pauline, Bill, taking the sandwiches round, got him to mix with everybody talk to people, all the thank yous made him feel good. He had a purpose in life, a direction. Wait till he starts selling eggs and receiving money. 'I think I'll borrow Mr Matsuda's buggy, he can start delivering eggs to homes.'

Virginia to be chucked out on a street, homeless, jobless, to get so attached to Chief's baby, and have the baby named after her, to have a home, a special friend in Helen, all the women folk she liked, not having to worry where her next plate of food was coming from. Her dream come true of designing and making clothes, to be able to sell her own clothing line and I'm pretty sure she's got a hot spot for Jimmy. You can just tell by the way she looks at him and blushes when he's around her. Running Bear (Chief) to be alone with a child to bring up, he makes no bones about how he wanted a son, but decided he could just as well teach his daughter, to ride, hunt, and of his family traditions and customs. He's so grateful to

Virginia, that he can carrying on doing what he's doing, and his child is being looked after he loves the woodland, his wigwam, nobody is going to move him on anymore, his child will get education, many people around her to guide and help her, a future, and he gets to chop wood and have fires dance, and his English language skills and words are getting better.

Father, who has helped so much of this happen, his face when we told him we were going to build him his own church, school and library, his own parish his own congregation, his own choir, kids to teach, adults to help read and write, he deserves all these things, because he's a loving, kind, generous person who cares deeply about people's feeling and ambitions, he's been guided here. Now he can guide others.

Juan and Too, all those years of wondering where the next meal is going to come from to feed his daughter. Those terrible places they've had to sleep in, dirt, squalor, horrible company, now a home for him and his daughter, regular meals, playmates for Too, she can go to Father's school, learn how to read and write, read books, religion. They have jobs, will get an income, she can ride horses, play in the woods, go swimming in the lake, sailing, she will be surrounded by loving honest people, maybe if he had more kids, he could call them Three and Four. Brad chuckled to himself.

Mr Matsuda, I must find out his first name. What an upstanding man with principles, dedication, accuracy, humble, I must ask him more about his past. Steve got the right man, for the right job. Him and Ching-Ching get on so well together like brothers. Their humour is contagious, side splitting, he likes to be kept busy and he will be a great asset.

Ah Jimmy, a right cheeky character full of life, full of beans, uplifts everyone around him, especially through his love of music, he'll have a change now to teach others, make instruments, entertain us all, he's got a ready-made fan club. Everyone adores him, I must ask him if he's settled, and does he have an eye for Virginia, what does he want out of life.

Then there's Cliff, the cowboy, probably happier with the horses than people, but I'll work on that. Working with Jimmy and George will bring him more into the fold, maybe one day I can make him sheriff of our town, with his own sheriff badge, he'd like that, and teaching people to ride would be a great reward for him.

George, we all love George, that man's journey in life is extraordinary, although years of working for a boss, not choosing his own name, but given one depending on his work, the conditions he lived under, punished, abused, lack of freedom, not a working wage lack of movement, disciplined every minute of every day, no love or relationships, no future, no hope, he held on to his belief in the Lord, and with a bit of luck, determination, heroism and boldness, he managed to escape his shackles, his enforced labour, he set himself free for the first time in his life. How he must have struggled to survive, in those early days of freedom, walking, running, hiding, lack of food, water, shoeless, his aches, pains and soreness must have been immense, but he kept his spirit, kept his faith, only to be captured, tied to a tree and whipped, for no crime committed, shameful.

When we came along, cut him down, Helen treated his wounds, he became a new man, freed, allowed to live his live, to choose, to walk anywhere, to have his own home, to work his way, no boss, to have friends around him who respect and love him, to be part of a community soon to get his own business and money, regular food, time off to do whatever he wants to.

George has been the best reason to do and start all this, a new change, a new beginning, Helen told him he would never be alone ever again, and I'll never forget his face, that smile, when Helen purchased his clothes for him, and the sucking of his lollipop.

Andy saved from the brink of disaster, a man going downhill fast, a drunk, dirty, dishevelled, no purpose in life, no hope, prospects or future, a man down on his luck. His wife had been killed, he was alone, sad and hurting, now the sky's the limit, I really believe he will never drink again, fingers crossed.

Ken, lovely, lovely Ken, huge man who wouldn't hurt a fly, loving, vulnerable, kind and thoughtful, sleeping in a barn, parents gone, sad, alone, picked on, he's so happy here just to have his own place, a job, people around him that love him, an amazing story and I'm sure many more treasured memories to come.

Just then his thoughts were interrupted, Ma had turned up with a hot cup of chocolate. 'Not interrupting, son, am I? I thought I'd find you here.'

'No Ma, lovely to see you please sit down. Well, Ma, what do you think of all the things that are happening around here?'

'Amazing, son, just amazing. Ma and Pa are loving this new life for us and for them, what a lovely completely different group of people, all needing a bit of help in life, all needing a home, a future, a change of luck. And you've done it, son, you've made it happen.'

'I didn't plan to, Ma, it just happened along the way. It was just me coming home by myself.' Brad went on to tell the stories how he came to meet everyone.

Ma said 'sounds as though you were guided. Everything was meant to be, you've given the ranch a new lease of life, a future and all the people a future to. Me and Pa have always loved all of our children, but we always knew you were going to turn out to be quite a special person. We love you and support you in anything and everything you do.'

'Thanks, Ma,' Brad said. 'How's Alan and Dianna? They do not feel pushed out in any way, do they?'

'No son,' said Ma. 'Alan's so pleased to have you back home, he's missed you, he's always looked up to you, you've always protected him, looked out for him, never played on his illness. He's had a heavy workload since you've been away. He can now relax more. You've taken a big weight off his shoulders, but he is still part of the team and progress. Alan and Dianna can spend more time together. Maybe we could have a new addition to the family. I'd love to be a grandma, and it doesn't look like you're going to make it happen.'

'You never know, Ma, you never know.'

'Is it, Helen, Virginia, anybody I know?'

'Not yet, Ma, I'll let you know all in good time.'

'Come on, son, let's get you in before you get too cold, they walked back to the house, one arm around each other.'

'I love you, Ma.'

'I love you too, Brad.'

Next morning after the sound of the gong they all met up for breakfast. Boiled eggs, toast, hot coffee and tea. Steve said 'thank you, Bill and Pauline. What's for lunch and dinner?'

'For lunch a bowl of vegetable soup, for dinner a meat, potato and vegetable pie and a pudding.'

'Sounds great,' said Steve.

Pauline said, 'I will be needing a grocery run soon to stock up, then I can write some menus up for next week, and find out what people would like to eat.'

'Great idea,' said Steve, 'tomorrow we'll all go into town, get your lists of things you need to Mr Matsuda, if you can't write them down, describe them to him, and he will write them down. Mr Matsuda, see Brad and he will sort the money out for you. We'll all go into town after breakfast tomorrow.'

A massive cheer went up, everybody was full of excitement, especially George.

'Right,' said Steve, 'how we doing on the job front?'

Jack and Lucy have got a lot of sorting out with the fishing tackle and boat.

**Steve said**

'Shout if you need any help. Ching-Ching, how's the flour mill coming along?'

'Good to go,' said Ching-Ching.

'Pauline, Bill, get your food list organised? Sarah, Ellis how's the medical centre coming along?' Helen said, 'Good we will soon be able to sew your mouth up.' A roar of laughter erupted. Steve thought that was quite funny so he winked at Helen, and she blushed again.

'Virginia how's it going?'

'I've been measuring people. I need certain material's.'

'OK,' Steve said, 'get your list to Mr Matsuda.'

'I've also made this.' She produced a white cotton all-in-one dress, and gave it to Too. Her face was so excited.

She said, 'Gracias. I mean thank you.' They hugged, Juan was so proud of his daughter and hugged Virginia.

'Awesome,' said Steve, 'Chief are you still chopping wood? Good, if you need help getting logs onto wagon, Brad will help, he's got nothing to do,' he said tongue in cheek. 'George and Ken, can help if needed.'

Mr Matsuda get the lists going.

'Jimmy, Cliff are you branding today?'

'Yes probably,' said Cliff.

'Good I'll help you, I've lassoed a few cattle in my time. James you can help after doing what you need to do. Andy, how's things?'

'The cot and crib are finished, they just were the bedding put in, then they're good to go.'

'After our shopping trip tomorrow, we'll get a plan of action, all hands to the pump, and start building the church and school.' A big hooray went up and clapping. 'Father if you could help Andy with the special surprise.'

Andy said, 'Oh and the partition is ready for Ellis and James.'

'OK,' said Steve, 'after lunch we'll got that fitted. OK everybody, have a good day, I'll see you all for lunch, don't forget your shopping lists.'

'Last thing, who's got any birthdays coming up?' Most didn't know or had forgotten. 'Don't worry,' said Steve, 'this Saturday well be birthday night for all those who have never had a birthday. There'll be singing and dancing and a big birthday cake and presents! Ye-ha!'

# Chapter 6

## The Shopping Trip

Today was Friday, the chance for everybody to go into town for the first time armed with their lists. Everybody was given two dollars to treat themselves, or others, bearing in mind it was birthday night tomorrow, a celebration of how far they had come, and what that all had achieved.

The excitement in the air was buzzing, Mr Matsuda had extra money for those who needed special items, he decided to set up accounts with local shop traders and settle accounts on a weekly basis. This would stop the group having to need money, they could buy whatever they needed and charge it to the ranch account. This shouldn't be a problem as the ranch had good credit against it.

He would also enquire at the bank, what he needed to do to set up bank accounts in everybody's names.

He'd been busy drawing up the posters, advertising products the ranch could supply, logs, fish, flour, bread, buns, cakes, apples, apple pies, clothes made to order, washing, cleaning, pressing service, repairs, shoe repairs (for George), metal working, blacksmith's horse and shoes, chickens, eggs, cattle, pigs, sheep, crops, vegetables, a medical centre, a school of music carpentry, wood planks for buildings, mention about the opening of a church and school, eventually, we'll have a cake shop, hopefully a restaurant, a dress shop, a butcher's, a fish monger's, hardware store.

He had seen Brad's drawing on the table, so knew what Brad was planning.

He would get all the youngsters to pin the posters up, then he thought we'll have launch day, and invite everybody around, to attend, we can have boat trips, fishing trips, a play area for children. Yes next Saturday we will have an open day with music, a barbecue, and sell sell sell, profit, profit profit, I must get Brad and Steve's approval, everybody will get excited and it's my idea, my project.

What a morning. Lists flying everywhere, money going out left and right, everybody was so grateful to have some cash in their hands, each had an idea of what they wanted buy.

'Right Brad stop everything. Let's get loaded up on the wagons, at this rate the shops will be shut.'

The horses were hitched up, Ma and Pa were going to go it their buggy, also Alan and Dianna, it had been ages since they had been in town together, Ching-Ching got in with Mr Matsuda.

Once everybody was loaded Brad poked his head out, looked that everybody was ready, they all gave him the thumbs up sign, he noticed the wagon train had got even longer now. 'Wagons roll,' he shouted.

'Wagon's roll,' came back with lots of vigour and excitement.

It brought a real smile to Brad and Father's faces. In town they parked at the back of the main street not to block all the buildings, straight away you could see what was going to happen. The ladies all gathered together, the men split up to go their separate ways.

Lucy said to Jack, 'Let's get an ice cream or lolly.'

'Great idea,' said Jack, thinking to himself I want to buy something nice for Lucy, maybe even something for their shack.

Ching-Ching and Mr Matsuda headed for the bank, closely followed by

Ma and Pa, Alan and Dianna decided to go straight for the cake shop, and have a cup of tea.

Bill and Pauline headed for the grocery store, Brad and Steve said they would meet them there later to help them load up. Virginia, Helen, Ellis headed for the materials shop. Jack stayed with Father as he went in hunt of a Bible, Chief was looking for the hardware store, as was Andy and Ken, Jimmy said to Cliff do you fancy a beer?

'That sounds good,' said Cliff, off they want to the saloon.

George was looking for gifts. He thought Helen, Ellis, Ma (flowers), maybe get everybody flowers just the ladies, also Pauline, Dianne, for cooking him such wonderful meals, get a big bunch of flowers, split them up, Lucy, Too, Baby Virginia a little present perhaps a doll, George thought he'll know what to get when he sees it.

He saw the florists, and went on. There were colourful flowers of all shapes, sizes, all colours under the rainbow, vases, ribbons, baskets. Standing there looking confused, a little soft voice, said 'Excuse me, sir, can I help you?'

He thought to himself I've never been called a sir before in my life. As he turned in front of him he saw a vision, this beautiful lady, petite gorgeous, long black hair, tied like a ponytail, luscious eyes, kissable lips, shiny white perfectly formed teeth, a smile to die for, cute little dimples, oh my God he thought, she's beautiful, she repeated, 'Can I help you, sir?' George couldn't think of one word to say, nothing, completely speechless, the silence seemed to go on for ages.

Eventually he blurted out, 'Flowers.'

'Yes sir,' she said, 'flowers, we sell flowers, it's a flower shop.'

George, trying to put words together, shouted, 'Buy.'

'Which ones,' she said, George was now starting to think this wasn't such a good idea after all, if only Helen was here George thought she'd know what to do.

George slapped his two dollar's on the counter, 'All of them,' he said.

She laughed, 'You can't buy all of these flowers for two dollars.'

'How many?' said George, feeling sick and dizzy.

She came from behind the counter, got him a chair, she said, 'Sit down slowly.' His head was spinning, he was sweating, his mouth had gone dry. 'Would you like a drink of water?' she asked.

'Yes please,' he said, thinking by the time she returned he might have composed himself better.

'Now who are they for?' she said.

'Everyone,' George blurted out.

'Now who's everyone?'

'Ma, Diana, Pauline, Helen, Ellis, Virginia, Too.'

'Is that all?' she said, 'are they all your girlfriends?' she asked.

'No,' George snapped. 'I don't have a girlfriend.'

'That's a shame,' she said, 'a handsome man like you should have a girlfriend.'

George felt like shouting, 'Do you want to be my girlfriend?' but he controlled himself.

'Now sweetie what's your name?'

'George,' he said.

'Nice to meet you George, my name is Maria.'

'Hello Maria,' said George. 'That's a lovely name.'

'Thank you, George. Is it a special occasion?'

'Yes tomorrow is my birthday.'

'Oh happy birthday for tomorrow,' she said.

'Thank you.'

'I wanted to get everybody a little present, a thank you gift for helping me. I wanted to get Ma a basket of flowers, Helen a vase with flowers in, you'd like Helen,' said George.

'I'm sure I would,' said Maria.

**Marie**

'How's this for an idea, I will individually wrap single flowers in tissue paper, attach a bow to each of them. Would you like me to put a card on them so you could write your name on to say who sent them?'

'I can't write,' said George.'

'That's OK,' said Maria, 'I'll write on most of them, the special vase for Helen, I'll show how to write George on it. You can copy what I write, and practise it.'

'Thank you, Maria. That sounds wonderful.' George thought what a lovely, caring lady, so smart, and she's going to help me write my name, and she's beautiful.

Time passed, the little bundles of flowers looked so good, George had been practising writing George. She held his hands to help him form the words, her hands were so soft, she smelt so good, and there it was, George in writing. The letters looked a bit wobbly, but it truly said George. The vase for Helen looked wonderful Ma had a lovely basket with baby plants in which would grow and bloom, just how he felt his life was growing and blooming. George said, 'Do I have enough money?'

Maria thought not enough money, but she would have done this gladly for nothing. 'Yes George, you even have some change.' She thought, I'll give him one of each coin, I bet he's never handled many coins before, George was fascinated by the colours and the hard metal in his hand. Maria thought I can tell this is a kind, caring, thoughtful man. 'Where do you live?' Maria asked.

'At the ranch. I have my own shack and a job.'

'What do you do?' she asked.

'Many things but my trade is I'm a blacksmith.' He was so proud.

'Oh!' she said, 'I'd love to see the ranch and your shack.'

'Why don't you come to our birthday party? You could meet Ma and Helen, Brad and Steve, Mr Matsuda, Cliff, Andy, Ken,' then he just stopped talking realising what he had asked.

'Yes I'd like that,' said Maria. George's heart missed a beat, he could feel his heart pounding, he started to shake and sweat again, then his brain kicked in. 'I'll pick you up Saturday, say late afternoon? Then I can give you a tour of the ranch, you can stay for the barbecue.'

'OK George,' she said. 'I'll see you Saturday.' As he got up to go, she said, 'Don't forget your flowers.'

'Thank you, Maria I'll see you Saturday,' and left the shop, he flopped against the shop wall. What am I going to wear? I'll see Virginia. Will Mr Matsuda let me borrow his buggy, what will I say to her?

Just then Brad and Steve were passing by. 'George, are you alright,' Brad asked.

'Never better, never better,' George replied.

'Good,' said Steve. 'We're going for a beer, would you like to join us?'

'Am I allowed to?'

'Yes of course,' came the reply.

George thought this day is just getting better and better. No, he thought, my life is getting better and better.

'Brad,' George asked 'can I bring someone for the birthday party?'

'Of cause you can, George you never need to ask,' Steve said. 'Have you met someone?'

Brad said, 'Mind your own business.'

As they went into the saloon, they saw Jimmy playing the piano, Cliff was slumped in a chair, as soon as he saw, Brad, Steve and George, he shouted, 'Barman, drinks for my friends,' then slumped over.

Steve said, 'Looks like we're going to have to carry him out'.

Jimmy came over, excited. He said, 'I've been offered a job here, some lunch times, evenings, whenever needed. He said I can write my own show and perform it!'

'Brilliant,' said Brad.

Jimmy shouted, 'Put these drinks on my tab, you can take it out of my wages.'

Steve turned to Brad and George and Jimmy. 'Cheers,' he said. 'I've waited a long time for this moment.'

'Cheers,' they said. George took a sip. This taste's different he thought, sort of bubbly with a strange taste.

'Drink up,' said Brad, 'we've got to get over to the grocery store to help Pauline and Bill load the stores up.'

Steve said, 'Someone's going to have to help Cliff,'

'Don't worry about that,' said Jimmy. 'I'll get him sorted and stick him in the wagon.'

Brad, Steve and George arrived just at the right time. All the boxes and bags were ready to load. Steve said, 'I'll bring my wagon round to the front, it will make it easier for us.' He turned to Pauline. 'Are these all mine?' he said.

'Get out of it,' she said, 'And hurry up and get the wagon, there's fresh things in here I want to get into the coolers and out of the sun.'

Once loaded Brad went walkabout to see if he could see anybody else straggling alone, he met the ladies. 'Would you like me to carry your bags?' he said.

'No we're fine,' said Helen. 'See if you can round up the others.'

By the time he got back to the wagons they were all loaded waiting for him. 'Last again,' said Father.

'Just collecting all the sheep,' said Brad. Father laughed.

Before he could say anything they all shouted, 'Wagons roll.' They all laughed, including Brad.

'Wagon's roll,' Brad said.

It was crazy at the ranch, people rushing everywhere, showing each other what they had purchased, the ladies trying things on, the men showing each other what they got. Cliff was put to bed.

Steve said, 'Pauline what have we got for dinner?'

'A surprise,' she said, and would from now on whenever he asked if she would answer 'a surprise'.

She already knew she was doing freshly cut ham and salad followed by a fresh fruit salad.

For the birthday party tomorrow, pork, lamb and beef all on the outside fire pit, with jacket potatoes.

Steve went to say goodbye to everyone but they'd all gone their separate ways.

George flew off to hide the flowers and put some water on them. Maria told him what to do, he'd already spoke to Mr Matsuda about borrowing his buggy.

'No problem,' said Mr Matsuda, 'any time.'

He just needed to talk to Virginia now and sort out what he could wear tomorrow to pick up Maria. He was excited but nervous at the same time, he probably wouldn't sleep tonight!

The gong sounded. Everybody made their way over to the canteen. Father asked Ma would she like to lead the prayers. 'Yes she said,' she would, 'it will be an honour.'

After dinner Brad stood up. 'After breakfast tomorrow, after we've done our chores for the day, we will have a day off (a big cheer went up). All those available can help build the fire, get the fire pits ready. See Pa, he has some bunting we can put up, tables and chairs to be got ready, and I'd like to build a little stove. There will be no work Sunday (big cheer). Go and do whatever you want to, Pauline and Bill will not be cooking, but they have agreed to leave leftovers for those of you who can't cook.

'Pauline and Bill, you are invited up to the house for dinner as you have cooked for everyone all week we would like to cook for you to show our appreciation. Every Sunday we would like to invite dinner courses for all groups so my family can get to know you better, and have a tour of the house, we would like to offer employee of the week, for someone who has going beyond the call of duty.

'Tomorrow is going to be an amazing day and night. Enjoy Sunday whatever you get up to, on Monday after breakfast all hands together we are going to start building the church and school.' Another big cheer and clapping.

Brad said, 'Right I'm off I've got things to do.'

George spoke to Virginia, she suggested a nice shirt, trousers with braces, a waistcoat and bow tie. 'Brilliant,' said George. 'I'll have a word with Pa, he's got all these things, they might need a bit of adjustment, but I can do that. We'll see if his shoes will fit. Thank you, Mam.'

'Don't worry,' Virginia said, 'We'll have you all sorted out by tomorrow. I understand you're bringing someone to the party.'

'Yes,' said George, 'she's beautiful. Her name's Maria.'

'Take things slowly, George.'

'I will, Virginia, I promise.'

Party day had arrived, Pauline announced, s they were having a huge meal later, all those who couldn't wait and would be hungry ham sandwiches were wrapped inside.

Steve stood up. 'Right we need to get organised today, all hands to the pump. Let's get the tables cleared, placed in a semi-circle facing our little stage, and enough room for dancing.' He winked at Helen again, she just smiled back at him.

'The fire pits and grows need to be built.' He put a thumbs up to cheers. 'All the bunting needs to go up, plates, grocery, glasses were to be got ready, the meat needs to be prepared. Jack, Lucy, a few nice grilling fish wouldn't go a miss, so all those that need to get their daily chores done, you go off and meet us back here when you can.

'George you just to and get ready, have a nice bath and shave, comb your hair, and get yourself looking real smart.'

George was embarrassed when everybody laughed, but inside he felt great.

'No Steve,' he said, 'I'd like to pull my weight, do my bit for the party. I've got plenty of time to get ready, any case I'm looking forward to them ham sandwiches.'

It was such a good effort from everybody, all pulling together as one team. Alan, Diana, Ching-Ching Ma, Pa, all joined in with what that needed doing.

It was soon ham sandwich time. George announced it was time for him to get ready, a big cheer went up as he walked away as soon as he was out of sight.

Brad stood up and said, 'We've got to get organised. As soon as George rides out in the buggy, all meet at Andy's workshop. We have a massive surprise for George, we have been working on a sign which says "Mr George the blacksmith" the ropes are already, we need to pull it up to the top of the blacksmith's. It needs to be fixed on and secured. What a surprise he will have when he returns with Maria.'

'What a way to impress her,' said Virginia.

'Not a word to anyone,' Brad said, 'once the signs up we can all start to get ready.'

George emerged from his shack, he looked dapper, he felt a million dollars, with his wonderful waistcoat, his white shirt, bow tie, long creased trousers, and shoes. Steve was first to see him and gave a wolf whistle. George just grinned. Steve walked up to George and squirted him with aftershave. It stung a little, but he smelled good. Bit by bit people gathered, all giving George compliments.

Virginia said, 'If Maria doesn't want you, I do.' They all laughed.

Mr Matsuda brought the buggy around, he'd cleaned it up. Brushed the horse done, with Virginia's help tied some bows to the harness, and on the passenger seat he'd left his best bowler hat, George was choked up with how kind people had been, he jumped up into the buggy, put Mr Matsuda's bowler on, everybody cheered and shouted 'Good luck, George,' waving him away as he left the ranch.

'Right,' said Brad, 'action stations. Let's get the sign up.' They all pulled together, got the sign up, secured it, then one by one left to get ready.

As George pulled into town, Maria was standing outside the flower shop. She looked amazing, thought George, she had a bright yellow dress, pulled in at the waist by a yellow ribbon, a matching yellow carousel opened, resting on her shoulder, with shoes with flowers attached to them. George, thought, she looked stunning, gorgeous, magnificent. What am I going to say? Don't forget what Virginia said, take it slowly.

George said, 'I'm sorry to keep you waiting, Maria.'

'Oh,' she said, 'I've only been waiting a short while.'

George jumped down from the buggy, took Maria's hand and helped her up into the buggy.

'You look wonderful,' was all he could think to say. He dashed around to the driver's side, got in.

Maria said, 'George you look so smart and handsome.'

He lent over and kissed Maria on the cheek, then wished he hadn't, too late now he thought then he remembered what Virginia had said, take things showed, oops.

'OK,' he said to Maria, 'let's head to the ranch.'

'Happy Birthday, George,' Maria said.

It had gone out of his mind. 'Thank you, Maria.'

When they arrived at the ranch, George pulled around to his shack. Nobody was about, probably everybody getting ready for this evening. He opened the door and said, 'After you, Maria.' Maria was pleasantly shocked of how clean and tidy everything was. George opened his bedroom door and said, 'This is my bedroom.'

Maria poked her nose in, saw that the bed had been made. 'Very nice,' she said as they walked past the table. She saw the vase, basket and flowers all laid out on the table.

George opened the second bedroom door. 'This is the spare bedroom,' he said.

'Is this where I'll be sleeping?'

George couldn't believe his ears. 'Pardon?' he said.

Maria said, 'Well, I thought I didn't want to be going home just as the party was starting to get going, besides,' she said, 'it will be getting dark, and we can't risk riding at night.'

'No,' said George, 'precisely.'

Maria carried on, 'Then I thought we could have a picnic together being as it's Sunday, do you have a day off?'

'Yes,' said George overwhelmed with emotion.

'Good,' said Maria, 'that's settled. George, would you mind bringing my case in from the buggy and putting it in my room?'

'Yes,' said George, stunned. He thought I don't remember putting a case in the buggy, but then his mind was so focused on Maria.

George said, 'Maria I thought I'd take you up to the lake, it's so pretty up there.'

'OK,' she said, they got back into the buggy.

George said, 'Andy lives there and Ken lives there you'll meet them all later. That's Cliff and Jimmy's shack, and the medical centre behind. That's Mr Matsuda's, he lent me this buggy and the bowler hat.'

'Very nice,' said Maria,

'That's Juan and Too.'

'Juan and Too,' Maria said laughing.

'Yes,' said George, 'it's a long story I'll tell you later. And this is where I work.' He stopped the buggy, then for the first time he saw the sign hanging up. George got out. He was shaking, flabbergasted, he'd seen blacksmith before, and written George, when Maria helped him to write it.

Maria read it out. 'Mr George the blacksmith,' she said.

George nearly crumbled to his knees. Luckily Maria was there to hold him, he turned to her and embraced each other, cuddling George as he just wept and wept.

Maria stroked the back of his head. 'Happy birthday, George, what a lovely surprise.'

George said, 'They are such lovely people here, I'm so happy, and I got you to share it all with.' They just carried on hugging for a while.

Eventually George said, 'OK let's try and make it to the lake without any more surprises.'

'That's Steve's office. Sometimes he sleeps there and sometimes in the house. That's Virginia's, she helped get all my clothes ready. Over the back is Father's home and Chief's and Baby Virginia's, but you'll often find Baby Virginia with Virginia.'

'Do you want children, George?' Maria asked.

'Hundreds and hundreds,' said George, hoping he hadn't gone over the top. 'What about you?' George asked.

'I'd be happy to start with one,' she replied.

'Over the back is the woodland and Chief's wigwam, the canteen, that's where the birthday party is later, then there's lovely Helen, Ellis and James, and the last one, Pauline and Bill. They've been looking after me and feeding me.'

'But that's kept them busy,' said Maria.

'Sure has,' said George. 'I like my food.'

'I can tell,' said Maria.

'This is the main house, Ma and Pa, Alan, Brad's brother, and his wife Dianna and Ching-Ching, he's amazingly funny.' As he pulled around, he pointed to the cowshed, barn and wood mill. 'Oh,' he said, 'I forgot to show you the cattle, pigs, sheep, chickens, the fields the crops, the horses, the corral.'

'Slow down, George there is plenty of time for that tomorrow,' Maria said.

Taking a breath in, George said, 'Yes you're right. Plenty of time for that tomorrow,' pinching himself that he got to be with Maria all day tomorrow. 'That's the flour mill and Jack and Lucy's lodge.'

How beautiful the lake looked. They sat on the branch together holding hands. 'This is where we'll have our picnic tomorrow,' Maria said.

'Yeah, I'll take you out in the rowing boat.' Their eyes met, and they passionately kissed for the first time. They kissed and kissed again. George felt like the luckiest man in the world.

By the time George and Maria arrived at the party the fire pits were alight. You could smell the meat cooking and spitting, the tables were laid, Jimmy was banging out some tunes. As soon as George and Maria arrived they were swamped with people gathering around them, everybody wanted to meet Maria. As they came forward, everybody hugged and kissed. Nice to meet you was said over and over again. George handed out his flowers, and when Helen received her vase of flowers she hugged and kissed George and Maria. Ma was over the moon with her growing basket, and told the couple, 'Next week you must come up to the house and join us for dinner.' They both said that would be wonderful and that they were both looking forward to that. 'And a tour of the house,' said Ma.

After lots of talking, chatting, music, laughter, finally the gong was clattered by Bill, 'Come and get it,' he shouted. The rush was on, queuing in a line, the selection was awesome, meats, sauces, bowls of salad, jacket potatoes, buns, rolls, tomatoes, a bowl of punch, a bowl of homemade cider, soft drinks, beer, et cetera. Just before everybody tucked in Father stood up and said, 'I would like to say prayers (they all nodded). Thank you, Lord, for the food we are about to eat. A special thank you to Pauline and Bill and the many helpers, Ma, Diana, Alan, Ching-Ching, Chief, Brad, Steve and all the others.

'I would also like to mention, I will be holding an assembly tomorrow morning after breakfast, to bless the sacred ground the church will be built on. There will be prayers and hymns in the open air.' Maria turned to George, and said, 'I would like to go to that.'

'So would I,' said George, then he kissed her again. They all said amen, then Mr Matsuda stood up, cleared his throat and said, 'And next Saturday I have been a advertising an open day at the ranch for all locals to visit the ranch, so start getting everything ready to show our products, and sell, sell, sell, profit, profit, profit.' A massive cheer went up.

'Well done, Mr Matsuda,' said Brad, 'and Steve, this is our chance to show everybody what we are capable of.'

Steve said, 'Wouldn't it be amazing if we could have the church and school finished by then!'

The party went on and on, singing, dancing, everybody swapped partners and danced, gifts were exchanged everywhere. Too wore her new dress Virginia had made for her. They drank, they ate, they were happy and loud and proud.

Then a strange thing happened, a little man appeared. He was dressed in a dark suit, a hat and carried a case in his hand, everybody stopped dancing. Jimmy stopped the music, everybody gathered around this little man. 'Who's in charge here?' he said.

'Brad,' said Ma and Pa.'

'Ma and Pa,' said Brad.

Steve said, 'We're all in charge.' Everybody roared with laughter.

'No seriously,' the little man said. 'I've come on very important business.'

'Go ahead,' said Brad. 'We are listening.'

'I represent the east to west railway line. Very soon the railway will extend from the west coast to the east coast. I was in town and saw your advertisement stating how much you could supply, the railway and the workers will need everything you can supply to feed the workers. We will need hundreds of chickens, thousands of eggs, meat, fish, veg, flour, the list went on and on. Your blacksmith, we will add extra furnaces, anvils, moulds, even help you with the extra workforce you may need.' Everybody was shocked, just standing there speechless.

Brad said, 'What we can't supply we can get all the local people to join in and supply our shortfall. This will be massive for the local community.'

'Good,' said the little man. 'I will be up Monday with some paperwork to sign, get planting, building, sewing, harvesting. This could be up to a two-year contract, as we move alone the line. Your products will be put on a train, and moved to where we are camped now.' He said, 'I must get going, I need to be back in town,' and left.

Everybody whooped, danced around in circles, Jimmy struck the music up, it was pure mayhem. George turned to Marie and said, 'Hallelujah, life doesn't get any better than this.'

'Oh yes it does, George,' she said, 'I'm never going to leave you, I'm going to marry you, have your children, but not a hundred, we're going to grow old together and I will always love you.'

'I love you too, Maria.' And they kissed

Next morning at breakfast everybody was chattering and chattering about last night's events. Eventually Father stood up. 'I don't know about you but I'm in shock.'

'Yes,' they all shouted, 'total shock.'

'Soon,' he said, 'I'll be going down to give thanks and offer up prayers. We've got a lot to be thank-full for. I'm going to bless the sacred ground, and I understand you all have a day off, Pauline and Bill have leftovers from last night, please take whatever you want, especially if you're going on a picnic today.' He looked in George's direction. 'If I don't see you for the rest of the day, have a lovely time. I'll see you Monday morning after breakfast, and let's get building the church and school.' A big cheer went up.

Every single person followed Father to the grounds where the church and school were going to be built just outside the crossroads to the left.

As Brad and Steve walked together, Brad said, 'We will get all the money we need to build our town.'

Steve said, 'I'll have to cancel my beach trip then.'

Brad said, 'I couldn't do it without you, buddy'.

Father had got a bottle of holy water in town from the old priest. He knew one day he would need it, and today was that day.

He sprinkled the soil with the holy water, said prayers as he went over the ground, blessing and swaying his arm from side to side, dropping drops of water as he walked.

They all joined in the Lord's prayer: 'Our Father who art in Heaven, hallowed be thy name …'

Everybody split up and went their separate ways, Pauline Bill to get ready for dinner at the house. Chief picked up little Virginia and went off into the woods.

George and Maria took a boat out on the lake. He faced Maria and said, 'I don't want you to go.'

'I don't want to go but I must.'

'Will you hurry back?' said George.

'As soon as I've shut my shop down, it's only rented, packed my things. I'm coming back to stay with you forever.'

'Will you marry me?' George said.

'Are you asking?' said Maria.

'Yes I'm asking,' said George.

'Yes,' said Maria, 'I will marry you as soon as possible.'

'Hallelujah, praise the Lord,' said George and kissed her.

# Chapter 7

## The Building of the Church

It was the start of a new week, everybody had finished breakfast and was talking to each other about what they did on Sunday on their day off. Pauline and Bill loved the tour of the house, stories, conversation and dinner. Maria and George had a lovely day around the lake, took a rowing boat and had a lovely picnic.

Just then Steve stood up. 'Good morning, everybody,' he said.

'Good morning,' came back.

'Well I hope you enjoyed your weekend. Saturday's birthday party was a resounding success.' A big cheer went up. 'We hope you all had a nice restful day Sunday, but now it's down to work. We've got a busy week ahead, all essential chores need to be done, then we're going to start building the church and school. (A big hooray went up.) Wouldn't it be awesome, if for next Sunday service we could be inside the church we had all built. (Another big hooray.) George may need help this week as he needs to mould a metal cross, and a weathervane, also a cross for the altar and metal drinking cups. We'll get that organised, we also need to build our little huts and stalls to display our products for sale for the big opening day, coming up at the end of the week.' Hooray went up.

'Mr Pullman is coming up to see Brad and the ranch today, the man from the railways, so get ready to show him what we are capable of doing. Pauline, what's for lunch and dinner?' Steve said.

Pauline shouted, 'A surprise, Brad, the menu.'

Steve took the hint. 'I'm sure it will be lovely,' he said. 'So why are you all still sitting here? Chop, chop, let's get at it.' They all laughed and clapped.

George and Maria went up to Father and said, 'May we speak to you in private?'

'Yes,' said Father, 'come with me to my shack.'

As soon as they all got inside Father's shack George blurted out, 'Father, Maria and I want to get married.'

Father jumped up and hugged and kissed the couple, so excited he said, 'When?'

George and Maria said together, 'As soon as possible.'

Father said, 'How soon?'

'By the end of the week if possible,' said George, 'I want to spend as little time as possible away from Maria, I love her Father with all of my heart.'

'I love George with all the heart and soul together,' Maria said, 'forever. And we would like the Lord's blessing upon our marriage.'

'Well um, well um,' said Father, 'what about next Sunday in our new church?' The three of them linked arms and danced around in a circle.

'That would be wonderful,' said George.

'OK.' Father said, 'We've got a lot to get organised and very little time to do it in.'

George butted in, 'I also have a very busy week ahead, our plan is to get Maria home, so she can sell off her remaining stock, get all her things packed up. I want to bring her home for Friday, so that she can be here for the opening day, then on the Sunday we can get married and never be apart ever again.'

'OK,' said Father, his brain twirling around at a hundred miles per hour, 'first things first, when Maria arrives Friday, I'll speak to Steve and borrow his shack for Maria to stay in, as it's unlucky to see the bride before on the day of the marriage, we'll go round to Virginia's now, get Maria measured up, I'm sure Virginia would love to make your wedding gown. If that's all right with you, Maria.'

'That would be lovely,' said Maria.

'Good, good, we'll make an announcement tonight after dinner, ask Pauline and Bill to put a spread on for you. Oh,' he said, 'everybody is going to be excited for you, and I get to marry you in our new church, the very first marriage, you will always be the first name forever in our marriage book. How exciting, right let's get around to Virginia's.'

They knocked Virginia's door. 'Come in,' she said.

George blurted out straight away, 'We're getting married, Maria and I are getting married.' He kissed Maria, Virginia stood up and screamed with delight.

'George,' she said, 'I told you take it slowly.'

'I did,' said George, 'I wanted to ask mark to marry me the first day I met her in the flower shop.' everybody laughed and hugged.

'Right,' said Father, 'we need to get organised, Maria is going home today, would you please make her wedding gown?'

'I would love to,' said Virginia.

Father continued, 'And a wedding suit for George.'

'It would be a pleasure,' said Virginia.

Father continued, 'If you could take the measurements you need from Virginia and George, I can take Maria home, so George can get on with his jobs. Virginia you come with us we can get the materials you need, and I've got to buy some things for Sunday, like the wedding book, et cetera.'

Virginia thought to herself, I'm going to make bridesmaid dresses for Too, Lucy, Ellis, what a great surprise that will be. I'll have to get all the ladies involved, Ma, Dianna, Helen, Lucy, Ellis, Too, oh maybe wedding dresses and suits for the menfolk, plus all the cousins and drapes for the church, and a special little gown for Baby Virginia, she'll look so cute.

Father said, 'We're going to stay hush until the evening meal tonight is over, then we will announce the wedding.'

Virginia said, 'I already have George's measurements so he can go.'

Father said, 'I'll get the wagon ready.'

'George you best say your goodbyes to Maria now and get to work. We've got a lot to do. And we'll arrange to pick Maria up later in the week.'

George turned to Maria, planted a big kiss on her lips and said, 'Maria, I love you.'

Maria kissed him back and said, 'George I love you.'

Both Father and Virginia said, 'Ah! That's lovely.'

Virginia thought I hope one day to find love like that for me, one day my prince will come.

Brad said to Steve and Mr Matsuda, 'I would like you to accompany me on the tour of the ranch with Mr Pullman. Mr Matsuda if you could take notes of his comments and requests, when we've finished the tour, we'll go back to the house for refreshments and look over the paperwork.'

Mr Pullman arrived quite early, eager to get stated. He had a few months to start getting ready for the laying of the railway, so much to organise, materials, tents, food-stocks, the list was endless, but he hoped this would be a good starting point.

They all shook hands. 'OK,' said Brad, 'let's get started.' They took him to the apple orchard first.

'Very impressive,' said Mr Pullman, onto the corral, pointing out where the church was going to be built, Brad mentioned about the future town he planned to build, with the cake shop, groceries, fishmonger's, butcher's, the hospital, hardware store, et cetera.

'Very impressing,' said Mr Pullman, to the cattle. 'We made need more,' said Mr Pullman.

'Don't worry,' said Brad.

**Brad said**

'I have a plan, as you know we have our opening day this Saturday, that gives us a week to organise all the local tradesmen, ranch owners, farmers, town folk, country folk, to attend and to tell you what they can provide.'

'Very interesting,' said Mr Pullman, 'my company can provide loans, so people can invest, in crops, cattle, poultry, pigs, sheep et cetera. We always pay in advance for things we will need, so nobody has to worry about money or bills.'

'That's amazing,' said Steve.

**Brad said**

'We would like you to be our guest of honour on Saturday, to meet everybody, and tell them of your plans.'

'I'm looking forward to that,' said Mr Pullman. They continued the tour, the fields with crops, the medical centre, past the blacksmith's, cowshed, the barn, wood sawmill, the woods to the left, canteen, the main house, onto the flour mill, and up to the lake, river and stream. 'Very impressive,' Mr Pullman kept saying.

'Let's go to the house get some refreshments, talk business, and have a look at your paperwork,' said Brad.

Back at the house Ma had made fresh cool juice, an apple pie was steaming on the table, Alan and Dianna were out working. Ma and Pa greeted Mr Pullman with handshakes, asked him to set down, which he did, removing his hat when he came into the house. Pa told him of the business he was running for the railway supplying nuts and bolts, Mr Pullman was very aware of that, and said, 'You can ever continue production. Increase your workforce, or sell the whole company to the railway to run.' Pa thanked him for the offer said he'd like to think about it and talk it over with Ma and that he would give him his answer this weekend on the open day, they shook hands in agreement.

'Now,' said Mr Pullman, 'I would like to try this tempting apple pie, mmm delicious, I already would like to place an order immediately.' They all laughed.

**Mr Pullman**

'Now on to business,' said Mr Pullman, 'the word contract scares the hell out of people. Let me explain, our contracts are not binding, we are not going to sue people or drag them through courts. This is why we us the word "endeavour", I know the good people who sign up for this will endeavour to do their upmost best, to deliver what they promised. We also recognise, weather, storms, material shortages, to be taken in to account, on the other side of the coin I can't have hundreds of men sitting in tents with nothing to eat, so we've come up with these contracts, which state to my best abilities and endeavours we will fulfil our commitments to the railways to our highest standard. My company is willing to invest early to make sure future needs are covered.'

Brad said, 'You have our fullest commitment to endeavour to meet all requirements of the railway.'

'That's good enough for me,' said Mr Pullman, 'we will draw up lists of requirements, for example how many chickens, how many eggs. We will give as much notice as possible if orders are to increase, as I know they will, with more people being involved. Any questions?' said Mr Pullman, 'and may I have another piece of apple pie?'

'Of course you can,' said Ma.

Mr Pullman left shaking everybody's hand and hugging Ma. She had wrapped a piece of apple pie for him to take away.

They all danced around the house together hugging, kissing, shaking hands. Pa said, 'This is amazing and so good for the whole area, and we're in the prime seat!'

Brad turned to Mr Matsuda, 'Get posters ready for town over the next days to get to as many ranches, farms, everybody you can, and get them here for Saturday.'

'Hu-wee,' said Steve, 'I'm off to get working on the church, you coming?'

'You bet,' said Brad, Ma, and Pa.

As they approached the location of the site of the church and school, they were amazed that the area had already been marked out for the two buildings. The main struts of the foundation were piled up ready to be laid, Andy, Ken, George, Cliff, Jimmy, Juan, Chief, Bill, James, Helen, Ellis, Lucy, Jack and Ching-Ching, Alan and Dianna, were all busy doing something.

Brad scanned the area, 'Where's Virginia and Father?'

'Gone into town to get some bits and pieces, and taken Maria home, but don't worry she'll be back for the weekend for the open day,' said George.

'Oh good,' said Brad, they started to lay the foundation planks, where the floor would be attached to, Pauline appeared with jugs of juice and sandwiches. They stopped for lunch, then carried on laying the flooring, hammering nails in, sawing, planning, rubbing, fixing, it was a great team effort. They were determined to get the flooring laid today. Pauline said she would prepare a salad. Meat and bits and bring it down so they wouldn't have to stop work for too long, and drinks, all you could hear for the rest of the day was hammering and sawing, Father arrived back with Virginia, went straight past the group to Virginia's shack and started onloading stuff from the wagon, nobody knew what it was except George. Mr Matsuda went flying out of the gate waving. 'Where's he going?' said Ching-Ching.

'I'll explain later,' said Brad.

'So many secretive things going on around here,' said Ching-Ching.

Finally at the end of the day, the flooring of the church and school had been laid. 'Congratulations everybody,' said Brad, 'at this rate we'll have it finished by Sunday for prayers.'

Father, Virginian Mr Matsuda, had rejoined the group as everybody sat on the flooring of the church.

Father stood up. 'Listen everybody, George has something he wants to say.' Hush came over everybody.

George gingerly stood up, and walked over to the middle of the floor. 'Thank you, everybody,' he said, 'I know on Sunday you all have a day off but I wondered if you could spare me some of your time, and come to me and Maria's wedding.' It took a second or two for the group for it to sink in what George had just said, then they went crazy, shouting and screaming they ran across the floor en masse and smothered George with bodies slapping his back, congratulating him, kissing him, hugging him, Father had to calm things down.

'Let George speak,' he said.

George continued, 'Virginia knows about the good news, and she is making the wedding dress for Maria,' clapping starred, 'and my wedding suit,' another clap. 'She may need some help,' said George.

All the women shouted. 'I'll help,' could be heard ringing around.

'I would also like to ask Brad, as Maria has no family, would he like to give Maria away?'

'I'd be honoured to, George.'

'And I also wondered would Steve stand by me and be my best man.'

'George,' Steve said, 'I'd love to.'

'Thank you, Brad and Steve, I wouldn't be alive if not for you two and Helen.' George blew Helen a kiss, she caught it and blew one back.

'That only leaves to ask Pauline Bill and the team could we have the biggest party ever?' They all cheered.

Virginia stood up, she said, 'I know how pleased we all are for Maria and George, could all ladies join me in my shack for a meeting and measurements? Men tomorrow.' Brad thought what a day it had been. Mr Pullman, I'll tell them tomorrow. George is getting married and the floor is laid of the church and school.

Father stood up and said, 'Let us pray.' His first prayer on the church grounds.

After breakfast next morning Brad stood up. 'Folks,' he said, 'You've made an amazing start on the church and school, let's push on so the church is ready for Sunday for Maria and George's wedding.' Big clap went up and hoots. 'As you know Mr Pullman visited for a tour of the ranch. He was well impressed.' More clapping and hooting. 'He will return on Saturday for our big opening, more clapping and hooting. He would like to meet you all individually to see what you can offer and where he can help you to reach our collective goals.

'Remember to build your little stalls, huts, or lay things on the grass, we hope to build little stalls for games for children, lucky dip, guess the wagon, how many grains of rice in a jar, everybody think of something to occupy the children, boat, rowing lessons, swings, knock down pins, anything that comes to mind, Saturday we will lay out our displays, Lucy and Jack fish, put them all in ice, Chief logs, cakes, pastries. Jimmy look after the music, Cliff gets ready to show cattle, sheep, pigs, James chickens and eggs. I don't need to tell you, you all know what you're doing and what you want to do. Steve anything to add?'

Steve stood up. 'I know we're all busy, Mr Matsuda is going around, farms, ranches, locals and drumming up support for Saturday. Cliff, when the wagons, buggy, horses arrive Saturday, park them up outside the crossroads. Now our lady folk are all busy helping Virginia. George will be melting the metal to make the crosses and other bits. To the men our goal today is to get up all the side struts of the church and school, tomorrow all the struts up for the roofs following day all the side panels, followed by furniture inside, roof on, weather proofing, finished by Friday.'

A big cheer and clap went up. 'Come on, come on,' said Steve, 'it won't build itself.' Everybody hurried away to get stuck into their allocated jobs.

The rest of the week went whizzing by, hardly anybody stopped for a moment, Virginia was on top of things, George had his fitting, she was just waiting for Maria, who was coming today, Steve had left his shack for

Maria and gone back to stay at the house, the ladies had changed all the bedding and put some flowers on the table.

Mr Matsuda had not stopped. He'd been to every location he could go, the interest shown was amazing.

Jack and Lucy were organised for the big fishing trip, the flour mill was churning away, apple pies were being made, along with, cakes, buns, sandwiches, drinks, logs were being chopped constantly, lines and lines of clothes were drying, eggs, chickens, pig, sheep, cattle, horses preened, washed and stalls and huts were popping up everywhere, the woodsaw and hammering never stopped, George had made the crosses and other bits and pieces, the cross was to be erected Friday.

At last Saturday came, opening day at the ranch, the church was finished, the cross and weather vane in place, games adorned the stalls, seating, bunting was all put out, drinks poured, food covered with clothes the animals in pens, bags of flour, vegetables, apples, crops, potatoes, lettuce, tomatoes, spring onions all displayed. Meat was cooking in the fire pits, the blacksmith's barn was opened for visitors, Maria put a flower stall outside the blacksmith's, Mr Matsuda was running around giving people change.

First to arrive was Mr Pullman, his wife and two boys. They were met and greeted and told to wander wherever they wished. Horses, carts, buggies, wagons began to arrive, Cliff showed them were to park, then it got busier, they were swamped with visitors, kids running everywhere, you could hear laughter, chatting, people meeting and greeting each other, hugs, kissing, the stalls were so busy, money was being exchanged left, right and centre, people were eating, drinking and having fun. Mr Pullman held a meeting and addressed the people, answered questions. Pa decided to sell his company, he only ever wanted to build the ranch and the money raised would go towards building the new town. Pa signed all paperwork Mr Pullman wanted.

By the end of the day everybody was shattered but happy and so much fun was had, meeting people taking orders for the future. Everybody tipped their bags of money onto Mr Matsuda's table every time he said, 'Profit, profit, profit.'

Brad stood up. 'Well done everybody, today has been a massive success.' Up went the clapping and hooting.

Our future has been secured by the railway, locals want our products, and everybody in the local area will gain from this.' Big cheer.

'We are planning to build you all a new town.' Gasps went up. 'Just outside the crossroads, by the church, we will have three rows of shops to begin with, which could grow. I will give you more details on Monday, as for now I'm ready for bed. And tomorrow is Maria and George's wedding.' Lots of hoots cheers and clapping went up. 'Goodnight everybody well done, a good job done by everybody.' Brad clapped them all. He turned to Matsuda. 'When you have the time, please take out our running costs, divvy up the profits into equal shares and divide amongst everybody. There's so much more to come without standing orders to fill, the railway investments, improvement on the largest of stocks, crops, cattle, chickens et cetera. We are on the right road for success.' Massive clap. 'Goodnight and God bless you all.'

'Goodnight and God bless you too, Brad.'

Brad thought to himself, what a week, what a group of people, all pulling together, they'd gone through homelessness, joblessness, no direction, no hope to a bright and prosperous future ahead. They'd made good long-term friendships, and now we have a marriage to celebrate. George who was near to death when we found him, this all seems meant to be. I'm so glad I took the leap of faith. Every day is a blessing, every day is a challenge, every day is special and rewarding thank you Lord for bringing this group of people to me.

The wedding day of Mr George Blacksmith to Maria Budd. George woke up to Brad and Steve knocking his door.

BRAD SHACK GOING HOME

**Steve said**

'You can't sleep in, buddy, or you'll miss your wedding.'

George said, 'Just leave me here, I'm too nervous to get up.'

'Come on, come on,' said Brad, 'today you're going to marry the girl of your dreams.'

Meanwhile Maria was already up fussing around with things to get every for the wedding, just then the door got knocked, the ladies had gathered outside the shack and brought Maria a wedding breakfast. Maria just cried and cried.

'What's the matter?' Helen said.

'No, no,' Maria said, 'these are tears of joy and happiness.'

The women all bundled in. 'Now we need to do your nails and hair,' said Helen, 'then we're going to get you dressed in the wonderful wedding gown that Virginia made.'

Time flew by, people were getting ready and dressed up, as a surprise the wedding reception was going to be at the house, their piano ha been moved down to the church so Jimmy could play music as the bride walked down the aisle to her future husband. Father was already in church saying prayers and practising his lines.

The gong was clattered for ages by Bill, a way of announcing the forthcoming wedding.

Brad knocked at Maria's door. Helen answered. Maria turned, she looked stunning in this white laced gown. Brad approached her. 'You look beautiful,' he said. 'Welcome to our family.'

That meant a lot to Maria, having no family of her own.

'I'm proud to give you away,' said Brad. 'You're marrying an amazing man.'

'I know,' said Maria, 'I know.'

With that Brad stuck his arm out. Maria held it and walked out the door, Mr Matsuda's buggy had been done up with flowers and ribbons flowing to the horse. They got in for the short ride down to the church.

George was inside and saw the rest of the congregation. Jimmy started playing a soft melody on the piano, which told George his wife-to-be was coming down the aisle.

Maria could see George ahead. She could smell the new wood, see the cross that George had made. She knew all eyes were on her, George turned his head and looked backward she could read him lip-reading saying wow! She got up alongside George, Father nodded to her, before she went off into a dream trance. She heard Father say, 'We are gathered here today to celebrate …'

She remembered saying I do, but not much else, she came back to earth when Father said, 'You may kiss the bride (in front of all of these people),' but George's kiss was sort of tender, a big cheer went up. George's face glowed. 'Pinch me, Maria. Am I dreaming? If so I don't want to wake up.'

'No, George, this is all real. We are husband and wife, married forever.'

When they got outside the church, Mr Matsuda was waiting in his buggy.

'Get in, get in,' he said. As they drove away the happily married couple turned backwards and waved to everyone, George said to Mr Matsuda, 'Where are we going?'

'You'll see,' said Mr Matsuda. They pulled up outside the house. Mr Matsuda helped them out, Ching-Ching was waiting to meet them with a refreshing drink. 'Follow me,' he said as they entered the main hall. All the tables were covered in white sheets, there were flowers everywhere, plates, crockery, everywhere was decorated and looking splendid. 'Wait here,' he said to the couple, 'you need to meet and greet everybody.'

Sure enough, one by one, all the people passed by the couple, shaking hands, hugging, kissing, congratulating the couple, then they all took their seats, Maria and George were led to the top table and seated. Plate after plate came out and was served to everyone, then George heard the words 'speech, speech,' George nervously got to his feet, everybody clapped.

George started with, 'My wife and I,' he got a big cheer. 'We just want to thank you from the bottom of our hearts. Everybody's been so kind, helpful and generous, a special thank you to Virginia, who's made us look so good, especially my beautiful wife. (Big cheer.) Ma and Pa for laying on this beautiful spread for us, Brad for giving Maria away, and Steve for making sure I got to the church on time. (Big cheer). Thank you all for making this the best day of our lives.' George went on to say, 'My wife is so beautiful, I'm so lucky.' He bent and kissed her. Big cheer.

'On the way in I was asked by Steve would I be taking his wife away for some alone time together, I told him I'm already in paradise.' He raised his glass to everyone and sat down shaking. The group remained standing, raised their glasses, and said, 'Bride and groom, bride and groom.'

Maria took George's hand and said, 'Well done, that was wonderful.'

Steve shouted right let's push all the table and chairs, back, strike up the music and let's dance, during the evening, every time there was a slow dance Steve made a beeline for Helen.

Eventually the couple were shattered and decided it was time to leave, they went around everybody thanking them, hugging, kissing, finally everybody formed an arch, the couple holding hands walked under the arch and out of the door. 'Do you need a ride?' said Steve.

'No sir, I'm going to walk in the moonlight with my beautiful wife.'

They kissed, Steve shouted, 'And I don't want to see you in the morning for work. Take as long as you want off.'

'Thanks, Steve goodnight.'

'Goodnight George, Goodnight Maria,' and disappeared back into the house.

George and Maria walked the short distance down to their shack, where they embraced and kissed. George kicked the door open, swooped Maria up in his arms, carried her over the threshold and kicked the door shut!

Back at the house, the dancing and singing went on till late, finally people drifted away. Ma said, 'We'll do the cleaning up tomorrow I'm off to my bed, come on Pa.'

It was a strange week, after all the recent activities it felt like a bit of a lull. Brad thought to himself the group had a lot of work coming up, and although they were quite happy to work and make their dreams come true. He didn't want them to just work, work and work, he wanted them to look forward to things, events, they all liked to celebrate and so they should for all their hard work. So he came up with a few ideas for the group to look forward to. One idea was to visit and camp out at the Grand Canyon. That would be fun, and the views would be spectacular. Secondly, he'd like to take everybody to the coast for a long weekend, he'd like to see Steve get his beach holiday finally. They could play on the sand, paddle in the sea, it would be a great time for all. Little Virginia could dip her toes into the sea for the first time. He would arrange games for the weekends, more shopping trips, build a big tree house, have boat races, hide and seek in the woods, treasure hunts, maybe some sports games, competition in teams, kite flying, a bake off for the best pie, cake, open fires, barbecues, singing contest, there legged races. His mind buzzed with ideas, I must go and crack on. The planning permission for the buildings, and get the deeds sorted out. I'll build their new homes above their shops, hopefully we will have more weddings, babies. I want to see this community grow and prosper, with a wonderful future ahead, I have my family. I only wish Molly was here to share it. I have my friends, my new family, business is booming. Maybe it's time I found a partner, to be in love, get married, and have children.

That would be nice, he thought, happy like Maria and George to share all this with someone special.

# Chapter 8

## The Future

Ma and Pa loved their new life. There was always someone popping in for a cup of tea, wanting to borrow something, they always had an open door policy. She would go to all the shacks, taking apple pie with her of course. She would always have a natter with everyone, a good morning, a goodnight, hugs and kisses. It was like an extended family. She would quite often babysit Baby Virginia, loved to cuddle her and put her to sleep.

They would sit out with Lucy and Jack, Pa would take her out in the little rowing boat, they'd have picnics by the lake, she loved cooking with Pauline and Bill, swapping recipes, trying out new dishes, baking cakes, she even gave her special apple pie recipe to Pauline, so that her apple pie would go on forever.

Helen, Ellis, James were such a lovely family, so kind and loving, Ma and Pa would quite often visit the medical centre, have a catch up talk about their aches and pains, Virginia would have sewing and knitting classes once a week, it was a good excuse for the women folk to have a good natter. Chief was always entertaining, always a log fire burning, they loved teaching him new words, his English was coming on very well. They loved Steve like another son, he was always so chirpy, happy, smiling, cracking jokes, he was organised at his job, organised others well, got the best out of people, knew how to motivate people always with a smile.

Juan and Too were brilliant. Too joined in with everybody, learning how to cook, sew, knit, chop wood, make fires, hammer hot metal, ride a horse, milk a cow, collect eggs, fish, play musical instruments, go to school and church, arrange flowers, pick vegetables, Juan was so proud of his daughter, and so happy to be part of this community.

Ma and Pa spent a lot of time with Mr Matsuda, writing up invoices, plans, advertising flyers, sorting the money out, he was so organised, so polite and so honest, good company. James was always in and out of the house, checking if they need eggs or meat or vegetables, he was such a nice lad, prepared to help out on anything they may need, so polite and charming, Jimmy was amazing always playing a tune, he was teaching them how to play the piano. When he and Virginia sang together it was magical.

They loved riding out with Cliff. He was now a real cowboy, he loved horses and his cattle. The railway had supplied as much help that Cliff needed to enhance his stock.

George and Maria were so happy, always holding hands, kissing. Maria helped out a lot with the vegetable patches, George did a lot of the digging. Maria introduced new variety of seeds, and was sewing them everywhere, she said how beautiful it would be next year when they would all be in full bloom with the sweet smell of the flowers.

Andy was forever measuring up things. He'd disappear for days at a time, than return with a new cabinet or table, or anything, Andy never touched a drop of alcohol again.

Then there was lovely Ken. When he bear hugged you, it took your breath away, he was kind and gentle, and loved to hug and kiss.

Alan, Dianna were much closer. They didn't have to work so hard, as the workload was shared by others.

Ching-Ching was always busy doing something, sometimes he'd come home covered in flour dust. His best mate was Mr Matsuda. They had loads of nights together playing these ancient Asian board games.

Pa was more relaxed now that his business had been sold to the railway, and he knew with that money he could invest it all in Brad's vision of a town, plus savings for a rainy day if needed by the family, he was so proud of his boys and the success of the ranch, and a good future for everybody.

Lucy, Ellis, Jack, James and Too were like a gang. They went everywhere together, they had sleepovers at the lodge, went out on the boats, picnics, attended school and church together, fished, climbed trees helped Chief, baby-sat Baby Virginia, took her for walks, helped with the chickens, collected eggs, rode horses, helped Ching-Ching in the flour mill, Alan, Diana, Maria in the vegetable patch, helped with the cooking, cleaning, washing, went into town together, picked apples, played music and sang in the choir, worked in the fields, helped in the barn, George showed them how to hammer hot iron, Virginia taught them how to saw and knit. They loved talking to Ma and Pa like they were their grandparents. Steve always made them laugh, gave them jobs and kept them busy, Brad was always talking about their futures and what they wanted out of life, what could he do to make their dreams come true. He was like their best uncle in the world, Mr Matsuda taught them sums, how to do invoicing and how to draw. They were busy happy kids, with a whole network of people around them with different personalities and skills to draw on. It was an amazing place to grow up. And they would always be grateful.

Lucy and Jack never looked into the possibly of their auntie being alive or visiting. They'd found their new home, friends and family and never wanted to leave, they knew they would become the next generation of the ranch and were up for any challenges to come. Ellis and James never forgot their dad. They would often pray for him in church. They really liked Steve and hoped one day their mum Helen and Steve would hook up. He was always round home laughing and joking together, they didn't want Mum to grow old alone, she deserved to be happy, she was a lovely mum to them, and shoulder all the burdens in life for them, and every day and night she told them how much she loved them.

Pauline and Bill gave thanks to the Lord every day, they'd gone from being evicted, homeless to a land of opportunity surrounded by lovely people. Pauling and Bill loved the fact that they helped feed God's hungry children. They had so much help, everybody mucked in to picking veg, apples, cutting up the meat, collecting eggs, building fires, dancing, singing, the open day, George and Maria's wedding feast, going to the house for dinner, Pauline got on with Ma like a sister. She loved the sewing and knitting club, Bill would sit with Chief and a roaring fire, smoking their pipes, the kids were brilliant doing anything possible to help. Steve was cheeky but she loved rearing him, always giving him extra. Brad was a true gentleman, thoughtful, caring, always putting other people's needs before his own. Alan and Diana had been brilliant giving so much help and guidance. Ching-Ching was always popping in and out bringing flour, trying her latest experiment in cooking out. He often said, 'Rubbish not as good as Chinese food.'

Mr Matsuda was always around writing lists of ingredients they needed, sorting out the money arranging shopping trips so they wouldn't have to do the heavy carrying. Ching-Ching and Mr Matsuda want to make a rice meal together with oriental flavourings, and Japanese cuisine, Chief wants to cook one night, the ladies want to have a go, Juan wants to do a Mexican dish, the kids want a pizza night, Cliff wants jacket potato and beans, Steve will just eat anything. It was an open kitchen, she loved sharing her skills with anybody that wanted to listen, and she loved new techniques of cooking, new styles, new menus, new ideas. She just loved it here, they couldn't believe their luck. Pauline's favourite was Ken. They wanted to adopt him, he always called them mum and dad, he would always hug and kiss them, always first to arrive, last to leave, cooked, washed up, served the tables, Pauline and Bill never had children, but if they had, they would have wanted a son like Ken.

For Helen this was a dream place to be, her kids were happy, they had friends, they were learning new skills, they had futures ahead of them, they were cared for, they were safe here, their education was amazing, one-on-one learning. Virginia was her best buddy ever, many a night she just poured her heart out above the loss of Wayne, they talked a lot about Steve, her feelings, was it too soon after losing Wayne? What would the children think, what if it didn't work out, would she have to leave? She couldn't cope with that. Was just friends enough, did she want to grow old alone, what if the children left her? Steve would sometimes fake an illness like his throat was sore, or he'd gone deaf in one ear, and kept saying sorry I can't hear you, he did come into the medical centre one day with a big wooden splinter in his hand. I'm sure he drove it in on purpose. He would always come in and take his shirt off, even for a splinter, he'd always say I don't want to get it dirty, it was obvious he was trying to get Helen's attention and show off his muscular body. It's amazing the amount of muscles he claimed to pull, just to get a massage or a kiss on his wound. She would always say to him as he was leaving to be careful and not to eat anything today. His little face would screw up like a child who's just had his candy stolen.

But he would come round most nights, they'd sit, chat and laugh. Sometimes he just fell asleep on the seats, Helen would just put a blanket over him.

From losing a husband, a home, the best thing that ever happened to her was getting stuck in that mud, and Brad and Steve coming along. Changing her world and her children's for the better. She loved nursing and helping people, and Brad had said they are going to build a hospital, Ellis was working and training with her, James was coming out of himself, he had a job, responsibilities, friends, Father was around for him to talk to.

Virginia, Virginia, Virginia, she would say to herself, how have I gone from a gutter life, to all of this? Nobody respected me, and I didn't have much respect for myself. I'll never forget the day, I was thrown out onto the street, with a bag on the floor, with my worldly belongings spilling out. When I met these people I didn't know who they were, where they were going. I took a chance, a gamble, it didn't seem I had much to lose. I saw Jimmy in the wagon, at least I knew somebody. When Brad opened the door to the shack and said this is your new home, I could have gasped with ecstasy, my own home, did they know what that meant to me, all my life I'd been shuffled around pillar to post, lived in squalid conditions, dirt, grime, dust, diseases, muck, rats, spiders, flies, and there in front of me was this lovely clean home, my own bed, sink, curtains, front door, cupboards, a table. Surely I'm in a dream this can't be real. Next door is my best friend ever and her kids, I've got a job, I love to sew, knit things. It's the one thing from my past. I'm good, I learned, I have regular meals, I'm surrounded by lovely people, I've got money in my pocket with more to come, I'm going to have a shop made for me, I've got loads of orders to fill for the local people. I'm so so happy.

I love being with Jimmy. I could listen to his music day and night, the first time we sang together we were in perfect harmony, we've had a few smoochy dances together, and the odd cheeky kiss, but I don't know what Jimmy would want from a relationship. Does he do commitment? In the past he was a bit of a philanderer, womaniser, but she said I must admit I do fancy Jimmy. I'd also like to have children. I've bonded with Baby Virginia, and miss her when Chief takes her. I'm not going to look back in life any more, only forward.

For Juan this was all a miracle, after railing to make a living, getting long-term employment, putting a roof over his daughter's head, a regular plate of food on the table, getting his daughter an education, clothing her properly, having friends, Ma and Pa. A mother, he felt such a failure he even considered going back to Mexico and begging on the streets, but he couldn't even afford the fare.

And then by chance if he wasn't kicked out of the restaurant at that precise moment, he might have missed the wagon train, miss the wagon train, miss this opportunity. I'm so happy here I feel like dancing every day. I'm so proud of my daughter too. To lose your mother at such a young age is devastating, never to moan at me or judge me, she put up with some very hard conditions, but look at her now she is blooming into a beautiful butterfly.

Every time she tries something new he worries. Boating, what if she falls in? Horse riding, what if she falls off? Don't get too near to the fire, worry worry worry that's all I do, I'm learning to worry less as she's surrounded by lovely people that will never let anything hurt her. It's like an instant family around her protecting her, Ma and Pa, Uncles Alan, Brad, Steve, Aunties Pauline, Helen, Dianna, Virginia, now Maria. She has friends in Lucy and Ellis and the boys, I'd better keep a close watch on the boys, there I go again worry, worry, worry. Her and my English improves every day, she has schooling, a church, never hungry, pocket money, lots of mums to help her grow into a beautiful woman. Myself, after a hard day's work, I love my job, plus building new homes, and shops, I love nothing more than sitting around the fire with my friends having a drink and a smoke.

'Will I ever meet a lady friend? That would be nice. Am I ever leaving here? Never, the only way I'm leaving here is in a box!'

Mr Matsuda, I'm a bit of a mystery nobody knows my real past or even my full name. 'Let me inform you a little bit,' he said to Ching-Ching one evening. His friend Ching-Ching came over every night to drink their homemade rice brews, play board games, talk about their lives. Mr Matsuda was brought up in New York state, a tough upbringing, his father was a very educated man through reading all sorts of books. He passed all of his knowledge onto his son, how to keep books, records, percentages, fractions, how to multiply, subtract, divide, even advanced mathematics, Mr Matsuda loved sitting with his father, calculating averages, predicting rise and falls, wages, investments.

But outside the home he never felt as though he fitted into society, he fell into gambling. Sometimes very successful sometimes he lost huge amounts, sometimes he won but they never paid him, threatening him with violence. Once his father passed away then his mother he saw no reason to stay in New York, but instead wanted to go on an adventure and visit different states, start a new life. That's when he came across Brad, Steve and the wagon train. I decided to follow them after watching how kind they were to Ken. Even if they did not want me to join them, it would have led to somewhere different, since I've been here with a home and friends, it feels as though my life has a purpose. I love looking after the people around here, sorting out their lists, getting materials for them, sorting out loose change, paying wages, banking, investing. Brad said they may even build me a bank to run investment or property development and sales, the profits we are making over the first couple of weeks are amazing, plus the railway investments are amazing. We are definitely going in the right direction. They'd had a few drinks. 'One last question,' said Ching-Ching, 'what is your first name?'

'I don't use it,' said Mr Matsuda, 'because you'll laugh at me.'

'I won't,' said Chin-Ching.

'You will,' said Mr Matsuda.

'It's a part of Matsuda that's a girl name,' blurted Ching-Ching and rolled around the floor laughing. 'Perhaps they wanted a girl,' said Ching-Ching still laughing. 'I'll always call you Mr Matsuda, because you're a good friend and respect you.'

Running Bear Chief, as he was now known, had seen many changes in his lifetime. The hostilities against him and his people, the cultural differences and how people always wanted to own land. His people liked to roam free, no barriers, to roam free to only hunt for what they needed.

His world changed when his daughter was born. He could no longer just think of himself. He'd always wanted a son to teach how to ride, hunt, fish, track, dance, but he'd adjusted now. He could still teach his daughter all those things. But to fit into society she also had to be modernised or she wouldn't fit into this new world.

After losing his wife, bringing up a baby was hard. How could he still hunt? He needed to provide for his daughter, but still wanted to do his own thing.

Trapped, his chance meeting with this group of people was amazing. His daughter had so many people to look after her. She was loved, she still had to be shown the modern way of living and how to survive in this tough world, and he knew if anything was to happen to him, she would be cared for and always have a home, love and friends.

He didn't know how to put into words what a saviour Virginia had been to him. Virginia was like a second mum to his daughter. He could live his life knowing his daughter was safe, well looked after, warm and loved. All the women here had pitched in to take care of her. It was right and fitting to name her after Virginia, modern ways, a modern name. He still would pick her up and show her their culture. He loved nothing more than felling trees, chopping wood, building fires, sitting around the fire at night with the men folk having a smoke. He no longer hunted so much, if he caught something he mostly let it go. He had more appreciation of life, and animals. Like Brad said, 'Cut a tree down, plant ten others for the future.' He enjoyed planting the saplings and watching them grow just like his daughter, a new life.

Mick O'Flanagan, he'll always remember that one tracker saying to him as a child that he would never amount to anything significant. Well, he thought, look at me now.

I've got my own church and school, my own congregation my own choir, my own home, and I'm surrounded by lovely people, I've got good company all around me, good food, mixed conversation, a group of people that pull together to get things done. I see them all as God's and my children. There's nothing I wouldn't do or sacrifice for these people.

I've given my first sermon in the church, I've done my first wedding, and I have a feeling it won't be long before I do my first christening. I hope and pray for more weddings and christenings. I dread the day I have to do my first funeral, but it's all part of the circle of life and death.

A few new practitioners will be attending church services this week, with a promise more children will be attending school. He loved teaching, it was his fashion. He loved to read to the children, and teaching them how to read and write. It was essential. He knew education was the way forward for a better society and advancement. He was in the perfect place for educating. He planned to do field trips to the woods, teach them about plants and trees, to the lake, teach them how to swim and fish take them out on boat rides, teach them where their wood came from, the use of garden, the crops and fields, teach them how to ride, to play music, to sing, how to cook and bake, other cultures, saving, knitting, he hoped to give them a well-rounded education not stuck in a classroom every day, but outside exploring. Make them inquisitive, interested in the world around them, build confidence, set goals for their future, he wanted people to come back in years to come and say he Father O'Flanagan was the best teacher they had ever had, that thanks to him they found religion in their lives and were better people for that knowledge and insight.

Jimmy, a drifter, no roots, no plans, no hope, all he ever had was his music, his singing voice and a violin. His granddad had left him. Granddad taught him to play and sing and write music. He never knew his dad, and his mother disappeared out of his life at an early age.

Once Grandpa died, he was lost, went from place to place, played music where he could, sometimes just for a meal. Never saved a penny in his life, never had a home or a future to look forward to. Ended up as a lover, no friends, no long-term relationship, never been in love, yes there were women in his life, but not the type he wanted to settle down with and start a family.

Virginia had always caught his eye, she was always friendly and nice to him, made sure he got his fair share of tips. Quite a time he laid a man out with one punch or threw them out of the door.

She was very grateful, and he was very grateful when she got into that wagon that day.

Since he'd been here, he had become fonder and fonder of her. He hoped in the future they would become a couple. Only time will tell, he thought.

He loved seeing her, to play music any time he wanted to, to see George and Maria's face in church as she walked up the aisle to his music, the nights around the campfire dancing, singing, were so special to him. The best reward was to teach others how to play instruments, sing notes, to play and sing for Father's choir, to have friends everywhere around him, good food, a music school being built for him, and most nights he could just sit and talk to Virginia, or go to the log fire with the men folk. Jimmy thought to himself he'd never been happier in his life than here right now

Cliff always thought everything in life he loved always died. His parents, his first horse, his dog, the butterfly he caught, everything, which always made him sad and lonely. His latest horse was won at a fair, he had to do rodeo, lasso cattle, shooting, quickest draw, shoot a bow and arrow, he was the best at everything, winning the horse and saddle outright.

That day was the day he became a cowboy. All he wanted to do was roam the countryside, herd cattle, he never got his chance. Yes he got to roam, his money ran out, when it was raining or cold he had no shelter, sometimes no food, or company, he worried for his future. He thought to himself he could die out there, nobody would find him and nobody would miss him.

When his horse went lame with a stone in his shoe these people picked him up, and fixed him. Everything he had ever wanted was right here, friends, family, cattle, sheep and company, they never left him out of anything. Barbecues, weddings, building work, lunch, dinner, dancing, singing, always someone to talk to. He was very busy, just how he liked it. Herding cattle, branding, breeding programme, the herd was being increased by the railway. He'd be head of the team around him, making all the decisions. They'd move the cattle around, stay out all night with the cowboys and eat beans around the fire.

Cliff was happy with his change in fortune. He knew how lucky he was, and wasn't going to screw up. He'd never let Brad, Steve and the gang down. He was in this for the long haul. He started to get savings and planned to buy more horses and saddles and maybe a dog for the lonely nights, perhaps he thought, maybe just maybe he might meet a cowgirl, but she must like beans.

Mr and Mrs George and Maria Blacksmith, blacksmith by name and blacksmith by trade, George always and faith in the Lord but now he had also seen his miracle, to have his past and background, to now his present and future is a miracle. George felt he was the happiest and luckiest man in the world, how could he have gone from having nothing to having everything in such a short space of time, to having a wife who he loved and adored, a new family, friends, food, his own business, singing, dancing, entertainment, fun, laughter, freedom, choices.

One night snuggled up to Maria, she whispered, 'I think I may be pregnant with our first child.'

'Pregnant? A baby, our first child, hallelujah,' he shouted. 'Hallelujah, praise the Lord, we've been blessed. First thing tomorrow,' he said, 'we'll go and see Helen, if so I'll ask her to be godmother.'

'That would be nice,' said Maria.

'Brad and Steve can be godfathers, we'll have to think of names,' said George.

'Slow down, George, it has to be confirmed first, then we need to know what sex before we start thinking of names.'

'Sorry, Maria,' he said, 'but I just can't sleep.'

George loved his work, hammering away at metals, it was a choice not a burden or enforced. Maria had fit in so well, everybody helping out with their veg, sowing her flower gardens, he felt like he never had an enemy in the world, just love and understanding, respect. He was part of a team, creating their own future, and now he would have children he could pass all his skills onto, watch them grow with an education with God in their lives and in their hearts. He would tell them of his background so they would appreciate their roots, but he would point them in the right direction to be good honest working folk, to be happy, but above all to be free to go wherever they wanted to and choose their own path in life. I'm so so lucky, thought George.

Andy, was a washed up alcoholic tramp going nowhere in life, only an early grave, and the quicker the better, thought Andy. Once his wife was killed, he died that day, only it was taking longer to die, but drink, no food, no hope would soon do it, nothing to live for, and he didn't want to live, but didn't have the guts to end it all by himself, a useless waste or a life and a person, hell-bent on killing himself.

That day he asked for change, he thought he might get a few coins. Instead he got a chance of a whole new life, a life where now he'd never let their people down, but most of all he'll never let himself down again.

All his life he loved to make things with his hands, especially out of wood. Here he'd been able to for fill his dreams and now other people's dreams, when they constructed the church and school, everybody working as a team gave him tremendous satisfaction. All the planning, cutting, sawing, hammering. To see it all come together was amazing, to have their first service and a wedding that he helped to construct was thrilling. Then to be told they were going to build a town, with houses on top for these good folk to live in would be amazing. Enough work to keep him busy for years to come, he thought how proud his wife would be of him, and only wished she was here to see it, and enjoy this place and people as much as he did. He had lovely George and Maria one side as neighbours and kind Ken the other, he often popped in for a cup of tea and a chat. He could join the men at the fire, take a boat out and go fishing. He felt he was never alone here, always someone around to talk to, often he would just sit in the church and talk to his wife about the day, what he'd seen, what somebody had said, where he was going or doing tomorrow. Andy would never be alone or lost ever again, and no alcohol ever again.

Ken had found a new family, a new life, a new hope. He loved being part of a team, lifting the struts and beams up, hammering nails in. He loved hammering.

Pauline and Bill felt like his mum and dad. They said that they loved him so much that they wanted to adopt him. They don't call him Ken, they call him son. He loves being in charge of the crops, planting, sowing, harvesting. He's part of the choir. Father said he and George had the deepest singing voices he'd ever heard. Jimmy lets him bang drums on music nights. He loved all the food he got to eat, Mum said he was a growing boy and always gave him extra.

He knew he was a bit different to others. All of his life people had poked fun at him, but not here. Not one person had made any remarks or comments, he was just accepted for himself no different to anyone else, he loved the way the women folk pulled him up to dance, or the kids would jump on his back for a piggyback ride.

Everybody was so kind. Always a good morning, goodnight, how are you today, Ken, anything you need. Ma always popped down for a chat and an apple pie. Quite often he'd go to Pauline and Bill's for an evening. They taught him how to play card games, he loved playing snap, they always had supper, usually a sandwich or a large slab of cake washed down with a cup of tea, or refreshing drink.

Ken thought of the days he slept in the bed of grandpa, now he had his own bed, a shack to live in, new friends, a family and a job he loved. He would never have to fight anyone ever again, he had money and loved to buy people surprise presents. Ken was happy, contented and would be for the rest of his days. The past had gone, his future was here.
*One morning Dianna said to Alan, 'I think I may be pregnant.'*

'Brilliant,' said Alan, 'it's what we always wanted. Ma and Pa can be grandparents, Brad will be an uncle and Molly an aunt.' They couldn't wait to tell the family. 'We'll go see Helen tomorrow, before we say anything.'

Next morning they went to the medical centre. They were surprised to see George and Maria sitting down waiting to see Helen. Both ladies looked at each other, rubbed their bellies, then both gave out a scream. George and Alan shook hands, they all hugged. Helen and Ellis came running out when they heard the scream, realised what was going on, also screamed with delight and also joined the hugging.

Helen thought to herself, she'd helped deliver babies before, but this would be a first for Ellis. The thrill of bringing a new baby into the world was exciting.

It wasn't long before the women began to show. George said 'you've got to take it easy, Maria. Maybe give your job up.'

She said, 'I'm pregnant not ill, I'll carry on for a while longer.'

George thought wow I'm going to be a father. Alan's family went wild, jumping up and down, Ma just cried with happiness she was going to be a grandma.

Brad was thrilled. He couldn't wait to be an uncle.

When everybody was told, the excitement around the ranch was electric, Andy thought I'd better get making cots and cribs. The girls all swooned. They'll get to cuddle and babysit the newborn. Virginia and Helen thought they'd like a baby, and laughed when they said, 'Well Virginia, there's always Jimmy.'

Virginia said, 'Well, Helen, there's always Steve.'

They both laughed, and said, 'Wouldn't it be lovely to be pregnant together and our children growing up together as neighbours and best friends?'

'Let's do it,' said Virginia.

Helen said, 'Maybe!'

# Chapter 9

# Reflections and Unanswered Questions

One Sunday Brad was sitting by the lake, fishing. He thought to himself how beautiful and peaceful it was here, birds flying around, files on the water.

His mind wandered, he was so looking forward to Alan and Dianna's baby in the house, the next generation, to keep Ma and Pa's and his own legacy going. We've got Too and Baby Virginia, what with the news that Maria and George might be expecting twins, and he was sure Helen and Steve would hook up and have a family, and Virginia and Jimmy. He thought he'd better get his finger out, he was getting older, but would love to have a wife and a family. He thought of Suzanne, who loved to be called Suzie. He'd met her downtown while he was sorting out paperwork for deeds and planning permission. He often thought about Suzie, that when they had to work closely together, she smelled so good, a hint of perfume, and freshness, she was a very intelligent woman, well spoken. Ah he thought, she wouldn't be interested in me, a ruffian, he was also so busy. I'll pluck the courage up and ask her to go on a picnic, or show her the ranch, go on a boat trip, maybe horse riding, his mind went back to the ranch.

We have the teenagers coming along nicely. They'll be able to pass the skills they have learned here onto the youngsters, he was sure that James fancied Lucy, and Jack fancied Ellis. They were always together, he could see budding romances happening there. You never know, maybe even weddings and children and families growing there, maybe even Chief, Juan, Mr Matsuda Cliff, Andy or Ken might meet someone, who knows.

So what might the next three to five years be like? he thought. Pa and Ma, she'll still be cooking her apple pies, Dianna and Alan's baby will be a toddler by then running around, they may even have more children. Ching-Ching will always be covered in flour dust he could see Pauline and Bill still cooking for everyone, and running their little cake shop. Maybe they'd even move out to above the shop, Virginia will carry on looking after Virginia. Jimmy I can see him moving in, maybe another marriage and children. Helen and Steve would make of great couple, I think I'll encourage him more, I want to see those two happy and married with children.

Chief is just happy where he is, I don't think he's ever going to go anywhere. He can just watch his daughter grow up and get old, like the rest of us. Father I don't think I've ever seen such a contented man, running the church and school. He's in his element, he keeps us all grounded, Juan, Mr Matsuda, Jimmy, Cliff, Andy and Ken.

All happy with their work, homes and food the backbone of the ranch, all helping and pulling together, they've all achieved so much together and their futures are bright and rewarding.

Then there's lovely Maria and George. What a story, what a journey they've been on, and now about to be parents. Mr Pullman has been brilliant, kept to his word, the orders and requests have come flooding in, money's all paid up front, this new town is starting to take shape. The plots are all marked out, the locals have prospered, they even wanted me to stand for mayor, but I'm so busy as it is. What an incredible journey we've all been on and it isn't over yet! There's so much more to come, I believe this was all meant to be, meeting the people when we did, how they all get on like a family. The railway contracts. I'm loving it and so are they.

Just then Ma and Pa came running over. 'Brad,' they were shouting, 'we've had a letter, a letter from Molly.' Exhausted they handed the letter to Brad it read:

*Hi folks, I'm sorry to say Ray has committed suicide, we've lost everything, our belongings, our home, our savings, we have nothing left, can I come home? If so can you come and get me? I'm staying at my friend Julie's house, just out of town, please hurry I'm desperate, love Molly xxx*

Brad said, 'How did you get this letter?'

Pa said, 'A travelling salesman. He knew Molly, was passing the ranch and said he'd deliver it for her.'

They all looked at each other stunned, Brad said, 'I'll go straight away and get her.'

Ma said crying, 'Molly's coming home, we'll all be back together just like it was years ago.'

Brad headed for Steve's. 'Buddy,' he said, 'I've got to go on a trip to Chicago to collect my sister, Molly, and bring her home. I'll leave you in charge to look after things, oh and you'll have to move out of the house as she'll have to have her room back.'

**Steve said**

'Buddy if you think you're going on a trip without me, you've got to be kidding. Where you go I go. Mr Matsuda and Ching-Ching can run things here, I'm coming with you and I won't take no for an answer, who knows, we may meet some new people along the way who need our help.'

Bard hugged him. 'Come on buddy,' he said. 'We need to hook the wagons up, get food and water and hit the road.'

Steve said, 'Where is Chicago?'

Brad said, 'Somewhere over that way!' Pointing north.

# Part Two

## The Creation of Bradville

Follow the characters and people through their new lives in the next chapter of their lives.

## PROFILE: KELLEE (COW PAT)

Kellee was born on the road, her parents being in a travelling rodeo troupe. They were always on the move, from place to place, she never had any roots, schooling, play friends. She learned how to ride from an early age, shoot lasso, draw, when she was young she competed against men and always lost, hence her nick name (cow pat), but she was determined to be the best. She trained and practised, all day until the sunset, until she became the best. She would beat all comers, young, old, trained soldiers, professionals, you name it she would beat them with perfect scores, but she longed for a home, no more travelling the countryside. She didn't want the loud-mouthed cowboy, she wanted a sensitive man, one that would treat her as a lady, with respect, the moment she met Cliff she knew he was the one she wanted to spend the rest of her life with and have little cowgirls and cowboys to pass her skills onto.

## PROFILE: DANIEL

Daniel was always a shy, sensitive boy, bullied at school, never allowed to join in any of the games, nobody ever came home with him to play games, or he was never invited to any other homes, even when they had birthday parties. He was no good at running, gym, skipping, ball games, the teachers use to worry about him not fitting in

But he had a gift, he could mould a piece of clay into a spectacular object, he could draw people, objects buildings, he loved working with colour, his essay writing was spectacular, his use of words to describe things. When he came to America he thought it would be a new start in life, but things were tough. He couldn't get the breaks in life he needed, until he met Brad, his life changed forever for the better.

## PROFILE: SUZIE

Suzie was the cutest baby most people had never seen, with her mop of blond hair all curly, and little kiss curls hanging. She was a very loving and sharing child. She was the apple in her dad's eye, he spoiled her rotten, but he always instilled in her education, education, education, at school she was so popular with both boys and girls. Everybody wanted to be her friend. Dad always told her that she would have to kiss a lot of frogs to find her prince. She studied so hard to gain the grades needed for her chosen career, and was one of the first women to achieve such a high level standard, she never really found time for boys as she was building up her business, and also found a lot of them immature, with no future plans or motivation. She was determined to meet Mr Right, and would wait a lifetime if she had to. Little did she know everything was about to change.

# Chapter 1

## Molly's Coming Home

Brad and Steve made good time, stopping only when they had to on a long and hazardous journey. It was quite easy to locate Molly once they had asked around a bit. Brad took a deep breath as he got out of the wagon and approached the door, before he could even knock the door it was pulled wide open. Molly stood there crying her heart out, bedraggled, scruffy, her hair in tatters, tears streaming down her face. Brad lifted her off her feet, and just hugged her, it seemed like ages, eventually Brad said, 'I've missed you, Molly.'

Molly said, 'I've missed you too, Brad.' They carried on hugging.

Eventually Brad said, 'Let's take you home, Molly.' More tears and hugs.

'Yes please,' said Molly.

'Is everything ready to go?'

'I haven't got much to take,' she said, 'Just one bag.'

**Brad said**

'By the way this is Steve, my best buddy.'

'Nice to meet you, Steve. I'll talk to you later, I just need to get out of this place as soon as possible.'

'Do you need to say goodbye to anybody or is there any outstanding money to be paid?'

'No everything been taken care of I just need to leave.'

As Brad and Molly disappeared upstairs to get the bag, Steve thought to himself that Molly had been through a hard time. She looked skinny, as though she was in need of a good hot meal, a bath, definitely in need of a change of clothes, and some love and understanding, This was his best buddy's sister, family to him, he didn't like seeing her so distressed, and would do anything to helps her, even if she just needed his time and help.

Once on board, Molly sat alongside Brad. Brad realised Molly was too upset to talk at this moment in time. There was plenty of time for talking on the journey homeward.

Just then Brad noticed ahead a man with a wooden easel, with a brush in hand, a palate of paint in the other, wearing a white tunic with different colours of paint splashed over it. He seemed to be painting a particular building.

'Just a second,' he said to Molly, 'I won't be long.' He jumped down and approached the man. 'Hi I'm Brad,' he said.

The man hesitated, looking Brad up and down. 'Oh hello,' he said, 'my name's Daniel, pleased to meet you,' put his brush on the easel, and held his hand out to shake Brad's. Brad thought it was a bit of a limp handshake, not butch and manly that he was used to. 'I notice you have an accent. Where are you, from?'

'From just outside London, England. I came here to make my fame and fortune. But it hasn't exactly worked out as I'd planned and dreamed of.'

'What do you mean?' Brad said.

'Well I planned to have a studio, and a gallery, I would paint landscapes. people, portraits, I'd be in such demand, and walk in elite circles, but instead nobody has no money, or certainly do not want paintings. I'm also a writer, but cannot get a chance to be read or signed up, instead I'm doing this painting to pay off my rent.'

'Is it finished?'

'Yes I was just signing my name. You never know one day I could be famous, and this painting would be worth a fortune to a collector.'

Brad said, 'I know you don't know me but I'd like to make you an offer.'

'Carry on, carry on,' Daniel said, 'sounds interesting.'

'Well my family own a ranch in California. It has lakes, a woodland, and thirteen shacks, owned by an incredible variety of wonderful people. I'd like to capture these people on canvas, for future reference, we also have a wonderful house I'd like you to paint, and portraits of my family and friends, I'd like a massive picture of Ma and Pa we could have over the fireplace, and a picture of my whole family together, plus the scenery around.'

'Sounds like a massive job. It might take me a while. California you say, I've heard the light is wonderful to paint in. So what are you offering?'

'Well obviously a place of your own to stay in, rent free, as much food as you want, cooked for you free of charge, running water, electrics, free of charge, part of a community. You'll love the people. We'll even work out a wage for you, or pay a commission on each work of art you do or both. We will supply you with everything you need, paints, brushes, canvas et cetera. You can paint at home, in the main house, outside, we even have a church, which Father would like some paintings in, and a school room. You could paint A–Z, or numbers, then, last thing, I will build you your own gallery to exhibit your own paintings for sale, and I would like you to capture the life stories of all the people on the ranch, so it's all written down for future generation to pass on to. What do you think, Daniel?'

'What do I think?' Daniel said. 'You had me hooked at California.'

'Great,' said Brad 'welcome to your new life about to begin.'

'Wonderful,' said Daniel, 'I've just got to deliver this painting, collect my bits, I'll be with you as soon as I can. Thank you.'

Steve appeared with some supplies. 'Collected another sheep?' he said.

'Yes, this one's going to paint your ugly mug and hang it up for all to see. Ha! Ha!'

'Daniel: Steve, Steve: Daniel.'

'Oh hello,' he said, 'I don't travel too well. I might be sick.'

'Plenty of room in the back to sleep if off.'

'Oh thank you.'

Brad and Molly had been travelling a few hours, when Brad said, 'How are you sis?'

'Broken hearted,' she said. 'I've made so many mistakes with my life. It just keeps getting worse. I'm a country girl at heart, I should never have left for city life, I thought money makes the world go round, you can buy nice things, mix with important intelligent people. It's all a sham. They were all back stabbing, greedy, only looked out for themselves, didn't care about anybody else. When we needed their help, they all went missing, making up feeble excuses. If you wanted to borrow some money, they would say their money was all tied up in stocks, bonds, gaining interest, and couldn't be touched. We did parties, dinners, dancing, yet when my husband passed away, nobody showed up at his funeral, they were not friends you could count on, but users like maggots on a body, I trusted these people, they were like vampires feasting on us.

'When we lost all of our money in investments shares, gambling, running costs, he then committed suicide, leaving me with nothing, all the problems, everything was reclaimed, sold off to cover our debts, no home, no future, no hope. You obviously got my letter, I was desperate, I didn't want to use anybody. Ma, Pa, you, Brad, but I didn't know what else to do, I'm so sorry for putting you through all this, wasting your time, coming all this way.' She burst into tears again.

'Molly, Molly, now you listen to me and listen good, you're family, you always will be, and as a family we will do whatever it takes to put things right and whatever help you need. Molly, do you remember when we were kids, you, me and Alan, we shared everything, that will never change. Ma and Pa brought us up to share everything, to love each other for our lifetimes, nothing has changed. I still love you, you are my family. I can't tell you how excited Ma, Pa, Alan and Dianna, even Ching-Ching are to see you, no one will ever judge you, you are family, we're just taking you home, you can do anything you want to, but you'll always have love and a home, forever and forever.'

'Thank you Brad, that's so reassuring. I'm really looking forward to seeing everybody again.'

**Brad said**

'Now there's been a few changes since you were last there, firstly the US Army have built shacks on our land, which are now occupied by the most amazing people I have ever had the pleasure to meet, we have all sorts of businesses running, industry, we make things, and sell them, we have more horses, cattle, chickens, sheep, we do a lot of supplies to the railways, crops, vegetables, the flour mill is open, so is the blacksmith's, all run by these amazing people. We have a church, a school, we do fetes, we have a doctor's surgery, cooks and a banker.'

**Molly said**

'This all sounds incredible, where did you get all these ideas from, and how did you meet all of these people?'

'I'll tell you all of their stories as we ride along, but first I must tell you this, we are building our own little town, just outside the main gate, next to the church and school, so Molly we will build you a building for any business you care to take up. You were always good at hairdressing, that's an idea to get you started.'

'Wow, Brad, the ranch is really going places.'

'Sure is, and Molly you'll always be part of its future. The love will always be there, you can count on it. Right,' he said, 'now I'll tell you the people's stories.'

Steve and Daniel didn't say too much to each other, Steve thought he was a kind, sensitive gentleman, obviously artistic. Steve asked about

154

England, Daniel asked him about the conflict. Then Daniel got into the back of the wagon. A few times he could hear him retching.

Time flew by. As they were reaching the ranch, Molly could see the church, with the cross on it George had made, Molly said to Brad, 'I think I need to spend a long time in there, I've got some sins I want to confess, and ask forgiveness for.'

'You'll love our Father, he's the best, an absolute lovely man. That's the school.' They entered the gate and Molly for the first time saw all the shacks. 'Wow,' she said, 'what a difference.'

As they pulled up Molly grabbed Brad's hand. 'I'm shaking,' she said.

Brad said, 'Don't worry, everything is going to be fine, you're home and they all love you. Come on, let's get some hugs and kisses and if you're lucky some apple pie.'

'Yummy,' she said.

Molly started crying even before she got down from the wagon, as she ran towards the house. Running in the opposite direction were Ma, Pa, Alan, Dianna and Ching-Ching. They all smashed into each other in a big huddle.

'Come on,' Brad said to Steve. 'Let's show Daniel where he will be staying. I'll sort the horses out and join you.'

Daniel was most impressed with what he'd already seen, everywhere was clean and tidy, fresh air, warm, not so windy.

'We'll just call at Pauline and Bill's to tell them one extra for dinner tonight, then we'll talk to Chief, let him know you'll be staying in his shack.'

'I don't want to put anybody out,' Daniel said. 'You won't be. Chief sleeps in a wigwam.'

'You have an Indian and a wigwam, I can't wait to paint those.'

'Wash and freshen up. When you hear the gong it's time for dinner, just out by the benches, you'll get to meet everyone.'

Back at the house it was crazy. Everybody chatting, laughing, crying, just like the old days. Brad walked in with Steve, a big clapping and cheering met them. Ma came up and held a hand of each of them, and said, 'Thank you very much for bringing Molly home, it has made my day. My family all back together again. Come on,' she said, 'apple pie is on the table.'

'Yeah ha,' shouted Steve.

'Molly,' Ma said, 'your room is just as you left it. Go up get your bearings, have a bath.'

'Thank God,' shouted Brad. They all laughed.

'Ignore him,' Ma said, 'I've laid some clothes on the bed for you, then we'll have a lovely dinner. You can meet everybody else tomorrow when you're more rested.'

'Yes Ma,' she said, 'Thank you, Ma.'

With a kiss she went to go upstairs when Ching-Ching shouted, 'And don't go away any more. I can't stand all these tears,' then cried again.

'Love you, Ching-Ching.'

'Love you, Molly,' he said.

When they heard the gong Brad and Steve took Daniel for his first meal. He was a bit shy, but everybody gave him a warm welcome.

Brad explained what Daniel would like to do. 'I want to capture these present moments in time, I want us all to look back in the future, to capture where we came from to where we are, what we have achieved, the fun, the laughter to watch each other grow, family.' Big clap and cheer.

'I would also like Daniel to capture in writing our stories, how you came to be here, and what you are doing now, and how your life has changed. You never know, one day somebody might write a book about us. Over to you, Daniel.'

'If it's OK with you, I'll spend some time with each of you and take some notes, and write them up, if you could pose for me for a few minutes, I'll sketch you, and paint afterwards. Thank you.' Then he sat down. Clapping.

**Brad said**

'Tomorrow, Daniel, we'll give you a tour of the ranch, show you your workplace. Mr Matsuda please make a list of all the things Daniel needs and go ahead and get them, thank you. As you may have heard our sister Molly has returned home, she's resting tonight, but can't wait to meet you all at breakfast tomorrow.' A big cheer and clap went up.

'Enjoy your meal I'm off to spend some time with my sis. Steve, would you like to join us?'

'Yeah sure thing,' said Steve, 'is there apple pie?'

'Yes.'

Back at the house everybody was waiting for Molly to come down. When she did appear, walking down the stairs, she looked like a princess. Ma had left out a beautiful white gown, and a flower was in her lapel, her hair was us in a bun with a bangle round the bun. Ma thought she looked underweight but she looked gorgeous, stunning, just like she used to look. How lovely to have Molly home.

Brad rushed forward and presented his arm, which Molly held. 'You look stunning,' Brad said to her.

'Thank you, Brad, you look half decent yourself.'

They both laughed, Ma beckoned Molly. 'Come and sit near me.' Every time Ching-Ching brought a dish in, he would kiss Molly on the forehead.

Pa said, 'Let us pray. Thank you for the food we are about to eat, thank you for bringing Molly home to us and making our family whole again. Amen.'

'Amen.'

Over dinner everybody was chatting and laughing, Molly found out she was to become an aunt. She was thrilled for Alan and Dianna, after a while Steve said, 'I'm ready for my bed.' Everybody thanked him, he thanked them, then he took Molly's hand and kissed the back of it, saying welcome home, which she thought was quite sweet.

'Goodnight everybody,' he shouted.

'Goodnight Steve,' they all shouted back.

'Right miss,' Ma said to Molly. 'Girls' time, say your goodnights. I'll be up in a moment.'

Ma just wanted Molly to know that she was loved, safe and secure, and that whatever decision she made, they would support her, this was her home, and this was her family, and she would always be welcome. Once Ma had left after a few hugs and tears, Molly got into bed. She thought she could not cry anymore and as the tears rolled down are face, she realised these were different tears, not pain or hurt but tears of joy and happiness. She was home with her family and loved and supportive, safe, secure, back where she belonged.

It was a beautiful morning, Molly was looking forward to meeting everybody, and everybody was looking forward to meeting Molly.

Bill gave an extra bang on the gong. Brad shouted, 'Everybody, this is Molly.' They all stood, cheered, and clapped. 'Carry on with your breakfast, Molly and I will visit each table, and you can introduce yourself.'

Steve stood up. 'I see you've all been slacking while I'm away.' Everybody booed him. 'No seriously, the new town is really taking shape, well done everybody, give yourself a clap.'

Pauline shouted, 'And we saved a fortune on food since you've been away.'

Steve said, 'I hope you've saved me some food, I'm starving.' They laughed.

Brad stood up. 'Daniel after the tour Molly will join us, we will go to the house meet Ma, Pa, Alan, Dianna and Ching-Ching, the first picture I would like you to do is one of Ma and Pa.'

'It will be a pleasure,' said Daniel.

'Tonight to welcome Molly home, we will have a knees up. music, dancing, a roast, singing and laughter. God,' he said, 'it's good to be back home, I've missed you all.'

'We've missed you too, Brad.'

'George, how's Maria?'

'She's getting big.' Maria elbowed him. 'Love you,' he said.

As Steve stood up and was getting everybody organised, for the day and night-time, Chief fire, Pauline Bill food, plus helpers, Brad, Molly and Daniel slipped away to go see the lake. Daniel always carried his sketch book with him, he also took notes of things he wanted to go back to sketch. Chief and the wigwam were on there, when he saw the lake and boats they were added, plus the boat house, fishing tackle, nets, all the people he had met this morning, then there was the writing of the stories. He was going to be a busy man.

As they walked along Molly said to Brad, 'Is the tree house still there?'

'Yes,' said Brad.

'Oh I must visit it later. It just reminds me so much of our childhood.'

'I know,' said Brad, 'such wonderful memories of growing up and playing. Doesn't the lake look so beautiful? It's wonderful when the moon shines across it.'

They then walked past the flour mill. Daniel made a note to revisit, then on to the house, Daniel was very interested and started sketching straight away.

Once inside the house, they showed him the large room. Brad showed him where he wanted the large picture of Ma and Pa to be hung, on the opposite wall the family portrait. 'Maybe one of the houses,' Daniel said.

'Great idea,' said Brad, 'Daniel just come and go as you see fit. Molly I've got to pop into town and see somebody, do you want to come?'

'Yes there are a few bits I need.'

'I'll saddle up the buggy and meet you outside.'

'What about money?' Molly said.

'I'll explain on the way there.'

'OK,' said Molly.

Walking down to get the buggy, Brad saw a lovely array of flowers. Shall I pick them for Suzie? he thought, and he hoped in his mind that Suzie could come tonight. Now all he had to do was to summon the courage and right words to ask her!

As Molly jumped into the buggy, the first thing she asked was, 'Who are the flowers for?'

**Brad said**

'It's the lady that's been sorting out planning permission, deeds, paperwork et cetera.'

'Does she have a name?'

'Suzie. She's beautiful, Molly, so kind, gentle, intelligent and she smells wonderful.'

'Wow, it sounds like your hooked, line and sinker.'

'I haven't told her yet. I'm hoping she'll come along to tonight's do.'

'What like a date?'

'Don't ask me that, I'm too nervous as it is.'

'Brad, just be yourself. I'm sure she'll love you just as we do.'

Brad said, 'Swap subject. Molly, every store in town has a credit against the ranch, so you can order whatever you like, get receipts, give them to Mr Matsuda, and he settles each invoice weekly.'

'Sounds a marvellous system.'

'Yes, and don't abuse it.'

'I won't, I promise.'

Once they got into town, Brad introduced Molly to a few stores, letting them know who she was and allowed to have credit. He pointed out where he would be, and said to come over when she was finished. 'Oh so I get to meet the mysterious Suzie.'

'I'm off,' said Brad. With his bunch of flowers in hand he headed for Suzie's office.

As he opened the door he saw Suzie sitting at her desk. Her eyes flicked upwards. Before he could say anything Suzie said, 'Hello stranger, I've missed you.'

Gob smacked, Brad said, 'I've got you some flowers.'

'Oh they're beautiful, thank you,' she said. 'I'll just pop them into a vase.' As she stood up, Brad couldn't help but watch her as she moved across the room.

'How's Molly?' Suzie said.

'She's fine, happy to be home, she's shopping at the moment, but will pop in to meet you before we go.'

'Oh that's good, I'd like to meet her. I can find out what you were like as a child and whether you were a good brother growing up. I'm sure you were. While you've been away, I've been very busy on your behalf. All the paperwork has been signed off by the judge and local authorities, there has been no opposition to your requests, so it's all systems go for the ranch. Each individual building and shop has the deeds attached, with all drawings and permits attached. They are all divided up. Let's take an example, George Blacksmith, you can hand him his folder, and everything he needs is in there. If anyone has trouble reading, I would be willing to sit down with them and talk it through.'

God, Brad thought, not only is she beautiful, intelligent, thoughtful, she's organised as well. 'Ummm brilliant,' Brad blurted out. Thinking that was not enough he blurted out, 'Magnificence. Wonderful, thank you very much.'

She giggled. 'Now because these documents are very important, of course I have copies of all documents in a safe. I've purchased you a briefcase to keep them all in.'

'You've put my initials on the case.'

'Yes, so everybody will know it's your case.'

'Thank you,' Brad said humbly. 'Uuum, we need you to meet Mr

Matsuda so we can sort out payment and fees. Thank you,' he said again.

'It's been a pleasure, but I do need to meet everyone to answer any questions. I also would like a tour of the ranch, and the new plots. Have you decided on a name for the new town?'

Brad by now was shellshocked, he wanted to speak but nothing came out of his mouth. He just nodded yes. Ask her about tonight, he thought, just then the door opened and in walked Molly.

'Hello,' she said, 'you must be Suzie.'

'Yes,' she said, 'you must be Molly, pleased to meet you.'

**Molly said**

'Has he got round to asking you to dinner tonight?'

'No.'

'Well, I'm asking, would you like to come to dinner tonight? You can stay over with me, in my room.'

'Yes I'd love to, I'll close the office for a day. I'll put a sign up "closed for repairs", and I can have a whole day off. If that's OK with you, Brad?' she said.

'Yes, fine,' said Brad, dumbstruck.

'Do you need picking up?' said Molly.

'No, no that's fine, I can find my own way there.'

'See you tomorrow, Suzie.'

'Yes can't wait, goodbye. Brad, see you tomorrow.'

'Yes,' said Brad.

Molly grabbed his arm. 'All finished here?' she said.

'Yes,' said Brad, 'goodbye.'

'Yes goodbye,' and they left.

Outside Brad turned to Molly and asked, 'What just happened there?'

'You, my brother, have just got your first date, and an opportunity to talk to her outside of work.'

'Oh wow,' said Brad, 'this has just made my day.'

'That's nothing, brother, wait until tonight.' They left arm in arm.

'Anything to pick up?'

'No no the nice man in the store has already loaded the buggy.'

Brad thought how lovely it was to have Molly home, then his mind turned to what he should wear.

The afternoon was busy as usual. The roast was on, the fire built, Jimmy was tuning up, spirits were high, everybody was excited to meet Suzie. Everybody wanted Brad to find love, he was a good man and deserved to share his life with someone special, and they wondered what the big news Brad wanted to tell them all.

What a lovely evening. Suzie turned up looking stunning in pink, Molly was outstanding in her new clothes. Helen, Virginia, Lucy, Ellis all looked wonderful. Maria was showing, so was Dianna. Ma looked so graceful, and the men folk didn't look too bad at all.

Suzie felt as though she's never met as many people in a short time in all of her life. Everybody said lovely and wonderful things about Brad. Just then Brad approached, 'Would you care to dance?'

'I'd love to.' Suzie said.

'It's a slow waltz,' he said.

'How lovely,' Suzie said. As he took her left hand and put his arm around her waist he was in heaven, and she smelled so good.

It felt like hours and hours Brad held her in his arms. Occasionally she would squeeze him, and he would squeeze her back, then that moment when there lips came together and they kissed for the very first time, a big cheer went up and clapping. Embarrassed, they pulled apart, than Brad dived back in a for a second smouldering kiss. He knew this was a special moment and wanted it to last forever. He started to think I'm in love. Suzie was thinking this is the man of my dreams, my prince.

Pa came over. 'Ahem,' he said, 'sorry to interrupt but I think it's time to announce the good news.'

'Sorry, Pa,' Brad said, 'I got distracted.'

'That's alright, son, she gets the nod of approval from all of the family.'

'Thanks Pa.' Brad jumped up onto a table. 'Quite please, everybody gather round. With Ma, Pa and Suzie's help I have some good news to announce.'

Steve shouted, 'Don't tell us your getting married.'

Everybody laughed.

'Well maybe, no that's for another day,' Suzie blushed.

'No it's about out new town, our property, our shacks, unbeknown to you, paperwork has been written up in your names, securing the land and homes and business we have created. In short it means you are now land and home owners, which can never be taken away from you. You're secure for life, and so are the next generation. Basically you never have to leave here if you don't want to!'

Stunned silence, then a massive cheer, and dancing around, clapping, tears, hugs and kisses, everybody wanted to hug and kiss Brad.

**Brad said**

'We will deliver the paperwork to you tomorrow. Suzie's here to answer any questions.' The clapping went on for ages. 'Jimmy strike up the music. Let's dance.' Everybody went twirling around.

What a night it had been. Brad grabbed Suzie hand.

'Come with me,' he said. They ran off towards the lake. The moon was shining across the lake, Brad grabbed and hugged Suzie, planting a tender kiss on her lips. 'Suzie,' he said, 'I think I'm falling in love with you.'

'What took you so long?' she said. 'I fell in love with you the moment you walked into my office and said hi, I'm Brad.' He kissed her again and again and again.

Breakfast was crazy. The paperwork was handed out. There was a big crowd around Suzie's table. As she explained what it all meant whoops of joy went up, tears of happiness.

Brad approached Suzie. 'I've arranged a boat trip and a picnic for later this afternoon, would that be alright with you?'

'That would be more than alright with me,' she said. He kissed her and went off to sort things out.

Mr Matsuda asked Ching-Ching and Daniel if they would like to join him on a trip, to get Daniel's paints and bits and pieces. Both said yes. Once he'd hitched the horses they set off.

Daniel sat in the back just listening to the two men's banter, chatter and laughter. He started to sketch them. It was a bit bumpy, but he could get a drawing out of it. Once in town Mr Matsuda showed Daniel the shop.

'I've got things to get.' he said. 'I'll be back to sort out the bill. Take your time, there's no rush.'

Ching-Ching and Mr Matsuda went off in different directions. Daniel thought this was like an Aladdin's cave, they had many new products Daniel had never seen before, putting all the bits to one side he wanted, he even got the big canvas for the portrait of Ma and Pa Brad wanted done first.

Mr Matsuda was back first. He sorted out the payment and arranged a credit facility for Daniel. Then they started to load up the buggy. They only had a few items left to load, when two drunks emerged from the saloon.

As they staggered past, one said, 'Hey nancy boy, are you doing some painting?'

'You can paint me if you like,' said the other.

Mr Matsuda just said, 'Just ignore them, they are drunken slobs.'

'What did you say?' said one man.

Mr Matsuda said, 'We are not looking for any trouble. We just want to go home.'

With that the two men jumped down and surrounded Mr Matsuda and Daniel. One pushed Daniel and he fell to the floor, the other went to punch Mr Matsuda, who caught his fist and swivelled up behind his back, crying out in pain. With Mr Matsuda's arm around his neck he was immobilised. Just then the second man went for his gun, but flying through the air came Ching-Ching. His foot landed directly in the man's stomach, which sent him sprawling, immediately being sick. His gun went flying, the second man went for his gun, Ching-Ching spun around and landed a kick where no-man wants to be kicked. Mr Matsuda took charge of his gun. As he let the man drop to the floor he also was sick. Ching-Ching picked up the other man's gun, just as the sheriff arrived.

'I saw everything. You were provoked, and only used self-defence. These two will spend the night in jail, then will be asked to leave town. We don't want trouble makers in our town,' he said, as they helped Daniel into the buggy. They got his last bits and pieces, thanking the sheriff before they left, and handing over the two guns.

Daniel, although shaken up by the whole experience, was extremely proud of Mr Matsuda and Ching-Ching. He even laughed when Mr Matsuda and Ching-Ching were arguing which was best, kung-fu, or Karate.

'It doesn't matter,' said Ching-Ching. 'You kick a man where it's going to hurt he'll go down like a fallen tree, no matter how big or tough he is.' They both laughed. 'Still Karate is better, not kung-fu.'

Daniel had never felt so protected in the whole of his life. He felt so safe, so adjusted, he'd found a very special place, with very special people. He couldn't wait to get started, sketching, drawing, painting, writing, this is the place for me.

Once they got back and unloaded Daniels bits he made a beeline for the house. He wanted to get started on Ma and Pa's portrait.

Ma said, 'Should we pose, or get dressed up for the occasion?

'No no,' Daniel said, 'I'll put you into position, say maybe an arm around Ma, or you can choose a stance that suits you, I'll start by getting the outline, sizes, background. At a later date we'll do faces, hair, then you can dress up and we'll capture the details of the clothing.'

Excited, Ma and Pa took up a pose, and Daniel was frantically sketching away. Ma showed Daniel the room he could paint in. They'd covered the floor in sheets, and told him to come in whenever he wanted to. It was an excellent room for painting, high ceilings, lots of windows and lots of natural light streaming in. Daniel made a start bringing his paints and brushes up.

Meanwhile Ching-Ching and Matsuda were demonstrating their fighting skills to Brad and Steve, telling them what had happened in town, exaggerating their moves and kicks. Brad said maybe they could teach classes in martial arts. 'Yes,' said Mr Matsuda, 'Karate.'

'No,' said Ching-Ching, 'Kung-fu.'

Brad said, 'Why don't you teach both?'

'Yes,' they both said and walked away with their arms around each other's shoulders.

After a lovely day together, eventually Suzie said to Brad, 'I have to go home, I've got a business to run.'

'I know,' said Brad, 'but I don't want you to go, I'm going to miss you so much.'

'And I'll miss you very much, but we're not far away from each other, we can see each other every day.' 'I'll come and stay the weekend here. How's that?'

'I'm missing you already and you haven't even gone yet!'

'Kiss me,' Suzie said.

'No,' Brad said, 'you kiss me,' and they rolled around on the grass laughing together.

Brad's heart and soul felt so good. This is the one, he thought, I want to marry her, settle down have children and be happy ever after. I'll build us our own home, with a back yard, with a swing in and a tree house just like Pa made.

'I love you, Suzie,' Brad said.

'I love you too, Brad.'

'Come on, I'll take you down to the buggy.'

'What about saying goodbyes to everyone?'

'Too many, in any case you'll be back soon.' As he kissed her goodbye, and they waved each other away, Brad felt so warm inside, and wanted to shout from the highest mountain 'I'm in love with Suzie'.

Steve arrived. 'Well, buddy, you've got a good one there.'

'Yeah keep your eyes off. I saw her first.' They walked away arm in arm. 'Tomorrow,' Brad said, 'we'll get stuck into our new town.'

'Yeah,' said Steve, 'we should give it a new name.'

'Yeah I'll ask everybody to put a name forward then we can vote on it, most votes wins.'

'What about Steve's?'

'No buddy, we're going to name the drains after you.' They laughed.

That night they put it to everybody to come up with a new name for the town. 'That's easy,' said Pa, 'Bradville.'

Everybody cheered, all hands went up in the air. 'Bradville,' they all shouted.

Brad was really touched with emotion. Ma and Pa came up and said, 'We're really proud of you, son, you deserve this.'

Pa said, 'Now go get Mrs Bradville, son.'

Ma said, 'Pa, leave the boy alone he'll figure it out.'

The next month flew by. Suzie had been awarded a major contract by the railways, with deadlines to meet, but she loved her breaks from work being with Brad. They went for coffees and cakes, walks, out on the boat, both were very busy people, what with the town being built. She loved how Brad planned ahead. He was going to build her an office in the new town so she would always be near here. He talked about their house, and the garden and the swing. She thought to herself this might be the last big contract she takes on, she wanted to be with Brad, the house, the kids, the community. She had been reading up on shareholders, how the business was one company, people purchased shares in the business, then got yearly dividends, depending on how the business was doing. People could buy and sell shares. This could help the capital flow. 'Interesting,' said Brad, 'worth looking into further.'

Brad said, 'Maybe we should get engaged to be married. We could have a big party. I could buy you a ring. I adore you Suzie will you marry me?'

'Yes Brad,' she said, 'what took you so long?' They kissed and laughed together.

'We'll tell my folks tonight.'

'And everybody else,' said Suzie.

At dinner Cliff also announced some good news, he would be taking part in a rodeo contest, including cattle driving, herding, roping, shooting, and invited everybody to come and watch him perform. Mr Matsuda said to Ching-Ching, 'We have bet on him to win with other punters.'

'Good idea,' Ching-Ching said.

Steve said, 'We'll all get dressed up as cowboys and cowgirls, yeeha!'

'And have meat and beans for supper, yeeha!'

Suzie said to Brad, 'I fancy dressing up as a cowgirl and lassoing you and tying you up.'

'Yeah and I might brand you with a big B on your butt, telling everybody hands off she's mine.'

It was rodeo day, Cliff was dressed up to the nines, everything was clean and shiny. He was ready to go, the support team all had hats, neckerchiefs, boots and they were loud and cheering. He was going to put on a good show for them, he wanted so badly to win.

Cliff went to check in, and saw this cowgirl standing there looking him up and down. 'So you think you can win?' she said,

'Yeah I hope so,' Cliff said.

'Well you'll have to beat me,' she said.

'Tell you what,' Cliff said, 'if you beat me I'll take you out for dinner, if I beat you I'll also take you out for dinner.' He couldn't believe he'd said all that.

'Ok,' she said, 'but I only like beans.' That was music to his ears. They shook hands. 'Let the best man or woman win.'

They started off pretty even. They both had a good rodeo ride, sitting at position one and two, Cliff at first place, with a smile on his face. They entered the lassoing contest. She was good, quick, strong and accurate, jumping over Cliff into first place.

'Losing your touch, cowboy,' she said. Cliff smiled. Win or lose he had a date lined up. Then it came to the tin shooting, twelve tins lined up, a six shooter in the left and one in the right. You had to be good at shooting with both hands. Cliff went first as he was in second place. Shots fired all over the place, the perfect score twelve tins down. She stood up, a blast of shots, eleven tins down. 'I missed that on purpose,' she said, 'to give you a chance.'

Last thing left, the quickest draw. After Cliff and she had beaten everybody else, it was just the two of them left for the draw off. They faced each other. The tension was high, then she walked over to Cliff, grabbed him around the neck and planted the biggest kiss on his lips Cliff had ever had. 'You win, cowboy,' she said, 'I'll be riding home with you.'

'Good,' Cliff said, 'we've got beans for supper.' A draw was declared, love had won here. The trophy was going home to the ranch.

## PROFILE: JULIE AND JULIA AND LITTLE FREE

Not much to say. They were born in a small village one week apart, life was very tough, the landscape very unforgiving. They lived hand to mouth, never knowing what the future held, but they had each other for strength and company. They were like two peas in one pod, never apart, like close sisters.

Free never knew any different. He couldn't remember his parents. Grandma was a lady that gave him scraps of food and where he slept. There was no attachment, no hugs, kisses, affection, it was just an existence from day to day.

How their lives were about to change for the better, they had no idea how good it was going to be.

# Chapter 2

## Love is in the Air

With long sunny days, beautiful evening sunsets, love seemed to be all around. You could feel it in the air, the beautiful smell of the flowers. The atmosphere was electric, Lucy and James announced they were courting, which was quite obvious, as you'd quite often see them walking about holding hands, or stopping for a kiss, the same with Jack and Ellis, although more shy. You could see they were getting closer and closer, one evening Lucy and Jack appeared at Helen's shack. Helen know something was going on, by the behaviour of Ellis and James, excited and twitching nervously. Helen let them in, they looked at each other and dropped their heads to break eye contact. Jack cleared his throat, obviously the selected spokesperson of the group, he started with, 'Er, um, how are you today Helen? Um sorry is it OK to call you Helen?'

'You always have in the past,' said Helen, 'why would it be any different now?'

The rest all sniggered, 'Um yes,' said Jack. Helen knew what was coming, but thought she'd string it out as long as possible. 'Yes well we, that is Lucy, Ellis and James,' he pointed at the three of them, 'well we was wondering ...'

'Spit it out, Jack, what are you trying to say?' said Helen.

Eventually Ellis stood up. 'Mum we were wondering if James and I could move in with Lucy and Jack, we all get on so well together we thought it would be fun. Like you always said, Mum, you're only young once.'

Jack butted in. 'Strictly girls' room and boys' room.

Helen said, 'I think it's a terrible idea.' All their little faces dropped in sadness. 'Of course you can,' said Helen. They all jumped up with joy, happiness, all hugging each other, dancing around, kissing Helen, Helen said, 'Thank you Jack for asking first. That shows true maturity.

'Well I didn't really,' then just petered out.

Helen said, 'I think we need some ground rules.'

'Yes,' they all agreed.

**Helen said**

'Now you might have some late nights, singing dancing, no alcohol, you must not let it interfere with your chores. I want you all to be on time for breakfast, work and study hard for your futures. You mustn't let anybody down. We are a team here. They're good people, you mustn't let anybody down.' 'We won't, Ma.'

'No, Helen, we won't let anybody down.'

Helen continued, 'I only wish I was young again, free as you kids are, on a beautiful place like here, right next to the lake, kind folks about, never having to worry where your next meal is coming from, safe, secure, brothers and sisters all good friends getting on together. Never take it for granted. We are so lucky, always appreciate what you have around you.' Realising then that she was going on a bit, Helen decided to shut up. She went around hugging all of them, saying, 'Be happy, and any problems talk to me, you can always come home. The door's always open to you.'

'Thanks, Ma.'

'When are you thinking of going?'

'Tomorrow.'

'That will be nice, I get to spend one more night with my kids, as you're all growing up now.'

'Ma, we won't forget you, we will still come and stay over.'

'And you can come and stay with us,' said Jack.

Helen said, 'I love you all, Lucy and Jack, I feel like you are my children too.' That meant a lot to Lucy and Jack. 'And I think all of you are a splendid match. Just don't rush into anything to quick. Take your time, but above all enjoy the journey of life, be happy, as I am so happy for all of you.'

'Thank you, Ma. Now what about Steve?' Ellis said.

'What about Steve?' said Helen.

Pauline and Bill had never had children, but if they did, they would have wanted a son like Ken, he was so loving and thoughtful. He always hugged Pauline and Bill calling them Ma and Pa, in return they always called him son. He would leave flowers on the table, which he had picked. He used to follow Pa around and copy what he did. Every night or morning they said goodnight, good morning, God bless you, we love you. Ken stopped going to his shack. This was home now with Ma and Pa. Pauline and Bill said to Ken that they would like to officially adopt Ken as their son. This made Ken so happy. He would have his own family, a ma and pa. Pauline said, 'I'll talk to Suzie and get the required paperwork drawn up for you to sign.' Ken's writing and reading was coming on leaps and bounds, thanks to Father's schooling, and homework he did at home.

They made it official and told the whole group that Ken now lived there, and that he was going to be their son. A big cheer went up. Brad thought straight away with Ken's shack free he'd get it all cleaned up and painted so if Suzie wanted to stay over for a night or even two she would have her own place to stay. He thought I'll put a double swing in the back garden and tied to the old tree, so they could swing together. Suzie loved the idea. When she did stay over some mornings Brad would appear from the shack and scuttle away, hoping not to be noticed.

Helen said to Steve, 'We need to talk.' They went off to the lake. 'As you know, Steve, the kids have moved out, I'm alone, I want to know do you have feelings for me? I want to know where I stand.'

Steve grabbed her and kissed her passionately. 'Does that answer your question?'

'No,' she said 'do it again and I'll give you my answer.'

No hesitation, Steve was straight in there kissing her lips, her neck, then he took her hand and kissed it. Holding her hand he said, 'Helen I've waited a long time to tell you how I feel about you. It was always about timing, I know you had to work through your grief and pain that you were suffering. I know time would heal a little, but I never knew when the time was right. Let me take you back to the first time I saw you, up to your knees in mud and water, desperate for help, even when you fell in and got covered in mud, you didn't get angry or annoyed, you just laughed it off. You're an amazing mother, so kind and understanding, that time you helped Jack out with his knee. You care for everybody and look after their wellbeing. Look how you treated George and his wounds. You're always helping people out, and I want to care for you, at the dances when we danced together, I could feel the magnetism between us, but always had to hold back. When I sneaked a kiss, I always wanted more. When I visited your shack or stayed over, I never wanted to leave. I wanted to hold you in my arms forever, but the kids were there, I had so much work on, so much to organise, but all I ever wanted to do was lie in bed with you, hold you and tell you how much I love you. I never want to be apart from you for the rest of my life. I want to have children with you, marry you and grow old together.'

As he looked into Helen's eye's she had tears rolling down her face. Steve hugged her and kissed her tears. 'Wow,' Helen said, 'my first impression of you was what a strong handsome man you are, willing to help anybody, always putting other people's needs before your own. I love the friendship you have with Brad, you're so organised and motivate others. They all love you and respect you. You are a good father to my children, and they love you dearly. I would like you to move in and let me love you forever.'

'Helen that would be awesome. Can you cook? I'm starving.'

'You also make me laugh a lot. Come on. Let's feed you.'

Steve couldn't wait to tell Brad, and Brad couldn't wait to tell him his news. Steve blurted out first, 'Helen and I are going to get married.'

'So are Suzie and I.'

They danced together going round in a circle, patting each other on the back. They hugged, then pushed each other apart, like real men, then hugged again.

Steve said, 'I'm moving in with Helen.'

'What about James and Ellis?'

'They're moving into Lucy and Jack's place.'

'I can't keep up with all this moving about. We'll have to re-do the map. Ken's moved into Bill and Pauline's. I'm going to do the shack up, so Suzie can stay over whenever she wants to.'

'Like a love shack.'

'Yeah hopefully,' said Brad. 'We're going to get engaged.'

'Let's have a double engagement party.'

'Yeah and what about a double wedding?'

'Yeah we've got all the bridesmaids, Too, Baby Virginia, Lucy, Ellis.'

'Yeah and I can be your best man, and you can be my best man.'

'Yeah and we can all go on honeymoon together.'

Pause. 'I don't know about that.'

'Let's get the engagement party organised.'

'Yeah we need to buy rings.'

'And presents for the girls. When do you think you might get wed?'

'Probably next year, Suzie's really busy with her work. She's got lots of deadlines to meet, once that's done she'll be more relaxed, and can take some time off.'

'Yeah Helen's going to be quiet busy what with all the babies that are coming.'

'Yeah next year sounds good, a beautiful spring wedding with two beautiful brides.'

'God Steve,' Brad said, 'we've been so lucky, look at this place thriving, everybody so happy. We've had a wedding, children to be born, Molly's back home, love is all around us, we've been so blessed.'

'The new town is taking shape, business is good just think it all started with our ride home, all these amazing people we met along the way, and they're all here, happy, content and prosperous.'

'Just think, I was going to lie on a beach now I'm going to have a wife and family yee ha.'

Brad said to Steve, 'Let's go down to Cliff's and see how he's getting on with his new cowgirl.'

'What's her name?'

'I heard someone call her Cow Pat.'

'It can't be.'

'Let's introduce ourselves and find out her name.'

As they approached the corral, sure enough the two of them were on their horses, doing tricks, lassoing each other and pulling each other together to kiss.

'Things look promising,' said Brad.

'Howdy partners,' Steve shouted.

They soon parted, got off their horses and walked over to Brad and Steve. 'Howdy,' they both said in tandem.

'How's things?' Brad asked.

'Couldn't be better,' Cliff said.

'I think it's about time you introduced us,' Brad said.

'Yeah sure this is Kellee.'

'Howdy,' she said, 'pleased to meet you.'

'Have you settled in?'

'Sure have. We've been riding, camped out and get beans.' They all laughed.

'Is Kellee coming to dinner tonight, as we need to let Bill and Pauline know one extra and Kellee can get to meet everybody else.'

'I hope Kellee will come to dinner every night,' Cliff said.

'I sure will,' said Kellee. 'I love it here, so peacefully with a full moon, cattle and horses to look after, and Cliff in my life.'

Cliff hugged her and kissed her on the cheek.

'Well we'll leave it to ya, see you tonight.'

They walked off. Steve said, 'That seems to be going well.'

Steve said, 'Have you heard Juan's planning a trip to Mexico to get his sister and her best friend to bring them here, for a better life?'

'All the more merrier,' said Brad. 'I bet he fancies the friend.'

'What about Too?'

'Virginia's offered to take her in and look after her.'

'Virginia's wonderful with kids. She should have some of her own. She'd make a lovely mother.'

'I think Jimmy's working on it, he seems to be staying there more often.'

'What with wedding, christenings, church and school, Father's going to be really busy.'

'He loves it.'

Alan and Dianna, Maria and George were regular visitors to Helen's clinic. They all got on so well, Helen was teaching the women some breathing techniques. She asked the men would they like to attend the births. Both Alan and George looked sheepish. Helen carried on to say they would be a great help holding their partners hand, and helping with the breathing and panting. She said, 'There will be a bit of blood, but you can close your eyes at that moment, and George you might have to go through it twice.'

'If Maria can put up with me fainting we will go through this together.'

Alan said, 'What if both babies come at the same time?'

'I've got that covered,' Helen said. 'Ellis is well up to speed with everything, and I'll be there to guide her. Also the town doctor will be staying in the clinic nearer the time, with his experience of delivering hundreds of babies, he will be nearby if needed.'

Helen went on to say, 'I'm thinking of turning a section of the clinic into a nursery. The mothers can rest, they will have company together. We can help the babies to feed, bathing, diapers to put on. George, Alan you can help with that! How to wind them, how to place them in the crib for sleep, lots of things you need to learn and practise.'

Everybody thought it was a marvellous idea, they wouldn't just be thrown out and told to get on with it!

'And no doubt there will be night feeds, so get as much rest as possible now, as you're going to have many a sleepiness night ahead, and George you're going to have double trouble.'

A bit shaken the men gingerly left, but they knew it would all be worthwhile. They were soon to be dads, their own family. They couldn't wait, and it all would be happening soon.

Andy had been very busy. What with all the wood needed for the town, the new cribs for the forthcoming babies, the request from Brad for a large swing, he'd also been working on a project in his spare time. He wanted to make everybody a small wooden cross to be hung around their necks, or perhaps placed on a Bible. He made extra to give to Father to put in his church to give away to anyone who wanted one. He started at the house. He knocked before entering, only Molly was in downstairs.

'Come in,' she said.

'I'm Andy,' he said.

'Yes I remember you at breakfast the other morning.'

That was nice he thought, all those people but she remembered him.

'Yes,' he said, 'I've made some little crosses, one for Ma and Pa, Brad, Alan and Dianna, the new little baby, Ching-Ching, and one for you.'

'Oh how kind,' she said, 'have you made them all?'

'Yes, all by hand.'

'How kind and thoughtful.' Andy blushed. 'Where are you going now?'

'Er I was going to go round and deliver them personally to each person.'

'Would you mind if I came with you? I'd like to spend some time with everybody, and get to know them.'

'Yes that would be splendid,' said Andy.

'I also need to spend some time with Father.'

'Oh that's good,' said Andy. 'I've got spares to give to Father for his church.'

'How thoughtful,' said Molly.

As they walked out together, Molly said, 'Do you mind if I hold your arm? The ground can be a bit bumpy.'

'Not at all,' said Andy, as proud as punch. He had a beautiful woman holding his arm. He hoped everyone would see them. Molly thought what a nice good man Andy was, good with his hands and a down to earth grafter. She thought I'd like to get to know him more, spend some time with him, he looks like he's had an interesting life. They passed Steve and Brad, gave them their crosses. They thanked them. As they walked away Steve said, 'Love is definitely in the air.'

Daniel had also been very busy, finally the portrait of Ma and Pa was finished. Andy had made an amazing frame and helped him to secure the picture. George had made a fixing in the house for the picture to be hung on and helped Daniel carry it up to the house, which George and Ching-Ching lifted into place. It was covered with a sheet, so nobody could have a peek. Daniel wanted to have a grand opening ceremony, and see his work of art for the very first time. I hope they like it, he thought to himself. Brad announced at dinner that after dinner everybody should go to the house to see the unveiling of the picture. As a surprise Daniel had stuck up sketches he'd done so far. The lake, Lucy and Jack, Brad and Suzie, Molly, Chief, the wigwam, Mr Matsuda and Ching-Ching, the mill, the house, all would be painted at a later date.

Everybody gathered around. Ching-Ching had made a drink for a toast. He called it a pair of teeth. Mr Matsuda corrected him, saying, 'It's an aperitif.'

'Yeah yeah,' said Ching-Ching, 'but not so funny.'

The moment came, Ma and Pa were asked to step forward, together they were to pull the sheet down. Everybody gave them a countdown. Five, four, three, two, one, the sheet came down. Total silence as people stared, it was magnificent, as though you were looking at real people. An amazing applause went up. They all slapped Daniel's back. It was a brilliant piece of artwork, such fine details, exuberant colours, he'd captured their souls, their smiles, their personality, their love for each other. Brad stepped forward clapping in Daniel's direction.

'Well done, Daniel, you've done a superb job.' Pa hugged Ma, who was crying. 'Don't worry,' said Brad. 'She likes it. Ma, Pa, you started this dynasty, without you two none of us would be here.'

'Three cheers,' shouted Steve. 'Hip-pip-hooray, hip-pip-hooray, hip-pip-hooray,' followed by loud applause. Pa bent and kissed Ma!

By now people were wandering to the walls to look at the sketches. They were amazing. He'd captured their lives, just as Brad had wanted. Daniel explained that colour would be added.

Ching-Ching said to Mr Matsuda, 'That's not me, I'm more handsome than that.'

'No you're not,' said Mr Matsuda, 'have you never looked in a mirror?'

Brad pulled Daniel to one side and told him what a marvellous job he had done and how happy he'd made everybody. 'There's lots more to come,' he said.

'Now payment,' Brad said, 'whatever you need talk to Mr Matsuda. He will sort it out, you can even open up your own bank account.'

'Brad,' he said, 'I can't tell you how happy I am here. This is not like a job, it's a pleasure. There will be no charge, on any drawings or paintings, people can take whatever they want.'

'OK,' said Brad, 'thank you. You will get a percentage cut at the end of each month just like everybody else. Living here you don't need money to survive. You're already rich with the pleasures of life.'

'Next I'll finish the whole family portrait, just waiting for Alan and Dianna's baby to be born.'

'We'd better add Steve. He's like family. Also could you do one of me and Suzie? I'd like to hang it in our shack.'

'No problem.'

'I can't wait for the new gallery to be opened so I can display all of my artwork.'

'Soon,' Brad said. 'Soon, fingers crossed.'

Just then a loud screech blasted out, it was Dianna standing in a pool of water between her legs.

'Don't worry,' said Helen, 'it's just her water breaking,' followed by another screech form Maria. 'Brad go get doctor, Mr Matsuda get the buggy, the men can walk down. Ellis you look after Maria, I'll look after Dianna, go go,' shouted Helen. Pa turned to Ma, 'We're going to be grandparents.'

George turned to Alan, 'We're going to fathers.'

What a long night this was going to be. Eventually the doctor arrived, checked a few things and said to Helen, everything seems to be fine. You're doing a splendid job carry on, I'll be in the background if you need me.

Time ticked by slowly for Alan and George. To see their women folk in such pain was a trauma to watch, but both women were strong and determined, helped by being told how much they were loved, with the panting. Finally Dianna gave birth first, a new baby boy. Alan and Dianna were over the moon with joy, as Alan picked his son up for the very first time. He said, 'I'd like to name him after Pa.'

'Yes,' said Dianna, 'and his middle names will be Alan and Brad.'

'That's a great idea, welcome to the world. Archie, Archie Alan Brad Shack. You are going to be so loved in life, surrounded by lovely people, a grandma and pa who will spoil you, Aunty Molly and Uncle Brad, and two loving parents,' he kissed Dianna. 'I love you,' he said, 'and I'm so proud of you.'

Then the noise started from Maria, George in his deep voice grunting, 'Breath one, two, pant one, two.'

'I can see a head,' shouted Ellis. 'Push, Maria, push.' George was in a daze as he was handed his firstborn son. 'Hallelujah' was all he could think to say. 'Hallelujah, praise the Lord.' Once his second son was placed in his other arm an identical twin, he just cried, 'Hallelujah praise the Lord.' He turned to Maria, placed both boys on her chest. You've delivered two beautiful boys. I love you, Maria.'

'I love you too, George.' All the babies were taken away, cleaned up, weighed. The doctor gave them the once over. 'Three fine and healthy boys, congratulations to the parents, congratulations to the fathers and mothers, congratulations to Helen and Ellis. My work here is done, time for bed.'

George and Alan both hugged and kissed Helen and Ellis, thanking them sincerely. Helen said to Ellis, 'That was your first birth, you've done very well, nice and calm and organised. How do you feel?'

'To bring new life into the world is amazing, to see the faces on the new mums and dads is outstanding, I want one.'

'Not yet young lady,' Helen said.

George said, 'What do we do now?'

Helen said, 'I suggest you men go home, and give these ladies some rest. You can go home as well, Ellis.'

'No I want to stay.'

'OK but get ready for some crying.'

'You men can come back first thing in the morning. Now say your goodnights and be off with you.'

George kissed Maria and his two boys. 'Love you. See you tomorrow,' he said.

Alan kissed his son and Dianna and also said, 'I love you. See you tomorrow.'

When George and Alan got outside, they hugged. 'Congratulations, Dad.'

'Yeah and congratulations back at you,' Alan said. 'Come up to the house. Everybody will still be up.'

George said, 'I don't think I could sleep anyway. everybody is going to want to hear our news.' The two men strolled arm around each other to the house.

Ma and Pa were up, Brad and Steve, Molly and Ching-Ching. Alan spoke first, 'Ma and Pa you have a grandson, Molly you're an auntie and Brad you're an uncle.' They all whooped with joy. 'His name is Archie Alan Brad.'

Brad was so touched by this gesture.

Molly said, 'What about me? I feel left out.'

'Don't worry, you're next on the list for names.'

They all swamped Alan.

'George, George, what's your news?'

'Two baby twin boys.'

'Way-hey.' They all swamped George. 'Any names yet?'

'No we've got to think about it.'

'Well done George and Alan. How are Maria and Dianna?'

'Both fine but tired, you can visit them tomorrow.'

'You try and stop me,' said Ma.

Steve said to George, 'How did Helen and Ellis cope?'

'Magnificently. Both were angels, you can be proud of them.'

Steve said, 'I am so proud of them.'

Next morning was crazy at breakfast. Everybody was so pleased about the news, everybody wanted to visit them. Brad said, 'In time. The ladies are quite exhausted, Ma and Pa are going down first followed by me, Molly and Steve. If they're up to it all the ladies next, followed by the men.'

As Ma and Pa went into the room they saw their little grandson asleep in the crib. They looked over to Maria and George, waved and whispered congratulations. Maria was trying to feed one of the babies. Ma kissed the baby's head and said they would come back later, when mum and baby were awake. She stopped Molly and Brad and Steve going in as they were both asleep.

Brad said, 'Ma and Pa we need to talk to you and you Molly.' They went back to the house, Brad then Steve told them about their up-coming engagements, how they were going to have a double engagement party, and planned to have a double wedding.

Ma said, 'I'm not sure if I can cope with any more good news. I'm exhausted, I can't keep up with all the going ons around here, it just keeps getting better and better.'

**Pa said**

'I think we should crack open a bottle of champagne, to wet the babies' heads, to celebrate the forthcoming engagements and the return of Molly home.'

'Cheers to that,' they all said.

What a night, what a day. Brad said, 'We've got our first baby in the house, the next generation the new town is nearly finished, we can put the sign up tomorrow. Bradville. It sounds so good, there are new romances happening everywhere, business is booming, Molly's home, and Steve and I have found love, they'll be a christening and weddings and more babies, let's drink to that!'

Steve said, 'Any chance of a piece of apple pie, Ma?'

'Help yourself, son.'

Ah, she called me son. That touched Steve.

Juan was packed and ready to go on his journey. Saying goodbye to Too was heartbreaking, but to have his sister in his life would be more important. Also he always fancied her best friend Julia, maybe some love or romance there, as he pulled out of the park. They had all gathered to wave him off. He was going to miss everybody, but wanted Julie his sister, and Julia to have a better life. He'd always promised his dad he would always look after her, now was his chance to make that happen. After days on the road, he finally saw his little home village. Nothing had much changed over the passing years. When he compared to where he lived now to where he'd come from there was no comparison. It reminded him of how lucky he had been, pulling up outside the little white hut, reminding him of the tough times they had had growing up, Ma and Pa working every day in the fields under the baking sun, no spare money for treats, just essentials.

He took a deep breath. 'Julie, Julie, Julie,' he shouted, tears rolling down his face.

Slowly the tattered old door slowly opened. 'Juan, Juan, Juan,' Julie shouted. 'Juan is that you? she said.

'Julie, Julie, Julie,' Juan shouted.

'Juan, Juan.'

They rushed into each other's arms hugging. They just sobbed and sobbed. 'What are you doing here, Juan?'

'I've come to get you, Julie.'

'What do you mean?'

'I've come to take you to a new world where the grass is green, lakes filled with water, fish, flowers, all the food you could ever eat, surrounded by wonderful people. I have my own business, making plenty of money, and a daughter. You are an aunty, she needs you to help bring her up.'

'But what happened to Roseanne?'

'She died,' said Juan. 'I have my own home, with plenty of room for you.'

'Juan, there is something you need to know. Mamma passed away few years ago, and Papa died last year. I had do way of letting you know. They are buried in the backyard, where they were born and raised. I thought it only fitting this should be there final resting place.'

Juan kissed Julie on the forehead. 'I like to visit their graves and pray, come,' Julie said. The room they passed through was very dark and dismal. Out the back were two very small crosses marking their graves.

Juan fell to his knees and started praying. At the end he said, 'Papa, I'm fulfilling my promise to you, to look after Julie. From now on she will be, safe, secure, and loved. Oh an also you are both grandparents to little Too. She is beautiful just like you, Mamma. I love you and wished I could have been here for you. Sorry.'

Julie picked Juan up. 'Come inside,' she said, 'please tell me what the hell are you talking about.'

'Julie it's true. I've come to take you to a new world, to a new life.'

'I can't just leave, Juan. What about the house, my job, my friends and neighbours?'

'The house is falling to pieces, I've already got you a new job, paying very well, friends, neighbours, you'll make new friends and neighbours.'

'What about the language?'

'I'll teach you. Too can teach you. She so wants to meet you, her aunty, family she's never met.'

'I can't leave Julie, my best friend from childhood. I can't leave her, Juan.'

'I know,' Juan said, 'that's why she's coming with us.'

'What?' said Julie.

'That's right, she's coming with us. Go get here and tell her the good news.'

Julie ran out of the door and brought Julia back with her. With tired eyes Julia said to Juan, 'What is she talking about? By the way, hello Juan, how are you?'

'Fine Julia, hello, please sit down and I will explain everything.'

Juan left the girls in a heap crying. 'Think about it, when I return I want your answer and I won't take no as your answer. I need to go attend to the horses, they need food and rest for the long journey home.' Juan went back into the house.

'Well what is your decision,' Julie crying, stood up, 'I want to meet Too, I want to swim in a lake and walk on grass. I'm coming with you, Juan.'

They hugged and cried together. 'Julia what have you decided? I don't want Julie not to be part of my life, If she's going I'm going too.'

Then they all hugged and cried. Juan said, 'Let's get busy packing all the things you want to take, Ma and Pa, personal things, food for our trip, we will all have our last meal together in this house. Julia pack your things. Do you have family to say goodbye to?'

'No they have all gone.'

'Just before you go tell me about the little boy standing by the well.'

Julie said, 'It's a sad story, his parents died of diseases, he has a very old grandma, who's very unwell and poor, she worries about his future.'

'If she were to die what would happen to him? Who would look after him? What's his name?'

'Free,' Julie said.

'What,' said Juan, 'is this some kind of a joke or a miracle?

'What do you mean, Juan?'

'Do you not get it? I'm called Juan, my daughter is called Too, and now

I meet a boy called Free.'

Altogether they said, 'Juan, Too, Free.'

He thought how Steve would laugh so much. 'Take me to his grandma,' Juan said. Juan spoke to his grandma for ages explaining how he could give Free a new life, safe, fed, schooling, play mates and part of a loving family. The grandma said this was a blessing from God. 'God bless you, son,' she said, 'please give free a good life,' and with that she rolled over and died. Free was very confused. What was going on? But he enjoyed the meal that evening. Juan gave the neighbours a few dollars to bury the old lady. In the morning they paid their last visit to their parents' grave and left, never to return.

Eventually it was time for the ladies and babies to go home. Most people had visited and left gifts, George had done the spare room up with the cribs, Alan had been busy decorating baby's room ready to receive his wife and child. Ma and Molly were excited.

Maria and George had decided on Biblical names Isaac and Isaiah. George often wondered how he would tell them apart, he'd make them a ring, each with different markings on, then he'd know which was which.

Steve picked Helen up and carried her home. She hadn't slept properly in days. He tucked her into bed, kissed her forehead. 'Sleep, baby, sleep. Love you.'

'Thank you, darling,' she said and was sound asleep before Steve had closed the door.

Cliff and Kellee were so loved up, they were never apart, as though they were stuck together with glue.

Brad was looking forward to the weekend as Suzie was going to stay over, and he wanted to talk to her about the engagement.

Virginia had her hands full with Baby Virginia and Too! Too was brilliant with Baby Virginia, and wished that she had a sister or brother to play with, little did she know what was coming her way.

Jimmy was so helpful too. He'd make a wonderful dad, she thought teaching the kids musical instruments.

Father was excited. He had three christenings coming up, Brad and Suzie's, Steve and Helen's wedding coming up next year, plus the engagements party. Maybe even Virginia and Jimmy or even Cliff and Kellee, exciting times. Love is definitely in the air, he thought. James, Lucy, Ellis and Jack are all living together. I must visit, he thought, make sure there's no monkey business going on there, and I'm sure I saw Molly and Andy holding hands by the lake.

It's a funny old world, he thought, you never know what's around the next corner. God works in mysterious ways. Amen.

A few days later Juan turned up with his new family. People rushed out to greet them, Juan said to everyone this is my sister Julie.'

'Hola,' they all said.

'This is her best friend Julia.'

'Hola,' they all said.

'And this little chap is called Free.'

'Hola.'

Steve said, 'You're kidding me. Juan, Too, Free. Are you joking?'

'No, it is true. He will be Too's little brother.' Just then Too burst through the crowd.

'Daddy, Daddy, I've missed you so much.'

'And I you, my little princess. Come meet your Aunty Julie, and friend Julia, and this is your little brother called Free.'

'Hola,' Too said.

'Hola,' Free said back.

'One big happy family,' Juan said.

Steve said, 'If you need more space, you can always use my shack. I've moved in with Helen.'

'Thank you, Steve, now we are going to rest up. It was a very weird journey and little Free needs a wash and some clothes.'

Steve said, 'Leave the wagon and horses to me to sort out. You get some rest.'

'Thank you, Steve.'

When Steve returned he popped in to see Helen. She was just waking up. Y

'You're not going to believe what's happened.'

'What,' Helen said, sitting up.

'Juan's family have moved into my shack, I'm just going to have to stay here with you forever.'

'Well,' she said, 'you'd better get under the covers with me. I'll keep you safe, and I'll never chuck you out.'

'Yee ha!' said Steve. 'I'll just bolt the door.'

Next morning there were lots of new faces to meet. Brad stood up, introduced everybody. 'Right,' he said, 'today's a big day. We are going to raise the sign on the new town. We will fill the stores available with our products and announce to everyone we are open for business with the big opening day this weekend, followed by a double engagement party for me, Suzie, Steve and Helen.' A big cheer went up. 'Ching-Ching and Mr Matsuda have got fireworks to let off and a celebration of the new babies. Let's get to it.'

Steve stood up. 'Right folks, we need to get organised today. All hands to the pump. There are two signs to go up, one at the entrance, saying welcome to Bradville. The bigger sign will be attached to a building, to make it safe for when the wind blows in. Once up, we'll start to move in display cabinets the fish counter, ice machine, flower stalls, the cafeteria, et cetera et cetera. You all know what you're doing, Mr Matsuda has the loose change purses, but will scope around, topping up loose change, taking away excess notes, to avoid temptation robbery.

'Hence why if Cliff and Kellee could come up we have elected our own town Sheriff Cliff,' they stood and clapped, 'and his very own Deputy Kellee (big clap). Anybody too rowdy gets slung into our jail, any fighting, stealing straight into jail.' Cliff was made up. He'd always wanted to be a sheriff, to have that shiny star on his waistcoat was all his dreams and desires come true, and to have the love of his life next to him as his deputy was the best feeling ever.

Steve went on. 'Now we're not expecting any trouble. Most folk around here are decent, it's more of a deterrent. You as shop keepers will always know there's help at hand if need be. Right I've got a dry mouth, so I'll shut up (which got a big cheer). Enjoy the day, and tonight we celebrate.'

Mr Matsuda stood up, saying, 'Profit, profit, profit.'

The hanging of the signs went well. They'd erected posts as an entrance to Bradville.

The larger sign had hundreds of nails hammered into it to make it safe. It had a little sliding window and above it: it read 'Population'. On an inserted slider it read 'thirty-five'. Brad was so proud of everybody, and now a town in his name, and tonight he gets engaged to the girl of his dreams.

Bradville had a steady flow of visitors all day, the main idea was to promote next week's grand opening. People were impressed with how clean everything was, what with everything being brand new. The standard of produce was high class.

All the fish was sold out, the vegetables had to be topped up as they were in great demand, the log pile went down and down. Molly was taking bookings for her hair saloon. The cafeteria was packed all day. Ma was baking apple pies all day, they were flying off the shelves. Bread, cakes, buns, disappeared quickly. Virginia had lots of enquiry for cloth ware, knitting, sewing. Daniel had art work on display, and sketches, characters. Juan organised a drop of point for laundry, and a time for pick up. Jimmy had lots of interest in his music, and booted up lessons. Helen and Ellis did a display on bandaging, health and diets. Maria, George and kids had displayed horse shoes, chains and a flower presentation taking orders. Andy had a wonderful display of frames, furniture. Father was everywhere promoting his school and church. Pauline, Bill, Ben where swamped in the kitchen, they managed to rope, Julie, Julia, Too and Free, plus Ching-Ching on the washing up. Mr Matsuda was buzzing around, collecting money, giving out change. Nobody was arrested, so Cliff and Kellee, gave horse rides. They also locked Steve in jail. Crime committed: eating too much of Ma's apple pie. Brad said, 'If you think this is busy wait till next weekend.'

After an amazing day they shut shop late afternoon, then all started getting ready for tonight. Virginia was helping Helen, Maria was helping Suzie, both women looked amazing. Brad and Steve were at the house getting suited and booted. 'Have you got your ring buddy?'

'Yep, you?'

'Yep.'

'Let's go get us our brides.' it was so romantic watching Brad and Steve on one knee asking their partners to marry them, to watch them kiss and hug, cry and dance was amazing. Everybody was so happy for them, with the music blasting out. All of a sudden a large bang appeared above their heads, it was louder than thunder, they all ducked down. It was Mr Matsuda and Ching-Ching letting off their fireworks, the kids started crying. As another erupted, Ma said, 'I think we need to stop them before they burn the whole place down.'

# Chapter 3

## The Grand Opening Day

A few weeks ago Lucy, Ellis, Jack and James were put in charge of entertainment. Young people with young ideas, it was put forward for people who wanted to do something on a Sunday, their at leisure day. The group had come up with this idea months ago, and had put it to the group. It went down as a big hit. The competitiveness came out in the group, the plan was to have rowing races. There would be three separate categories, men's race, ladies' race and mixed pairs. Over a period of time people had been out on the lake practising. The standard was improving weekly, Chief was carving out a canoe while Andy was working on a new rowing boat.

Once the rowing was finished there would be a three-legged race, followed by an egg and spoon race, a mixed relay race, a fishing competition, horseshoe throwing finished off by a rounders competition, men versus women.

Everybody worked so hard on the Saturday, getting everything just right. The displays were amazing, they'd learned from last week to have spares extras lined up to replace the outgoing products. Orders were flying in for George, Maria, Andy, Molly, Chief. The cafe was buzzing, but had a great team behind them. Virginia had lots to do with measuring up. Jimmy's violin lessons, started it made such a noise they had to shut the front door. Alan and Dianna were running a play area, where babies could be dropped off while the parents shopped, Molly washing and cutting hair, Juan and family were giving washing back, and taking in more. Ma, Pa, Bill, Pauline and Ben were all cooking away and serving. Cliff and Kellee were locking kids in the jail. Daniel was sketching away. Mr Matsuda was tearing around.

Brad turned to Steve, 'Can you believe what we've created? A while ago there were only five people here: Ma, Pa, Alan, Dianna, and Ching-Ching, now look at the place. It's thriving, bustling with life and atmosphere. It's all down to you, buddy.'

'I couldn't have done it without you.'

The competitors were warming up their limbs, so wired but striking costumes were on display. Jack took charge. 'Can I have your attention please? We would like to start off with the ladies pair race first. Row up the lake to the body, go round the buoy, first past the line on the grass wins. We have six teams entered, two races of three boats, first boat home in each race goes through to the final where the tow boats will race to decide the winner. Ladies, please get into your boats. The first heat is between Ma and Pauline, Lucy and Ellis, Julie and Julia.'

Mr Matsuda and Ching-Ching were laying off bets.

'What do you think?' said Mr Matsuda.

'Well Ma has the experience and Pauline has the power, Lucy and Ellis have youth on their side, Julie and Julia unknown quantity. Two to one Ma, three to one Lucy, four to one Julia and Julie.'

Cliff was the starter with his gun. 'On your marks, get ready, go.'

Bang, his gun went off. Ma and Pauline took an early start. They had rhythm and power and began to pull away from Lucy and Ellis. Julie and Julia were strong but going in the wrong direction. Ma and Pauline rounded the buoy first, closely followed by Lucy and Ellis. Julie and Julia were way of course going way past the buoy. Coming into the home straight Lucy and Ellis were catching Ma and Pauline, who were tiring quickly. Eventually Lucy and Ellis crossed the finish line first and were going through to the final. It was so exciting for the spectators, cheering everybody on. The biggest applause was when Julie and Julia finally finished.

Brad said, 'It's not the winning that counts, it's the taking part.'

'It's all about the winning for Mr Steve,' said the ladies.

'The second race is between Molly and Suzie, Helen and Virginia, and Maria and Dianna. Ladies please get into your boats.'

Mr Matsuda said, 'What do you think?'

'Hmm, Molly has rowed all her life knows the water well. Suzie, soft office worker, not outdoor type. Virginia, as tough as old boots. Helen, strong mum, proud. Maria, Dianna tough mums. Maria, powerful, Diana knows the lake well.'

'Make a decision.'

'OK, everybody two to one favourites.'

Bang. The gun went off. All three boats were neck and neck going up the first strip, Virginia and Helen were on the inside, Maria and Dianna in the middle, Molly and Suzie on the left outside. The buoy would be the defining factor, no boat gave an inch. It was stride for stride, Maria and Dianna didn't get their turn quite right, bumping into Molly and Suzie's boat slightly knocking them off course, and disrupting their rhythm, while Virginia and Helen went up on the inside and did the perfect turn, putting them into the lead, which they never lost. The roar from the crowd was amazing. Steve went up and hugged Helen and Virginia.

'That's my girl,' he said.

Molly got out of the boat fuming. 'I demand a re-match,' she said, 'they should be disqualified.'

Jack said, 'First across the line.'

So Molly said, 'Right no rules, that changes everything.'

Brad said to her, 'Don't get upset, it's only a bit of fun.'

'Fun,' she said, 'do I look like I'm having fun?'

'They'll always be a next time.'

'Yes,' she said, 'and I'm going to win.'

'You were always like this as a child. Very competitive. Didn't like to lose.'

'What do you expect? I was up against you and Alan. I blame Suzie,' she said, and they all roared with laughter.

'OK folks, the ladies final. Ellis and Lucy versus Helen and Virginia.'

Bang, the gun went. A very even first leg, but Helen and Virginia got it all wrong at the turn, walking each other's oars, knocking them out of their stride. Lucy and Ellis were as smooth as swans gliding along, and got a monstrous cheer as they crossed the line. Helen was so proud of her daughter Ellis, Jack was chuffed his sister and girlfriend had won.

Andy had made little wooden shields that stood up by themselves. Printed on them first place, one each, presented by Ma and Pa. Their names were called out. As they walked up to receive their shields they got a standing ovation.

'Right,' said Jack, 'now it's the men's turn.'

'Right suckers eat our dirt,' said Steve.

**Jack said**

'There will be three heats of three, each winner going through to the final. Gentleman let's keep it clean and fair race. One Chief and George, Pa and Alan, Father and Daniel.'

**Mr Matsuda said**

'What do you think, Ching-Ching? Easy win for Chief and George?'

'George built like an ox, Chief fit as a fiddle. Problem is Father may have God on his side.'

Little did they know Father was a strong rower in Ireland, and Daniel rowed as a student.

'What about Pa and Alan? Both know these waters well and have rowed this lake many times.'

'Ok,' he said, 'Chief, George two to one, Pa and Alan three to one, four to one Father and Daniel.'

**Mr Matsuda said**

'You haven't got one right yet. We're losing money.'

'Don't worry, this one is a banker for us.'

'Gentlemen, take to your boats. On your marks, set, go.'

Bang, the gun went off. Although Chief and George were strong and powerful they weren't rowing in sync, Chief was used to a one-man canoe, George was all power no rhythm. Pa and Alan were competitive. Pa was struggling with his age a bit, and Alan's breathing was panting a bit. Father and Daniel eased off in the end save energy and glided home.

**Jack said**

'Race two: Brad and Steve, Jimmy and Cliff, Jack and James. Oh that's me.'

**Mr Matsuda said**

'Well you idiot, you said that was a banker race, worst odds four to one. We're losing a fortune. What about we turn your predictions upside down? Maybe we have chance of winning. What about this race?'

'Brad and Steve, fit, strong, friends know their strengths and weaknesses, Jimmy and Cliff unknown element, Jack and James live on the water, young, strong, virile. It's a hard one. What do you think?'

Mr Matsuda said, 'Two to one Brad and Steve, three to one Jack and James, four to one Cliff and Jimmy.'

Bang, they were off, splashing everywhere, oars colliding, boats bumping into each other, total mayhem, by the busy it was anyone's race, then Steve lost his oar. That was them out of the race. Jimmy and Cliff took the buoy too wide, which gave the advantage to Jack and James, who stormed home. Ellis and Lucy were all over them, jumping for joy. What with the girls win in the women's race, the young team ruled supreme. Just the final to go to both be champions. Steve couldn't believe his luck. Brad just smiled and said to him, 'Loser, I'd be better off with Baby Virginia in the boat.'

Jack said, 'The third and final men's heat, Bill and Ken, Juan and Andy, Mr Matsuda and Ching-Ching.'

Mr Matsuda said, 'We can't bet against ourselves. Surely we are favourites.'

'I don't know,' said Ching-Ching, 'you a bit over weight.'

'You calling me fat?'

'No I say more cuddly.'

'Well you skinny and old, no strength no direction.'

'Well are we favourites or not?'

'Well Bill getting old but strong, Ken very powerful, knowledge and strength, Juan nippy, Andy hands like a boulder.'

'OK,' he said, 'two to one me and you, three to one Juan and Andy, four to one Bill and Ken.'

'You sure?'

'Well you got it wrong last time, let's win the race and clear up on the betting.'

'Gentlemen get in your boats. Ready, set, go.'

Bang. They all flew off the line. Mr Matsuda and Ching-Ching got the best start, just ahead of Juan and Andy. Although slow to start Bill and Ken were catching up, Ken was so powerful, Mr Matsuda and Ching-Ching rounded the buoy first closely followed by Juan and Andy. Bill and Ken were going so fast they had trouble getting round the buoy, as they were coming down the home straight, Mr Matsuda did an air shot, which catapulted him on top of Ching-Ching. Juan and Andy overtook them, but Bill and Ken were coming fast, but not enough distance left. Andy and Juan were winners. Julie, Julia, Too and Free were going wild on the sidelines jumping up and down. When Juan got out he was mobbed. Too was saying, 'Well done, Daddy.' Julie and Julia were hugging and kissing

199

him. Juan felt so proud of him and his family.

Molly said to Andy, 'Me and you in the mixed race, we're going to kick arse.'

**Jack said**

'Ladies and gentlemen, the final of the men's race, me and James, Father and Daniel, Juan and Andy.'

Ching-Ching said, 'We could have won that race, you falling on me we lost and we lost money to. This is our last chance to get it right. We know the form as we've seen them race. Andy, Juan lucky, we should have beat them. Jack, James, young, strong, fast, determined, but Father might still have God on his side.'

'OK, Jack and James two to one, Father and Daniel three to one, Juan and Andy four to one.'

'Gentlemen take to your boats,' Brad shouted. 'On your marks, set, go.'

Bang. Father and Daniel had already decided they didn't need to win. It was more important to others. Juan and Andy gave the boys a good race but also wanted the boys to win, so held back a little but not enough to be noticed. Lucy and Ellis went wild as they went up to collect their shields. Steve said to them, 'Congratulations, but next time I'm going to whoop your arses.'

Everybody was having so much fun. Cool drinks were served, snacks, the babies had to be fed, a few went swimming, eventually Jack stood up. 'Last but not least the mixed rowing event, this had been drawn out of a hat:

| | |
|---|---|
| First heat | Ma and Pa, Pauline and Bill, Maria and George |
| Second | Brad and Suzie, Virginia and Jimmy, Ken and Julie |
| Third | Molly and Andy, Helen and Steve, Cliff and Keller Juan Julia |
| Fourth | Jack and Lucy, James and Ellis, Mr Matsuda and Ching-Ching |
| Fifth | scrapped Juan and Julia, Ben and Julie, Alan and Sarah (withdrawn) |

Chief will be racing in a single canoe in all races. If he can win a race he will be in the semi-final. There will be two semi-finals, and two for the final.'

Mr Matsuda said, 'OK, we don't bet on each race. We give a price on the whole field, everybody will bet on themselves, only one winner we clean up.'

'Yeah only one winner, us.'

'Right give prices, who's favourite?

'We start two to one Jack and Lucy, two to one James and Ellis, three to one Brad and Suzie, three to one Steve and Helen, four to one Virginia and Jimmy, Cliff and Keller, and Juan and Julia, five to one Ken and Julie, five to one Molly and Andy, six to one Ma and Pa, six to one Pauline Bill, six to one Maria George, ten to one Mr Matsuda and Ching-Ching. Some idiot might bet on us.'

| | |
|---|---|
| First heat winner | Pauline and Bill (withdrawn) |
| Second heat winner | Ken and Julie |
| Third heat winner | Molly and Andy |
| Fourth heat | Mr Matsuda and Ching-Ching (disqualified) |

'As Ching-Ching dressed as a woman (this is not allowed in the rules) Juan and Julia took their place and were the winners. The fifth heat was cancelled. Alan and Sarah withdraw as Chief won his heat. Instead of a semi-final one big massive final, ladies and gentlemen take to your boats.'

Chief in canoe, Ken and Julie, Molly and Andy, Juan and Julia, instead of it being a dash for the line, Chief did a display rolling backwards, Juan and Julia kissed most of the way round, Andy acted as a brake so Molly couldn't win, as he knew how much this would mean to Ken, and Julie had never won anything in her life.

'You're a good man,' Molly said to Andy. 'That was the right thing to do.'

Steve said to Helen, 'I haven't won anything today.'

'You have,' she said, 'you've won my heart.'

Mr Matsuda said to Ching-Ching, 'You're crap at odds.'

'Yeah, you're crap at rowing.'

Ken gave his shield to Pauline and Bill. Julie slept with hers under her pillow.

Ding-Ding lunchtime.

'Oh good,' said Steve, 'something I can win at: eating. Why don't we have an eating contest?'

The youngsters wanted to carry on playing games, they'd organised a three-legged race, egg and spoon race, archery, horseshoe throwing, fishing contest, relay race, and a game of rounders, but Ma and Pa after yesterday and today went off for a cat-nap. Alan and Dianna disappeared as well to put baby down for a sleep, as did Maria and George. Chief was taking Baby Virginia to the woods. Pauline, Bill and Ken were going to rustle up some hamburgers. Brad and Suzie went for a walk. Suzie said to Brad, 'You've created a wonderland. Everybody has a job, it's a real community, everybody is happy. You've created events, games, parties, you're amazing.'

'Not,' he said, 'as amazing as you. You are my world, the centre of the universe, since you came into my life, my world is whole. I adore you and can't wait to marry you.'

Jimmy and Virginia had time to talk about their relationship. Jimmy asked if he could move in full time, Virginia said that would be wonderful. 'I need you, Jimmy, in my life.'

Mr Matsuda and Ching-Ching slipped away. He'd bought a bottle of spirit and wanted Ching-Ching to try it. Cliff and Keller were off on their horses, they were going to follow the river and may camp out for the night, an open fire and beans for supper. Molly and Andy took a buggy, she wanted to show Andy a hillside with a beautiful view, which Ma and

Pa used to take her to. Steve and Helen just wanted to snuggle up in bed. Juan was taking the whole family through the thick grass he had promised Julie, and into the woods, he asked Julie and Julia, 'Are you missing home?'

'No,' they both said. 'This is home now, and we are very happy. Our family together forever.'

Father was busy for his sermon tonight, Daniel was just finishing the family portrait so it could be hung tomorrow. As the stories started to build up every evening after dinner he would read what he had written so far to anyone who wanted to listen.

This was going to be another special week. Ma and Pa's fiftieth wedding anniversary. Brad, Molly, Alan and Dianna and Ching-Ching wanted to do something special for Ma and Pa. Father suggested, 'Why don't we get them to say their marriage vows again?'

Brilliant idea thought the family, but we'll keep it a secret.

'Great idea. The ladies can look after Ma and get her ready. Alan and I will get Pa ready. We'll tell them they've got to pose for Daniel to sketch.'

Ching-Ching said, 'I have another idea. There is a very special place down by a waterfall and lake they always talk about. I think it was where you were conceived, Brad,' he said laughing.

Brad, ignoring his comment, said, 'OK you get that sorted out and booked, we will let everybody else know and have a reception party at the house.'

'Yeah we decorate everywhere,' said Ching-Ching, 'mum's the word, keep it secret.'

'I'll tell Father,' said Brad.

Alan spoke up, 'Why don't we have baby Archie's christening on the same day? That will be an excellent cover why they need to get dressed up. I'll talk to Maria and George to see if they would also like to christen their boys at the same time.'

The day came, Ching-Ching had everything ready in the back room. It was going to be tight time wise, after the christening and wedding vows that he didn't want to miss, he had to get back to the house with an army of people to bring the food in, drinks, banners, plates, seats, cutlery. These were special people, he'd get it all done on time. To see the three babies get anointed and blessed was so special, but the look on Ma and Pa's face when they were told they were to say their vows again was spectacular. Pa made everyone laugh when he said, 'Not another fifty years.'

The party was excellent Ma and Pa were told they were being taken somewhere special tomorrow. It had been a wonderful day all-round, Daniel was sketching away to capture events.

As you can see over a period of time there had been some exceptional events, partners, sports days, wedding, christenings, Bradville too many to mention but as in life, there can always be a sting in the tail. It's part of life, swings and roundabouts, ups and downs, highs and lows, the group so far had only experienced ups. Their world was about to come crashing down on one particular day.

It was lovely sunny day, breakfast as normal, with all the usual chitter chatter. The only thing absent was Virginia and Jimmy and Baby Virginia. Brad, Steve and Helen thought this was odd. 'Perhaps they've slept in,' said Steve.

'Let's go round and check,' said Brad. They headed for the shack, Jimmy was on his way out. '

I'm just coming to find you,' he said. 'It's Baby Virginia, she's burning up.'

Helen pushed to the front and went in. Brad, Steve and Jimmy stayed out side, Jimmy was so emotional, crying he said, 'It doesn't look good.'

Helen reappeared. 'Brad, go get the doctor.' They stripped Baby Virginia down and applied a wet bandage to her head. Virginia kept saying, 'Is she going to be alright? Is she OK?'

Outside Steve said, 'I'm going to get Chief.'

Helen said to Virginia, 'Tell me her symptoms.'

'She's had a slight tickly cough, been off her food a little, restless not her normal giggly self. I've been up all night with her, watching her, dabbing her. Should I have got you sooner? I'm sorry it is all my fault.'

'Virginia calm down. Let's get baby sorted first, you've done nothing wrong.' Just then the door opened and in walked Chief. He went to his knees, placed his hand on his daughter's head, kissed her forehead and left the shack. He returned a little while later with a mixture wrapped in a skin from his old Indian days, and placed it on his daughter's chest, saying, 'Medicine, fever.' Soon the doctor arrived, it didn't take him long to diagnose whooping cough.

'I thought so,' said Helen.

'What can we do?' said Virginia tearfully.

'Pray,' said the doctor.

The sad news spread fast around the ranch. There wasn't a dry eye to be seen. People walked about quietly, or stayed indoors. Once the news hit the house Ma and Molly were in pieces. Dianna and Alan held their baby and knew what Virginia and Chief most be going through, dreading that such a thing could befall them. Maria and George held a baby each and just cried. Their hearts went out to the family and they got down on their knees and prayed. Father was also on his knees in the church saying prayer after prayer, hoping that she would pull through this. Jimmy couldn't go into the shack it was too emotional. He sat with Steve in silence. He knew Virginia would need his support, but at this moment in time Chief and Helen were with her. He turned to Steve and said, 'I know she was not my child, but I love her as though she's mine, she was part of Virginia I grew to love.'

'I know,' said Steve, 'everybody knows how happy you are as a family.'

In the shack Helen sat in the corner, attending to Baby Virginia as and when she needed, Virginia sat talking to Baby Virginia telling her how much she loved her. Chief was chanting and going in and out of trances. Sometimes he would hold Virginia's hand and kept saying thank you, Virginia kept saying sorry.

The doctor had to go on a call that was also urgent but promised to come back as soon as possible.

Finally Baby Virginia breathed her last breath on this earth. Virginia let out a scream that could be heard all over the ranch. Everybody knew the end had come for Baby Virginia. Virginia was inconsolable, Helen held her as tight as possible as the tears streamed down from both women. The whole ranch and its occupants could have filled the lake with their tears. Father in church said, 'God bless you Baby Virginia, may you rest in peace. Amen.' Steve held Jimmy as they sobbed together. The whole ranch was in bits.

Chief left the shack, threw himself on to his knees wailing. His body went up and down towards the earth. He collapsed the wigwam, loaded up his wagon, drove around to Virginia's shack, pulled up outside, and got out carrying a pouch-like sewn up skinned bag. He entered the shack, put a hand-made necklace over Virginia's head, hugged her, kissed her forehead, thanked her and thanked Helen, then he gently put Baby Virginia into the pouch and sewed the remaining pouch up so the baby was completely cocooned. He picked her up and said to Virginia, 'I must go now, to our ancient burial site, where young Virginia will be amongst our spiritual ancestors.' Without hesitation he placed the pouch in the wagon, rode off, never looking back.

Helen and Virginia were gobsmacked, Helen said, 'it's just Chief's way, passed down to him from generations before.'

'I know,' she said.

Jimmy arrived and held Virginia. Steve took Helen back to their shack. Father came up to Virginia's and asked them to pray with him, he didn't want to stay too long, but said he would like to hold a service tonight in the church. Virginia said she would like that. Father left and went across to Andy's, and asked if could he make a cross for Baby Virginia to bring to the service tonight.

'Please spread the word around.'

'I will,' said Andy. Father always knew the sacred burial ground behind the church would slowly fill up even to the point where his own body would be laid to rest, but for future generations it would tell the stories of those that had gone before them, a history of the past, and now the first cross to be put into the ground. The congregation was very solemn, candles were lit everywhere, they sang and gathered at the river, prayers were offered up. Virginia read psalms from the Bible, then they went outside. Virginia, with Jimmy's help, gently tapped the cross into the ground, wreaths and flowers were laid all around the cross which simply read: 'Baby Virginia, loved, gone but not forgotten.'

There was no big breakfast gathering the next morning, most people stayed at home. For the next couple of days people had gone into mourning. Nobody approached Virginia because nobody knew what to say and didn't want to upset Virginia by saying the wrong thing. Helen popped in a few times, but Virginia stayed in bed, clutching some of Baby Virginia's things. Helen brought in some soup, but Virginia hardly touched it. Jimmy said to Helen, 'I don't know what to do for the best.'

'Just be there for her, Jimmy. She's grieving. The only cure is time and understanding, just support and listen to her, she'll get out of bed when she can.'

Little did anybody know that when Chief left the ranch, they would never see him again. Once he'd lost his daughter, he also lost his way in life. Although the experience of the ranch was amazing, the friends he had made, watching his daughter grow, the help from Virginia, chopping logs, the big roaring fires, at heart he was a loner, like a free spirit that couldn't be tied down, free to roam the fields, mountains, streams, to hunt, to be with his own kind. He had tried civilisation and wanted his daughter to be educated in the white man's ways. This was not meant to be. Chief now had to make his own way in life. Daniel had captured Chief is so many ways, one in particular captured the essence of Chief, four feathers protruding from his headband, piercing eyes, no smile on his face, his tattooed arms crossed upon his chest, the beautifully coloured wigwam, the canoe he had carved for himself, the roaring fire with people sitting around, and a pile of logs Chief had chopped. But his favourite was one of Chief holding Baby Virginia in his arms smiling down at her, capturing all his crinkles in his neck, love pouring out of his eyes. Daniel put the picture of Chief alone in the house, the one with Baby Virginia in the church, the wigwam and canoe into the art gallery, along with some sketches he had drawn of Chief (Running Bear).

Brad, Steve, Helen and Suzie were all sitting around the lake.

Brad said, 'I don't know how to lift the gloom. It's like a blanket of sadness lying across the whole ranch.'

Steve said, 'It's not your job or responsibility. In the war we saw many a good man lying in the mud. Friends, fathers, brothers, uncles, good Christian men. How did we cope then? Well it was about survival, you could easily have taken that bullet or shell fire that killed that man, and how did we cope and carry on? We had their memories, of days gone by, laughing, eating, spitting out tobacco, yes,' he said. 'We learned that death was part of life. One day we will all die, nobody can live forever. What is left is our memories, close your eyes, think of little Baby Virginia. Can you see her? Yes, as clear as day. What is she doing? Laughing and smiling, you see, Brad, you carry her images and spirit in your heart and mind, just like we do our fallen comrades. The whole ranch is grieving, bit by bit over time things will get easier, we have our past, we have our present, but we can only look forward to our future. As we get older in life, we will experience more pain and loss and suffering, it's the way of the world. But a new generation will take over with new ideas and new challenges, we will be a thing of the past resigned to history.'

Brad turned to Steve. 'When did you get so clever?'

'It's all the apple pie, it's good for your brain.' They tumbled together.

'Steve's right,' said Helen, 'this is our time, the memories we created today I hope when we are old we look back and remember the faces, the good times and what we have achieved in life, and pass on to others.'

Suzie said, 'You're right. Where would people be without the ranch? We're building memories with every day. Yes at times it will be tinged with sadness, but we are a community, we'll help each other through it.'

'As a group we are strong. We do not stand alone,' Brad said. 'I really miss Baby Virginia and Chief. It's left a gap in my heart.'

Slowly the group came back together. People left flowers at Virginia's shack. Then one morning Jimmy and Virginia went to breakfast. People tried to carry on as normal, all the women folk went over and hugged Virginia and Jimmy. She thanked them all, as they all said, 'If there's anything I can do please don't hesitate to ask.'

Virginia said to Jimmy, 'Please take me down to the little cross at the back of the church. I want to lay some flowers and talk to Baby Virginia.'

This brought a lump to everybody's throat and the tears followed.

When Virginia and Jimmy walked into the church they saw the picture Daniel had hung on the wall. Instead of bursting into tears, Virginia gently touched the picture. Stroking it she said to Jimmy, 'Isn't she beautiful? Thanks to Father and Daniel I can come see her every day and talk to her.'

Jimmy said, 'Everybody has been amazing. They have shared our grief, with little touches with the cross, the painting and flowers, it's probably completely the wrong timing, but I'm in a church. Baby Pauline and Chief are looking down on us, along with God I hope.' He fell to one knee. 'Virginia I love you, I want us to have a family, a baby of our own. Will you marry me?'

Even Father had a tear in his eye.

'Yes Jimmy, I'll marry you, I want all those things as well.'

They kissed, Father said, 'Shall we all pray together?'

'That would be nice, they said.'

Brad had a great idea after breakfast. He asked everyone available to join to cut logs, fill Chief's store as a legacy, cut trees as Andy needed more wood, and build a fire in honour for Chief that would never be lit. They would build it on the site of where Chief's wigwam sat. Everybody would put a splinter or log of wood onto the fire to remind them of all the things Chief had done for them. It would be a good bonding exercise. Virginia wanted a log. Most did, Ma and some others only cut a splinter but everybody got involved. The mound got to over six feet high and on top was a plaque Andy made just saying 'Chief.' Ken was splitting wood in one swing. Brad asked him to take over Chief's role, Ken was happy to.

Pa said to Brad, 'You've done a clever thing there, son, you've galvanised the group again.'

It took the group three days to accomplish what they set out to do, the store was chock-a-block. Andy had loads of wood to work on. But most of all the wood pile looked amazing, so much effort, anger, release went into the chopping, as a group they let out all their pent-up emotions, and a wonderful tribute to Chief would always be there. They even dragged over some big offcuts, and placed them in a circle around the fire to sit on, if you wanted to talk to Chief.

Now that was out of their system, Steve stood up and said, 'Right, let's finish Bradville, then we're going to have a summer break and go off to the Grand Canyon, camp up and chill out for a few days.'

'What about the chickens, cattle, horses? Don't worry, all taken care of. Old farmer Graham and his team of workmen will be coming up to take care of things and keep an eye on the place, reading, watering, et cetera.'

Ma said, 'Tell him not to forget the vegetable patch and flowers.'

'I won't forget, Ma,' he said.

'Good or there's no apple pie for you.'

'I'll go tell him now,' Steve joked.

The team got stuck into Bradville. For all those who wanted to move in above the shops could, although the uptake was slow as everybody loved where they lived and felt part of the community. George realised in time he was going to need more space, Daniel wanted to move so he could do more sketching and painting and fill his gallery. Virginia and Jimmy wanted to move, as the shack held too many memories of Baby Virginia. Virginia and Jimmy saw this as a new start, Mr Matsuda wanted his banking office. Lucy, Jack, Ellis, James were happy where they were at the moment, but if things developed in the relationship, they saw the possibility of each couple living together. Andy was wondering whether to ask Molly to marry him. If so would they live in the house or Bradville? Juan couldn't wait to move his family in, as overcrowding was becoming a problem, and he was getting closer to Julia.

Pauline, Bill and Ken, although happy where they were, thought if everybody else was in Bradville, maybe the main kitchen for food should be down there. Chief and Keller were also happy living near the horses but thought when they were married with kids the sheriff office looked appealing. Father had already put up a makeshift camp bed in the school. He quite liked sleeping there next to the church, every night he said, 'Goodnight Baby Virginia, Chief, goodnight. God bless.'

Steve said to Brad, 'Everybody seems to be moving on to better things except you and me, and we're both going to be married next year, and I've got no real home to offer my wife.'

'Is that a fact?' Brad said. 'Come with me. I always save the best to last.'

They walked out of the main gate out through the town cut to the left and climbed an embankment which had a large flat plateau at the top. They climbed up. From the top they could see the lake, the mill, the house, the woodland, the shacks, wood mill, blacksmith's, Helen's surgery, all of Bradville, the cattle sheds, the corral.

Steve said, 'I've never been up here before, it is beautiful.'

'Yes,' said Brad, 'everything we've helped to create is in view, and this is where we are going to live my friend, we are going to build two detached houses side by side, with swings in the garden, and a porch out front each so we can grow old together watching our kids playing together.'

**Steve said**

'Buddy, you just broke my heart strings. This is awesome. We've got to get the ladies up here to see this.'

'We will, but first let's mark it all out so they can picture it better. New homes for new brides and my best buddy as my neighbour. It's the best idea I've ever had, let's get marking up. Are you sure this is what you want?'

'What do you mean am I sure? It's perfect Helen and Suzie will love it.'

'Oh I just thought you might want to go lie on a beach.' They wrestled to the ground and rolled a bit down the hill.

The slope leading up to the mound, only gently raised up, easy to walk up, ride a horse or a buggy, they'd have to work out water supplies, a generator. Pa and Ma already knew about Brad's plan and thought it was a terrific idea.

'When are you going to tell the ladies?'

'This weekend when Suzie comes over.'

'Yeah,' Steve said, 'we'll ride out through town on horseback then take a left out of town up the slope to the top. The houses will be all marked out. We'll just sit there admiring the views until the coin drops on Helen and Suzie.'

Ma said, 'I can't wait to see what they think. Still making people's dreams come true, Brad, eh!'

'Ma, it's a gift I got from you and Pa.'

Suzie arrived. She said to Brad, 'I'm exhausted, I've had such a busy week, I'd just like to lay in a hot bath soak and relax and one of your massages.'

'Plenty of time for that later,' said Brad, 'I promised Helen and Steve a little ride.'

'OK,' she said, 'but I wanted a double massage.'

'I'll even rub your feet.'

'Deal,' said Suzie.

Helen and Steve were on their horses leading Brad and Suzie's. They jumped on. 'Where are we going?' asked Helen.

'We're just going to feel the breeze in our hair, come on then,' they said.

They took off at a canter, out of the gate through the town, and up the slope, they stopped at the top. Brad and Steve said nothing, just sat on the horses looking at the view.

Helen said, 'It's a beautiful view from here. You can see for miles.'

Suzie said, 'It's stunning. Can you imagine the sunsets from here?'

Brad said, 'Wouldn't it be brilliant to have that view everyday looking out your window, or even sitting on your porch! Look behind you.'

'What?' Helen said, jumping off her horses.

All of a sudden the coin dropped for Suzie. 'No way, no way,' she kept saying, 'this can't be true.' She also dismounted.

Steve grabbed Helen's arm. 'Allow me to help you up the steps.'

'Thank you, kind sir,' Helen said.

Brad said to Suzie, 'Allow me to open your front door to your new house.'

'Thank you, kind sir,' said Suzie.

'Allow me to walk you into your new kitchen.'

'Thank you, kind sir,' she said,

Brad held Suzie's hand. 'Allow me to walk you into your new lounge.'

'Thank you, kind sir.'

'As you can see we have identical swings in the garden and we both have a master bedroom, and children's rooms,' said Steve.

That was enough for Helen and Suzie they grabbed Brad and Steve and danced around in a circle. They were hugging and kissing each other.

**Helen said**

'This is what dreams are made of and with a man that I love.'

**Suzie said**

'I'm speechless. This is amazing. You two are amazing. Let's get married today and move in, we could have a pretend marriage.'

'Down boy,' said Helen, 'you've got to wait.'

All four agreed life doesn't get much better than this. 'We've got our best buddy's next door, we are all in love, let's have lots and lot's of babies,' Steve said.

'Down tiger,' Helen said.

They all roared with laughter.

'Well get working,' said Suzie. 'It's not going to build itself, any case you promised me a hot bath and massage.'

'And you promised me apple pie,' said Steve.

They all eventually finished Bradville. Juan and family were first to move in, the foundation flooring was laid for the two houses, then it was time for their summer break. The Grand Canyon, everybody was busy packing their bits and pieces, most or the men on horses plus Keller, the women folk in the wagons and buggies. They set off really early to get a good start. They might have to camp out tonight so rations and food, cooking pots, firewood, plenty or water and a few apple pies. The views were magnificent, with the Colorado river running through it! First to go down on one knee was Brad, followed by Steve, followed by Andy, followed by Jimmy, followed by Juan, followed by Cliff. 'Will you marry me,' the men all said.

'Yes,' was the resounding reply.

Father said, 'God be Jesus, what's going on here?'

Ching-Ching got on one knee and said to Mr Matsuda, 'Will you marry me? Everybody else is doing it.'

'Get up,' said Mr Matsuda.

The men had arranged everything. It was Steve's idea. Not one couple would ever forget where they were proposed to, on top of the Grand Canyon.

'Did you see Father's face? All those weddings. Shall we make it easy for him? One big massive wedding, one massive wedding reception, say aye if you're up for that.'

'Aye,' they all said. 'Did you see Ma's face when Molly said yes to Andy? She wasn't expecting that. No, Juan hasn't wasted much time on Julia.'

Father said, 'Now all gather around, we should pray on this moment us occasion. So many lives have been changed coming to the ranch, so much love is bring shared, God bless us all, amen, amen.'

It was so refreshing, all being together, leaving work and their worry behind them, just enjoying the simple pleasures of life.

Brad said to Steve, 'I've got an idea we'll talk to Mr Pullman about. The machinery he has, they've had to dig through rock, under mountains, streams, rivers, he might have the tools we need to find the well we need.'

'Good idea, and if not we'll dynamite it.'

'We'll have no mound left if you were in charge!'

'We'll have to work out a sewage system, especially with the amount of apple pies I eat.'

'You're impossible,' said Brad.

'Relax,' said Steve, 'enjoy the views, we'll get on it as soon as we get back. I'm off to do some smooching.'

'Yeah me too,' said Brad.

It was a fantastic trip. Everybody loved it. Just what they all needed. Everybody was looking forward to building the houses for Brad, Suzie, Steve and Helen. They couldn't think of more deserving couples. All their lives had been changed for the better by these people, they had put everybody before themselves building the church, the school, the town, securing orders, jobs, profits and only taken their fair share, no rents, no greed or slave driving, just planning ahead motivation. This was the group's chance to do something for them, to show their appreciation and build them a future, just like the future they had built for them.

Brad went to visit Mr Pullman, who was very pleased to see him. Mr Pullman thanked him for all the reliable deliveries, high standard of products.

'Without your team and partners we would never had made such success as we have done, I also hear you're engaged to be married to Suzie. My God,' he said, 'you've got a good one! She's beautiful, clever, intelligent, smells divine.'

'You're right there,' said Brad.

'I hope I'm invited to the wedding.'

'You sure will be,' said Brad.

'Now what can I do for you? I'm sure you didn't just come for a chat and a catch up.'

Brad explained about the mound and how they needed to find the well, and a sewage system.

'No problem,' said Mr Pullman, 'I've got all the top water people in the country working for the railways, I've got drilling experts, mining engineers, surveyors, water finders with sticks, you name it we've got it. I'll send a few chaps over tomorrow to do the initial work. They'll order up the men and machinery needed to do the job and we'll get started straight away. How does that sound?'

'Amazing,' said Brad, 'thank you. Could you also give me an idea on price?'

Mr Pullman said, 'pay? After all you've done for us. There's no charge involved, see it as a good community gesture. Do you have anywhere my men can stay over?'

'Yes,' Brad said, 'we now have a few empty shacks, now the new town is up and running.'

'Yes,' he said.

Suzie said, 'it's called Bradville.'

'Nice touch, you deserve it young man. You're an inspiration to us all.'

'Would you like me to at least pay the men's wages?'

'No, wouldn't hear of it, see it as a wedding present to you and Suzie. You're one hell of a lucky guy.'

'Tell me about it,' said Brad.

'There is one thing you could do for me.'

'Anything, name it.'

'Could you send me one of Ma's apple pies?'

'I can do better than that. I'll send you two.'

'Marvellous!'

# Chapter 4

## The Fire

Mr Pullman's men arrived as promised. They went all over the mound, sticking rods and all sorts of instruments into the ground. They saw Brad before they left. 'It's looking good at moment,' they said, 'we'll be back as soon as possible.' They disappeared. A couple of days later they were back, with generators, drilling equipment, rods, pumps and things most people had never seen, you could hear them banging and clunking for days, the men stayed in the empty shacks, but they had rigged up massive lighting system and seemed to have kept working right through the night. Eventually the foreman approached Brad.

'All done,' he said, 'we managed to hit water. A deep well, you now have a bore hole directly into the water, we've also managed to redirect the water to your town, and even taken it across to the other side. We've installed three generators one on the church side, one on this side, and one where the two houses are to be built. We've also installed lighting up the mound to the two houses, and in the main street of the town, cables run from the generators to each individual building, so you'll have lighting, water and drainage in every building and house.'

Brad said, 'You've done an amazing job, above and well beyond what we'd expected.'

'You're welcome,' he said. 'All courtesy of the railways, we all wanted to give something back to you, for the wonderful food and drinks you've supplied to us over a long period and of time, on many a cold night, I've sat there eating Ma's apple pie, which reminds me, I've got to take two back or he'll kill me.

'We've parcelled up more than two, Ma's baked a whole tray full.'

'That will do for me,' he said. They packed everything up and left.

Now the tram could get on and finish the houses, the town could be lit up at night, all the buildings had running water and lights, the whole town was alive.

What a terrible night was brewing, you could hear the lightning crackle, the thunder roar and rumble, the wind got up and the rain came down. Brad and Steve had joined Cliff and Keller to get the horses and as much livestock as possible to safety. Ma and Pa were covering the vegetable patch and flowers.

'Better batten down the hatches,' Brad shouted, the small sign in the town was swaying all about. Jack and James had pulled all the boats in and tipped them upside down, as sheets of rain fell from the skies. Too and Free got into Juan's bed. He told them not to worry, it was just God playing marbles. The twins were restless, waking up and crying. Mr Matsuda and Ching-Ching were outside watching the lightning show.

'It's better than a firework display,' said Ching-Ching, then boom a great big thunderclap directly overhead and made them jump.

'Probably time to go in,' said Mr Matsuda. Ching-Ching was first through the door. Up at the house was more calm, bigger stronger timbers made them all feel safer, it seemed to rain and thunder and lightning all night.

'It will be good for the ground to get a good watering, of the crops I'm sure some will get destroyed,' said Brad.

People slept as and when they could, Steve said, 'I don't think we'll get an early start tomorrow everything will be to wet, and everybody tired through lack of sleep, let's hope the shacks and town stay water proofed, and there's not too much damage.'

'My only worry,' said Brad is lightning strings. They can do so much damage just from a lightning bolt.'

'I know,' said Steve, 'we'll do a night shift keep an eye out for any such thing, we built well. Fingers crossed everything should be alright.'

As Brad and Steve were outside having a cup of coffee a huge lightning strike went off behind them.

'That was in the woodland we need to check that tomorrow must've brought a tree or two down.'

'Yeah,' said Steve, 'what with all this rain any fire should be put out quickly.'

Just then Steve threw himself to the ground. His coffee went flying as the biggest thunder clap roared out.

'Bit nervous there, buddy,' said Brad.

'Old habits die hard,' Steve said as he stood up covered in mud. 'That reminded me of the canons going off, the first thing you did was to hit the deck.'

'You'd better get yourself cleaned up, and another cup of coffee.'

As Steve went in doors, Brad thought to himself you never forget the noises of cannons roaring out, and men screaming out in agony or an explosion if it hit the gunpowder store, or men with arms and legs blown off, or a head missing or a man's stomach spilled out. How lucky he was to be alive. By the time Steve returned the rain had stopped. It looked like the storm was blowing over, the lightning was striking far in the distance, you could just hear a tiny rumble of thunder.

'That's it,' Brad said, 'the worst is over, we might get our heads down for a few hours, but I've just had another cup of coffee. I'm buzzing I'll never be able to sleep, maybe now's a good time to snuggle up to Helen.'

'You're joking, she's sound asleep, slept through it all.'

'Unlucky,' said Brad, 'see you later buddy.'

That big lightning strike they heard had done some damage the power was so great, even though everything was so wet a fire had started, not helped by the rain stopping. At around the same time it started as a small glow in the woods, but gained momentum, the heat increased, which gave the fire its power, as there was a light breeze picking up the flames started to increase gaining speed at an alarming rate, being fanned by the wind, the direction of the fire was heading towards the ranch and shacks.

Ken was first up, he was always an early riser, as grandpa would always get him up to feed the animals before school, many a time he went to school reeking of manure, or pie and cow dung, everyone gave him a wide berth, except one lad who had no sense of smell, as Ken stretched his body yawning, he was sure he could smell smoke. He sniffed the air. Yes definitely smoke, he didn't want to raise the alarm and wake everybody up, as they'd all had a bad night's sleep, and were catching up.

So he decided to go have a look, perhaps it was small enough for him to put out, and he wouldn't have to wake everybody, as he went into the woods smoke got heavier, so he used his rag in his pocket to cover his nose and mouth. The deeper he went he went he could hear the crackling of wood, and trees falling down like an explosion as they hit the ground. Eventually as he made his way through the thick thicket, he could see the glow of the fire, it was shooting up high catching the top of the tree's alight, which then caught other branches alight, he turned on his heels, and ran as fast as he could through the thicket getting cuts and scrapes as he ran

As he reached the shacks his mind said to him what should he do, warn Pauline and Bill, or hit the gong and make sure everybody knew, this was urgent and help was needed. Quickly he choose the gong, banging it as loud as he could shouting fire, fire, fire, continually banging the gong fire, fire, fire.

Bill came out first, 'What's happening, Ken?'

'Fire, fire in the woods.

'What, a small fire?'

'No a big fire and it's coming our way, I'll get changed, keep banging the gong until everybody get's here.'

'Yes, Bill,' Ken said.

It could be heard all over the ranch, even in Bradville, people got up, something's wrong as they got outside they could hear people calling fire, fire, fire.

Pa, Brad and Alan heard the gong clanging.

'Fire in the woods. Not the first time we've had fire in the woods, Brad, Alan you know where the fire dampening brushes are, yes behind the canteen, Ma you stay with Dianna and Baby.'

'No,' she said. 'I'm coming you're going to need all the help we can muster.'

'Must have been that have strike last night,' Brad said. 'I knew I should have checked it out straight away.'

'Don't worry about that now, son, we've got a job to do, mother nature has a way of culling the old trees for the new saplings to grow, let's just hope it's not coming our way, and rain is in the forecast.'

As they ran towards the gong Steve was on his way out with Helen, Jack, James, Lucy, Ellis, were running along. Juan had dropped Too and Free with Maria so George, Juan and Father joined up, Cliff told Keller to stay with the horses and be careful. If the cattle get spooked they would stampede. Andy was running alone, Mr Matsuda, Molly and Ching-Ching were heading in that direction, Virginia and Jimmy were running towards the gong, as were Julie and Julia as they gathered near the gong.

Brad stood on a bench. 'Can I have your attention, please. Ken you can stop banging the gong now. Thank you, behind the canteen is lots of fire beating sticks, grab one. Ma has soaked towels in water, keep it to your face, smoke inhaled can be as bad as the fire, as we approach the fire the heat may be so extreme that we cannot get anywhere near it. We may have to go to the side of the fire to contain it's spread, if so we need to dig fire defence ditches to stop the flames. Shovels are next to the brushes, there are plenty of buckets behind the shower block. Julie, Julia start filling the buckets once the trenches are due start pouring the water this side of the trench, never work alone stay in a group. Steve you go to the left with Juan, George and Cliff, Pa you go right with Mr Matsuda, Ching-Ching, Bill, Andy Ken, Jimmy, Alan, Father, Daniel, Jack, James with me in front of the oncoming flames. Ladies if you can keep those buckets of water coming, let's go, stay safe.'

The fire had gained strength, Brad took the front line way back from the fire, the heat was too intense to get to near, Steve and gang started digging their trenches to the side to stop it spreading to the left. Pa and team did the same on the right, the ladies shuffled bucket after bucket to the trenches, pouring them on the ground behind the trenches hoping it was too wet for the fire to jump the trench and carry on burning. Father said, 'I'm going to pray for rain.'

**Steve said**

'Where's Chief when you need him? He could have done a rain dance.'

They threw the earth towards the advancing flames hoping that would stop the fire in its tracks, the men dug and dug as fast as they could, the women were brilliant. The furthest to go was Pa's team, so they started taking buckets of water from the canteen as it was nearer, Brad heard wagons pulling up behind, out jumped Graham and his workers from the farm down the road. 'Thought you could need some help we saw the smoke from afar and knew this was a big one.'

'Thank you,' said Brad, 'join the men at the front, this is the biggest section to cover.' They all had their own shovels and picks, and got stuck in straight away.

**Brad said**

'I just hope now the wind doesn't change direction.' More and more wagons arrived from the surrounding area, each jumping out and getting stock in. More women arrived to help with the buckets of water.

Brad looked the fire straight in the eye of the storm. 'You're not taking our ranch, not with all the work we've put in, come on fire we're ready for you whatever you throw at us, you won't break us.'

The good work that had been done, with all the water laid down, the fire had nowhere to go, they'd contained the sides so it couldn't spread out. The main ditch at the front did its job, the fire never jumped over it, although still roaring, it would eventually burn itself out with no new wood to feed it! The cheer and clapping was tremendous. The ranch had been saved!

Black faced, dripping with sweat, tired, exhausted, they all sat around the branches, lots of water and lemonade were brought out, along with apple pies. Brad approached Graham and his men, and all the volunteers that had turned up.

'Thank you,' he said. 'Thank you, you have all helped to save the day.'

Everybody stood cheered and clapped, Graham stood up, 'I'm sure you'd all do the same for us. Plus you've created a community here, we were just a sleepy outback, before you guys got started, bringing the railway orders sharing the products around. We were struggling to make a living, now we're all healthy, well fed with money in the bank. My loans are paid off, my herds have increased along with my crops, you've brought wealth and prosperity to the whole area, and we salute and clap you.' All neighbours, all the volunteers stood up and cheered and clapped the team.

One old timer stood up. 'For over forty years I've never been able to fence my land off, thanks to ye all I've got a brand and banking new fence yeeha!'

Brad said, 'I don't know how to repay you all.'

Graham stood up and interrupted Brad, 'You owe us nothing, it's we that owe you!' More clapping, 'What say all this weekend we have a right old shin-dig, food, dancing, music, yeeha!'

They all shouted, the old timer said, 'I'll bring some of my moon-shine.'

Mr Matsuda said to Ching-Ching, 'What's moon-shine?'

'You're about to find out, and it will blow your socks off,' Ching-Ching shouted. 'We will have homemade fireworks.'

'No,' Brad said, 'we've had enough of fire thank you very much.' Just then the heavens opened up and poured with rain. 'That will quell the rest of the fire.'

Father looked upwards and said, 'Thank you, Lord.'

Steve looked upwards and said, 'Thank you, Chief!'

As the volunteers left and the group sat around a sense of achievement flowed over the group.

'Well done, everybody that was great team work.'

Daniel stood up as black as the ace of spades and said, 'Well at least I've got plenty of charcoal to work with.'

The group roared with laughter and relief.

'Well,' Brad said, 'let's get cleaned, up, go to church and give thanks. Pauline, Bill, Ken let's have a slap up meal tonight. Ken, today you did very well, today you saved the ranch. Three cheers for Ken. Hip-pip-hooray.'

Pauline and Bill went up to Ken. 'We're very proud of you, son.'

'Thank you Ma and Pa,' he said.

After a super meal, and Daniel reading Ken's life story, he thought it appropriate to do Ken's story as he was the hero today.

Father stood up. 'Orphans,' he said, 'orphans, have you ever thought about orphans?' The group looked puzzled. 'No fault of their own, there are children out there living in hostel and homes, sometimes with no parents to love them, struggling to find food. We have an abundance, could you see it in your heart to share with someone less fortunate? I've been doing my homework. These are the available shacks. Chire has moved on. Daniel is in Bradville, that's one. I'm sleeping in the school house that's two. Juan and family have moved to Bradville that's three. Helen will be moving to the new house that's four. Virginia and Jimmy are in Bradville, five. Pauline, Bill and Ken are moving to Bradville, six. Mr Matsuda is moving to Bradville, seven. Andy might be moving to the house, nine. Maria, George and the twins have moved to Bradville, ten. Steve's office can be in Bradville, eleven. Helen will be moving into the new house, twelve, and Cliff and Keller will be moving into the sheriff's office above, thirteen. That's thirteen original shacks all empty, all empty, most are double roomed, two beds in each room, that's over fifty children we could accommodate. Fifty children we could help with education, pass on our skills, invest in their futures, feed and clothe them, share what we have with them.'

**Brad said**

'It's food for thought, but who's going to look after them? Be responsible?'

'All of us and the Lord, Father said.

'We'll talk about it,' Brad said.

The family sat down around the table at the house. 'What do you think of Father's idea, I like it in principle and I think we can all help out. But fifty children is a lot to start with. Maybe we could take say a few less to start with to see how it goes. Father said we will have thirteen empty shacks, what if we take ten, one for each shack.'

'No, no,' Ma said. 'They might get scared at nights on their own, any case you can't split up brothers and sisters, or youngsters from their siblings.'

Pa said, 'I think we can do something. Remember these kids will grow in to teenagers, and will eventually need their own shack, good point,' said Ma. 'What if we used six shacks, two in each, that way when they grow, if they want to be separated we would have enough shacks for one each. The thirteenth shack could be a visitor's shack for anyone who wants to stay over, say Mr Pullman and his family.'

'Great idea, Ma,' said Brad. 'I'll tell Father we'll take twelve to start with, shall we say six girls and six boys. Do you want to be involved in the selection process on shall we leave it to Father?'

Ma, Pa and Molly said they'd like to be involved.

'I'm also interested in these children, maybe we could send on our unused food, or even make a regular donation to help out. Even toys, chalk boards might help, especially at Christmas time.'

All agreed to go down tomorrow to see what they could do. Father was very pleased on behalf of the children. 'I would like to thank you, sometimes,' he said, 'we get so involved in our own lives, we forget what others may be going then, on the trousers they have. I think twelve is a sensible start, but it's not going to be easy picking the twelve lucky ones, leaving the rest behind.'

Pa said to Ma, 'We've been so fortunate in a lovely home, the range, a kind and caring family, I'd like to build our orphanage, with matrons and teachers living in. But for handicapped children, the forgotten ones, you're a lovely caring person Pa and I love you.'

They rode out of town to the orphanage, it was in the middle of nowhere, no facilities or children to go anywhere, a run down old hovel with a broken swing in the front yard and the grass growing high in the play area. As they pulled up a frumpy oldish woman met them at the door. Ma couldn't help noticing how bad her teeth were. You certainly wouldn't want a goodnight kiss from her, I bet her breath smells terrible. They went in it was dark and murky, cobwebs everywhere and dusty as though it had never been cleaned.

'We rely on donations,' she said. 'We're not government funded, the church helps out when it can, now come on children get in a line, these nice people want to talk to you.'

There were ten children in a line ranging from approx. five to ten year olds, six girls, four boys.

'Where is Michael and Johnny?' matron shouted. The boys joined the line. 'You're late,' matron said.

'Sorry, matron,' Michael shyly said. What a bedraggled little bunch they looked, ripped or patched clothing, no socks, holes in the shoes that didn't look like they fitted. Unwashed hair and uncut, scratching their heads often as thou they had fleas.

Ma said to matron, 'Would you mind if we talked to the children alone, the might be more relaxed if you were not here.'

'Behave yourselves,' she bellowed and headed for the kitchen.

'Children,' Ma said, 'can you tell us your names and how old you are, and whether you have a brother or sister here.'

They all looked dumbstruck. Johnny spoke first. 'I'm Johnny,' he said, 'I don't know how old I am, but this my best friend, Michael.'

'Yeah,' said Michael, 'we are always in trouble with matron.' They grouped together. 'Do you know how old you are Michael?

'Nope, I'm as old as him,' pointing to Johnny.

'Yeah,' Johnny said. 'We're the same age.'

'When's your birthday,' asked Molly.

'Same as his.'

**Johnny said**

'Yeah same as his.'

Molly said, 'Poor litter darlings they have no idea do they, they just copy what the other one is saying.'

A little girl stepped forward holding another little girl's hand. In the other hand she had what looked like a rag which she used as a comfort blanket. She put her hand up and said, 'Please miss my name and Janet and this is my sister Ann, I'm eight years old and I don't know how old Ann is, she doesn't talk.'

The little girl started crying. Molly said, 'Do you mean she can't talk, or just doesn't want to talk at the moment.'

'Sometimes she talks to me but nobody else.'

'I'm Brenda, another girl stepped out I'm ten years old, I've been here for three years. Daddy is very busy and I've got to wait for Mummy.' 'I'm Brandon.' A little hand went up. 'And I'm Robert,' 'I'm Mary,' 'I'm Joe,' 'I'm Theresa,' 'I'm George,' 'I'm Cindy.'

'Well hello everybody,' said Ma, 'I'm pleased to meet you all, do you like it here?'

Silence.

Johnny said. 'I like fighting with Michael.' They nudged each other.

Brenda said, 'School's a bit boring, yeah said a few others.'

Brandon said, 'I don't like vegetables.'

Michael said, 'When I'm naughty I have to stand in the corner.'

Robert said, 'I don't like taking a bath the waters too cold.'

'Yeah,' someone else said. 'I don't like the dark.

'Yeah,' someone else said.

'I don't like prayers,' Joe said.

Mary said, 'I don't like the boys pulling my hair.'

Johnny and Michael laughed, as though guilty of the crime.

'Janet, Ann is there anything you like?'

Pause, 'No.'

'George, I like jumping on my bed.'

.Cindy I like talking but matron tells me to be quiet.'

Just then the door opened in walked Father. 'Sorry I'm late I got distracted. Good morning children how are you all today?' They all rushed towards Father. They knew he would have candy bars for them, which he got out of his pockets. 'Well you've met the children what do you think?'

Molly spoke first 'I'd like to wrap them all up in a warm blanket and keep them all to myself.'

Ma said, 'They're adorable such little characters, some need some love and some need a little understanding.'

Pa said 'I'm blown away, look at these conditions, but the children are so cute, loveable, funny, reminds me of our kids growing up, finding their way in the world just that these kids need a break a helping hand.'

Father said, 'Let me go down the list of children and give you an insight to these backgrounds. Let me start with Janet and Ann, their parents had been drinking. They were out on a balcony, when the balcony railings gave way and they fell to their deaths, Janet and Ann went out onto the balcony looked down and saw their parents motionless on the floor, that was the day that Ann stopped talking, she's never let go of her piece of rag, they both need time to heal, love and understanding.' Molly said, 'I just want to take those two home with me right now and give them all the love they need.'

She then cried. Father said, 'There's a procedure we have to go through, if the parents or parent is a live, they have to sign a form giving their permission for their children or child to be placed, secondly the church have to grant permission of any movement of children, checking out conditions et cetera for the child to be placed, and thirdly, we have to present a recommendation to the judge, who considers the move in the interest of the child.'

Pa said, 'Red tape, these children need love and a good home now.'

Father said, 'I will get all the local documents ready, you may have to visit the church council and probably the judge if requested.'

| Children | Notes | Paperwork | Church | Judge | Tick means they can go |
|---|---|---|---|---|---|
| Janet and Ann | Parents dead, no family. | | ✓ | | ☐ |
| Michael and Johnny | Abandoned at birth, they are like brothers, in situations all of their lives. | | ✓ | | ☐ |
| Brenda | Parents alcoholics, never visit, I know where they live, money talks for them. | | * | | ☐ |
| Brandon | Has an old grandma who can't cope. I'll visit her, shouldn't be a problem. | | * | | ☐ |
| Robert | Parents divorced, remarried, unknown whereabouts (We'll chance it with him). | | ✓ | | ☐ |
| Mary | Was found roaming the streets, no information on parents. | | ✓ | | ☐ |
| Joe | Was a result of a teenage pregnancy. Family given up all rights on him. | | ✓ | | ☐ |
| Theresa | Wife raped, husband wants nothing to do with the child. | | ✓ | | ☐ |
| George | Been rescued several times. Father hits him, long prison sentence. | | ✓ | | ☐ |
| Cindy | Family killed by Indians, found in Indian camp and rescued. | | ✓ | | ☐ |

Father said, 'I need to do two visits, get signatures, then present to church council, I have an inside track on that, the judge is an old friend of mine, shouldn't be a problem. I'm sorry I haven't asked you if you want all of the children.'

Ma, Pa and Molly were in bits. 'Of course we do,' said Ma. 'We want all of them and as soon as possible.'

Pa said, 'I wished we'd done this years ago.'

On the way home Pa turned to Ma. He said, 'I know my future now, I'm going to leave a legacy for me and the ranch, I'm going to build an orphanage, on the other side of the lake, it will be modern with dormitories so no child will ever be alone. And I know just the people to run it, Virginia with her caring ways, Jimmy a male influence in their lives Lucy and Ellis and Too, to bring the young influence, obviously Molly, we'll do charitable events to fund the expenses, if we find the right families, people who can't have children of their own we can run an adoption facility.'

Molly said, 'I want to adopt Janet and Ann immediately.'

Pa said, 'Excellent, Ma just think of the future, we can give these children new lives, new hope, if they are happy here and want to stay, they will be the future of the ranch, as Andy and George get older, we can have apprentices learning their trades, passing their knowledge on to a younger generation, this group of people can look after the next group of children, I'm thinking two dormitories each with six beds, one for the girls, one for the boys, we'll teach them English to speak and write, sums geography, history, how to sew and knit, how to design clothes and make clothing how to cook, how to plant vegetables, how to ride a horse, how to make a horses shoe and put it on, how to row a boat and fish, how to make flour, pick apples, banking, how to play music and sing, first aid, it's endless the life skills we could pass onto the next generation, there would always be jobs for them all, a future, safe and secure, but above all to have fun, love and sharing, how to enjoy the simple pleasures in life, friendship bring part of a community watching the ranch grow and develop.'

## Ma said

'You lovely man, you have my full support, we'll talk to Brad, get the building arrangements sorted, talk to all those you mentioned to see if they would be interested in the process, wait for Father to do his bit, get the shacks ready for our first children to arrive. This is so exciting I think I'm going to cry tears of happiness.'

'I'm going to join you,' said Molly.

The very next day, Father visited Brandon's grandma. He explained all about the ranch and the wonderful people living there, of the opportunity's available for Brandon, she said to Father, 'I'm old, I cannot look artier Brandon the way they should be looked after, Father, if you say it's a good place, I believe you and I want to sign the paperwork.'

'Thank you,' said Father, 'you can always visit him.'

'I'm too old,' she said, 'thank you, Father,' and he left.

Just one to go Father thought but this could be a tricky one. He knew where Branda's parents would be drunk in their dirty old home, he banged the door, a voice shouted out 'What do you want?'

Father said, 'I have some money for you.' He knew they would open the door if money was involved, otherwise he would be told to sod off.

'What do you mean money?' said the drunken swaggering man.

'Yes,' said Father, 'all I need is two signatures on a piece of paper and I give you money.'

'How much,' the man said, 'and what paper?'

'Well you and your wife sign this piece of paper each and I'll explain everything.'

'I'm not signing anything,' said the wife sprawled out on the bed face down.

'Oh that's a shame,' said Father, 'because once you've signed I was going to give you a nice of bottle tequila.'

'Just sign, women,' the man said.

Father said, 'May I come in, it's about Brenda.'

'What about her,' the woman said, 'she ruined my life, always demanding things, wanting food and clothing, did she think we were made of money?'

'No no no,' Father said, 'it's just a silly little bit of paper, that needs signing from you, so we can move her to a better place.'

'She doesn't deserve it,' said the woman.

'How much?' the man said again.

'Both sign it and I'll tell you.'

'Give it here,' the man said I'll sign it, how much?

'Just the lady to sign first.'

'Sign it,' the man shouted, 'then we can have some tequila.'

'Give it here,' she said, 'there you are now how much?'

'Well,' Father said, 'I know you would like to make contribution towards your daughter's upbringing, food, clothes, et cetera.'

'Get out,' the man said, 'and don't come back, give me that bottle.'

'I hope you enjoy it,' said Father. 'It's full of water, good day to you.' Father left, the man smashed the bottle and slammed the door shut. 'Yes,' said Father, 'all signed for.'

Father got back to the ranch and headed straight for the house. To tell everyone the good news, he'd got the consent and signatures he needed, Pa, Brad, Alan and Steve were already drawing up plans for the orphanage. Next they were going to mark out the area.

'I'll speak to Pullman, we might need his men again. Well the water shouldn't be a problem,' said Alan, 'it's right next to the lake, but we will need another generator.'

The women folk had been busy, cleaning the shack, fresh bedding. In each of the girls shacks, they had put hand-knitted dolls from Virginia, and Andy had made some wooden toys for the boys, the whole ranch was excited about the children coming. Lucy and Ellis were on board as they had plenty of time on their hands. Virginia was over the moon, Helen was happy to help, Jimmy couldn't wait to teach his music and everybody even was happy to pitch in, including Too. Molly asked Father would it be alright if Janet and Ann moved into the house to start with, into her bedroom. 'The children need a lot of attention and time, and I've got that in abundance, I want to help Ann speak again, if they miss the other children, we can easily move them back in.'

'Sounds fine to me,' said Father. Molly hugged him.

'Tomorrow,' he said, 'is the church's monthly meeting, I will be attending with all the paperwork ready to be signed off. Only tricky one is Robert, but I'll slip it in saying we can't just leave one child at the old orphanage. Now Ma, Pa and Molly, you need to be with me if called for, also it looks good if they need to visit.'

Ma said, 'Would an apple pie help?'

'It certainly couldn't do any harm, could you write out all the activities and skills the children would be, doing, I'll cover the education, ask Helen to come she can cover their health care, with her nursing background, now we just need a head, a matron someone who would the full responsibility for the children umm any suggestions?' said Father.

'Me, me,' said Molly, 'I'd love to do it.'

'What about your hair dressing?'

'Oh I can fit that in around everything.'

'Let's vote on it,' said Father. Up went Ma and Pa's hand and up went Father's. 'Be prepared tomorrow to answer questions.'

'I was born prepared.'

'We can vouch for that,' said Ma and Pa.

The time came to go in to the church meeting. Father said just stand to the back of the hall they will call you forward if needed, everybody was so nervous, all wanting this to go well. Father approached the bench. 'Good afternoon, fathers and mothers,' he said. 'I have here an application to relocate children from the old orphanage to the ranch, where the children will be located in their own homes. They will attend my school and church services (Father knew that would go down well) a whole community would be looking out for them and helping with their education and guidance. I have here a list of all activities and skills they will learn. Father Benjamin, i know you have visited the ranch and Bradville town were very impressed,' said Father.

'Yes,' said Father Benjamin.

'In view of the welfare of the children, health, diets, cleanness, may I introduce our very own doctor and her daughter a trainee nurse who will visit the children daily, and adhere to any of their needs or ailments, furthermore Ma and Pa, the sponsors and supporters of the whole scheme, who also wish to get your permission to build an orphanage on the ranch's ground which they would like you to take into consideration.'

The panel did a bit of murmuring. 'That's a wonderful idea,' a mother said, 'there would be extra rooms, for any of the fathers and mothers to stay over, to watch the daily activities unfold and report back to the church council. In charge and taking full responsibility for the children will be Ma and Pa's daughter Molly, who's been responsible in running a profitable business in Chicago, and she adores children.'

Pause. The council asks, 'Does she have any experience bring up children?'

'Molly would you like to step forward and answer this question?'

Molly stepped forward, 'I was brought up in a warm and loving family, I had two brothers to contend with, I have just become an auntie, and I've always got Ma's guidance and experience to fall back on, also Helen has her own children, and I can always lean on her, I also was a child once, so know that them and love is all a child really needs, education is a bonus.'

'Thank you,' said the council.

As Molly went to step back, she said, 'there is always Father to guide me.' She thought that was important to put in.

'Thank you,' they said again, as Molly got back to Ma and Pa. They said to her well done well spoken, you've done really well, we're proud of you.

The council said, 'Would you give us a few minutes to gather our thoughts, please wait outside, Father would you join us.'

Ma, Pa, Molly, Helen went outside all hugging each other. 'Wasn't Father brilliant in there? and so were you, Molly,' said Helen, 'the perfect words, fingers crossed I hate this waiting and not knowing.'

It seemed like a short while, but it seemed like ages, eventually the door opened.

'Would you come inside please,' Father said.

'Approach the bench please,' the spokesman said. 'They all lined up waiting in anticipation. We have given your application considerable thought. What we have decided is, of course with the judge's approval, to arrange a visit to the said premises providing we are satisfied with all arrangements you will have our blessing and can proceed ahead.'

The group couldn't help but cheer and hug each other.

'The application to build another orphanage has been approved subject to our visit and documents to be provided for our consideration, we will draw the meeting to conclusion now and all meet tomorrow at mid-day at the ranch, thank you for attending this meeting and look forward to meeting you all, goodnight and thank you.'

They all bundled outside hugging and kissing. Pa said, 'You were magnificent in there Father.'

'Yes,' said Ma, Molly and Helen.

'Yes,' Father said, 'it's a gift, with some help from above, now it's all down to tomorrow. We must put our best foot forward and impress them but so far so good, everything looks promising. Molly you were excellent, Ma and Pa your stature in the community is outstanding, Helen I think you swung it for us.' They all hugged again.

'I can't wait till tomorrow,' said Molly.

As the church council walked them the town, Juan was excited Too and Free would have new playmates, they stopped off at the school and went into the church, crossing their chests and kneeling. They moved onto the corral, saw the cattle, sheep, chickens, stopped off at the clinic, were impressed with the blacksmith's, and wood saw mill, inspected the shacks, were impressed with the little knitted toys, met Virginia and Jimmy and Mr Matsuda, up to the canteen meeting Pauline, Bill, and Ken, Daniel told them how he would teach them to draw and paint and read and write past the woodlands up to the house and went inside. Molly showed them the two little beds she'd put in her room, for Janet and Anne, as Anne needed one to one to start with, and not be left alone in a shack. They saw the flour mill, and saw Ching-Ching covered in flour, they were impressed by the orchard veg patch, crops and flowers, onto the lake, then they took them to where the new orphanage was going to be built, Brad and Steve had streaked it all out for them to see the layout with it's beautiful views.

'Right,' Ma said, 'let's go back to the house for refreshments and some apple pie.' Suzie had arranged for Mr Pullman to be there to add some clout to the proceedings.

Mr Pullman was introduced to the church council. He started by saying, 'I highly recommend these good people to take into their care the children, they are devoted God, loving people, kind, generous and organised with compassion. The railway would like to sponsor the planned orphanage on the ranch, no cost to the owners, we will also grant a yearly subscription for its running costs, and we would like to totally rebuild the old orphanage with a play area and an abundance of toys, trained staff, a cook and a medical assistant will be stationed in all homes. We would also like to take this conception across America as we go from town to town, city to city, each orphanage shall be called Ma's and Pa's sponsored by the railway underneath, of course, and a yearly budget will be set which the railway will pick up the tab for.'

He went on to say, 'Our Suzie will sort out all the documentation needed, and payment system, thank you.'

The church council were blown away, everybody in the room was blown away speechless, all they could do was applaud Mr Pullman.

'Yes thank you,' he said, 'all courtesy of the railways, by the way work starts on the new orphanage tomorrow and the old orphanage once the children have moved in here (making it sound as though the whole agreement was subject to the ranch getting the children).'

'You're amazing,' said Suzie to Mr Pullman.

'I know,' he said. 'I know, by the way I've been meaning to talk to you.'

'Go ahead,' she said, 'I'm all ears. Well you know most of all the contracts have been done.'

'Yes,' she said, 'thank you for that and I'm very happy to do all the paperwork needed for the orphanages including the adoption paperwork.'

'Yes,' he said.

'But.'

'I knew there was a but coming.'

'When I marry Brad. The love of my life, I'm going to retire.'

'Oh Suzie this is the saddest day of my life.'

'Brad and I want to start a family straight away, I'll always help you if you need me or you get stuck on something, but I want to put all of my time into our marriage, home and children.'

'I envy you and Brad. You've found the perfect love, not many people get to experience that, go with my blessing, I'll miss you but wish you all the best in your new adventure, thank you for the magnificent work you have done I could not have achieved half of this success without you. One day I will step down and entire and spend more time with the wife and kids but I'll never forget this ranch and the people in it.'

They hugged and kissed, Brad came over. 'Hello,' he said, 'have I got competition?'

'No,' said Mr Pullman, 'luckily she's all yours. You're the luckiest man in the whole wide world.'

'I know,' said Brad and grabbed Suzie and kissed her.

'I've just told Mr Pullman when I marry you, I'm going to retire and spend all my time loving you and our children.'

'Right back at ya,' said Brad.

'Did I tell you Mr Pullman and his family are coming to the wedding? I'll fetch him myself if he doesn't turn up,' said Suzie.

'Quiet please, quiet please,' said the church council spokesman, 'we would like to personally thank Mr Pullman and the railways, this is going to help so many children across America, for years to come, Ma and Pa's Orphanage sounds so warm and friendly and inviting. You have the church council's approval (big clap), our visit today has set the highest standard we have ever seen, this should be the role model to be sent across America, with support and love and understanding and knowledge we are building our next generation of Americans and our orphans will be part of it with the help from people like you caring and sharing.

'It gives us great pleasure to say that the said orphans can come to the ranch, immediately tomorrow, and the new orphanage to be built has our seal of approval. I will be accompanying Father to see the judge tomorrow to get his signature. Congratulations everybody you deserve it and I'm sure the children will be happy here.'

'Hooray,' went the cry. Tears, laughter, joy, hugs excitement, everybody else was outside the house, when they heard the noise they also hugged and jumped for joy. Ma and Pa looked at each other. 'We've done it, we've made dreams come true.'

Molly, Alan, Dianna, Brad and Ching-Ching surrounded them and congratulated them.

'What an added bonus for the children beyond my wildest dreams,' said Pa, 'just amazing.'

After everybody had left, Ma, Pa, Brad, Molly, Alan, Dianna, Helen and Steve and Ching-Ching sat around the table.

Pa said, 'We've been on an amazing journey and it's not over yet, these are amazing hard-working, loving people, they deserve all the happiness they get, I'm so proud of all of my family, all of their achievements and I just want to say Mr and Ma love you all. Our future looks bright and tomorrow we get our extended family, I hope they all turn out as good as you all have.'

The fathers went to see the judge, the judge knew both men well. He looked through the paperwork, and said, 'Everything looks in order here. I trust your judgements and signed the required documents.'

The fathers thanked each other shook hands and parted. Father couldn't wait to get back to the ranch to speak the good news, he will hold service tonight to give thanks and blessings.

# Chapter 5

## The Dilemma

'Today was the day they were going to collect the children,' Ma said.

'We mustn't spook the children, they're already going to be scared stiff. Not knowing where they're going, strangers, a new environment, new patterns. If we take Too and Free with us, and Lucy and Ellis they might relate to the children better. We'll give each of the girls a doll, something to hold if they get scared; give the boys their wooden toys. This will help distract them. Boys will just play anywhere, we don't need to enthuse. They're moving home, let's just say would they like to go to a party, with jelly, cakes, buns, candy? We'll play music and games, we'll wrap a present up for pass the parcel, musical chairs. Let's make it lots of fun for them instead of a major trauma, or upheaval, then the first night they can all crash on the floor once we've worn them out. We'll put blankets and pillows down, and they can all sleep together as though nothing has changed. We'll have breakfast in the house, boiled eggs, toast, most kids like these items. We won't force the adults on to them straight away, but slowly introduce them. Wait until the kids find their bearings, we'll take them down to where the horses are, and we've just taken delivery of six ponies. I'm sure Cliff and Kellee could take them for little rides, or at least sit on them. We'll go to the chickens next, let them collect eggs, that will be fun for them, then up to the lake, a couple in each boat and a rower and swimmer, in case somebody falls in. We don't want to lose anybody on the first day. We'll show them the shacks, but tell them they don't have to sleep there straight away. Get them used to playing in the shacks, all those that want to sleep at the house can, we'll put no pressure on them. After lunch, we'll take them to the town, introduce them to the school and tell them they are going to be taught to read and write, and sums and singing and to play music. Get Daniel down there, he can start them drawing, and playing with colours.'

'I used to like playing with mud,' said Steve.

'Yes good idea, we'll put a bucket of mud in. They can make shapes and bits and pieces, they'll need to be washed after that. We'll take them up to the shower block, get them all cleaned and put on their new clothing. Then back here for more food and games then see who wants to sleep in the shacks.'

Ma said, 'Molly you've thought of everything, I wish I was one of your children.'

'You are silly. Oh yes Ma, I forgot just how much love we got from you and Pa.'

'And Ching-Ching,' he said.

'And Ching-Ching,' Molly said.

'Right,' said Ma. 'Are we ready to go? This is so exciting.'

The kids were lined up ready to go, nervous, anxious. They sent in Too and Free first with the toys, that broke the ice, followed by Ellis and Lucy, the kids were talking to them, showing them their new toys. Lucy said to the kids, 'Would you all like to go to a party, with jelly and candy and party games?'

'Yes!' they all shouted except Ann.

'OK,' Lucy said, 'don't be scared, but we need to get there so outside are some wagons and a buggy, and some lovely horses. Who wants to go for a ride in a wagon.'

'Yeah!' came the voices back except Ann. She held Janet's hand tightly and her red rag.

'Ok,' said Lucy all hold hands like a chain. 'We all go together. There are some nice people who are going to lift you up into the wagons. Don't be scared, they are my friends, Janet and Ann would you like to travel in the buggy with auntie Molly?'

'Yes,' said Janet, Ann just looked terrified.

'Come on,' Lucy said, 'let's go get some jelly and candy.'

'Hooray,' shouted the children. Holding hands they walked outside and got lifted into the wagons.

Ma turned to Molly. 'Step one accomplished without any drama. Sending the kids in first was an ace stroke, well done, Ma.'

The ranch was a beehive of activity, Mr Pullman's men had arrived and occupied the remaining empty shacks. The big light was erected off the generator, so they could continue work while some men slept, others worked, the orphanage was going to be built. Unbeknownst to Brad and Steve, once finished the men were going to help finish Brad and Steve's homes, as a retirement gift to Suzie for all the hard work she had put in for the railways. Wagons and wagons of wood arrived to help finish the orphanage and two homes. Andy was very relieved as this cut his workload down a lot. He could just concentrate on beds and other bits and pieces.

Then the children arrived but went straight to the house, there was plenty of time later to meet everyone.

The kids were having a great time. Molly sat next to Ann, and was putting things on her plate to eat, Janet was just jumping in like the rest of them, Ching-Ching was loving bringing all the dishes in, watching the food disappear so quickly. 'They're so hungry,' he said.

Ma said, 'Ignore table manners today. But that's high on my agenda. It's just so great to watch them pig-out.' Afterwards Jimmy was playing his music, and mucking about dancing, mainly swinging around on one leg.

Jimmy organised the musical chairs, stopping the music, taking a chair away, and eliminating a person at a time. Ann didn't join in but was getting more comfortable sitting next to Molly, then they sat them in a circle. Jimmy played the music, when it stopped, the person holding the parcel took one layer off, the music started again and the parcel moved on. Jimmy tried to get everybody to have at least one go, even Ann. This is progress, thought Molly, she's joining in and looks to be having fun. Once finished Molly said, 'Who wants to go see the horses and ponies?'

Kellee, Cliff, Brad, Steve, were all there to help so the kids would get used to their ranch and friendliness.

Pa said to Ma, 'Have you ever seen this place so busy? Do you miss those days just peace and quiet listening to the crickets in your rocking chair?'

'Never,' Ma said, 'this is life at full pelt. You never know from one minute to the next what's going to happen. Are you coming down to see the kids with the horses and ponies?'

'Wouldn't miss it for the world,' he said. They all walked down with a child holding their hands.

Molly said to Ann, 'I'll go in the middle, that way I can hold Janet and your hand.' Ann made no comment but allowed Molly to do this. At the corral some horses and ponies were saddled.

Cliff said for all those daring enough, we can put a child in front of us and hold them and give them a little ride the ponies, put the kids on and we'll have to hold them. Actually there were two ponies two donkeys, and two miniature horses called Shetland ponies. The kid's faces lit up stroking the animals, Michael and Johnny were up for going on the big horse, but also wanted to go on the donkeys. Brenda wanted to go on a pony, the more the other kids saw the stronger personalities going for it, the more the courage built up. Brandon, Robert. Joe and George wanted to go on all of them, the girls mainly the donkeys. Ann kept stroking the miniature horses.

Molly said to Ann, 'Would you like to ride him? What if we put Janet on first and you sit in front of Janet and she can hold you. Don't worry,' she said, 'I'll be right next to you, you won't fall off.'

Ann nodded yes. Molly thought this was a major breakthrough. When the rides were done, Molly said, 'Children, say thank you to Kellee and Cliff.'

The children all said thank you Kellee and Cliff.

Keller thought they were so cute. 'If you come down tomorrow you can help feed the animals.'

'Goody,' said some of the girls.

'Right,' Molly said, 'we've off to collect chicken eggs.'

A big cheer went up. Straw was flying everywhere, Brandon found the first egg, but in his excitement to show Molly, fell over and smashed the egg. All the other children laughed. Don't worry Brandon, there's plenty more. See if you can find another one. Molly was in her element watching the kids playing, have fun and laughing. She thought to herself, this if the happiest moment of my life, and I've got Andy to love it with, he looked at her and gave her a wink

Molly said, 'Right who wants to play in mud?'

The boys all screeched, 'Yes!'

Not so much the girls.

'Right, everybody say "thank you" to James.'

'Thank you, James,' they all said.

Molly thought this way they would get used to the names. They marched on down to the schoolhouse play yard. Small buckets of watery mud were placed around, Daniel was to do a demonstration first of things the kids could make. He rolled a piece up and said, 'A sausage.' That got a laugh from the kids. 'A donut.' Another laugh, then he rolled a piece around in his hand, making a snowball. He added legs a tail, ears and pulled at the ball and made a snout. 'A pig,' he said. Another laugh. Daniel was enjoying this. 'OK kids,' he said, 'you have a go.'

The kid's got mud all over their hands and clothing. The girls were more refined, any only picked smaller bits out, even Ann dipped her finger into the mud. Most of the boys rolled sausages, copying each other, whereas the girls copied Brenda and made donuts.

'Right children,' said Molly. 'Say thank you to Daniel.'

'Thank you, Daniel,' they said.

'Right we're going off to get showered and cleaned.'

'Boo,' said Johnny, Michael copied him.

'Listen,' said Molly, 'you can't stay dirty all day, and haircuts.'

'Boo,' the boys said.

'Girls you can have yours in a ponytail or up in a bun, anything you want to try.' That brought smiles to the girls. 'Lucy, Ellis, Virginia and Helen are going to help, then Helen and Ellis are going to give you a health check over, and you're all going to wear lovely new clothes.' This pleased the girls, but the boys didn't seem bothered. Once they were washed and cleaned Helen and Ellis checked their ears, their eyesight, their mouths, their heads, their bodies. Most were underweight for their age.

Once dressed and finished they all said, 'Thank you, Helen, thank you, Ellis.'

'Right,' Molly said, 'we're off to get some food.' They walked around to the canteen, where sandwiches and drinks were already on the tables and apply pie. The kids got stuck in, what with all the workmen, kids and the rest of the residents, Juan, Too, Free, Julie and Julia, were helping out Pauline, Bill and Ken.

After lunch Molly said, 'We're off to the lake to feed the ducks, moorhens and swans. First of all say thank you to the cooks.' There were too many to say for the kids to remember. They had a lovely afternoon at the lakes. Not all of them wanted to go on the water, those that did Brad, Steve and Jack took out.

'Right,' Molly said, 'time for dinner, but Ma is going to teach you some dos and don'ts, say thank you to, Jack.'

'Thank you, Jack.'

Back at the house the table was all laid. Ma said, 'First of all everybody go wash their hands.' Ching-Ching was out there with towels, and stools for those that couldn't reach the sinks. 'Now all sit down on the chairs, pick up the cloth in front of you and place it on your legs, so if you drop anything it will go on the cloth, not your clothes. You can also use the cloth to wipe your hands.' Molly put the cloth on Ann, she liked the cloth and dropped her rag on the floor, realising this was bigger and cleaner. Molly kicked the cloth away and under her breath she said yes.

Ma continued, 'In front of you, you have a plate, a knife for cutting and a fork to put food into your mouths. If the fork is too difficult to use you may use the spoon, but do not touch the food with your hands. Put your hand up if you need help cutting your food, or need help feeding, we do not climb all over the table to get what we want.' She was looking at Johnny and Michael when she said that. 'What we do is ask the nearest person to the thing you want to pass it to you. For example, Brenda, could you pass the salt please? The please is very important. Let's practise that.'

The kids said, 'Could you pass the salt please,' and added a name. It was mayhem, water was getting knocked over, meat fell off plates, the gravy boat was dropped.

'Stop, stop,' said Ma, 'this is never going to work in a million years. Right, Molly, Father, Alan, Dianna, Ching-Ching, Pa, grab a dish and go around and serve each person. We will have to work on this slowly.'

Ching-Ching said, 'I don't know why you bother with plates, knife, forks, spoons, just a bowl and chop sticks is all you need. Less washing up as well. Even emperor China uses chopsticks and you can't get more high society than that.'

'Good luck, Father, they're all yours tomorrow,' Ma said.

'Don't worry,' said Father, 'I'm used to it. Besides, I have a cunning plan.'

'Please share,' said Ma.

'I read a particular book. It said divide and conquer, and that's my plan. Divide them into smaller groups, Daniel will teach they younger ones, with sketches and drawings introducing one letter at a time and saying the letter out loud. Mr Matsuda will introduce numbers, saying them out loud. I'll be taking the older group first of all to help them spell their own names out, and say the spellings.'

'Brilliant idea,' said Ma, 'and we will always finish with a children's story read by Daniel, maybe we should do that at meal times. Split them up.'

'Good idea,' said Molly, 'what about Ann?'

'We'll get her playing with things, drawing with charcoal, chalk, et cetera, no demands on her. We'll ease her in as just part of the group playing.'

Just then Brenda came up, hugged Molly and said, 'Thank you for a lovely day, I love it here.'

It broke everybody's hearts. Tears flowed. 'What was your favourite part?'

She thought for a second, then said, 'The horses and ponies was my favourite.'

They all started school the next morning. They were to get a break to go feed the horses and ponies, with apples and carrots, then they had their sandwiches outside under a tree. Brenda said, 'Why is there a cross in that garden?'

'Sit down,' said Father. 'I'm going to tell you a story about a little girl called Baby Virginia. Once upon a time there was this big strong Indian

man. His name was Running Bear.' Michael and Johnny sniggered. 'He
had a baby daughter whose mother had passed away. When Running Bear
met Virginia, do you remember Virginia, the lady that knitted your doll's
and made clothes for you? He asked Virginia to help look after baby so he
could hunt and build fires, Virginia loved the baby so much that Running
Bear named his daughter Virginia. She was known as Baby Virginia,
Running Bear changed his name to Chief, and lived in a wigwam. Baby
Virginia got very sick and passed away, Chief had to leave the ranch, and
that's why there is a pile of wood with Chief on near the canteen, And a
little cross was placed in the garden.'

Cindy said, 'If I die, do I get a cross?'

Over a period of time they started to sleep in the shacks. Six boys
in one shack, four girls in another and Janet and Ann with Molly. The
table manners improved with time. They all started to spell their names,
their A, B, Cs, one, two, threes. Too and Free joined in slowly. They got
to remember faces and names. Molly was called auntie Molly, Ma was
Grandma and Pa Grandpa. Everybody loved the kids and interacted
whenever they could. They all said how well the children had settled in,
and what a good job the team was doing and how happy the children
looked. They were visited by the church council, who gave them a vote
of confidence. They could see the improvements in their health, tidiness
and education. All the children seemed happy, even Ann had got rid of
that rag. Molly would replace it with a clean one, Ann never caught on.
Every night Molly would always say to Janet and Ann, 'Shall we say our
prayers?' Molly would lead, Janet would say her bit and they finish with
amen. One night to Molly's astonishment Ann said amen. Molly did not
make a big thing of it, but inside she was bursting with joy. The same the
next day, Molly gave the girls a little treat. Janet said thank you and Ann
said thank you. It was joy to Molly's ears, each day she encouraged Ann
to speak more, hold the doll up and say doll, Ann would say doll and clap

her little hands. She was still shy and reserved but she was getting there one step at a time

Daniel had been busy sketching, drawing and colouring. He'd sketched all the children, and horses, ponies, pigs, chickens and posted them on the school wall along with all letters and numbers, then he got every child to stand against the wall with a piece of charcoal. He marked the tops of their heads where they came to on the wall and wrote their names. 'We'll do this every year and watch how much you've grown, and years to come when you are adults you'll be able to look at the markings to see how tall you were when you first came here. These markings will always be here.' He also arranged for some pet rabbits to be brought in. It helped with learning. One ear, two ears. He had to laugh when the children drew the rabbits they looked like monsters from outer space.

The orphanage was gaining pace quickly. They were working on the second layer already, which meant the men were working at height off ladders, hauling heavy materials up. One day there was a nasty accident. One of the hoists swing and knocked into a ladder, knocking both men off. Helen was informed, and got the clinic ready, the two men were brought in on a stretcher. One seemed to have a broken arm and bruises, the other was unconscious bleeding from a head wound.

Helen said, 'Steve can you please fetch the doctor?' She went to the unconscious man first, he was covered in dirt and blood, then slowly he came around, dazed and confused. He looked very sleepy, muttering something. Helen couldn't make out what he was saying, so she decided to clean his wounds and wash his face, and get a bandage on to maybe stop the bleeding. As she was washing his face he started to look familiar to her. Confused, she started to stare at him, then the realisation hit her, maybe this was her husband. It can't be she thought. As it sunk in she dropped the wash bowl, which made the other man jump. 'You alright, miss?' he asked.

'Yes, yes,' said Helen, 'just came over a bit dizzy with the sight of blood,' she said foolishly, holding onto a bed.

'You're in the wrong game if you don't like the sight of blood,' the other man said.

Helen eased off his shirt, he had so many scars on his body. One looked like a bullet hole, badly sewn up, she noticed a massive indentation on his head were maybe shrapnel or something sharp had hit his head. Doctor came in, checked out the now sleeping man. 'Yes I'm going to have to give this man a few stitches. He needs bed rest and looking after for a few days.' Moving to the second man he said 'We'll have to mark a splint for his arm and bed rest for a few days.'

'Excuse me a minute, Doctor,' Helen said. She flew out the door and was instantly sick and shaking.

As she went in the doctor said, 'Are you alright, Helen? You look as white as a sheet as though you'd seen a ghost.'

'Just tired, Doctor, just tired,' Helen said.

Doctor finished the stitching, 'You wrap him up with bandages, Helen. I'll fix this man's arm.'

Helen thought she put as many bandages as she could on him, covering as much of his face as possible, under his chin, over his chin, over his ears, over as much of his head as possible. All she could think was would her children recognise him?

'Wow,' said doctor, 'you've bandaged him up like an ancient Egyptian mummy. Never mind, too much is better than too little. If you can bandage this man's arm, there's nothing more I can do here. I'll pop back in tomorrow to see how they're getting on and I suggest you get a goodnight's sleep, Helen, you look worn out.'

'Thank you, Doctor. I will see you tomorrow.'

'I'll let myself out, goodnight,' he said.

'Goodnight,' Helen said.

She just stood there looking at him on the bed. Tomorrow would he recognise her? If he did what would she tell Steve? What about the wedding? What about my kids? Her thoughts were interrupted by the other man, 'Any chance of a drink? My mouth is so dry?'

'I'm sorry,' she said flustered, 'will coffee do?'

'Anything a bit stronger?' the man said, 'to help take away the pain.'

'Only warm drinks for you,' Helen said, 'you've got a nasty bump on your head.'

Helen went to make the coffee, which gave her time to think. I've got to stop Ellis coming in here. Luckily she's been busy with the children. I'll tell her they've got to have complete bed rest and mustn't be disturbed, until I can think this all out.

I know, she thought, I'll question the other man. See If he knows his name, or where's he from, is he married, where he's living. I'll make it out that I need it for my records so that he doesn't get suspicious.

'Sugar?' she said.

'Just one, my dear.'

'I have to ask you some questions for my records, can you tell me this man's name?'

'We call him John. His background is a bit vague. Apparently in the war he got injured, left for dead. The confeds found him, done him up a bit, apparently he was hospitalised for months, completely lost his memory. He got hit in the head and shot. Eventually they sent him back to the north, for rehabilitation. Our boss was looking for workers for the railways, came across him and said he was a war hero. Didn't know his name, where he'd came from, whether he had a family, was married, children nobody knows.'

'Did they say his memory would come back in time?'

'Don't know, love, I ain't no doctor. But I do know no one came looking for him.'

Helen paused for thought. 'Do you want my details, love?'

'Urm yes,' said Helen.

'I'm Bob Mortimer, married with two kids ...' Blah! Blah! Blah! Helen wasn't listening to him. She just sat looking at this man named John. Her husband the father of the children, once the love of her life, lying there in a heap motionless, no memory, a war hero back from the dead, no one to love him, nurture him, heal his wounds, tell him they loved him, to see his children, and thinking all along nobody cared, nobody came looking for him. What am I going to do? she thought.

Just then Steve knocked the door. Helen panicked, stopped Steve coming in and pushed him outside.

'I've just come to see if you're all right. Do you need anything? Food, drinks, do the men need anything?'

Helen's mind was blown. 'Umm, if you could bring some soup and Brad, that will be good.'

'OK,' Steve said, 'how are they doing?'

'Umm one man needs to rest he has a broken arm, the other man is in a bad way, needs complete rest. Can you tell Ellis to stay away for a day or so? He must not be disturbed. I can't come home tonight he needs all-night observation.'

Steve said, 'Are you all right? You look worn out.'

'I'll be fine,' she said, 'just get the soup, leave it outside, give a gentle knock and go away. Sorry, Steve,' she said. 'I'm just worried about the man, and want to do my best for him.'

'OK,' said Steve. He went to kiss her on the cheek but she pulled back from him.

'I'm sorry, Steve, I'm just a bit tired.'

'Take it easy, Helen,' he said. Steve had never seen her before like this and left confused.

She realised quickly she had been a bit short and maybe rude to Steve. She must act as normal as possible. He knows her well. He will suspect something is wrong. She was not ready at this moment in time to have a deep conversation with Steve, when she couldn't even fathom her own thoughts. Steve gentle knocked the door, Helen went outside, gave Steve a big hug.

'Sorry I was bit short with you earlier, I didn't mean to be. Just got a lot on my mind.'

Steve said, 'Good I was getting a bit worked for a moment, I thought you'd gone off me.'

'Don't be silly, just that one man is quite critically ill and needs all my attention.'

'I need all of your attention too,' said Steve.

'Everything will be calmer tomorrow,' Helen said, 'and we can get back to normal. Did you tell Ellis to stay away for a while?'

'Yes, I had to stop her coming down. She said that's not like Mum.'

'Tell her I'll explain everything tomorrow.'

'Virginia asked, would you like her to come down to watch the men, while you get some rest?

'No no I'll be fine. Thank her, and ask her to pop in tomorrow.'

'Well goodnight, love,' Steve said.

'Yes goodnight, love. See you tomorrow, sleep tight. Night.'

As Steve walked away he thought she never kissed me goodnight. She always kisses me goodnight. Something's not right, he thought. I'll talk to her tomorrow when she's less stressed. Behind the door Helen thought at this moment in time I just can't kiss Steve. She gave the awake man his soup and bread.

'While you eat that,' she said, 'I'm going to push John's bed into the other room so you both get a goodnight's sleep.'

'My dear,' he said, 'is there anywhere I can use a toilet?'

'Yes,' Helen said, 'the cubicles are just behind you. Mind you don't bang your arm.'

'Thank you, my dear,' he said.

Helen pushed the so-called John into the other room. She thought if John started talking, she didn't want the other man to hear anything, she waited a while, checked on the other man. He was snoring fast asleep.

As Helen sat there thinking what to do, an idea came into her head. Why don't I write everything down? Maybe things will become clearer in writing, and my head wouldn't be so jumbled. She started. First things first is this really my husband or did he die in the war?

What will I do if this is my husband?

How do I feel about him?

When should I tell Steve?

Do I need to tell Steve?

Do I tell Ellis and James?

If I don't am I stopping them having a father?

Am I stopping my husband having a wife and a family?

Should I tell this man who I think he is?

Should I not tell him and let him go away?

Should I stop the wedding?

If I marry Steve knowing this man is alive, that makes the marriage null and void. I'd be a bigamist and could end up in jail.

Should I tell Virginia? Get her point of view or keep everything a secret? So many questions, Helen thought, but no answers. Finally she fell asleep, exhausted, with her head on the man's bed.

As she woke up with a stiff neck she looked at the man. He was just lying still with his eyes open.

'How are you feeling?' Helen said.

'I've had better days and nights.'

Helen tried to work out if this sound like her husband. It had been over five years since she last heard his voice.

'Are you hungry?' she said.

'I would like a glass of water,' he said.

'I've got some soup I can warm up, or you can wait a while and have eggs and toast.'

'My head hurts,' he said.

'I'm not surprised you had quite a bang on it yesterday.'

'I'll have the water please and maybe a coffee with my eggs and toast. Thank you for looking after me,' he said. 'What's your name?'

Helen hesitated, 'Umm you can just call me nurse if you'd like to.'

Virginia was first to call, Helen met her at the door. 'Is there anything you need?'

'Yes,' said Helen. 'Two eggs on toast, pot of coffee, sugar cups et cetera.'

'Anything you need?'

'No I'm not hungry at this minute.'

'How are they doing?'

'They're both awake. Can you tell Ellis to pop in ASAP?' She wanted Ellis out of the way quickly, in case doctor took the bandages off to have a look at the wound.

Virginia and Ellis reappeared. Virginia set to feeding the man and pouring his coffee. Helen took Ellis to the door. Stood in front of her so she could only peek in.

Helen said, 'He needs lots of rest and re-cooperation.'

'I can help, Mum,' she said.

'There's not much to do here,' she said, closing the door, 'besides, the children need you more at this moment in time. I'll call you if I need you.'

'Is everything OK, Mum?'

'Yes fine nothing to worry about, but he's had quite a serious injury.'

'OK, Mum, love you. Call me if you need me.'

'Love you,' Helen said.

Virginia said, 'Do you want me to feed the other chap?'

'No, no,' said Helen, 'we have to be careful with him,' keeping Virginia away from him.

'OK,' she said, 'I'll come back later pick up the plates and bits and see if they want any dinner.'

'Thank you, Virginia.' Helen felt like telling her everything but resisted. 'See you later, tell Steve everything's all right.'

'Will do,' said Virginia.

Next to arrive was the doctor. 'Ah good, nice to see both men are awake. How are you doing?'

'A bit sore,' he replied.

'Well you're in good hands, I think we'll leave the bandage on your head for another day. Let it heal. We'll have a look tomorrow, any other aches and pains?'

'No just my head,

'Good good,' said the doctor. 'Get plenty of rest, and how are you young man, arm a bit sore?'

'Yes, Doc.'

'Are they looking after you well here?'

'Yes fine,' he said, 'am I allowed any alcohol?'

'No afraid not, no drinking in the clinic, you can get up today but don't knock your arm. It needs to set.'

'Thank you, Helen, you're doing a fine job. See you tomorrow.'

'Thank you, Doctor, see you tomorrow,' said Helen.

Helen sorted out toilet visits, as John got up he put his arm around Helen for support. It sent shivers up her spine, and the hairs on her neck stood upright. In no time Virginia was back.

'Pauline's made a lovely vegetable soup, to keep their strength up and Ma's sent some apple pie. She said you must eat as well or your be no good to anyone. Oh and Steve sends his love. He says he missed you last night and he'll pop in later, to see if you need anything and a kiss.'

'Tell him I missed him too and will see him later, and she blew a kiss, 'send him that.'

'I will,' said Virginia.

I need to put on my thinking cap, thought Helen. She looked at her list. First on it was make sure who this man was. He might not know himself. I know, I can trust Suzie. I'll get her involved she knows people in high places, maybe she can get hold of medical records, or service records or medical reports. What excuse can I use to get her here? I'll tell Brad and Steve it's about co-ordinating our colour schemes for the new house's furniture and fittings.

Helen thought this man needs to be washed. Ah she remembered the birth mark her husband had on the left side of his body. She helped him remove his shirt, and looked straight away for the mark. it was about half way down his ribcage on the right hand side. Right where it should have been was a massive scar, ugly and protruding, as though sewn up in a rush, or botched up in a field tent by untrained nurses or trainers. No help there, she thought. What about his chest hair? Chunks missing, a bit greyer than she remembered, but years had gone by, definitely thinner, but most men who came out of the wars were thinner than when they went in, except the cooks. She just didn't know, none the wiser, definitely similar, but different, but then we all change as we get older. No, Suzie, was the only way around this problem.

'Do I get a bed bath, nurse?' said the other man.

'No,' Helen said, 'you can use your good hand.'

'Aahh,' he said, 'I wish I'd bumped my head.'

'If you're not careful,' Helen said, 'you will get a bump on the head with a frying pan.'

Steve popped around later. 'Sorry I've been a bit distant lately,' Helen said, 'you know I love you, don't you?'

'Yes I love you, you know you can talk to me about anything.'

'I know, and you can talk to me about anything. Yes when I get everything sorted in my mind I promise to tell you everything.'

'Anything I should worry about?'

'No,' she said, 'just something I need to do alone.'

'Can I help in any way?'

'No just be there for me and be patient. I'm starting to worry about it now.'

'Don't,' she said, 'everything will be fine.'

'You're not ill,' said Steve.

'No just need to sort something, do you know when Suzie is next coming over.'

'She's just arrived.'

'Could you ask her to come on over as soon as possible please?'

'Now I'm definitely worried, but I won't add any more pressure. I'll just do as you ask, but always remember that I love you no matter what, and I'll always be by your side, through thick and thin, highs and lows, always there for you.'

'Thank you, darling, now go and get Suzie for me.'

By the time Suzie arrived Helen had written down everything she could remember about her husband, his regiment, name, rank serving officer, where he was stationed, some of the battles he had fought in, everything she could remember.

Suzie arrived. What's the matter, hun?' she said. 'I gather it must urgent or—'

'Can I trust you?'

'You know you can. You can trust me with like your—'

'My whole life and future is at risk, can you promise me you won't tell a soul, not even Brad.'

'I tell Brad everything, but if you ask me not to I won't.'

Helen said, 'I need you to check something out for me, no questions asked.'

'Right,' said Suzie, 'mum's the word.'

She handed Suzie the list. Suzie read it. 'I know exactly where to go. You know the big town down the road, they have a records room in the library. I'll start there tomorrow.'

'Thank you, Suzie, I can't wait to hear the whole story, love you.'

'Love you too.'

Helen thought I mustn't let this man out or my sight until I get to the bottom of this, and the truth. I'm not having him disappear never to be seen again, even if I have to break his legs. Ellis came around again. Helen said she had a sterile area, and mustn't allow any germs in. She hated lying to Ellis. It was only a little white lie, only to protect her daughter from any harm.

Virginia came around again and sorted the meals out.

'If you need a break, Helen,' she said, 'I'm quite willing to step in for you.'

'You're a good friend, Virginia,' Helen said, 'but I'm coping thank you. The doctor's coming today to take the bandages off and I need to be here.'

'OK,' Virginia said, 'but let me know if you change your mind.'

'I will, thank you.'

The patient said, 'Can I get up and stretch my legs? I'm feeling a bit stiff.'

'You can go to the toilet,' said Helen, thinking quickly, 'but you mustn't walk about, because you might start the bleeding off, or even get a dizzy spell. Let's wait for the doctor to see you first.'

'OK,' he said. Helen started to think more and more this was not her husband. The mannerisms, were not right, but then maybe all he had been through, left for dead in a field, seriously injured, loss of memory would change any person. She decided to do some probing.

'I understand you're a war hero.'

'I don't know about that,' he said.

Helen went for it, hoping to get a glint of information. Maybe his memory had come back a little. 'What do you remember?' she said.

'Not very much,' he said.

Pressing, 'Do you have any memories.'

'Not really,' he said. She was getting nowhere.

'Do you remember where you were when the war was over?'

'Not really,' he said. She felt like shaking him. You do know, she thought, you're just not telling. Try a different approach Helen thought.

'Where were you when you got this job?' Work backwards, Helen thought.

'I was just wandering around.'

'Where were you living?'

'I'd been taken ill, I was in an army medical unit.'

'Where were you before that?'

'I don't know, I can't remember. Can I get a coffee?' he had all the answers.

Helen had all the questions. 'Yes you can, try to remember,' she said.

Eventually the doctor arrived. 'Hello, Helen, how are you?'

'Fine thank you, Doctor.'

'I see you've got bags under your eyes. Been up all night again?'

'I'm fine, Doctor, really.'

'Bed for you when this is all over.'

'I promise,' Helen said.

'Now let's have a look at this chap,' he said unwinding the bandages. He said, 'His head wouldn't get cold with all these bandages on. Yes the stitching has taken well, still looks very sore you've been a lucky man.'

Helen butted in. 'Do they keep records of surgery men had in the war?' Doctor looked at her. She carried on, 'Well it's just that this man has obviously had surgery in the past, but has complete memory loss, and I wondered if he wanted to find out, where would he go?'

'Do you know where the records office is down town?'

'Yes the one in the main library.'

'That's the one. If there's any information it will be in there. I'll leave you to sort this man out with dressing.' He approached the other man. 'And how are you doing young man?'

'A bit bored,' he said.

'Well not to worry, you'll be out of here tomorrow. Your company is sending you both to a convalescent home to recuperate, and to give lovely Helen a rest from you to, I won't be seeing you again so take care,' said the doctor.

'Thank you, Doc,' said the man.

Helen panicked. I must get the answers I need before they leave, I'm so close now. I'll rebandage him up so Ellis doesn't she him. Hopefully if his boss comes I can find out what he knows, and Suzie is in the right place. If she were to find something, the one person who could find out what I need is Suzie. Her mind went off to Steve, the wedding, the new house and how Suzie and Brad will be her next door neighbour. Surely this dream and my new life cannot fall apart. She'd been through a lot, looked after children alone, moved areas, fell in love. I absolutely adore this place and the people. My kids are happy with jobs and friends. All this is not going to come tumbling down. God help me, I need answers. Come on, Suzie, she thought you're my last hope. I'll be glad when this is over one way or another, imagining having to tell Steve, this is hell and torture.

Suzie arrived late afternoon. 'Is there anywhere we can talk?' she said.

'In this room,' Helen said.

Suzie started, 'Now hear me out, I'm not going to judge you or pry, I'm just going to give you the facts as I know them. Some things will be hard to listen to, but we'll get through it together. I know what this is all about, you want to know who this man is, could he be your husband. I can tell you he is not.' Helen nearly fainted but needed to hear more. 'Reports were written at the time, by both sides of the conflict, due to the confusion after the war. Now have these documents finally come together, this man was a confederate soldier, seriously injured. He took your husband's uniform hoping that his treatment for his injuries would be better in the north. Unfortunately for him as the north pulled back the confeds found him and took him south to treat him, he spent months and months being treated, too ill to be transferred north. Other soldiers had witnessed what he had done, but were also receiving treatment. Their commanding officer was informed and reports were written and filed, there are two books written by officers which I've taken out of the library for you to read. each covers the incident from a different angle, the South were considering a court martial for desertion and corruption, deception, the North for deception, possible murder with no proof that the man's uniform was taken dead or alive. It was considered the man had suffered enough, his only real crime was to put on another man's uniform, never heard of before, hence why it was written about in the books and reports, it set a precedent in law.

'Questioned about the body of the soldier, the eye witnesses could not confirm one way or another whether the man was alive or dead when buried, but the charges were dropped when they said that they had laid there for two days and there was no movement in the said body at that time. The lady from the library has let me have all the correspondents, reports and statements referring to the case.'

Helen said, 'So my husband is dead, buried in an unknown grave.'

'Yes, most men could not pick out the precise location. The areas were searched but there were so many bodies. They were collected and put under the tomb of the unknown soldier.'

Helen literally collapsed onto the floor. Suzie helped her onto a chair. Suzie said, 'It's over, honey, you now have the full truth.'

'I'm dumbstruck,' said Helen, 'I have no thoughts. My mind is just blank. I have no ill feelings for that man in the other room lying on a bed. He was just doing his best to survive, war does horrible things to mankind. As for my husband, he was a hero. He died for his beliefs. I've got some comfort from the fact he had some sort of a burial when many others did not, and now I'd like to think he is with his comrades in arms buried in the tomb of the unknown soldiers, which I will visit one day. Tonight I want to sit down with Steve and my children, Ellis and James, and tell them the whole story from beginning to the end. I'm going to ask for their forgiveness in all the secret and lies and hope they forgive me.'

Suzie said, 'I'm sure they will. Let's face it, nobody could have known all of this.'

'And Suzie,' Helen said, 'I don't have the words to thank you enough. There's only one person in this world that could have got to the truth and that is you. I love you, thank you.' And she hugged Suzie. 'That's what neighbours are for, a friend in need, a friend for life. You'll always be my friend, Suzie, I owe you so much.'

They were interrupted by the boss of the two men coming into the clinic. He had a big bunch of flowers for Helen and thanked her for looking after his men. Helen said, 'What will happen to these men?'

'They'll go off to a convalescence home. This one once his arm is healed, he'll get some compensation and probably be back at work in a few weeks. John, however, we think he's been through enough in life, so were going to retire him. He can live in the home for the rest of his days on a pension scheme, the railways look after their own,' he said.

Helen helped pack the men's things up, the man with the arm said, 'Thank you, nurse,' and left.

She went up to John held his hand and said, 'I forgive you; God bless and enjoy the rest of your life.'

A bit confused, John said, 'Thank you for all that you have done for me.'

'I'll visit you one day,' said Helen.

'That would be nice,' said John.

Once everybody had left Helen got into one of her clinic's beds and cried herself to sleep, when she woke up she had only one thing on her mind: talk to Steve and her children.

# Chapter 6

## New Life, New Beginnings

Helen had arranged for Steve, Ellis and James to meet her at the clinic. She didn't want any interruptions. As they entered they could all see Helen had been crying. Everybody was concerned and wondered what was going on.

'Sit down, please,' she said. They all sat in silence, waiting for Helen's words. 'First of all,' she said, 'I want to apologise for my abnormal behaviour over their last few days, if you think I've been a bit offish, strange, even wired you'd be right. I'll get straight to the heart of the matter. The man that had the accident on the building site, the one with the head injury, showed signs that he may have been my husband, your father.'

They gasped. 'Let me continue, I over-bandaged him, in case Ellis came in and recognised him, and got upset.'

'I thought so,' said Ellis. 'All that garbage about sterile area and germs, I knew that was a cover up.'

'I'm sorry, Ellis,' said Helen, 'but I was only trying to protect you. I'll never mislead you again. I promise. I love you.'

'I forgive you, Mum. Love you.'

'Right, back to the story, the other man with the arm injury said they had no money, and was a war hero. Nobody came looking for him after the war. He slightly resembled my husband, your father, He always had a mole on his side I looked for it but a massive scar was there in its place, that's when I saw you, Steve. I was so upset confused I didn't know what to think, and I apologise for the way I spoke to you and treated you. I was so worried about losing you. Not being able to marry you, love you, set up home with you, have children, that we might have to leave and go live with this man I didn't know any more. I couldn't tell you, Steve, I would have fallen apart but I needed to stay strong. I wrote a note she got it out of her pocket and gave it to them. Now everybody was in tears, I had to find the truth. That's when Suzie stepped in, my super woman.

'She knew all about the records office and the library. She spent most of the day there going through, records, information. Finally she got a breakthrough. There was information on this man from eye witnesses, officer reports, and two books written by the involved officers at the time. It was to go to court as what happened was unprecedented at the time, hence why documents were made for records to be kept. To cut a long story short, that man is not my husband or your father.' The emotions just expended in them. They all jumped up and hugged each other. 'Not just yet there's more.' They all sat down again. 'Your father did die in the battle.' The room went silent again. 'He died a war hero. This man John took his uniform and tried to pass as a northern soldier, instead of a southern soldier. Things got mixed up.' She could she their little faces all upset and decided to miss a bit out of the story. 'Your father's body was found and he's now buried in the tomb of the unknown soldier, which we will visit one day.' Silence fell while they gathered themselves and wiped their eyes.

James spoke first. 'I'll always be proud of my dad,' he said, 'but through no fault of his own, he was away from us for a long time and we were so young. I always believed he would come home to us, but as time went by I knew this wasn't possible. I believe this has put closure to our family story, I'll never forget him, and wish I could tell him that I love him. I will one day when I stand at the tomb, but things move on. I'm happy here I have a new life, a job, friends, a girlfriend who I hope to marry one day. We love Steve also, we are glad he is joining our family. We are sure he's going to make you very happy and you have our blessing for your forthcoming wedding.'

Helen hugged James. 'Those were beautiful words, well spoken. I'm so proud of you.'

Ellis stood up and said, 'James has captured the moment perfectly. I've got nothing to add except to say I love you Mum and Steve and wish you all the happiness in the world in your forthcoming marriage, and I can't wait to be your bridesmaid.'

Helen hugged her and told her how much she loved and how proud she was of her. 'Now if you don't mind I'd like to talk to Steve alone.'

'We understand.'

They both hugged Mum and Steve and left.

Once the door had closed Helen grabbed Steve and planted a kiss on his lips he'd never forget. It nearly blew his socks off. 'Wow,' he said.

'I'm so so sorry putting you through all of this. I love you so much. I just didn't want to lose you.'

Steve kissed her. 'And I love you so much and I can't wait to marry you.' They kissed again. Steve continued, 'Don't you ever go through something like this again alone. We are a couple, we are supposed to share everything. If you get a splinter in your hand I want to know about it, understood?'

'Yes, understood,' said Helen. 'But James is right, this is closure. My old life can be left behind. I can close the page on it an end to a chapter, a new line ahead with the man I love.' She kiss smacked him again.

'I could get used to this,' he said.

'Right let's move on. We need to go talk to Suzie and thank her. She's an amazing woman and Brad is so lucky. Not as lucky as you're about to be.' She went across the room and bolted the door Steve took her in his arms.

'I thought I'd lost you Helen, I thought you'd changed your mind. I thought I'd done something wrong. I was going out of my mind. I couldn't bear to lose you, Helen.'

'Shut up and kiss me.' She started to rip his clothes off.

'What about Suzie?' he said.

'She can wait, I can't.'

'Wow,' Steve said.

Later on they went to Suzie's and Brad's. They knocked, Brad opened the door sheepishly.

'It's over,' blurted Steve.

'What's over?' said Brad.

'Me and Helen, it's over, we're finished, the weddings off. She's already married.'

'No, no,' said Brad. 'You've got it all wrong. Helen's got to marry you.'

'Ah got ya,' said Steve. 'It saved me asking if you knew the story.'

'You pillock,' said Brad, 'get in here.'

The men hugged the women hugged everybody hugged. 'No seriously,' said Steve, 'Suzie you're a diamond. You saved the day. Helen calls you super woman, you're even better than apple pie. We love you and thank you from the bottom of our hearts.'

Brad stood up. 'I can confirm she is super woman, and is definitely better than apple pie, but don't tell Ma I said that. Here's to our forthcoming marriages, and apple pie for life.'

Finally the orphanage was finished. It looked magnificent in its setting by the lake, with the big Ma and Pa's sign to be seen from a distance, underneath sponsored by the railways.

'It looks brilliant,' said Pa, 'the first of many. But who do we move in? Our existing children who look so comfortable where they are, or being new children in who need love and understanding? We'll give each child a choice. Now the men have nearly gone, we'll have empty shacks again.

A twelve bedded-orphanage, Janet and Ann are going to be adopted by Molly and Andy, they just can't let them kids go, and the kids don't want to go. Molly's done a remarkable job with Ann, she's flourishing every day, gaining confidence, speaking a few words. Isn't life wonderful? It warms the cockles of my heart.'

'Look,' said Ma, 'the men have even made a roadway up to the orphanage around the house and the mill, Lucy and Jack's, right up to the front door. That Mr Pullman is amazing. He deserves an award.'

'Yes,' said Pa, 'we'll make him president of our orphanage, and give him a framed certificate he can keep for the rest of his life.'

'Great idea, Pa,' Ma said.

'And now onto the two remaining houses, it won't take too long now,' said Brad.

'Right,' said Ma to Brad and Steve. 'I'm pleased the houses are coming along well, but you will not be moving in together until after the marriages.'

Steve said, 'I was hoping to marry Helen not Brad.'

'You're not too big for a clip, my boy,' she said. 'You know what I mean, yes you can be together sorting out furniture, curtains et cetera, but no staying over until your married. I'll have no shenanigans going on here. We've got to set a good example to the children.'

'But Ma,' Steve said, 'I already live with Helen.'

'Right,' she said, 'I want you moved out tomorrow. We've got standards to maintain especially with the church council lurking about.'

'OK Ma. Whatever you say,' said Steve. 'I love you more than apple pie.'

'I wish I could believe that,' said Ma, 'but do as you're told.'

'Yes Ma,' said Steve.

'That's you told,' said Brad.

'And the same goes for you too, Brad.'

'Yes Ma,' said Brad. 'Love you.'

One morning after breakfast Brad said to Alan and Molly, 'Let's go see the old tree house.'

'Yes,' said Molly, 'Ma can take care of Janet and Ann.'

'Yes,' said Alan, 'I get a break from chores.' They clambered through the woods. There had been a lot of fire damage. Most things were black or ash or tears had come down. Now there were open skies whereas before it was thick with the tops of trees then they came to the opening where the old tree house had stood, with its see-saw. It was completely burnt out, destroyed. 'The memories,' said Brad, 'it was as though it was only yesterday.'

Molly said, 'I can see us all clambering up the rope, with Ma and Pa saying be careful you don't fall. Such happy days, carefree innocent. Who could have known what paths we would take in life.'

'I remember you two tying me up, saying I was the Indian and had to be tortured,' said Alan.

'Yeah you were a good Indian,' said Brad, 'until Ma said we had to untie you, as you kept crying.'

Molly said, 'Do you remember the picnics under the tree?'

Alan said, 'Yeah and we always had apple pie.' They all laughed.

'Look,' said Brad, 'a new sapling is growing, it's a new life, just like the three of us. Alan you now have a baby, Molly you're getting married next year and are adopting Janet and Ann, and I'm moving out of the house and getting married. New beginnings just like this sapling.'

'You know what we should do?' said Molly. 'We should build a tree house next to the orphanage, a big play area with swings, see-saws, a picnic area with benches and tables. Let's give the children lifelong memories like we have.'

Alan said, 'That would be fantastic. We could watch our kids do what we did.'

'Yeah, but who would be the Indian this time?' The three of them hugged together.

'Happy days,' Brad said. 'As soon as the houses are finished that will be our next project.' They walked out of the woods, never to return to that spot.

Mr Pullman had heard the orphanage had been finished. The wanted a grand opening, the publicity would be good for the railway. Ma and Pa had organised the certificate, declaring Mr Pullman as honorary president of Ma and Pa's Orphanage. It was a surprise.

The big day came, there was lots of reporters, book men, recorders present. A ribbon had been placed across the doorway ready to be cut. Mr Pullman had a little speech written, the whole ranch turned out, plus the children and church council.

Mr Pullman went up and gave his speech that this was the first of many, that the railways took care of the community. Ma and Pa stepped forward and were asked to cut the ribbon. 'I declare this building open.' They cut the ribbon together and an almighty cheer went up and clapping.

Once it calmed down, Pa said, 'I would like to present, sorry I mean my wife and I (big cheer) would like to present this certificate to Mr Pullman for all the help and development the he has given us. It says Mr Pullman, sorry, the honourable Mr Pullman, a lifetime president of Ma and Pa's Orphanage, and may there be many more. There cheers for Mr Pullman hip-pip-hooray, hip-pip-hooray, hip-pip-hooray.' Then they sang 'For he's a jolly good fellow, for he's a jolly good fellow, and so say all of us.' Cheering and clapping.

Mr Pullman said to Ma and Pa, 'Thank you. I'm really touched by this gesture. I've achieved many things in my lifetime and awards but this certificate tops them all. I will treasure it for the rest of my life, it will take pride of place on my deck. Oh by the way I have got some children lined up for you, as you know the railways always takes care of its own. There have been accidents in the workplace. It can be a dangerous jobs. Some have been tragic, a loss of lives leaving families devastated, sometimes children left with no parents or families. I would like to help them, I have a few lined up for tomorrow, would that be OK?'

Pa said, 'We are open for business. We're ready.'

After dinner Pa stood up. 'Can I have your attention please? As you may or may not know, we have children arriving tomorrow to live in the new orphanage (clap). We need to be organised, I have a few suggestions. Please tell me if you don't like the jobs I've allocated.'

'Food,' Steve shouted out. When he lot a laugh, 'Sorry Pa.'

'What with our regular folk, the workmen, the first kids and now the second kids, although they are coping well it could become a bit of a strain on Pauline, Bill and Ken. I know others have been helping out, but we're going to try and streamline. Divide the cooking, Pauline, Bill, Ken you will be in charge of all of the children's meals. You can move into the orphanage if you so wish, or stay where you are, it's up to you. Juan, Julie, Julia will run the restaurant from town for all other meals, including the restaurant, obviously helping out will be Alan, Ma, me, Ching-Ching, Virginia, Jimmy, Lucy and Jack, and Mr Matsuda. Molly has full responsibility for the orphanage. Any problems, suggestions, go to her first. Virginia and Jimmy are going to be in charge of the orphanage, looking after the children's welfare, organising games, play time et cetera. Helping them out is Helen, Ellis, James, Lucy, Jack and of course education Father and Daniel. Daniel teaching the younger children, Father the older children. Now I know some of you have other jobs that need seeing, to that's fine, complete your chores first, but any help you can give will be appreciated, and Ma and me are always available. Thank you for listening. This will be a team effort enjoy.' Pa got a standing ovation. 'Thank you,' he said.

Mid-morning the wagons arrived, drove straight to the orphanage, where a party was laid on for the children, the same format as before, but this time there were twenty-two children plus Too, and Free. It was mayhem, kids running upstairs jumping on the beds, running outside, Pa said to Ma, 'Just how I wanted it, children at play.'

'Well good luck trying to get them to sleep!'

The sand had arrived. All filtered no stones in. 'Only the best for our children,' said Mr Pullman.

It was a hot and sticky day, one of the workman, a Mexican boy, had taken his shirt off as it got so wet from the sweat. He was ripped with muscles. Julia said to Julie, 'Go offer him a cold drink.'

'No,' she said, 'you do it.'

'No I'm busy you do it.' Julia walked out with a tray with a pitcher of lemonade juice and some glasses, as she approached the man she couldn't help notice his body and bulging muscles. He was also very handsome. 'Would you like a cold drink?' asked Julie.

'Yes thank you very much, Julie.'

She slammed the drinks down and ran off, she went to Julia. 'He knows my name,' she said, 'he knows my name. You, you told him.'

'Yes he asked Ma for your name, I didn't think you'd mind him knowing.'

'You should have told me, I can't face him again. I'm too embarrassed.'

'Hola,' he said. He stood behind them, Julie thought how much did he hear?

'I bring the glasses back.'

'Thank you,' said Julie as red as a beetroot.

Julia said, 'What's your name, Gonzalez?'

He said, 'Gonzalez Fortune.'

The girls exploded with laughter, they laughed and laughed until they were crying laughing.

'What's so funny with my name?' he said.

'No, no, sorry,' Julie said composing herself. 'It's not your name, well in some ways it is. Let me explain, my brother is called Juan, his daughter is called Too, his adopted son is called Free and you are Mr For-Tune.' The girls exploded again. Even Gonzalez joined in.

'Does that mean I can take you on a date?'

Julia answered for her. 'Yes,' she said, 'she would love to go on a date with you.'

'That's for me to answer,' she said. 'Yes I would like that.'

'Good,' Gonzalez said, 'I will pick you up at four.'

The girls and Gonzalez exploded into laughter. 'You see,' said Julia, 'he has a sense of humour as well as a good body.'

He left.

'I wonder where he will take you.'

'I don't know,' said Julie.

'Wherever it is I want you home by five.'

The girls erupted again with laughter.

The sand was being put in, plus an extra sand pit for the kids to play in. All the wood and ropes were waiting to be erected, and the tree house, extra netting had been added, so if a child fell, the netting would break their fall. A little shed was on the side like a changing room, where the kids could put on their canvass shoes to play on the sand, then change their footwear so sand didn't go all over tile orphanage.

The two houses were nearly complete, just the final small details. Brad and Steve were standing outside the houses.

'Beautiful,' said Steve, 'absolutely beautiful. What are you going to call yours?'

'What do you mean?'

'You know, like Shangri-la, or Ponderosa.'

'Well,' said Brad, 'I was thinking of numbering them.'

'What do you mean? I was going to get George to make two numbers, one and two, to put on the front doors like delivery men, yes make number one on the mound.'

Silence. Steve said, 'So what house is number one and what is two?'

'There's one way we could decide it. Yeah, arm wrestling, like we did in the army for bottom or top bunk.'

'Yeah let's do it.'

They lay on the floor, took the hand grip. 'Take the strain, pull,' shouted Steve. Both men gave it their all, trying to flatten the other man's arm. There was no movement so with his other arm Brad slapped Steve around the face. He lost his concentration and Brad pinned his arm.

'The winner,' shouted Brad.

'No, no it was always best of three.'

So the man re-connected their grip. Take the strain, pull. Steve pulled Brad's hat over his eyes so he couldn't see and Steve flattened his arm. 'One one, equalised,' said Steve.

'This is no good, let's draw for it. I'll get two different stones one will be one and the other two. I'll put them behind my back, mix them up and you choose one.'

'OK,' said Steve, 'but if I win I want you to choose.'

'What do you mean?' said Brad.

'Well, I think you should be number one, because in my eyes you'll always be my number one.'

Brad said, 'Yeah and in my eyes you'll always be a number two.' They rolled around laughing. Brad said, 'Why didn't you say that at the beginning? We wouldn't have had to go through all that.'

'Well, you didn't ask,' said Steve.

After breakfast Steve stood up. 'First of all, me, Brad, Helen and Suzie would like to thank you for all the effort that has been put in to get the houses finished.'

Brad stood up and clapped everybody. Steve said, 'As like Ma and Pa's house you don't need an invite, pop in any time for a coffee or just a chat. We've decided to number them one and two, the first one being number one, this will be Brad and Suzie's home. Next door number two will be mine and Helen's house. But Ma said the girls can't move in till after the marriage.' That got a giggle.

'That's right,' said Ma. 'No hanky-panky.'

That got another giggle.

'Late today we will be nailing on the numbers. Thank you, George.' Another clap. 'So anybody who wants to have a good nosey around is welcome to, but please take your shoes off, otherwise I'm going to have to wash the floor.'

'Can you do mine as well?' shouted Brad.

'Our next project is to help finish the play area at the orphanage, a tree house needs to be fitted and soft nets to catch anybody falling or who may have been pushed. And now I would like to ask Julie how her date with Gonzalez Four-tune went, where he took her and will she be seeing him again.'

Her face was redder than a beetroot this time. She turned to Julia. 'I'm going to kill you.'

'Yes, yes, yes,' said Julie.

Sitting down, 'Well I hope you say no sometimes.' Big roar of laughter. 'Now Pauline, Bill and Ken would like to say something.'

The three stood together. 'Go on Bill, say something.'

'OK woman,' he said, 'I'm just getting composed. As you all know we've had many a good night, here, breakfast, lunch, dinners, celebrations, parties, so tonight we'd like to have one more big bash, everybody invited including all the kids, a big fire, a roast, music and dancing, as tomorrow we move to the orphanage. Have I missed anything, dear?'

'No, you've done very well. Now don't go on to much.'

'So my wife and son will see you all later, thank you.' Big cheering and clapping. 'Oh, when you hear the gong for the last time, thank you,' said Bill.

The usual busy day but everybody's mind was on tonight, there was lots of food to prepare, especially as so many children would be there.

They decided on sausages, hot potatoes, beans, cakes, buns, cookies, jelly, trifles. Ma had baked a special cake for Pauline, Bill and Ken, with thank you in icing on the top.

The fire was stacked up ready, the roast was on late in the afternoon when everything looked ready Pauline said to Bill, 'Go ring that gong as hard as you can for the very last time.'

Bill loved it clanging away. He was sure it could be heard in the next town.

Everybody started to arrive, the children were sat down in anticipation of the food, everybody was milling around saying hello to each other. Juan's family arrived, and Too and Free joined the kids. Julie had brought Gonzalez along to meet everybody. Mt Matsuda and Ching-Ching had been strictly told no fireworks as it might scare the babies and children. Everybody was eating, chatting, Jimmy started the music up, people were dancing as the kids ran in and out of them. It was getting late, time to round the children up and get them off to bed, time for the babies to be laid down for the night, so the party started to dwindled away. Pauline, Bill and Ken loved the cake.

Bill said, 'Shall we do the cleaning up tomorrow?'

Pauline said, 'No the party's never over till the cleaning's done. Besides we won't have time in the morning what with breakfast. Then we've got to move into the orphanage, and the children will want feeding.'

'OK, OK,' Bill said, 'You're right. Let's get stuck in and leave it all nice and clean for the last time.'

Pauline said, 'I'll wash, Bill and Ken, wipe and put away, then we'll have a nice slice of Ma's cake, and give the rest to the children tomorrow.'

'Sounds good to us,' said Bill and Ken. They all worked fast and efficiently, like they'd always done in the past. They lit the candles on the cake, took a slice each and went outside to eat it, and cool down.

They sat outside reminiscing about all the good times they'd had here.

'Well, love,' he said, 'we're not getting any younger. Time to step back and let the young'uns have a go. I'm sure they'll be times when we strike the fire again. I miss sitting outside with Chief and the gang, and I'm sure the kids are going to keep us busy.'

'Yes,' said Pauline, 'a new challenge, do you know how lucky we are finding this peace? Ken becoming our son, we love you, son.'

'I love you too, Ma and Pa.'

Bill said, 'Can you smell something burning?'

Pauline and Ken sniffed the air. 'Yes,' they both said, 'I think something's on fire.'

As they turned around they saw the curtains on fire in the kitchen. Bill said to Ken, 'Go get some water buckets.'

The flames caught hold very quickly, and started to spread around the kitchen. 'It must have been the candles on the cake,' said Pauline. Ken arrived with two buckets of water. Bill chucked them into the kitchen. 'Get more, Pauline, help him.' As they went to get more buckets of water Bill went into the building, coughing from all the smoke he tripped on something on the floor, fell forward and banged his head on the wall, knocking him out. When Pauline and Ken got back with more buckets of water they couldn't see Bill. Pauline screamed, 'He's inside.'

Ken chucked the four buckets of water inside, then went in to get Bill. The water had put the fire out, but there was still a lot of smoke, Ken covered his mouth but his eyes were streaming. He saw Bill lying on the floor not moving, Ken picked him up and got him outside and laid him on the floor. 'Go get Helen,' Pauline shouted. Ken rushed off. Pauline picked Bill's head up. 'You silly, silly man, why did you go in there?'

Bill showed Pauline in his hand the shield Ken had won. He murmured, 'It meant so much to him and so much to us.'

'You silly, loveable old man, we could have replaced the shield, but I can't replace you.'

Pauline felt his body go limp. She screamed, 'Lord, not my Bill, not my beloved Bill.'

Helen and Steve arrived, 'Help me get him to the clinic.'

Steve and Ken carried him to the clinic, Helen put her arm around Pauline and followed.

Once inside Helen said to Steve, 'Please go and get Doc.' She needed to get Ken to do something as he was getting hysterical. 'Ken go and get Brad.' That would give her some time, from the moment Helen had seen Bill she knew he had passed away. Pauline just sat there crying. She knew in her heart of hearts her beloved Bill had gone, Helen checked all his vitals: breathing, circulation, pulse, it was without doubt Bill had passed.

'I think he has gone,' Helen said to Pauline.

She let out a scream that could have woken the dead. Helen went to hold her but Pauline ran out of the clinic, Helen turned back towards Bill, mystified to see the rowing shield in his hand on top of his body. She got a sheet out and covered his head and body. Just then Brad and Ken arrived. 'He's gone,' Helen said.

Ken chucked himself to the floor, kicking his fest and pounding his fists. 'No, no, no, no, no,' he kept saying over and over again.

'Brad,' Helen said, 'we need to find Pauline. She's just run off.'

'Come on, big guy,' Brad said, helping Ken off the floor. 'We need to go find your ma, right now she needs us. Are you up for that?'

'Yes,' said Ken. Through his blackened face from the fire, tears had made clear lines down his face where they had run. With a hand around his shoulder Brad and Ken walked out.

Where would Pauline go? thought Brad. Then it came to him, she would go where he always sat with Chief around the fire. Sure enough she was there sat with her head in her hands crying. When she saw Ken she got up and hugged him. 'Thank God you're safe, I couldn't have lost you as well.'

The two of them just hugged each other and cried. 'I'm sorry, Ma,' he said.

'It's not your fault. You were ever so brave going in and rescuing Pa like you did.'

Brad decided to walk away to leave them together just hugging and grieving. He went back to Helen, he said to her, 'Are you OK?'

Then she burst into tears, Brad hugged her and said, 'This is a sad, sad day.'

Steve and the doctor arrived, the doctor pulled the sheet down and did all the checks Helen had previously done.

'It is with great sadness,' said the doc, 'that this man is deceased.' He could tell he had been in a fire, from his clothing and smell of the fire on him. 'Probably caused by smoke installation. It's not always the fine that kills but the smoke. I will do the death certificate you will need. I'm sorry for your sad loss.'

He scribbled and left the piece of paper and left, Steve hugged Helen. Brad said, 'I'm going to get Father, maybe he could say a few words and go and speak to Pauline and Ken.'

'Where are they?' said Steve.

'Up by Chief's fire.'

'They must be devastated,' said Steve, 'and just think tomorrow they would have been living in a different place, what a tragic thing to happen on their last night at the canteen.'

'So sad,' said Helen, 'so sad. We will really miss Bill, with all his banter, hard work and the banging of the gong. He loved to do that.'

Brad fetched Father, who said a few words over Bill's body and made the sign of the cross over his body. Now he said, 'Let's go and find Pauline and Ken.' As they approached Pauline and Ken they were still hugging and crying off and on.

Father approached. 'I'm so sorry to hear of your said news. Bill was a fine upstanding man with principles and a good work attitude. He will be surely missed. Would you pray with me?' Father said. After talking for some time Father said, 'There are some things that need to be sorted out tonight. I'm sorry to push you, but decisions have to be made. Bill's body,' Father said, 'would you like him to be moved to the church, and maybe placed in a coffin for his burial tomorrow?'

Pauline, fighting back the tears, said, 'Father would it be alright if I went down to the clinic and washed Bill's body and changed his clothes? He wouldn't want to go to church looking like he does.'

'That would be fine, if you let me know when you're finished we'll get Bill placed in a coffin, and have a last procession from the clinic to the church so people can pay their last respects.'

'Oh Father,' Pauline said, 'tomorrow we would have been moving to the orphanage, now we're having Bill's funeral.'

That morning nobody went to breakfast. Instead they formed a line both sides of the road from the clinic to the church. All the children and workman turned out, everybody knew and loved Bill. With their heads bowed and their hands crossed in front of them and total silence, Bill's coffin was carried out by Brad and Steve, and placed on the open topped wagon which had been covered in a silk material. Kellee and Cliff had chosen two black horses to pull the wagon, and had attached a massive white feather to each of their heads. Brad and Steve rejoined the line next to Suzie and Helen. Father and Pauline stood behind the wagon and Pa was to drive the wagon down, but there was no sign of Ken. Just then the gong sounded, twelve slow gongs. Ken wanted to do this for the last time for his Pa. This started the tears rolling for everybody, then Ken joined Pauline with his arm around her. The wagon pulled out with Father in front and Pauline and Ken together behind the wagon. Slowly the wagon started to pass by the people. Stems of flowers were thrown onto the wagon and coffin, an applause started, and gained momentum till everybody was clapping loudly for the appreciation of Bill. He was clapped all the way to the church, Pauline turned to Ken. Bill would really have appreciated that Ken said he was loved by so many, as Father walked behind he'd dreaded this day coming. He knew it would and he also knew it wouldn't be the last. He'd now had a wedding, christening, a blessing for Baby Virginia and now a funeral in the new church. How dignified, a community pulling together in times of need. Brad and Steve had scuttled down the outside to be there to unload the coffin, which was placed on a table inside the church, those that could get in the church did, those that couldn't waited outside the church.

Father said, 'Let us pray,' and they all sang.

Now they were gathered at the river, the coffin was taken outside and lowered into the grave that George had dug. As the coffin was lowered people chucked handfuls of soil on top of the coffin and Pauline laid a red rose on the coffin saying, 'I love you, Bill, and will miss you, thank you for loving me.'

'Wait for me.' Ken stepped forward also placing a red rose on the coffin. 'I love you, Pa,' he said then he placed the shield onto the coffin and said, 'Look after this for me, Pa.'

Everybody was shattered emotionally and physically, George gently filled the grave in, Andy stepped forward with the big cross he had made and gently tapped it into the ground. It read 'Beloved husband Bill, much loved and missed. Wife Pauline and son Ken.' The people slowly drifted away. Father said a prayer over the grave, and told Pauline and Ken, 'Ma and Pa have invited you up to the house when you are ready.'

Pauline said, 'Thank you, Father. It was a wonderful service. Everybody has said such kind words. Would you thank them for us. Me and my son are going to stand here I while and say our final good-eyes to Bill.'

'Yes by all means take your time. There's no rush and with your permission Daniel has drawn a wonderful picture of Bill smiling at us all, just as we are all going to remember him smiling. He's placed it in the church alongside Baby Virginia and Chief. Please look at it on your way out. It's heart warming.' And there we have it, thought Father, the funeral was over. In the graveyard at the back of the church stood Baby Virginia's little cross and alongside the cross of Bill.

As they walked through the church they stopped at Daniel's picture. 'Daniel's captured him so well with his big smiling face,' she said, and she kissed two fingers and put it to his lips on the picture.

Ken said, 'And Ma, we can come visit him every day.'

'We will, son,' she said. We will visit him every day. I don't really want to go to the house I'm so tired I just want to rest but we've got so many people to thank. Then we're going to move into the orphanage. Those kids need us and Bill wouldn't want us to let anybody down, so let's go face everybody.' She turned to the picture. 'We will be back tomorrow, darling, and every day after. See you tomorrow.'

Ken said, 'And look after our shield.' They walked away arm in arm.

The very next day Pauline and Ken moved into the orphanage. Pauline became the matron of the home, always there for any of the children's needs. She liked to be kept busy as it took her mind off things. Ken was called Uncle Ken by the children. He always organised games, dressed as a clown and was there play mate. They never missed a day without visiting the church, stopping at the picture and talking to him about the day's event. Then always placing a flower on Bill's and Baby Virginia's crosses, Ken everyday said, 'Are you still looking after Pa?'

Over the next few day's Ma and Pa had noticed a lot more travelling wagons were passing through the area. Some were stopping to top up their supplies. Ma asked one wagon where they were all going.

'Have you not heard? There's been a gold strike north of here. We're going to make our fortune.' Some children looked worn out, hungry, thirsty. Ma said to Brad and Steve, 'Bring me some tables and stalls down with a supply of water, juice, bread, buns, cakes, vegetables, lettuce et cetera, any leftovers, old clothes from the orphanage, leftovers from the restaurant, blankets, pillows, get people to help you, and bring everything back as soon as possible.'

Bits started to arrive, the stools and tables, Father and Daniel turned up to help so did Kellee and Cliff. They brought food for the horses and dragged a water trough over and filled it, George brought horse shoes down in case they were needed. Cliff brought wheel spindles in case any were broken and needed replacing. A message was sent to the house, bring all available apple pies, get a new batch in the oven, get cooking more loaves, bring flour down, vegetables and fruit.

It looked amazing all set out, Ma beckoned the first few wagons along to come over. They pulled over, got out and wandered over. 'I'm sorry, mam,' one man said, 'but we've got a very low budget to live off.'

'Help yourselves, take only what you need, leave some for others that are following you. There is no charge,' said Ma.

People had been travelling days, weeks to get to their new destination, not knowing what they would find when they get there. Housing, jobs, water, diseases, they were risking everything, even their lives in the hope of striking it rich. People could not believe the hospitality shown to them at the ranch. 'Make sure,' said Ma, 'every child gets at least a bun a cooked a sandwich, clothes, blankets for the chilly nights.'

Some people wanted to pay for their goods. Those that were insistent Ma said, 'Make a donation to our orphanage.' She said, 'If you strike it lucky you can always come back another day and pay us. I can't let these people supper so much, especially the children.'

One chap arrived with his wife and five children, and told the story of a boy he found. 'His parents had died of hunger, he was all alone starving, many wagons just passed him by, my wife insisted we stopped, bury his parents and tar him with us, the problem is I have enough problems feeding my own family without an additional mouth to feed.'

Ma quick as a flash said, 'We have an orphanage here and would be only too happy to take him in and give him a food and happy home.' The man thought about it, I'll have to ask the wife, he came back with the boy. He said his name was Peter, the boy had brownish hair, cute little dimples and smile but was as dirty as coal, with tattered clothes hanging off, his little under-fed body. 'Would you buy him off us? You know, to pay for our food he has already eaten.'

'We don't have money to give you but we will trade for him, extra food, clothing, horse, reeds whatever you need.' The man took as much as they could carry.

'Hello Peter,' said Ma, 'would you like a nice piece of apple pie, and some candy and jelly and a nice warm bed to sleep in?'

'Yes please,' said Peter, 'can I go to the toilet please?'

Ma thought he's so cute and went off with him to the house.

Over the next couple of weeks the flow of wagons was quite steady. Ma and Pa were out there every day, helping whoever they could. One day in particular was very strange. A man turned up who said that they had helped him on his way through there the first time round. Ma and Pa couldn't remember him, as so many had passed through.

He said, 'You gave me food and water, fed my horse and watered him. I'm sure I could not have made it without your help, you helped me on my way with no charge. Your name is legendary at the camp-site, everybody talks about how kind you are and the handouts, clothes et cetera and your apple pies are talk of the town. You should go commercial with them you'd make a fortune. Well thanks to your help I've struck it lucky. I hit a rich vein of gold. Now I'm not a greedy man. I only took what I need, enough for me to have a comfortable life. I passed it onto this chap who had four children, he said you took in a little boy named Peter. He gave me a nugget of pure gold to give to you to donate to the orphanage for his upkeeping. He said one good turn deserves another.'

He handed over the nugget, Ma said, 'We didn't do this for reward or payment.'

'I know, I know,' said the man, 'but I'm not sure you know how grateful, how many people owe you so much and appreciate what you have done for them out of the kindness of your hearts. And here is the second nugget from me, because you told me at the time, that if I couldn't pay for the goods at the time if I were to strike it lucky to come back and pay you. Well you passed your good luck onto me, so now I'm paying my debt.'

Ma said, 'You don't have a debt now.'

'Now Mrs,' he interrupted, 'I want to pay to help others like you helped me and many others. The conditions up there are appalling so with your permission here's a third nugget. Not so many wagons are coming up now. The last strangers, could you fill these wagons with supplies to send up there, telling them this is from a lucky old timer.'

'Yes,' Ma said, 'but we don't need your gold.'

The man said, 'A deal's a deal, and I'll not take it back,' and left.

Ma and Pa were speechless. 'Right,' Ma said, 'get everything we've got to give and start filling the wagons,' telling them that they must share it out and not to sell it on.

Just before the last wagons rolled through these was an incident, where a few families were fighting over a stolen loaf. Luckily Brad, Steve Cliff and Kellee run over and stopped the fighting. Ma caught up. 'What are you fighting over? A loaf of bread, when if you walk over these they are free of charge.'

This made the man feel stupid, they shook hands and apologised to Ma. When they walked back Ma said to Pa, 'This world is changing, people are starting only to look out for themselves, and not caring and sharing with others. I'm afraid, Pa, we might be the last generation that help people.'

'Ma, I think you're right, I'm glad we won't be around to see all that happen.'

'You aren't going anywhere without me, Pa. Love you.'

'Love you too. Just stand a minute and look at this place. We have these wonderful children, a daughter-in-law, two granddaughters and a grandson, we have a new daughter-in-law joining the family soon, and a son-in law joining to, and on top of that we have Ching-Ching. Pa do you realise how lucky we have been? When I saw those families with so little, desperate, homeless, my heart went out to them.'

'You're a good woman,' said Pa, 'and I'm very proud of you, and love you dearly.'

'And what are we going to do with these three nuggets of pure gold?'

'I have an idea,' said Pa, 'we'll give a nugget each to our children. I'm hoping they will make gold rings for themselves, their partners, wives and husbands to be, anything over stick in a bank for a rainy day.'

'Brilliant idea,' said Ma, 'you're not just handsome, but clever too Pa.'

'I don't know about handsome, but I am clever. I was clever enough to have you as my life partner and marry you. I'm the lucky one, I got you to love a whole lifetime.'

'Love you.'

'Love you more.'

# Chapter 7

## Something's in the Water

## (Baby Boom)

Gonzalez never left when the other workmen left. He was staying with Juan's family. It was a bit cramped with four adults and two children, so they went and saw Brad and Steve. They asked what with the loss of Bill, could Gonzalez help out in the cooking area plus the restaurant. Brad said he'd be a great asset what with all his maintenance skills as well. 'Great to have you on board, welcome to the club. You know our motto, the more the merrier.'

Julie also asked was it possible for them to have a shack, as they wanted to set up home together. Brad said, 'Why don't you move in to Juan's shack that he left?'

'That would be wonderful,' said Julie and thanked them.

Steve said, 'Ma might not be too happy. She's already stopped Brad and me living with our partners that we are engaged to and are going to marry.'

'That's no problem,' said Gonzalez he dropped to one knee. 'Julie,' he said, 'I adore you, you've made my life so complete, will you do me the honour of marrying me and becoming my wife?'

Julie dived on him, knocking him to the floor, smothering him with kisses. Steve said,' I think that's a yes!'

'Yes yes,' Julie kept saying, 'Yes I love you too, let's get married as soon as possible so you don't get time to change your mind.'

'I'll never change my mind, I love you.'

'Come on,' she said dragging him up. 'Let's go tell Juan, Julia, Too and Free.' They ran off shouting, 'Thank you.'

'I don't know about you, Brad, but I think there's something in the water around here, so many people in love and getting married.'

'Happy days,' said Brad, 'happy days.'

Steve said, 'You do realise she's going to make a fortune.' Both men laughed.

'You do realise they now have Juan, Too, Free and two fortunes.' They laughed again.

Steve said, 'I can't wait to move into the new house.'

'I'm the same,' said Brad. 'I've been meaning to talk to you, we might have to bring the wedding forward.'

'But buddy, I thought we were going to have a double wedding, I was looking forward to that.'

'So was I buddy, but we think Suzie is pregnant.'

'Pregnant!' shouted Steve.

'Shhh! Keep your voice down, I haven't told Ma and Pa yet.'

'She's going to kill you, she warned you no hanky-panky until after you're married, you're in big trouble, buddy.'

'I know, I know. Suzie's going to see Helen today. I'll wait for conformation until I tell Ma, Pa.'

'Congratulations, buddy, never knew you had it in you.'

'Thanks, buddy, but don't tell anybody until we know for sure.'

'Yes,' said Steve, 'I'm going to be an uncle. That's right ain't it, Brad.'

'Yes you'll always be, all off my children's uncle.'

'And you mine,' said Steve, 'how many are you going to have?'

'At least three like Ma and Pa had.'

'I was thinking more like five,' Steve said.

'Does Helen know this?'

'Not yet but I'm working on it.'

Steve couldn't wait to tell Helen, even though he'd promised. But he knew Helen would find out before anyone else anyway, he rushed into the clinic. Helen was alone. 'You'll never guess, you'll never guess,' Steve shouted.

'Calm down,' she said.

'Brad just told me, they think Suzie pregnant, but I'm not allowed to tell anyone, and Suzie's coming to see you today.'

'Well,' said Helen, 'that's not the only secret, someone else on the ranch is definitely pregnant.'

'Who?' Steve butted in.

'Guess,' said Helen.

'Molly, Virginia, Keller, Julia, Julie, not Maria again, Dianna, not Lucy or Ellis, it can't be Ma, who?' said Steve, sitting back on the chair looking puzzled. Helen gently rubbed her stomach around in circles. 'You,' Steve said. 'You.'

He got up dancing around and around. 'I'm going to be a dad, I'm going to be a dad,' and flumped back down on the chair.

'Are you pleased?' said Helen.

'Am I pleased? I'm over the moon, congratulations, I mean well done I'm going to be a dad,' then he burst out crying.

Helen put her arm around him. 'Calm down,' she said. 'There's a while to come yet. Now this time keep the promise, don't tell anybody. I need to talk to James and Ellis first.'

'I won't but can I tell Brad?'

'Yes but tell him not to tell anybody else. OK?'

Steve flew up to Brad, 'She's pregnant,' he said, 'I'm going to be a father. Helen, she's pregnant.' Then he dropped to the floor.

'Breathe, buddy,' Brad said.

'She's pregnant, Brad.'

'I know,' said Brad, 'calm down, you've already told me there times.'

'She's pregnant. That means we'll have to being our wedding forward. If Suzie's pregnant we can still have our double wedding as planned.'

'I need to wait first to find out what the situation is with Suzie. You haven't told anybody have you?'

'No,' said Steve, 'only Helen.'

'And you haven't told anybody have you?' asked Steve.

'I've only just found out how could I have told anybody yet?'

'Oh yeah,' said Steve, 'but you can't tell anybody yet because she wants to tell Ellis and James first.'

'I won't.'

'You promise.'

'Yeah just like you promised, Helen was going to find out anyway. I'll have to tell Suzie.'

'Yeah but get her to promise not to tell anyone yet.'

'All these promises,' Brad said, 'at least you'll take some of the heat of me with Ma. Ma's going to kill you, no more apple pie for you.'

'No,' said Steve, 'I'll tell her it was the apple pies' fault.'

'What?' said Brad.

'I'll tell her I've had so much apple pie that it made me fruity.' They fell about laughing.

'Congrats buddy. I want to go and see Helen.'

'Me top,' said Steve, 'I've just left her all alone and ran out to tell you.'

They both went to the clinic. Brad congratulated Helen, Steve said, 'Now sit down and rest.'

'I'm pregnant,' she said, 'not an invalid.'

'I want to marry you as soon as possible,' said Steve, 'and if Suzie is pregnant, we can still have our double wedding as planned and move into the house a lot sooner, and our baby can be born in the new house.'

Both Helen and Brad said, 'You're the one that needs to lie down, you're hyperventilating, calm down, rest.'

'I can't,' said Steve. 'I've got so much to do, Brad, would you mind getting Ellis and James for me and asking them to come over here. I'd like them to know first, and not hear it from somebody else, as bigmouth here can't keep a secret.'

'Tell me about it,' said Brad.

'I want the world to know,' said Steve.

'If he's like this now, what's he going to be like when the baby comes?'

Lucy, Helen and James came in with smiles on their faces. It wasn't too hard to work out what was going on, with Steve's white face and gasping for air.

'Ellis, James I'm pregnant. Me and Steve are going to have a baby.'

'I thought so,' said Ellis. 'There's a glow about you.' Both hugged Mum and Steve. 'We wanted you both to know first,' said Steve, 'but blubber mouth here has already told Brad.'

'Sorry,' said Steve, 'I just couldn't keep it in, when he told me they think Suzie is pregnant, I had to tell him Helen was pregnant.'

'Suzie's pregnant?' said Ellis.

'You've done it again,' said Helen. 'You promised Brad you wouldn't say anything.'

'Ah! Shoot me,' said Steve, 'my hormones are all over the place,' which made everyone laugh.

'Now we don't know about Suzie yet she's coming in today so mum's the word at the moment, and just because everyone's pregnant, doesn't mean that you,\ pointing at Ellis and Lucy pointing at James, 'need to get pregnant. Get married first,' Steve said.

'Oh like you and Mum did,' said James.

'You know what I mean,' said Steve, 'and that leads me to the next topic. Your mum and I are going to get married asap.'

Helen said, 'Will you be my bridesmaid, Ellis, and James will you give me away?'

'Of course, Mum,' they both said and hugged her.

'I can't wait to deliver your baby,' said Ellis.

'That sounds a bit weird, my daughter delivering her mum's baby. Just as weird as your mum delivering her daughter's baby. But not yet,' said Steve.

'Let's get one out of the way first, Steve. I'd love you to deliver my baby,' said Helen, 'and wouldn't want anybody else delivering my baby,' said Ellis.

'But not yet,' said Steve.

'Now everybody hooo! Suzie might be here any minute, and remember mum's the word including you, Steve.'

They left, Helen sat down rubbed her belly and thought wow I'm going to be a mum again, I'll be marrying the man I love, and moving into a beautiful new home, with my best friends living next door, and all because I got stuck in some mud. Funny how things happen in life it's all meant to be, like every things mapped out for you in life.

Suzie arrived later in the day. Slightly embarrassed she went into the clinic.

'Hello Suzie,' said Helen, 'do you have a cold?'

'No,' said Suzie, 'I just wanted to come and talk to you.'

'Do you have a swelling in your stomach?'

'You know,' she said.

'Yeah, Brad told Steve, Steve told me. It's supposed to be a secret. You know men they can't keep a secret, now a simple test and we'll know for sure. You can tell you are because you're glowing just like me.'

'You're not,' said Suzie.

'I am,' said Helen, 'We're both going to have babies, get married and live next door to each other, and have coffee mornings and watch our children grow up and play together, stop take a breath, get married.'

'Brad hasn't asked me yet.'

'He will now you're pregnant.'

The girls hugged and whooped around. Brad and Steve came to the clinic went in, all you could hear was whopping and congrats all around.

'Let's go and see Father and get things organised for next week a double wedding.'

'Wait a minute,' said Suzie. 'Brad hasn't asked me, and don't think you're getting away with it, Steve,' said Helen, 'down on your knees the both of you and ask us properly.'

'You go first,' said Steve, 'I might get some tips.'

'Suzie,' Brad said, 'from the moment I met you I fell in love with you. You're now having my baby. I love you. Will you marry me.'

'Yes,' said Suzie, 'from the moment I met you I knew you were the one. I love you, I want to marry you and have our baby.' They hugged and kissed.

Tears were rolling down Steve's face. 'That was beautiful,' he said, 'so moving. What he said, but change Suzie to Helen. Will you marry me, Helen?'

'No,' she said, 'ask me properly like Brad did.'

'I'm sorry Helen, shoot me, my hormones are all over the place.' That made them all laugh. Steve cleared his throat ahum, he said, 'Serious face, from the moment I saw you in the muddy water, you had kids, you just lost your husband, then you didn't know if he was still alive, and now you're pregnant with my baby. I'm making a right mess of this.'

'Calm down,' said Helen, 'and start again.'

'I love you, Helen, with all my heart. Will you please marry me?'

'Yes,' said Helen. 'That wasn't so hard was it?'

'I'm never doing that again,' said Steve.

'I hope not,' said Helen.

**Steve said**

'Let's go down and see Father and arrange a date for the marriages.'

'Yeah we can tell Ma we're getting married, then we can tell her you're pregnant after the marriage.'

'Ma is not that stupid,' said Brad, 'honesty is the best policy.'

'It's alright for you, you're her son.'

'So are you!'

They eventually found Father. 'Father, Father, great news,' Steve said, 'we would like to being our double marriage forward.'

'Oh and why is this?' said Father.

'Umm,' Steve stuttered, 'we'd like to move into the house sooner, but Ma won't let us until we're married.'

'Good on her,' Father said, 'principles, protocol, the right away to do things. Would you also like to book the christenings in advance?' That made them all giggle. 'Us old people are not as stupid as you youngsters think we are.'

Brad pulled Steve backwards as he was making a right pig's ear out of this. 'Father, we love our ladies very much, and we would like God's blessing on our marriage.'

'Well spoken, Brad, but I repeat, would you also like to book the christening?'

'He knows,' Steve said. 'Yes Father, both Helen and Suzie are pregnant and we all want to get married as soon as possible, before Ma finds out.'

'Yeah something like that now let me see,' said Father, 'I'm very busy next week, I already have two weddings to do.' He looked at the four of them in silence.

'Do we know them?' said Steve.

'Yes, yes you know them.'

'Who?' said Brad.

'Well I don't think it's a secret, but then it's not my place to say.'

'Go on, Father, then we can congratulate them, better still we'll all get married on the same day and save time,' said Steve.

'Well I'll think I'll wait,' said Father. 'Helen I suggest you get back to the clinic, I've a feeling two more ladies will be visiting you today.'

'Who?' said Helen. 'Urr I mean I need to write their names in the book.'

'You'll have to get up a lot more earlier to catch me out like that,' said Father.

Helen said, 'I need to get back to the clinic.'

I'm coming too even if I have to wait outside, I want to see who turns up.' The four of them headed for the clinic.

First to turn up was Virginia and Jimmy. 'Hi guys,' said Brad, Suzie and Steve, which made Virginia and Jimmy jump. 'Helen's inside if you want to go in.'

Virginia started to go in Jimmy hung back, not going in.

'Women's things, you know,' said Jimmy.

'We've had some good news today,' said Brad. 'Both Helen and Suzie are pregnant.'

'Oh that's great,' said Jimmy, but not really listening as he was waiting for his own good news.

'Yes,' said Steve, 'we were hoping to get married next week but Father's already got bookings.'

'Ah guys,' Jimmy said, 'you already know we're just waiting for confirmation if Virginia is pregnant. But we want to get married any case.'

Just then Virginia screamed out. 'Yes, yes, yes congrats,' said Brad, before they knew it Virginia come out and ran straight into Jimmy's arms.

'I'm pregnant,' she said, 'and I don't care who knows it.'

They all gathered in a group Helen joined them. Virginia said, 'We're getting married next week and you're all invited.'

'Funny you should say that,' said Brad, 'but I think we should have a massive wedding all together, what do you say?'

'Brilliant,' said Virginia and Jimmy. But wait a few moments there's another surprise on the way.

It wasn't long before Kellee and Cliff walked up, surprised to see so many outside the clinic Kellee said, 'Let's come back later.'

Cliff said, 'We've come so far I'm dying to know, I'll make up some excuse.'

'OK,' Kellee said, 'I also want to know.'

'Howdy folks,' Cliff said, 'is Helen in?'

'Yeah, she's expecting you.' The group laughed.

'What you all doing out here?'

'We're having a mother's meeting,' said Virginia. 'More grocers not going in, Cliff,' said Steve.

'Ah no women's things,' he said. Before long they heard Kellee, 'Yeeha, yeeha.'

Cliff roared, 'Yeeha,' and the rest of the group roared 'yeeha.'

Kellee came flying out jumped on Cliff with her legs around his waist. 'I'm pregnant,' she said, 'and we're getting married.'

'I know,' said the whole group, 'and so are we.'

Kellee and Cliff were up for a massive wedding and joint celebration. 'Right let's all go and tell Ma and Pa at the house.' The whole group walked up there holding each other's hands. As they got near the house Steve said, 'You go first, Brad, I'll be behind you to catch you if she knocks you out.'

'Funny,' said Brad. 'Everybody come. In this is going to be a big surprise,' said Brad, as they entered Ma came running out.

'Come in, come in everybody we've got great news, Alan take it away.'

'Dianna and I are going to have another baby, she thinks she's pregnant again, and will go and see Helen tomorrow. Oh Helen's here, will that be OK with you?'

Everybody congratulated the couple. 'I'm going to be a grandma again,'

Ma said, 'plus Janet and Anne that's four grandchildren.'

'Well actually, Ma you'd better make it five,' said Brad. 'Suzie's pregnant but we're getting married next week.'

'You better had,' said Ma.

**Molly said**

'Actually, Ma you might have to make it six, I think I'm pregnant and was going to see Helen tomorrow. Sorry Ma,' said Andy, 'but we also want to get married next week. Pa get Ma a drink I need one. Apple juice, Ma, have we got anything stronger? And that's why Virginia and Jimmy, Kellee and Cliff are here. They are getting married next week as well because Virginia and Kellee are pregnant.'

'Oh,' said Ma, 'I can't take any more, drink quick drink.'

Once she'd got over the shock, Ma and Pa went around every couple congratulating them, and wishing them the very best for the future, their forthcoming marriages and the births of their children.

'Right,' said Ma, 'we'll hold a massive reception celebration here in the house and outside in the garden.'

Pa said to Ma, 'I told you there was something special here in the water.'

'Yeah it's filled with love,' said Ma. That got a clap.

Steve couldn't resist his joke again, 'Ma I think it's in your apple pies as well. They'd all heard it before, so said together, 'Because it makes us fruity.' Big laugh.

'So Helen was seeing Molly and Dianna tomorrow. If all the ladies are roughly pregnant at the same time, and I am myself there's no way Ellis could cope with everyone at the same time, the doctor will have to move in here for a week or so. I'd better organise two agency nurses to cover.'

Helen was busy in the morning in the clinic getting everything spotlessly clean waiting for Molly and Dianna to arrive. There was a knock on the door.

'Come in,' she said. She turned it was Maria. 'I think that George has gone got me pregnant again,' making out it was all his fault.

'Well you know the procedure,' said Helen, 'let's do it. Yes, Maria your definitely pregnant.'

'Oh Lord,' she said, 'a little girl this time would be nice. There's too many boys in the home now. I'd like a little girl.'

'So long as it's healthy,' said Helen, 'and the wedding's next week and the invites, at this rate we'll be able to open up our own nursery.' Both laughed.

Maria left. Not long after Dianna and Molly arrived. 'Yes, I can confirm ladies you are both pregnant.' More whoops of joy.

'Is it going to hurt?' asked Molly.

Both women had already had children. Helen said, 'Well imagine passing a melon.'

Dianna said, Getting your top lip and pulling it our your head.' The two laughed. 'We're joking. It's the best experience in the world and at the end of it you get a little baby worth all the pain in the world. It's when they're born the pain starts.' Laughing again.

'When do we know what sex it is?' asked Molly.

'When God decides,' said Helen, 'I have a book here. You can read. It might answer some of your questions.'

'Thank you,' said Molly, 'don't forget we're all meeting at the house tonight to discuss the wedding plans.'

'I'll be there.'

'This has got to be some sort of a record. So many,' said Helen, 'pregnant women getting married on the same day.'

It wasn't long after Dianna and Molly left, there was another knock at the door, surely not, thought Helen. This better not be Ellis or Lucy. Doesn't anyone round here just cut their finger? Giggling away outside were Julie and Julia. 'Can we come in?' said Julia, 'I thing I might be pregnant.'

Helen now was taking all this in her stride. 'Yes I can confirm Julia you're pregnant.'

The girls giggled together. 'Julie would you like a test?'

'No, I can't be,' said Julie.

Helen said, 'Have you been having sex with gorgeous Gonzalez?'

'Maybe,' said Julie, the girls laughed again. 'It doesn't take long, OK,' said Julie.

'Let's see, Julie you're pregnant.'

The girls collapsed with laughter. 'We can have our babies together?' said Julie, 'and they can be friends and family just like we are.'

Helen said, 'You're not the only ladies pregnant on site.' She went through the names, Molly, Dianna, Suzie, Kellee, Virginia, Maria and myself and now Julie and Julia. 'Wow,' said Julie, 'everyone's been very busy.'

Julia said, 'Who's going to wash all the diapers?' They collapsed in laughter again.

Helen explained about the meeting tonight at the house. 'Bring, Juan, Too, Free, Mr Fortune and yourselves tonight, as next week there's going to be a massive wedding day, followed by a reception at the house.'

Julia said, 'I'm sure Juan would want to be part of that.'

'I do,' Julie said, 'Gonzalez doesn't even know I'm pregnant yet let alone wanting me to marry him. He might run away.'

'Don't worry, Juan would track him down and bring him back. I can only ask we will see you tonight.' The girls walked away arm in arm still giggling.

At the house the place was buzzing. Wedding and baby talk was in the air.

'Right,' said Ma standing up, 'let's get this meeting started. We've got a lot to talk about. I think Father should start.'

He stood up. 'Let us pray for good healthy children, love and long strong relationships and the best multiple wedding ever, amen.'

'Amen,' they all said.

'Now let's see,' producing his list, 'I make it seven wedding. That is if Gonzalez and Julie are on board.'

'Easy,' Gonzalez, 'I mean yes.'

'Good,' said Father, 'now a mass wedding like this takes some organising otherwise it will be chaos. I suggest that all brides get ready in the main house along with all bridesmaids, the men will get ready in the school and if any page boys they will be with the men. We will need to hire some buggies. Each bride will be free led down to the church by the person giving a bride away, example Pa and Molly, et cetera. The congregation and choir will be in the church, the first bridegroom will be in the church waiting for his bride, I will say the vows laid down by the good Lord. If you wish to say something to each other you may but please keep it short as others will be waiting. I will announce you man and wife after you have said I dos to each other. That couple will leave through the back door to the garden behind the church, then the second couple will come in and repeat the procedure till every couple are married. I will then give you all a blessing and you may kiss the brides.' A big cheer went up.

'I suggest this order, subject to change:

| Couple: | Giving away: |
|---|---|
| Brad and Suzie first | Ma |
| (as none of us would be here without Brad) | |
| Molly and Andy | Pa |
| Helen and Steve | Ellis and James |
| Virginia and Jimmy | Mr Matsuda, Ching-Ching |
| Kellee and Cliff | Ken and Daniel |
| Juan and Julia | Too, Pauline and George |
| Gonzalez and Julie | Free, Lucy and Jack |

Bridesmaids: Janet, Ann, Ellis, Too and all the other girls lining the route. Page boys: James, Jack, Free, and Ken, all other boys to line the route to the church, boy-girl alternating each side of the road all the way to the church.'

Father got a standing ovation. So well organised they all thought.

Virginia was next to stand up. 'Thank you, Father, that sounds wonderful. Now we only have a short time to get gowns, dresses, bridesmaid dresses all the page boys outfits.'

Ma, Molly, Suzie and Helen stood up. 'Sorry to interrupt you, Virginia, but now that you're pregnant we don't want you under any stress, besides you've done so much for others its time you sat back and let other's help you. As you know it's traditional for the mother of the bride to get her daughter's wedding dress and bridesmaid's dresses. Suzie's going to be our daughter-in-law which we're very pleased about, so we would like to get her dress and pageboy outfits.'

Helen then said, 'Virginia, you have always been my best friend from day one, and I would like to get your wedding gown for all the things you've done for my family and our friendship for like.'

Brad stood up, 'I'd like to get Helen's wedding gown because she's marrying my best buddy.'

Pa stood up. 'We would like to get Julie's and Julia's wedding gown for the way they have stepped up and helped the orphanage in the time of need and done a splendid job. Also Kellee you've gone above and beyond helping those kids with riding, petting, you've made them so happy.'

Suzie said with all the tears in the room, 'I hope you don't mind but I've pre-booked appointments tomorrow for our fittings with a lady downtown who has a team of workers and has promised to have everything ready in time.'

A big cheer and a clap went up. Virginia sat down emotional.

Ma was next. 'Food.' She paused, waiting for Steve to shout something out.

'Yes please,' shouted Steve.

'Food and drink, we will all pitch in with anything you think. Others like Molly will coordinate, so we get a good mixture, especially jelly, for the kids drink option there will be plenty of fruit juices. No alcohol, especially for the pregnant women, Mr Matsuda and Ching-Ching we would like you to arrange the buggies all dressed up to the wings.'

'And fireworks too,' said Ching-Ching.

'No fireworks,' said Ma.

'Rings, said Steve, 'what shall we do about rings?'

Pa stood up. 'Do you remember all the help you gave to those wagons that past by? George, Cliff, Andy and others were out there every day helping. Well one man returned, he'd struck it lucky with a gold strike, and so did the man with four children and a wife, the ones that left little Peter here. The man left us three gold nuggets for all the help we'd given him and others. I wanted to give each child of ours a nugget each to do with whatever they wanted to, but I wanted them to make their wedding rings out of gold. An old friend of mine is coming here tomorrow to get ring sizes of your fingers and make the rings. That means all brides and bridegrooms will have a ring each. That includes Maria and George as we didn't have the gold when they got married. All gold will go into trust for any future weddings. Thank you,' said Pa and sat down. A big cheer and clap went up.

'Cake, cake,' shouted out Steve.

Suzie stood up. 'As you know, Mr Pullman has always wanted to come to our weddings and we've all wanted him here, so he's coming to the wedding day. He's bringing his family and their going to stay over for two nights at the orphanage, to experience what the children experience, to see if he can make any adjustments or add any improvements, as seen through the eyes of his own children. Anyway to cut a long story short ...'

'Which you would,' shouted Steve. That got a giggle. Suzie's eyes blazed him down.

'Mr Pullman would like to supply us with the wedding cake. All he asks for is a sturdy table with screening around it so nobody can see it until the big day.'

Suzie sat down. Big clap. Brad stood up. 'That just leaves the music, Jimmy needs a night off. Gonzalez knows a band called the Swing Five. He said they're very good, very upbeat. Good dancing group, lively. So I told him to book them.'

Steve stood up. 'I can't believe this,' he said, 'not only have we got Juan, Too, Free, Mr Fortune, we've now got the swings. What time do they start, six o'clock?'

Ma and Pa stood up. 'This has been an awesome meeting. We've sorted out everything that needs doing. I knew we would, you people are fantastic, all pulling together when needed, we applaud you all, now all we've got to do is enjoy the day and night.' Big cheers. Clapping.

Steve stood up. 'As you know as our ladies get bigger,' he expanded his hands out from his stomach, 'the man have got to step up and cover their workload. For example the orphanage, luckily we have Pauline and Ken as permanent residents (big applause) they are supported by Ellis, Lucy, Jack and James, also covering the restaurant are Mr Matsuda and Ching-Ching, Ma and Pa, Brad and Steve. Plus we have Father and Daniel, back-up force, Cliff, Andy, George, Jimmy, Juan and Gonzalez. Now we've still got to get our products out on time. You might find yourselves doing jobs you haven't done before, like Brad mucking out the pigs.'

Brad jumped up. 'Like Steve mucking out the cattle and horses.'

'Point taken,' said Steve, 'but you know what I mean, all mucking in together.'

'No, that's your job, Steve.' Big laughter and clapping.

Steve said, 'I'm just going to get a gun and shoot myself, I don't know what I'm talking about.'

'Wish you would,' shouted Brad. More laughter. 'Goodnight everyone.'

The following week was hectic sorting out what people were to wear, including all the kids. The ladies and men went for their measurements and fittings, the old lady that ran the shop took on extra workers. Pa's old friend turned up to take finger measurements, he was going to melt the gold down, and pour into moulds, then polish the rings up. When the extra buggies arrived, Mr Matsuda and Ching-Ching and anybody else they could rope in washed the horses down and started decorating the buggies with ribbons and bows. The table and screen were in place for Mr Pullman's wedding cake. Tables inside and outside the house were laid out and sheets laid over them, and the vows and speeches were being written, the smell of cooking was in the air.

Mr Pullman and his family arrived a day early. He said it's about time he had a few days off, and spend some time with his family. He planned to take a boat ride, teach the children how to fish with Jack's help, go for a walk in the woods, let the children play in the sand pit, and on the climbing frame and tree house. Ma and Pa invited them all over for drinks and a piece of apple pie. Pa asked how the railways were doing.

'Railways,' said Mr Pullman, 'are going to change the world. Do you know how long it took to get a herd of cattle half way across America? Days and days. Now we get them there in hours. They had losses along the way, stampedes, trouble finding water sometimes, a whole group of men, the cattle lost weight along the journey. Now we just load them up, then take them off easy. Take money,' said Mr Pullman, 'always moved around by stage coach, you needed different drivers along the way, break downs, horse fatigue, hold ups, bandits, theft. Now we load it on, a few security guards, and it's there in hours. Less men and delivered safely. The horses and bandits can't keep up with the train. Take your products and goods you supply to us. It goes on fresh, a few hours it comes off fresh and the shareholders and government are so pleased with the cash rolling in. Yes they had to pay out early days, with no returns, but now we have paying customers getting on suited and booted, getting off refreshed, clean and no bumpy ride in between and no delays. Our trains leave on time and arrive on time. Cargo and supplies have increased dramatically, one day you'll be able to travel from the west coast right across America to the east coast and back. In the future north to south, and anywhere in between. Invest in the railways, you can't go wrong. Investments will go up and up, and we will get a bigger bonus,' he laughed. 'Now where's Ma's apple pie?'

'Enough about trains,' Mr Pullman said, 'Ma, Pa let's go have a sneaky look at the cake.' They checked nobody else was around, and pulled the screen back. It was magnificent it stood six feet tall, had a three foot base and five tiers. 'I wanted seven tiers, one for each wedding, but was told it would be too heavy. Well,' he said, 'there's enough cake there to feed an army, at least two slices each. It was completely white. Trimmed with pink icing on the edges, and on top made of liquorish was a little bride and groom in their top hat and tails, and wedding dress.'

Ma said, 'It's beautiful, everybody will love it. They've done a magnificent job, the cake makers, it can't have been easy erecting it either.'

'Perfect,' said Mr Pullman.

As they walked away Mr Pullman said, 'I hear there's going to be a lot of babies around here soon. You're going to be a grandma and grandpa again.'

'Yes,' Ma said, 'Andy our carpenter has got to make I think seven cribs and cots.'

'I must say the orphanage is splendid. So clean and organised, so efficient and well run, a happy atmosphere, all the children clean, well fed, happy, playful. Their education is coming on leaps and bound, there's all sorts of drawings on the walls, everybody is talking about the horse's and ponies riding and grooming, collecting chicken eggs, cooking, sawing, on the boats, in the woods, the sand pit, and climbing frame, tree house, school, a, b, c, one, two, three, music and they're looking forward to the big wedding day, jelly and cakes. You've all created a magical world for them, a future, safe and secure, with lots of interaction, with so many characters, so many aunts and uncles, Ma and Pa. It's an amazing place. My kids even want to go here.'

'There's plenty of room,' said Ma.

When Steve came in Mr Pullman congratulated him on his forthcoming marriage and baby.

Steve said, 'Be careful, I think it's all down to Ma's apple pies, they make me fruity (same old joke).'

Mr Pullman said, 'I don't need extra, but perhaps I'll slip the wife an extra slice.'

Steve roared. He thought that was very funny

The night before the big day, people were putting finishing touches for things, laying clothes out to be worn, finishing off the food dishes, cleaning shoes, ironing, everybody was hoping for an early night, as it was going to be a long day tomorrow, starting early and finishing late. Pauline and Ken were first up. They wanted to get breakfast out or the way before starting to get the kids ready, plus Mr Pullman and his family stayed over so Pauline wanted to get everything just right.

The house was busy, getting cutlery, plates, glasses, drinks all out and ready. The brides all arrived to get ready, plus all the bridesmaids.

The men started to make their way down to the school along with the pages. Each shack was getting ready. Father was putting everything in place that he needed, back doors to the garden were opened up, he had his book register for each couple to sign.

The children and those not involved in the wedding ceremony, like the Pullman family and Graham and his family from the farm down the road, started to form a line either side of the road. The bridesmaids were the first to appear, one in each buggy. Ellis, Lucy, Too, Janet, Ann, Brenda representing the orphanage, driving the buggies were Mr Matsuda, Ching-Ching, Pa, Jack, George and Daniel.

Everybody waved and cheered as each buggy rode by, with each bridesmaid waving back at them. Molly was so proud of her girls. Even Ann had the confidence to sit in a buggy all by herself. They all looked so splendid, sitting up high, dressed beautifully with their hair up in a bun. Molly had purchased a white bead necklace to wear and to keep to remind them all of this day. Mr Matsuda, Ching-Ching and others had done a splendid job with the buggies all decorated with ribbons and bows. Each buggy had a different colour, blue, red, yellow, green, pink, purple and the lead buggy to be white.

Once the bridesmaids had been dropped off they were paired up with the pageboys, Free, Peter from the orphanage. The bridegrooms were put in a line, in order they were to get married, Brad, Andy, Steve, Jimmy, Cliff, Juan and Gonzalez. Brad went into the church first. Father greeted him and they stood facing each other waiting for Suzie to arrive.

'Nervous?' Father said.

'No,' said Brad, 'I'm marrying my dream girl.'

'Good to hear,' said Father.

Suzie was in the lead off buggy ridden by Mr Matsuda. She looked stunning with her hair up, earrings, a necklace, she looked so radiant up there in the buggy. As she waved to both sides or the line of people, she felt a million dollars and she was off to the church to married her soul mate and dream husband. Ma was waiting at the door, held her arm out for Suzie to hold.

Ma said to Suzie, 'You look so beautiful. Brad's a very lucky man.'

'Thank you, Ma,' she said, 'but I'm a very lucky lady.'

Father greeted the couple, then he started. 'We are gathered here today to join this couple in holy matrimony et cetera et cetera, I now pronounce you man and wife, you may kiss the bride.' Once finished they went to the back garden. Andy stepped in, Pa was driving his daughter Molly down. He was so pleased to have her back home.

'You look stunning,' he said to her.

'I know,' she said. 'Didn't Janet and Ann look wonderful?'

'Come on,' he said, 'let's get you married before you change your mind.' Father again, we are gathered here today, et cetera.

Helen was driven down by her son James, and her daughter Ellis was her bridesmaid. 'Mum you look beautiful and we're so proud of you, and Steve is a lovely man.'

Next was Virginia driven down by Ching-Ching, as Jimmy waited in the church for his bride followed by Kellee and Cliff waiting in the church, Daniel drove her down, followed by Julia and Juan waiting, then Julie and Gonzalez waiting, ridden down by George. Once all the I dos, kissing the brides was over, they were all in the garden.'

Father said, 'Have you even seen such a gathering of beautiful brides? And the grooms don't look too bad either. I'll tell you one thing for sure we are going to have beautiful babies around here.'

Each bride and groom were ferried up to the house. Mr Matsuda and Ching-Ching rode them down to the corral, unhitched them and watered and fed the horses.

'I pick up all the manure in buckets, good for the plants,' said Ching-Ching.

Everybody was mulling around chatting, complementing each other on how lovely they all looked, then Pa stood up. 'Ladies and gentlemen and children, the food is now ready. Children first, some may need help, followed by the ladies through the men. Thank you.' The kids made a beeline for the food, the little ones were helped by the ladies, then the men. There were stacks and stacks of food, plenty to go around. Ding-ding on the glass. Pa said, 'And now some speeches. I'll start. Never have I seen so many beautiful brides in one room. Stunning (clap). The grooms have washed up pretty well, some of them I didn't recognise (clap). I would like to thank Father, didn't he do a marvellous job (clap)? Everything was so well organised give yourself a clap (clap). Mr Matsuda and Ching-Ching you both did an incredible job on the buggies well done (clap). A special thank you must go out to Pauline and Ken, getting all those children ready could not have been easy, and they were all so well behaved (loud clapping). The food you all have helped to lay out is incredible and tasty (clap).'

'The bridesmaids,' said Ma.

'Oh yes and I've saved the best to last, the beautiful bridesmaids and pageboys (clap) and now I'll hand you over to my son Brad (clap).'

Brad stood up. 'Thank you, Pa (clap). I have to echo everything Pa has said. It's been an amazing day for everyone, thank you for all your reports put in to make this such a special day that we all will remember for the rest of our lives (clap). Thank you Ma and Pa for everything you do for so many (clap). Everybody loves their gold rings. It was a lovely gesture (clap). Oh and thank you Suzie for marrying me, you've made me the happiest man in the world (big clap). Have I for gotten anything?'

Suzie stood up. 'We also would like to thank our distinguished guests Mr Pullman and family and Graham and his family (clap). Thank you everyone for coming, and you my husband have made me very happy. I love you (clap).'

Brad stood up. 'Thank you, dear wife (clap). Now just before I hand you over to Steve, the best man for all of us, I just wished you'd made more of a report. Sorry Helen you got the valet one.'

Roar of laughter and clapping. Steve stood up. 'Thank you, buddy. Thanks to Ma's apple pie. Who do you think got all these ladies pregnant?' Massive roar of the night. 'Now to the serious stuff,' he changed his voice level. 'I noticed today, a lot of people were slacking off work. Today, I've made a list of names, Mr Matsuda, Ching-Ching, especially Brad, James, Jimmy, Jack, George, Andy, Juan hunky Gonzalez and Cliff. This will not be tolerated also the ladies haven't done so well either Helen, Ellis, Virginia, Lucy, Julia, Julie and even little Too! We cannot put up with this terrible behaviour.' Boo, boo, came from everybody. 'The only way to solve this problem is to announce two days off for everyone (big cheer), but all the married men and women get five days off (massive cheer). Looking at my beautiful wife I'm going to need a month. (Massive cheering off and clapping) Now I'll hand you over to Mr Pullman.'

He stood up. 'Thank you for inviting us. It's been an absolutely wonderful day, my whole family have enjoyed themselves. You are a very special bunch of people and I applaud you all (clap). I only have one good piece of advice for a happy and content marriage, and that is always do what the wife says, and remember she's always right. Is that what you wanted me to say dear? (Massive cheer and clap.) And now ladies, gentlemen, children, brides and grooms.' A toast to the bridegrooms, brides and grooms came back. 'And now let's cut the cake.' A big cheer went up, every couple cut a slice each and gave it to their wives, then the wives cut a piece and gave it to their husbands. Then the kids got stuck in, while the adults cleared away getting ready for the band to strike up. They all danced the night away, bit by bit they all disappeared. Brad, Suzie Steve and Helen walked hand-in-hand up towards their new homes on the mound.

'Hasn't it been an amazing day?'

'Yes,' they all said, 'amazing.'

'And now for an amazing night.'

'Careful tiger, I don't want you pulling a muscle,' said Steve.

'I think I did the best speech,' said Steve.

'Yeah only because I wrote it out for you,' said Brad. They got to the doors and carried their new brides over the threshold and shut the doors. Steve reappeared and on both doors stuck a sign saying 'do not disturb' then went back in.

# Chapter 8

## Baby Time

The seconds rolled into minutes, the minutes rolled into hours, the hours rolled into days, the days rolled into weeks, the weeks rolled into months, the ladies got bigger and heavier. The men stepped up and filled the gaps, baby talk was in the air, all the pregnant women met every week with Helen running the seminar, talking about breathing techniques at birth, breast-feeding, diets, baby food and any questions that popped up. They introduced the two extra nurses that would be assisting with the births, so they could all get to know each other. They would be living in one of the shacks so would always be available. The older nurse was Ruth, years of experience under her belt, delivered many babies in the past, highly recommend by the doctor, the second a bit younger, but had studied a lot more on child birth, new techniques, problems on births, so they complemented each other very well. Doctor said he was well impressed, and said he would just take a back seat and watch, only stepping in if needed. He also decided to stay that week, and would only leave the ranch for emergencies, people could come to him in the clinic. He wanted to enjoy the ranch's facilities and do a bit of fishing, and of course, Ellis was checking pulses, picking up tips from the nurses.

Andy had been very busy making up the cribs and cots. George helped him a lot, the ladies were knitting baby clothes, blankets, hats, mittens. The children played their part, knitting and sewing under Virginia's guidance. Ma was back-up nurse, mainly for the cuddling,

The excitement was growing. The time was getting nearer and nearer. Some were more nervous than others, but Helen calmed them all, having already had two children, what to expect, what to do, and a good team be in place to help them. Helen was determined every baby under her watch was going to survive. She couldn't bear losing one or two. Also joining the team was Kitty. She was Graham's daughter from the farm down the road, she'd been to the big wedding day, loved what she'd seen, loved the people, loved the children and the orphanage, loved Pauline and Ken, and wanted to work in the orphanage as she loved children. Pa was over the moon, another hand to help out, securing the future of the orphanage. He was sure there was a spark between Kitty and Ken. Both were big people. Both loved their food, and both loved children. 'Mark my words,' said Pa, 'what with them two working together all the time they will grow close together.' Kitty was given her own shack, but loved sleeping over at the orphanage. It was Kitty's idea, after talking to the children most didn't know their birth dates, or had for gotten, lots had never had a birthday party or a present. Kitty said to Pa they would like to give a special birthday day, so all children in the future would have one day in the year to have a birthday on. They would roughly calculate their ages and that would be added each year to work out their ages. Pa loved the idea. 'What day shall we choose?'

'I've done my homework,' said Kitty, 'your birthday is next week and as founder or the orphanage, we all think it's right to have your birth date to celebrate.'

'I'm honoured,' said Pa, 'let's have a massive celebration.' When news spread around Mr Pullman got to hear of it. Coincidentally it was the same day as his own birthday. This greatly pleased him, as president they would all have his birthdate.

'Excellent, I must buy everyone a present. No child will be left over, everybody on the ranch including Too, Free, Janet, Ann, Dianna's child and George and Maria's twins will get a present and a party, and while we're at it, I want new toys, baby clothes, anything relating to babies buy it and arrange, flowers for all the mums to be, plus every lady on sight including the nurses. They've all worked so hard this year, and the first cigars for the men folk, everybody included.'

One day Andy was in fits of laughter. He saw George carrying his twins, holding them dangling so the children looked like they were flying, lying horizontally facing the floor. Andy said to George, 'What are you doing?'

'They're getting so heavy, man,' he said, 'it's the easiest way to carry them. They love it like flying! What are you going to do when you've got three, or it could even be four?'

'Oh man I need to grow to more pairs of arms.'

'I have an idea,' said Andy. 'I read this book Pa has, the women in Switzerland, Europe, carry two big buckets of milk on a thing called a yolk, the yolk goes across their shoulders, the chains go down, which are attached to the buckets, which equalises the weight.'

'Are you saying, Andy, I should put my children in a bucket?'

'No, no, but we should take the principal of building something along those lines.'

'Couldn't you make something I could just push along? These kids are going to get heavier and heavier, plus I've got more to come.'

'Good idea,' said Andy, 'let's say a light weight chair, with wheels on, you can push along.'

'Yeah you'd better make something for four children just in case. No but we could make something for two children, and you and Maria could push two children each, or for the other parents to be a chair they could push around with wheels on like a push chair. Yes, George, a push chair, I know I would love something as easy as that and I'm sure all the other mothers would want one, and maybe a way of strapping the baby to the mothers or fathers, so it's hands free. No weight to carry and baby is good and safe snuggled up next to Mum looking at her. She would know if baby was awake or a sleep, you know when a baby is awake you hear them. Mine is double, plus more to come. The Indians carry their children behind them, leave it with me. I'll design something. I might need your help with some metal work.'

'Anything,' George said, 'anything to make this a lot easier.'

Meanwhile Mr Matsuda and Ching-Ching were plotting a gambling system, to recuperate their big losses from the rowing day. 'We run three betting choices on what order babies are born in, number two what day and time, number three what names,' said Matsuda.

'That's stupid,' said Ching-Ching. 'Each couple knows what name they're going to call their baby, Brad tell Steve, Steve tell Brad, etc, etc, etc.'

'Good point,' said Mr Matsuda, 'OK, order, day, time, three bets. Yeah we tell them all profits go towards orphanage yeah after we have our cut and profit. Yeah we make donation fifty per cent or profit.'

'How much is fifty per cent?' said Ching-Ching.'

'One in two,' said Mr Matsuda. 'OK we give good odds, that way more people gamble more profit. OK let's look at the order: names Helen, Dianna, Molly, Maria, Virginia, Keller, Suzie, Julie, Julia.

OK favourites: Helen, Sarah, Molly, Maria.

Second favourites: Virginia, Suzie, Kellee.

Third favourites: Julie, Julia.'

'Why this order?' Ching-Ching said.

'These were the first to announce it, and to go to Helen, then Virginia, Kellee, Suzie, last was Julie, Julia.'

'Yeah but not every lady go full term.'

'Yeah that's to our advantage, one early, one upset all the apple cart. OK, give good prices, sucker them all in. OK four to one on first favourites, that means three bets will lose. Profit. Six to one second favourites, two will lose, ten to one, one will lose. OK good prices I have one dollar on Julie.'

'You idiot, if you win we have to pay you.'

'Oh yeah,' said Ching-Ching.

'OK,' Mr Matsuda said, 'we only take bets on first, second, third, that means seven bets guaranteed to lose. What about last baby born, nine to none, this means eight bets lose.'

'I like it,' said Mr Matsuda.

'OK if someone bets one dollar we give him a betting slip with name on or time or order we write down same bet, total, how much betting money we collect, minus what we have to pay out, rest all profit.' The two men danced around.

'Don't tell Ma and Pa, she will kill us gambling.'

Meanwhile Andy had been working on his prototype. It was a chair fixed to what looked like a pair of skis. George laughed, he said, 'If we had snow it would be ideal.'

'Try it on the grass,' said Andy.

'I'm not putting my kid in that,' he said, 'it could be a death trap, put a boulder in about the weight of a child and try that.'

George put the strap around his chest and launched off, it was a bit cheeky. The skis collected a lot of mud, and left tracks across the grass.

'All right for humping wood,' said George, 'but not babies.'

'OK,' said Andy, 'prototype number two. You know how a wagon wheel goes around, if we made smaller wheels and had an axis going through them with a chair on ...'

George said, 'Keep working on it, I've got to get these two fed.'

318

So the next big event would be some of the children's first ever birthday party, and their official birth date. It wouldn't matter if they were days, weeks or months out, it would be an event every year they could look forward to and celebrate. Lucy, Ellis, Jack, James were to retry the game they didn't get around to doing last time, with extras added. They were going to start with a sports day. They mapped an area out for racing, dividing the children into groups, fastest wins, egg and spoon race, three-legged race, furthest jump in the sand pit, relay race, and adults racing if they wanted to join in, buried treasure in the sand pit, pass the parcel, musical chairs, present time, finished off with a big game of rounders followed by food, and dancing. The kids were going to love it, meanwhile Brad, Steve, Helen and Suzie, were having a great time in their new houses. They were all always together, sitting out at night watching the sunsets.

Steve said to Brad, 'Have you heard Mr Matsuda and Ching-Ching are running bets on baby times? First, second, et cetera. We have an advantage here. Helen gave us some information those two won't know. We'll clean them out. Helen said to know you'd have more change than going to the moon, anything can happen and probably will.'

Everybody had a lovely day at the annual children's birthday, the children especially, sports, games, presents, wonderful food as much as they could eat, horse and pony riding and lots of fun at the rounders. Now most things were out of the way, it was all concentrating on the pregnant women, the two nurses had moved in, so had Doc, but occasionally left for calls. Ma was on standby, Ellis was graded up, all the cribs were in place, with all sorts of bedding in, diapers, bottles, towels, wiping cloths, you name it, it was there ready.

Helen said, 'Shall we move the ladies into the main ward to give each other support? Then with contractions, move them into the middle-room for births. We have four beds, each bed will have a nurse each, Ma and Ellis for support and delivery, with Doc in the background. Once they've given birth, move them to the second ward for recovery and visitors.'

'Sounds a good plan,' they all said. 'Now who's going to be first?' The men got involved as well, Juan, Too, Free moved in with Gonzalez, so they could be near the ladies. If Juan had to go first, Gonzalez could look after the children, Alan, Brad, Steve, moved into the next shack, Pa was left to look after Janet, Ann and baby Archie. The next shack was Jimmy, Cliff, Andy and George, again if George had to go first, either Andy, Jimmy or Cliff could look after the twins. It was all about the time waiting for the scream, or the first man's name to be called, in Brad, Steve and Alan's shack.

They talked about the birth, about being there. Alan reassured them it was an incredible experience not to be missed having been through it, and at the end of it all you get to hold your newly born child for the first time. Steve said, 'I'm worried more about screaming than Helen does.' Juan was calming Gonzalez, as he'd been through it before with Too! And George was doing the same for Jimmy, Cliff and Andy, telling them about the twins' birth. Twice as much trouble. 'Oh Lord,' he said, 'just one nice healthy baby would be enough this time thank you.'

The men all sat nervously but excited. No one could sleep, but this could go on for hours, even days. Brad said, 'Famous last words.' Doc had brought in a hand bell, ding -ding, followed by the word's Steve, Steve. Steve was as white as a shirt. 'Go buddy go, this is what you've been waiting for your whole life, a child.'

Steve was frozen to the spot. Couldn't move. 'Go on, buddy, Helen needs you.'

Steve snapped out of his trance. 'See you soon,' he said.

'Good luck, buddy, give our regards to Helen.' With that he was out of the door like lightning.

Doc met him at the door. 'Put this gown on, mask and hat, and shoes,' Doc said, 'we don't want any germs coming in here.'

Everybody was masked up, he approached Helen. 'How you doing, sweetheart?' he said, not looking down to the foot of the bed, where all the action was taking place. He held her hand just as the command came push, push, push. Helen's hand and finger nails clamped into Steve's. He gave a little yelp.

'Don't you dare,' said Helen.

'Breathe, sweetheart,' he said, 'Pant one, two, three, pant one, two, three. You can do it sweetheart push, push, push, sweetheart, one, two, three,' then Steve fainted like a sack of spuds to the floor.

'Don't worry,' said Doc, 'I've got smelling salts here. Always happens.'

They got Steve back on a chair, made him smell the salts. He was back in the game.

'We won't mention that incident to the other men, don't worry,' said Doc, 'you not the first and you won't be the last, just hold Helen's hand.'

'Have you got any thicker gloves?' Steve asked. Push sweetheart one, two, three.'

'I can see the head,' said Ellis. 'Push Mum. Push.'

Helen sat up a little grabbed her knees and gave one almighty push. 'The baby's here,' Ellis said, 'the baby's here.' Helen flopped back into the bed, exhausted. Steve was back on the floor.

'We've got a right fainter here,' said Doc. More smelling salts. 'Breathe,' said Steve, 'One, two, three.'

'You're a father, Steve. Baby is already here.'

'What?' said Steve.

'Say hello to your son.'

'A son,' Steve said, 'a son.'

'They're just going to clean him up a bit, check him over, then you can hold him, a boy.'

Steve said, 'A boy.' All the ladies clapped next door.

Steve said to Helen, 'I'm so proud of you, I love you very much. The best day of my life was when I met you in that puddle, the icing on the cake was when I married you. Today is beyond my wildest dreams. Look,' he said, 'a boy, my little son.' He kissed the baby's forehead, and said, 'You are going to be so loved. I'll teach you how to ride, swim, go fishing, and so many other things.' He looked across at Helen, who was fast asleep. He placed his son into the crib, kissed baby and Helen and quietly left. He went to see all the other ladies and gave a thumbs up sign.

'Good luck,' he said. He then turned to Doc, shook his hand and thanked him for all his help. He then thanked the two nurses. Then hugged Ellis, 'I'm so proud of you, you were brilliant, and now you have a baby brother, well done and I love you.'

Ellis was choked. It had been so emotional, helping to deliver her mum's baby, seeing how happy Steve was.

Steve whispered, 'I'm off to tell James he has a baby brother, mother and son are well, and he can visit tomorrow. I'm so happy,' he said.

'I can see it,' said Ellis. Steve went straight around to Brad and Alan, banging on the door so loudly he probably woke half the ranch up.

The three men were jumping for joy together. 'A baby boy, I've got a son, a boy, a son.'

'How's Helen?' said Brad.

'Fast asleep, a boy, Brad I've got a son.'

'Brilliant,' said Brad, 'I wonder who's next.'

'I just want to go back and look at Helen and my son all night.'

'Best let them rest, buddy.'

'I know I just don't want to be away from them both for a second.'

Alan said, 'I told you, it's the most memorable moment in your life, and it just keeps getting better and better.'

Meanwhile Mr Matsuda and Ching-Ching were spying on who went in and who came out.

'Jackpot,' said Mr Matsuda, 'one of the favourites, Helen, is first, that means all bets on firstborn except Helen have lost. How many on Helen.'

'Three, Steve, Brad and George, at four to one, twelve dollars. The rest is all profit. OK we don't need Virginia, Suzie or Kellee to be next, anybody else is all profit. Come on ladies, we could get a clean sweep here.'

No more activity came the rest of the night. Everybody was cat napping whenever possible, early morning. The doc rang the bell, all the men froze on the spot. Brad, Brad. Brad went around in a circle looking for something but he didn't know what. 'Go, go,' Steve said, 'good luck, buddy, good luck, bruv,' they said.

Brad was out of the door like a greyhound. Doc stopped him. 'Put these on. We don't want any germs in here.'

As he went in he saw Suzie with sweat rolling down her face, straining, her face was red, and her teeth were clamped together. 'Love you,' Brad said as he grabbed her hand. 'Push, baby, push, breathe, baby, breathe.'

Ellis shouted, 'I can see the head. Big push, Suzie.'

'Big push, baby,' Brad said.

'It's a boy,' said Ellis.

'A boy,' Brad said, 'a baby boy.' He also went a bit faint and dizzy.

'Smelling salts,' said Doc. Baby was whisked away to be cleaned up and checked out, then placed on Suzie's chest.

Brad gaining his faculties said, 'Oh baby, you don't know how much I love you, and now we have our very own little family. I'm so proud of you, and love you so much.'

Suzie said, 'Hold our boy.'

Brad picked him up so gently, and looked into his eyes. 'He's so beautiful, he's even got hair, and your beautiful eyes.' Then Brad cried uncontrollably which made Suzie cry and Ellis.

'Thank you, everybody,' he said, 'Ellis you were amazing just like your mum. Wow,' Brad said, 'can life get any better than this? Suzie the woman I love and adore and now a baby son, and my best buddy and Helen have a son, only born hours apart.'

'Right,' said Doc, 'into the room with Helen.'

Suzie, and baby were pushed, then all the ladies in the other room clapped and shouted out, 'Well done Suzie and Brad.'

Once in the other room Brad hugged Helen and took a look at their baby. 'Hello, little buddy,' he said, 'meet your best friend in life, you two will grow up together and have so much fun, just like your dads do. Ladies I know you two need rest, I love you both, well done, goodbye, son. I'll come and see you as soon as they let me, and you little buddy.' Brad kissed everybody in the room, then went into the other ward. 'Good luck, ladies,' he said, 'who's next?'

Brad also went banging on the shack. 'A boy,' he shouted, 'a boy, I've got a son.' Everybody came out, shaking his hand and congratulating him. Steve said, 'Isn't it an amazing feeling? It's unbelievable, I can't find the words to describe it.' They hugged.

'Our boys will grow up together, Alan,' Brad said, 'You're now an uncle.'

They all hugged together. Well done they kept saying, 'Ma and Pa now have another grandson, Molly's an aunt and Dianna, Janet, Ann are cousins. This is an amazing day already and there's still more to come.'

Ma, Pa and the children arrived. They hugged Brad and Steve, and gave baby Archie to Alan, he said, 'You're going to have a brother or sister to play with soon, you've already got a cousin and another cousin coming soon. I'm going in when Molly and Dianna are having their babies. I wouldn't miss this occasion for anything in the world, and I want to see Brad and Steve's son.'

Mr Matsuda and Ching-Ching were dancing around. 'A second favourite, Suzie, six to one, how many on Suzie for second baby? Only Brad and Steve, the rest all losers. That Brad and Steve clever boys, they had a good spread across the board. Next we need another favourite like Molly or Maria, then it's all down to last baby. We don't need Julie or Julia last baby nine to one, a lot of bets riding on that.'

Ding, Ding, Andy, Andy, Alan, Alan. 'Oh my God,' said Ma.

'Oh my God,' said Andy. Good luck they all said.

'Come on, sons,' Ma said, 'let's go get us some more grandchildren.' She held Alan and Andy's hand, and made a beeline for the clinic. 'Look after the kids, Pa,' she shouted, 'we'll let you know what's happening as soon as we can.'

'Good luck everybody,' Pa shouted, 'so I've got another grandson. Another heir to the ranch, the future looks good, and Steve, your family, so another grandson, and more to come. Molly gave birth to a little girl, and so did Dianna, so far two boys and two girls, which now meant Molly and Andy had three girls. Dianna and Alan had a boy and a girl, Ma said we've gone from having one grandson, two adopted granddaughters to having a grandson, and two granddaughters, plus Helen and Steve that's seven children.'

Molly and Dianna were pushed into the room with Helen and Suzie in. Ma said, 'This is perfect. Amazing timing. All my new family in one room.' She picked up Brad and Suzie's baby first, 'Isn't he handsome?' she said, 'just like Brad was as a baby.' Then she picked up Helen and Steve's, hugged him and said, 'You can see it in his eyes he's going to be a handful, just like his dad.' Then she picked up Molly and Andy's baby, 'She's beautiful just like her mum.' Then Dianna's and Alan's baby. 'You're absolutely beautiful, just like your mum. Now ladies I'm going to clear everybody out of here so you can all get a good rest, but tonight all your men folk can't wait to come and see you, and the babies, so does Pa and the children. We all can't wait to come back, congratulations everybody, you've made one very old lady very happy. Love you all see, you all see you soon.'

She left, thanking everybody in the delivery room, and especially hugging Ellis. 'You've done an amazing job, we're all so proud of you. You deserve a medal, you've helped make my family so complete and happy, we'll never forget what you've done for us all. We will be eternally grateful. We love you.' They hugged. She popped her head in to the ward of the expectant mums. 'Good luck, everybody, who's going to be next?!'

Luckily a few hours passed by, which gave everybody a rest and a chance of some food and drink, Ma and Pauline sorted out food, mainly so Pauline could have a look at the babies, Father popped in and blessed all the children and congratulated all the mums, dads and grandparents. Daniel gave Father a message to pass on, that he wanted to capture all the parents and children in their arms, sketching and drawing the happy couples and babies to go into the art gallery, James, Jack, Lucy were visiting later.

Father said when they had names sorted for the babies he needed to know, so he could write them in his book along with the children he already had. It will be like a family tree, were we all came from, and who was related to who and in one year's time a massive one year birthday celebration of all these children, plus christenings to come.

Ding-ding. Jimmy, Cliff. 'Here we go again,' said Steve. 'Good luck, fellas.' Jimmy and Cliff went running.

'Put these on fellas,' Doc said, 'we don't want any germs in here.' Virginia was first, a little baby girl, followed later by Kellee, a little baby girl, the other smaller ward was so packed, the ladies and babies where wheeled back into the original ward, which allowed Pa and the kids, Brad, Steve, Alan and Andy to visit their wives and babies plus Ma. There was a lot of hugging, kissing, picking up babies, congratulating. Daniel popped in making a few sketches of parents and babies. He said to him all the babies looked the same.

'Any names yet?' said Pa, most had an idea, but were not ready to say just yet.

'Let's get all babies born first, then we'll have a massive celebration at the house and announce the names, and plan a massive christening day.'

Brad said, 'I've won a few dollars off Mr Matsuda and Ching-Ching.'

'Yeah,' said Steve, 'I've got a few dollar's coming back.'

Pa said, 'I've lost a few bets but Molly has saved my bacon.'

Ma said, 'You've been gambling on babies? Shame on you all.'

Helen and Suzie said, 'Yeah I've had a little wager as well and won.'

'Right,' Ma said, 'wait here I've be right back.' She stormed out of the clinic and banged on Mr Matsuda's door loudly.

'Come in, Ma,' Mr Matsuda said.

'You two should be ashamed,' she said, 'gambling on babies. I want you to pay all those that have won their money, any profit left over you will not make a cent out of. All profit will go to the orphanage. I allow you to have a little tipple, but from now on there will be no more gambling and no fireworks, do you understand?'

'Yes, Ma,' Mr Matsuda and Ching-Ching said, 'it's only a bit of fun.'

'Ching-Ching, gambling is not fun,' said Ma, 'it can lead to many a man's down fall; and I don't want it happening on this ranch understood?'

'Yes understood, now how much has Pa got coming back, and Brad and Steve? Because it's all going to go to the orphanage, give it to me, plus your profits.'

'Yes, Ma,' they both said.

The rest of the day was quiet and relaxing, then early evening, ding, ding, 'Juan, Gonzalez,' Doc shouted. The boys were buzzing around. Ma arrived to look after Too and Free.

'Go, Go,' she said to the two men.

'Sí, sí,' they both said. Squeezing out or the door together, Juan said, 'My wife and sister are going to have their babies together.'

Gonzalez said, 'We're going to be papas, let's go.'

Doc stopped them at the door. 'Put these gowns on,' he said, 'we don't want any germs in here.' A lot or Spanish was spoken and shouted and screamed, but when the first baby was born, olé was shouted. It was a little baby boy for Julia, followed by olé, a little baby boy for Julie, the whole family was over the moon. The girls said, 'Our boys will grow up together, best mates just like we did, but in this amazing place and these people.'

Which just left Maria. George said, 'Are you too tired to push?'

'No,' said Maria, 'I'm just enjoying the rest, but I think it's time.'

'Hallelujah,' shouted George, 'make way, make way, pregnant woman coming through.'

'Ah I didn't get the bell like everyone else.'

'I'm sure Doc will let you ring it later.'

'From now on,' said Maria, 'you're sleeping in the other room until I call you.'

'Yes honey,' he said, 'you won't be able to wait too long.' They laughed. 'Go on, Maria,' he kept shouting, 'go on Maria, you're an old hand at this.'

'Don't call me old.'

'Sorry, dear,' he said, 'push, push, Maria.'

She delivered a baby girl, George was looking. 'Any more?' he said.

'No just the one,' Ellis said.

'Hallelujah,' said George.

Maria said, 'Look George we've got a beautiful baby girl.'

George held her crying and thanked the Lord.

Maria said, 'When she grows up, me and her are going to rule the house and knock you boys in to shape. We are going to be the bosses.'

'Yes dear whatever you say, dear, you're the boss.'

'Good,' said Maria, 'now get out of here feed and change the twins. Give them my love, I need to get some rest, but bring yourself and the boys back tomorrow, because I've missed you all.'

'Yes dear whatever you say,' said George.

The doctor, the two nurses, and Ellis got a standing ovation. Well done, flying around everywhere. Helen was so proud or Ellis, James had met his new brother. Doc said, 'Never have I seen such organisation, cleanliness, dedication to duty, happiness than I've seen here. You were all brilliant, nurses, mums, fathers, grandparents and friends. This has been the best experience of my life, I'll never forget it, what a team. Nine pregnant ladies, nine babies born. Good and healthy mothers and babies all doing fine. I will back tomorrow for another check up, just to make sure. Now I'm off for some rest, I suggest my team get some best as well, we only had two major incidents and that was with the fathers Steve passed out twice and Brad only the once.' That got a big cheer.

Brad said, 'Steve, twice.'

'Yeah and you buddy passed out once, but for longer.'

The next few days were all about visiting, people coming and going all day, the nurses had time off to rest. Ma and Pauline did the running around. Babies all throughout the day were feeding and being chanced. Ma had sleep times organised throughout the day, so mums and babies could sleep. Doc came back often, he was well pleased. He said they all could go home soon, the ladies moaned that they would miss each other so organised daily visits to the house to kept it touch.

Father arranged to meet at the house to finalise names and set a date for the christenings. In a couple of days' time, Steve said to Brad, 'Have you decided on a name yet?

'Yep,' said Brad, 'have you?'

'Yep,' said Steve, 'but we'll all have to wait a few days to find out.' All the couples discussed with each other what names they would give their child, and couldn't wait to find out all the other names which had been chosen.

And would it matter if someone had chosen the same name, they would all have to wait. Mr Matsuda said to Ching-Ching, 'We would have made an absolute fortune, what with Maria being the last baby born.'

As the ladies and babies went home one by one and started family life all together, Steve said to Brad, 'Good job we've had experience mucking out the animals.'

'I know,' said Brad, 'how can a little bundle of joy produce so much.'

'Have you tried the um baby milk yet?'

'No.' said Brad, 'well a little. You?'

They diffused. 'Yeah a little.'

'So this afternoon we're all going up to the house to tell our chosen names for the babies. What's yours?' Steve said.

'You'll just have to wait, buddy, like everyone else. Daniel's finished a lot of the sketches, can't wait to see them. Hope he does a couple. I like to keep one in the house of a constant reminder of that special day. Yeah we'll get them framed and have them on the wall.'

The afternoon came, most babies had been fed, and were asleep, they all gathered at the house, Father called order quietly. Steve shouted, 'You can shout as loud as you like, even light dynamite. It wouldn't wake our Stevie.' Everybody laughed, then Steve realised he'd let his son's name out.

Helen said, 'You can't help yourself can you?'

'Sorry, Helen, it just slipped out.'

'So close,' said Helen, 'so close.'

Father said. 'I think it might be a good idea if Helen and Steve go first.' Big clap and laugh.

Steve stood up. 'Some of you might have guessed by now our son's first name, Steve, we've chosen this name because it's always been lucky for me, surviving a war, meeting Helen, living at the ranch with all of you lovely people. Stevie's middle name will be Brad, since I've met you my life's got better and better. You're the best buddy any man could ever have. I love you, buddy and have named my son after you. Stevie Brad.' There were tears all around the room. Steve and Brad hugged.

'Thank you buddy that means a lot to me,' said Brad.

Father said, 'Brad while you're up why don't you go next?'

'For exactly the same reasons Suzie and I have named our son Bradley Steve. I hope they grow up together, and get as close as Steve and I are. I hope they have the bond, fun and laughter we have every day of our lives, living here with all of you. It is the best place in the world to bring children up in and I hope they find beautiful, wonderful wives like we both have.'

Father said, 'I don't know about you but this is quite emotional, I thought we were just going to write names down and that was it. Let's continue. Alan would you go?'

Alan stood up. 'So we've been blessed with a beautiful son which we named Archie after Pa, now we've been blessed with a beautiful daughter. Her name is Mary Anna, which we've named after Ma and Dianna her mum, Ma short for Mary, Anna short for Dianna.

'Wow,' said Father. There was clapping of delight. Ma was in tears and hugged Alan and Dianna, and blew a kiss to her namesake.

Pa said, 'That's wonderful. Our names will live on here a bit longer even after we've gone. Molly, Andy would you like to go next.'

Andy stood up. 'Not only have I been blessed with marrying Molly, and joining this amazing family, we now have a family of our own, little Janet and Ann, and I would like to present to them their little sister Mandy. I now have a beautiful wife, three beautiful daughters, I've joined a wonderful family with amazing friends and neighbours and a job I love. I couldn't be happier.'

Then he broke down in to tears, Molly stood up and hugged Andy. 'We love you too, Andy,' she said, 'and you're a wonderful father to our beautiful babies. Just to add the reason we named her Mandy was the M of Molly followed by Andy Mandy.' Big clap.

Steve stood up. 'Are you sure the M is not for Ma?' Big laugh. 'Also do you realise Ma's influence because if you take all of the initials and put them together you get M for Ma, A for Andy, J for Janet, A for Ann and M for Mandy which spells out Ma Jam.'

People cried with laughter. 'Trust you,' said Helen, 'but that very cleverly works out, now just sit there and say nothing.'

Jimmy, said, 'Virginia, I'm not sure I can follow that, but I also adore my wife Virginia, and our baby. As you all know we've been through a tough time after losing Baby Virginia. There was an empty void in our lives, a sadness that was so hard to overcome but with our marriage, our love, and this little bundle of joy it has given us new hope, new love, we will never forget little Baby Virginia she will always be in our hearts, but this little one means the world to us and we love her very much, therefore we will be naming her Finny.'

Big clap. Everybody was in tears including Father. 'Quite often people called Virginia are shortened to Ginny or Jenny, so it's a mix tore of her mother Virginia, a name they all share.'

'Wow,' said Father, 'this is all so moving. Who'd have thought names would mean so much, so far you've all chosen amazing names with such meanings and sentiment attached. Even Ma Jam (clap). Cliff, Kellee.'

Cliff said, 'We also adore our baby girl. Since I've met Kellee, my life has changed for the better, once I was irresponsible, now I have a beautiful wife and daughter to care about, they are my world, we've named her Tyler. No real reason we just like the name.' Clap.

Maria, George. George stood up. 'Thank you,' he said, 'today you have said some beautiful stories, for Maria and I, and two twin boys, we have been blessed by the Lord, and given a beautiful baby daughter. A our boys have names out of the Bible. We thought it only right for our baby girl to follow suit so we are going to name her Isabelle. I can't tell you how happy we are as a family and our extended family around us. I only have one word to say and that it Hallelujah praise the Lord.'

Everybody said hallelujah back to Maria and George. 'Which leaves Juan and Julia.'

Juan said, 'I cannot believe that just a short time ago, I and my beautiful daughter Too, were out on the streets homeless. Then we met Brad, Steve and Father, and within a short period of time, we have a home a job, neighbours, friends, a beautiful wife, an adoptive son, my wife's best friend, a brother-in-law and a beautiful baby boy who we are naming Jay. Jay standing for J for Juan and J for Julia. JJ.' Clap.

And that just leaves Julie and Gonzalez. Gonzalez stood up a bit nervous. 'Thank you,' he said, 'I came to work here on the orphanages. I met and fell in love with Julie instantly. It was love at first sight. (Aah, they said.) We got married and have had a beautiful baby boy named Five (lots of laughter), no I'm kidding his name is Julian like his mother and best friend Julia. We're so happy here, we never want to leave. Thank you Juan and family for bring part of our family and thank you everybody for being part of our family.'

Father stood up and said, 'That was amazing by everybody well done, shall we pray, blessing all the children, hoping they would be happy and healthy in life. Now Daniel.'

He stood up with a pile of sketches all framed by Andy. He gave one each to each couple, and to Ma and Pa, one of Alan, Dianna, Archie, Mary, Anna, one of Andy, Molly, Janet, Ann and Mandy, one of Suzie, Brad, and Bradley, and one of Steve, Helen and Steve. He said these are all for you to keep. But I've also done a second copy which we are going to hang in the gallery for all to see, everybody was so happy. Daniel had captured the parents and babies so well Ma and Pa were over the moon.

'Now,' Ma said, 'we have our children captured for ever and our children's children captured forever, thank you.'

Pa stood up. 'This is a momentous day, not only have we secured the ranch's future, but have created our next generation to keep this ranch going well into the future, God willing. We are so proud of you all, and the wonderful community you have all helped to create, good luck, good health, good memories.' Love clap and cheering.

Father again. 'So our last bit of business is planning the christenings. Any ideas?'

Brad stood up. 'The sooner the better,' he said, big cheer.

'Shall we say next week, maybe on the Sunday, our Lord's day, we can have a service, prayers, blessing, hymns and I'd like to christen, all of our children from the orphanage, the first children including Janet and Ann, and every child here.'

Brad stood up. 'What a wonderful idea, Father,' he said, 'every child needs a father a mother a brother a sister, an aunt, an uncle, a grandma, a grandpa, a cousin, a family a neighbour, a friend. I believe every child here has that in some shape or form, the only thing missing is that every child here should have our Father as their godfather. All those in favour say aye.'

'Aye,' they all shouted back.

Father was overwhelmed. 'Thank you,' he said, 'it would be a pleasure.'

Ken and Kitty stood up, both shaking like a leaf. Ken said, 'Kitty and I are courting (big cheer and clap). we love each other very much, and next year we want to get married (big cheer) and have a family. If we have a boy we would like to name him Billy after my Pa who we sadly lost, and miss him very much. The boy would be called Billy Graham. Graham after Kitty's father, and if we have a girl it will be named Paula after my Ma. Thank you.' He sat down.

Next up was Jack and Ellis. 'We are also courting and want to get married next year, we haven't talked about babies yet as we need to talk to Helen and Steve first.'

Then Lucy and James stood up. 'We are also courting,' said James, 'and would also like to get married next year and have a double wedding like Helen, Steve, Brad and Suzie, as we're also all going to be friends for life.'

They sat down stunned silence. 'Anybody else?' said Father, 'as it seems line confession day.'

Ching-Ching and Mr Matsuda stood up. People looked shocked.

Ching-Ching said 'I know you can't marry us, but we was wondering, Father, could you give us a blessing, because I've never had such a good friend in my life.'

Mr Matsuda said, 'You're the best, although you can be annoying sometimes.' They hugged and got the biggest cheer of the day.

Mr Matsuda continued, 'As you know this has been a very busy year. It started with Mr Pullman's contracts, which we have successfully fulfilled. With the help of the surrounding farmers, Bradville has been very successful, with a steady stream of customers growing by the day, we've had very good opening days, and we have collected a huge amount of money. The running of the orphanage is mainly taken care of by Mr Pullman and the railway. We obviously have running costs, materials, spares, bits and pieces we've needed to buy. This has to be subtracted from the profit then we put a percentage away for future outgoings, and rainy days. Each individual gets an equal share, as we are a team of equals. You will all be notified of the final total, which will go into your bank accounts. I can tell you his over a thousand dollars each. Well done everybody.' Massive cheer and clapping.

Ma, Pa, Brad, Steve all stood up. 'Well done everybody, an amazing result for our first year trading. Thank you, Mr Matsuda, you've been amazing, here's to another great year.' The cheering and clapping started to wake a few babies up, and the crying started and snowballed.

Father said, 'Thank you everybody. See you all Sunday for the christenings.'

'And a party back at the house,' Ma said. As George and Maria walked away, George said, 'Over a thousand dollars, I've never even seen a hundred dollar's now we've got over a thousand. What we going to do with it?'

'Spend it,' said Maria. 'We haven't just got a thousand dollars, we've got two thousand dollars.'

'Hallelujah,' said George. Everybody was the same. Each couldn't believe they all had over a thousand dollars each to spend. It hasn't been that much work either. It's been more of a pleasure all working together. It's been enjoyable and fun, time has gone by so quickly and it hasn't all been work, work, and no play. We've had loads of time off, parties celebrations, weddings, christenings, so much to enjoy.

Brad and Steve said, 'Did you see their faces when Mr Matsuda told them how much they were all getting? They've deserved it, they've worked hard, pulled together when needed, built a church, a school, Bradville, helped with the orphanage and our houses. I don't know how we're going to top that next year, more of the same,' Brad said, 'more of the same.'

'Just think,' said Steve, 'what if on our journey from Florida to California, we'd have gone a different route, do you think we would have met different people?'

Brad said, 'I believe this was all meant to be, the people we met along the way, were the people we were meant to meet. Helen, George, Father, Jimmy Virginia, Juan, Too! All were meant to be where they were meant to be for us to meet them. They're all amazing, and you got a wife and child out of it,' Brad said. 'Steve, they're not just the lucky ones, we are the lucky ones as well.'

'Never a truer word spoken, buddy.'

# Chapter 9

## What's Next

One day the family was just sitting around the table, Ma, Pa, Alan, Dianna, Molly, Andy, Ching-Ching Brad, Suzie, and Baby Bradley, Steve, Helen, and Baby Stevie. Father and Daniel popped in, Daniel had some more sketches he had done and wanted to show everybody.

Pa said to Daniel, 'You've been an amazing asset to this community. Not only have you captured our amazing events, you've captured our very souls, through your stories will live on, to tell a period in history, in generations to come when they look back in time, our little community, our struggles, our highs and lows all captured in your sketches and pictures. Not only are we enjoying your work, but others will enjoy it for years to come. Well done, Daniel.' Little clap.

'It's all been a pleasure,' he said, 'never have I had such good material to work with, babies, children, weddings, the landscape, the people, teaching a, b, c, one, two, three, is so rewarding for me. I love being here, thank you so much for the opportunity. This was what my life was missing, a purpose, a reason to exist to achieve something special, and of course the book I am writing will capture every background, every moment, past, present and future.'

'Thank you, Daniel,' Pa said. 'I've been having dreams. They're more than just a dream they're visions, they feel real to me.'

'Share them with us,' said Molly.

'You all know how amazing we've done up to this point, our past has brought us to the present, but I want to talk about everybody's future. At this moment in time, were all very comfortable, the future looks good, Bradville has a great reputation and is growing on a weekly basis, the railway contracts are very secure at the moment, but what if we lost the contract, because a bigger company took over, cut our prices, or were nearer for their needs? With Mr Pullman there he has an affection to us, but what if areas were divided up, or Mr Pullman retired or moved on to a different job? Would we struggle? We've got more mouths to feed, we must keep creating jobs for our up and coming community. Think of your own children and families. We have a responsibility to every family and child on this ranch.

'We have started and planted a small acorn here, if we nurture it, it can grow into a large oak tree, the branches being the views of this country, I want our children's children's children to play a huge roll in building this country to one of the greatest countries of the world every day, week, month, year. Our population is growing, they come from Europe, Asia, South America, North America, from all around the globe, some arrive with next to nothing in their pockets, nowhere to live, no job, they need shelter, food for their families, clothing, prospects, futures, every man and woman wants to work for a living to provide for his family, to have a better or a food standard of living, they went their children to be well educated, happy, leisure time, have their own families to have money in the bank, to buy nice things. Let's look at what every human being needs, the basics: food, water, clothing, shelter, jobs, money.

'So I've broken down in sections where we could help and prosper. Let's take food, what if we purchased land in mid-America and turned it into vast fields of wheat, barley, corn, sugar, rice, vegetables, all sorts of crops. California, Florida, where the sunshine nearly every day, fruit orchards, apples, oranges, potatoes, strawberries, lemon, limes, build near rivers, lakes, streams, ponds, irrigation is the key to all planting and growth. Land at this moment in time is probably the cheapest it's ever going to be, as we get more populated, and people start to buy land, it will go up and up in price, we need to strike now. Housing, town, factories will start to spring up everywhere, which will create jobs, more babies, more children, more food needed. Brad, Alan, Molly, Steve, what are the plans for your children in say five years' time, ten years' time, twenty years' time, fifty years' time, your children's children a one hundred years' time? Wouldn't you like to know that what you've all started here grows and grows and looks after the next after the next generation and the generations after that.'

'So, Pa,' Brad said, 'what's the plan of action? Let's get started.'

Pa said, 'Small steps, one project pays for the next project.'

'Land,' Pa said, 'you can't expand without land, you need to know your soil, to know what plants will grow, which way the sun shines. No good buying land the wrong said of a mountain, where the sun don't shine. Water, the most treasured commodity on God's earth. Workers, jobs, housing, food, contracts, money, take cotton, we have an abundance on our doorsteps in the south. Cotton mills, we must think big, not just supplying our country but exports, world trade, it's bringing in new money from abroad. Take cities they will always grow fast first, but they won't have fields to grow their food, they'll have to bring it in. If we could have a location in the centre of the country, we could reach all corners of America.'

'Just like the roots of a great oak tree,' said Steve.

'Yes Steve, just like the roots of an oak tree. Feeding south, the branches west and east.'

'So what's next, Pa?' Brad said. 'First of all we have to secure the hub.'
Steve looked puzzled.

'The hub being here. We know the format and we know it works, now we have to roll the format out let's take five years' time, some of our children will be reaching fifteen years old, most will be ten years old, add five years the majority will hit fifteen years old. Your own children will be ten years old, everywhere needs to double up. As our generation gets older, we must train up our natural replacements, look for certain skills in our children, find out what they like to do, what are their passions in life, what career path do they want to take, what skill's do we need to teach them, do they see their futures with us? Our expansions will create more and more jobs, housing, I've got a plan, trees are the future, not only are they good for the environment, yes, you don't get quick rewards, but once planted, there's not much you need to do to them. Our next generations will reap the rewards of what we start now, in years to come. There will be more housing, more furniture, more fencing, more huts and more shacks, you mark my words.'

'So what's next, Pa?' said Brad.

'Well, I've been thinking, what's the one thing that might make our young generation leave the ranch? Housing, everybody needs a home, especially as they get older, or married with families, so I propose building thirty houses on our property. I estimate thirty children at this moment in time, which could rise. I would like to build fifteen either side of the lake, beautiful views, easy access to water, as Jack, Ellis and Lucy, James are an item with plans to marry and probably have children, I would like to build them more lake houses. It will keep the families nearby, but also give them room for any expansions. In the house we have Alan, Dianna and two children, Molly, Andy and their children and of course Ching-Ching, and me and Ma. I'd always like to think a family member will always live in this building, but sometimes we all need our own space, so we have some options. Ma and I are getting older, the stairs can be an effort going up and down. We don't need this much space, we were thinking a nice well-built shack with all mod-cons near the lake would suit us fine. Molly and Alan can decide who wants to remain in the house. Fine if they both want to, if one family want to move, we would build a grand house just like this one just behind us, with room for additional housing for their children so they can always be nearby. The mound is Brad and Suzie, Steve and Helen's domain, so we will build around the mound in a circle, for all their future children's children, again keeping all the families close, which only leaves the shacks that are a feature of the ranch and have served us well, but in time will have to be replaced, updated and modernised. Also retirement homes for Ching-Ching, Mr Matsuda, Pauline, Father, and anybody else that needs one, when they are ready.'

**Brad said**

'Pa to me you've always been amazing, I've always looked up to you, you've always been my role model, my inspiration, you've instilled into all of us good principles, work effort, how to balance life, between work and pleasure. But this is truly amazing, you've managed to foresee the next one hundred years, and you're so right. If you don't move with the times you get left behind, others will step in if you don't step up. It's not just about us here in the present, it's about those coming behind us, that what we do today they will reap the rewards in the future. Our own children, our friends and work mates' children, our adoptive children. Pa your vision has gone way beyond them, to their children's children. OK we may be comfortable now, but who knows what the future holds, but we can certainly plan ahead to help any situation that may arise.'

**Steve said**

'I agree Pa, this is an amazing insight to the future. I struggle to plan what I'm doing tomorrow but I'm onboard with your ideas and plans. It makes so much sense when you explain it like you do, you can count on my whole family's support.'

'Thank you,' Pa said.

**Father said**

'This has to be the most unselfish words from a man I've ever heard,

Ma and Pa could easily take a back seat, they've already achieved so much, but no they want to inspire you, thought provoking, motivate you not just to think about yourself but others' way into the future. We're in the presence of a pure genius, a kind, considerate man.'

'Thank you,' said Pa, 'such high praise from people I love and respect, but I'm just the ideas man. You guys have all the planning and hard work to do.'

Steve said, 'It's not hard work, especially when you see why you're doing it. Nothing is more special to a man or woman than their family and friends and our community. Long may it live and prosper, here's to the future. I don't know about you, all this brain work makes me hungry, so what's next?'

'Apple pie,' said Ma.

'Yes it might help me think better, thank Ma.'

'So what's the plan of action, Pa?' said Brad.

'It's all about priorities,' said Pa. 'I'm thinking of building a workforce, I'll have a word with our friend Mr Pullman. He must have men knocking on his door everyday looking for work. I'm thinking a gang of twelve men, mainly carpenters or labourers, or men who want to work with wood, they can stay two to a shack. I don't expect you guys to do all the work, you've got enough on your plate for filling all the orders we already have. We'll place Andy in charge, he knows what needs doing. OK Andy?'

'Fine, Pa,' he said.

'Suzie, if you could take on the legal side of things, you know planning permission, paperwork et cetera. Is that OK, Suzie?'

'Fine, Pa,' Suzie said.

'Brad, Steve, vet the guys, get them settled in, start by getting all the wood we need, put two men on the sawmills. Gonzalez, can sort out water supplies, sewage, we'll rent or even buy the equipment we need. We'll leave that to Suzie to sort out Mr Pullman. I'd like our first priority to build a third, second lake side home for Jack, Lucy, James, Ellis. They've all worked so hard with fishing, chickens, the orphanage, Ellis delivering all the babies, and what with their future plans of marriage and families, this would be a major way of thanking them. I have an old friend I used to do a lot of business with. He was the one that actually told me about this ranch. He's into land, renovations, properties, developments. I'll have him scout around for arable farmland, potential woodlands, orchards, anything that might interest us. Second plan of action the retirement homes. They don't need a second floor, just comfortable lounge, kitchen, bedrooms, tomorrow Brad, Steve, Alan and myself will walk the grounds to see what we can fit in, and how many, then we'll look at another main house behind this one, then we'll build around the mound, then mark out our row of housing alongside the orphanage, then in time the shacks to come down and replace with modernised housing. Any questions?'

'Brilliant,' said Steve, 'now what shall we have for dinner?' What's next?'

'Well first of all we call a meeting, announce some of the good news, explain our long-term plan, and find out if people are interested in it, and do they want to support it, do they want to invest in it, or just carry on as they are?'

'Who wouldn't want to support it?' said Steve.

'Different folks different strokes. Some might want to stay comfortable with no risks, this planning may appeal more to the younger generation, or those with children, then there's a section, like Father, Daniel, Mr Matsuda, Ching-Ching, Pauline maybe thinking shorter team, with no children to benefit from the long-term scheme, so the fairest scheme would be to divide the two companies into two different companies, still keep our profit-share scheme, which is working very well, then the second company would have a hundred shares. This would be divided up with each person buying shares. This would give us the capital we need to start investing in our plans. People can opt in and out of the company by buying shares or selling shares. For example I would like our family to own fifty-one per cent of the shares. We would have shareholders meetings and vote on ideas, investments, projects, providing the fifty-one per cent all agree, and vote. It will always get carried as a majority. If people are not happy they can always sell their shares, which if successful should go up and up. It saves time and delays, lack of information may confuse people, we as a family will always guarantee their share prices, if anyone invests a thousand dollars, they will get back a guaranteed thousand dollars, each year they will get a percentage or the profits, plus our next project or investment will be explained, with an option to sell if they don't want to take part, or simply want their money back it's all optional.

'So this is what I'd like to do, that is with everyone's support. We have three children and Steve, seven grandchildren, which may increase, and me and Ma, so let's say for example me and Ma would be fifty-one per cent. That breaks down to thirty children who cannot vote or take any money out until they are adults, for argument's sake let's say eighteen. It would cost them nothing to buy a share, me and Ma would put in fifty thousand dollars, this is our business profits and sale of the business to the railway. That means with nothing coming out, we will have every year fifty-one thousand dollars to invest on the following year. Over time the value will increase, plus profits, anything over the fifty-one thousand will be put into the orphanage fund. One share per child, including all other children on the ranch. Maria and George's children, Kellee and Cliff, Virginia and Jimmy, Juan, and Gonzalez's children, Brad, Steve, Molly's, including any increases. This would amount to twenty thousand dollars plus the thirty-one thousand allocated to the children and orphanage fund because the children are so young, and at this stage in life don't need money, every year, the amounts should rise. The more successful, the more the profits, the bigger the investments, that leaves forty-nine thousand dollars to sell as shares, giving us a hundred thousand dollars to start our business. So basically we have forty-nine shares to sell at a thousand dollars each, if we only get twenty-five people interested then we make them two thousand dollar each. Let's take Maria and George as an example, if they buy two shares at two thousand dollars, they get yearly premiums from the shares. Their money is guaranteed, plus they get three children shares extra, and a guaranteed home and jobs for their children as house prices rise. Maria and George will already have their children's homes built for them, with no other costs involved.'

Steve said, 'I've got a headache, but I did follow what you were saying. But the more children you have, the more you benefit as a family.'

'Yes,' said Pa, 'children are our future.'

'Come on, Helen, we've got work to do.'

'My lasts example,' said Pa, 'if anybody puts their savings into a bank, they will get a small amount of interest, but if we combine our savings we will get a much greater interest rate, so everybody will be getting better interest rates from day one, meaning they all earn more immediately.'

Steve said, 'Pa with my looks and your brains we will go far (laughter). No seriously, Pa, you're a genius. Helen and I would like to invest in your scheme to start the ball rolling. That is OK isn't it, Helen?'

'Well,' she said, 'if you hadn't said it I would, it's excellent.'

Ma and Pa called a meeting at the house. He started by saying, 'I've been asked many times by many people what should they do with the profit-share money they received. As most people have already got everything they need and want right here, a lot of you feel in some way they want to give back. They don't pay for housing, food, land, the shops, you all feel you want to give back and help others. As a family we've taken on board what you have said but want to tell you you owe us nothing. We can't tell you how much of a pleasure it is to us to have you all here. We know how hard you all work, and you all deserve the rewards, but there is one thing we all could do, and that is secure the futures of our next generation and the next generation to come. We can invest in the future, if you want the generations to come to enjoy what you have, to have the opportunities you have, the security, the way of life you enjoy. It may become a tough world out there, with many changes, but what we all do today will affect the children of tomorrow. This community we have created, I want it to go on for years and years to come, for you and your children's children. By investing today we secure their tomorrows (massive clap). So I've come up with an idea I'd like to present to all.'

Pa went on to explain, 'In this great country we live in a land of opportunities and dreams, to expand and grow and prosper. It will have and need certain needs and requirements, wood for their fires, wood for their housing, furniture, sheds. We are lucky here we have an abundance of wood on our doorstep. Our policy has always been, if you fell a tree, plant ten in its place. I would like to buy land and plant as many trees as possible. Food supplies will increase the more the population grows, the more food will be needed so I would like to increase our food crops, vegetables, cattle, chickens, pigs, fish. I would like more land for fields of crops, possibly in mid-America, so it will be more easily accessible for the whole of America. What with the railways constantly expanding, there will be no limit or destination that we cannot reach. Now for some of these projects there is no quick or short term rewards, this is planning for the future. It's like planting seeds, watching them grow, but the next generation will reap the rewards and hopefully they also will plant and nurture for their next generation (clap). I also have short term plans up by the lake. I would like to build retirement homes for Ma and me, Pauline, Mr Matsuda, Ching-Ching, Father for their senior years, a beautiful setting, still part of the community, but never having to worry about their future lives, help always at hand. Helen, Ellis always there for them. Opposite on the other side will be a row of houses for your future families, each couple will have a family house for them or for their children, which they can pass on to. I would like to build, two more lake chalets one for Jack and Ellis, and one for Lucy and James, for their futures and children, at the back or this house will be either two houses, one for Andy and Molly and their children, and one for Dianna, Alan and their family. Cliff and Kellee are happy where they are but I want to extend their home, or even build a new one on their site for their family. Eventually the old shacks will come down and more housing will be built for our children in the orphanage. Now I know what you're thinking, that's a lot of work, but I'd like to hire a gang of carpenters living in the shacks but completing the building work.

'Andy, Brad, Steve, Alan will be supervising the work. We will have a workforce to take the heavy load, the same with planting. We will use local people. As you know more and more ships are arriving every day with people, families, with no homes, jobs, food, clothing. We can help them, with all of these things they need. In return we will increase our productivity, the company will grow. Have I still got your interest?'

They all stood and clapped and cheered.

'OK,' Pa said. 'I'll continue, this is how it will work, we will all invest in the company, it will be divided up into one hundred shares, Ma and me will put in fifty-one thousand dollar's owning fifty-one per cent of the company. The main shareholder, it's not that we want more profit than anybody else, we actually will not be taking out any money for ourselves. It means that each year fifty-one thousand dollars will be available every year for our new projects. We won't have to generate more money each year. It will already be there, that leaves forty-nine per cent or forty-nine thousand dollars to generate as shares. If you want to you can take this out yearly, or let it grow with the company as the share prices increase. For example if you put one thousand dollars in a bank, you will get an interest rate, but if you put our money together, we will get a much higher investment rate so you are earning more money and interest from in this scheme day one. Please put your hand up if you are interested in this scheme.'

Every hand in the room went up, clapped, cheers.

'Good, thank you,' said Pa, 'so here's how it's divided up. Now remember you can withdraw your stake at any time, your money is guaranteed. But if possible, if you could not touch it for a full year, you will already have increased your share money, so buying four shares Brad, Suzie and Jimmy, Virginia, Alan, Dianna and Molly, Andy and Helen, Steve and Kellee, Cliff, Maria, George two shares, Mr Matsuda, Ching-Ching, Jack, Ellis, Luck, James and Julie, Juan, Julia, Gonzalez, Ken, Pauline, Daniel, and Father, which adds up to forty-eight shares, I would like to offer this one share to Mr Pullman, for all the amazing work and help he has given us. Suzie has kindly offered to do all the paperwork required and Mr Matsuda will be taking care of all banking arrangements needed.

'So to summarise,' said Pa, 'you now all own part of this ranch, not just for you, but for your future generations and generations to come.' Massive standing ovation and clapping and cheering.

Brad stood up. 'Pa,' he said, 'you've always been an amazing father to me, Alan and Molly, but to give your life savings, your land, your ideas and foresight has been an experience none of us will ever forget. Your generosity, kindness, motivation, a future for all these people here and their families is beyond belief, and on behalf of everybody here an amazing thank you.' Massive cheering, clapping. 'If I end up only half the man you are, I will be a very happy person (big clap). It's been amazing how we've all come together, how we've all gelled together, how we've all become one big happy family. Now we have a future to look forward to, our children will be safe, secure, with real potential in their futures, and always loved and helped by this amazing community, I give you Ma and Pa, and to the future.' They all stood, clapped, cheered and hugged each other.

Mr Matsuda shouted, 'Now all we need is your money.' Big laughter then booing.

Father stood up. 'Quiet please,' he said, 'first of all there are so many people I need to thank. Brad, Steve, when you started home on your journey, collecting all the sheep (laughter) there had been a lot of hard time and misfortunes with the people. You picked them up and gave them hope, your family welcomed them in with open arms, love, support, a roof over their heads, food on their plates, jobs, an income, and now a future for them and their children. Every person here has worked so hard, and achieved so much. Yes we've had our ups and downs, losing Baby Virginia and Bill, but we've created a strong community here with love and support. We've given lots of children a home, food, education, a chance in life. It can be a hard life out there but we've all built something special here, so thank you to everyone, thank you to this incredible family, and Steve and Suzie, long may it continue, now please join me in prayers, and let's also thank the Lord.'

They had a lovely meeting with Mr Pullman. He was straight on board with the share scheme, but insisted he purchase his share, but thanked them for the gesture. He gave them an update on the orphanage purchase. They had acquired ten buildings to date, renovations were taking place at this very moment. The first orphanage had been completely redone and was ready for its first instalment of children. All the homes were in place. It had the full backing of the railway, which they used for advertising and promotions.

They spoke about the workforce they needed for the ranch. Mr Pullman said he had the prefect candidates for the jobs. Some men were getting near to retirement age, the strain of the job, the demands of the job, forever on the move, no families, these men would love a home, a job they could take their time over and have pride in. 'A good community like yours, having beautiful surroundings, a place to call home, also there are a few younger men that are getting a bit bullied. They are good workers, trying to make their way in the world, but would be much better suited to your way of life.'

'I also would like to put my children into your care. They love the ranch, friends they've got to know, education is very good, with variety, and one-to-one teaching. All of their lives they've been moved from pillar to post because of my job, not putting down roots or sustaining friendships. This will be an excellent move for them, also for my wife and I, I can make sure every weekend we visit, so we can spend more time with the children. My wife also likes the idea of living there, she would like to help out at the orphanage, and we both agree that when I eventually retire, this is where we would like to live, amongst your amazing community, spending our last years at the ranch, watching our children grow, so I'd like to purchase one of those new houses you mentioned.'

'We would love to have you here, and your wife and children, but you don't need to purchase a home it's already yours. We've just got to build it.'

It was a busy time at the ranch, the new men arrived and fitted in very well. They had a tour of the ranch and were very impressed. Pa said if they worked hard, there would always be a home for them all on the ranch. Each day wagons and wagons turned up loaded with all sorts of things sent from Mr Pullman. Wagons of wood, doors, frames, table chairs, cutlery, plates. A lot was recycled from the old orphanages. He'd put notes on them, for example, 'for the houses', 'could you keep this one for my house' (a piece of antique furniture). There was even an old chandelier, with 'mine' on. Mr Pullman informed the ranch that acres and acres of land had been purchased in mid-America to grow crops, being Pa's idea. He would get a percentage of the profits every year, to go into the share scheme.

Mr Pullman wrote 'don't forget my one share'. Already the ranch was making a profit, plus the interest from the bank. The railway also likes his idea on replanting. As they were using a lot of wood for their sleepers, it would be wrong to take it all and leave nothing for the future generations, so they also purchased a lot of land, just to grow trees on, also it helped prevent pollution, the trees naturally absorbing carbon dioxide and replacing it with oxygen. They would be sending a substantial amount yearly as a bonus payment, more profit for the ranch and another yearly income, and for helping out their senior workforce, who had served the railways well in their time. They would like to pay their wages for the next five years, then they would go onto a pension scheme. As Mr Pullman said, they like to look after their own. All contracts for food deliveries were signed, along with the local farmers and community all paid for in advance. As agreed the orphanage payment was paid in full and in advance.

Brad said to Pa, 'Well old man, you've done it. You've started an amazing legacy. You'll never be forgotten.'

'I couldn't have done it without you and my family, and Steve and the others. Now all you've got to do is keep it all going, and Ma said let's have some more babies.'

'I promise you that, Pa and Ma, God willing.'

Jack, Ellis, Lucy, James were so excited watching the foundations of their new homes being built. Later everybody was excited for them, looking forward to their forthcoming marriages, and living next door to their best friends and family. Pa said, 'It won't be long before we see babies there, they deserve it.' Brenda and Too became best friends, and asked could they live together in Lucy and Jack's lake shack. Nobody objected. The girls thought they were getting a bit old to be around the children any more, although they went there every day to help out, and their meals. Gonzalez was brilliant at sorting out water supplies and sewage. Mr Pullman made sure all generators needed were supplied, his children moved in along with his wife, and to his word every weekend he would turn up and spend time with his family. He kept an eye on all developments, anything the ranch needed would soon turn up a few days later. Lots and lots of baby new trees would turn up. Everybody got involved in planting them, even the children. Andy made little plaques, which the children placed in front of the tree, so they could watch their trees grow, and in years to come they could revisit and see how much the tree had grown. Part of their weekly activity was to water the plants.

Mrs Pullman was a great help at the orphanage. She was brilliant with the children. They all loved her. It also helped Pauline to take it a bit faster, Pauline befriended two of the workmen, Ted and Bob. They would sit together in the evenings, swap stories of their lives. Both men were very entertaining, chatty and full of fun, how she wished Bill was still here to enjoy this together. She knew Bill would have got on with Ted and Bob very well. Her and Ken still went every day to the church and his grave.

So that was it really. Business continued to grow, and so did all of the children, the new buildings came along bit by bit, the team had finished Kellee and Cliff's new extension, Suzie and Mr Matsuda sorted out banking and the share certificates.

Ma, Pa, Brad, Steve and Ching-Ching were just sitting around one day.

Ma said, 'Can you believe what we've all achieved here? We started with a house, an orchard, barns, corral, vegetable patch, it was just a sleepy old outback, not connected to anything or anyone. There was me and Pa, Alan, Dianna, and Ching-Ching. That was it, no excitement, no growth, no laughter, no parties no rowing competitions, no music, no barbecues, no church, no school, no Bradville. A few chickens, pigs, horses, cattle. First Brad came home bringing with him Steve and rest of the gang, a father, a carpenter, a blacksmith, a cowboy, fisherman, chefs, cooks, teachers, artist, intellectuals like Suzie, and Mr Pullman and family, bankers, clothesmakers, knitting, sewing, a clinic with nurses, shops selling wares, an orphanage, and marriages, babies, christening, and a lot of love. You've all helped make this place what it is, home, we could not have assembled a finer group of people if we tried.'

Pa said, 'You're right, Ma. If I could dream this is what I would have dreamed for the ranch for my family, my grandsons and granddaughter. When you returned home, Brad, you brought life with you, and an amazing group of people, that also call this home and their families, I would love to be able to come back here in say fifty years or one hundred years' time, to see what happens to the ranch.'

Steve said, 'Ching-Ching will probably still be here.' Big laughter.

'So it will be your responsibility, make good decisions, keep growing, think of the future not just for yourselves, but for your family's families, and everyone else here. I know it's a big responsibility but you two together are the perfect team to make it happen and when you are old and grey like me and Ma are ...'

'Speak for yourself,' said Ma.

'You've both got good, clever women to support you, just like I had Ma. And the two boys Bradley and Stevie, teach them everything you've learned so they can carry on after you.'

'Any pie left?' said Steve.

# Chapter 10

## Life and Death on the Ranch

The first main event of the year was Ellis to Jack, Lucy to James, Kitty to Ken spring wedding. Kitty and Ken were going to wait a little longer, but didn't want any fuss, so it was easier to add to the other wedding and let them steal the limelight. Both Kitty and Ken were happy to be in the background, although Pauline made a massive fuss of them.

The brides all looked so beautiful, the grooms handsome. Mr Matsuda and Ching-Ching, decorated the buggies, all the children and guests lined the pathway to the church, Father loved doing weddings and christenings. Daniel was there sketching away, Graham gave his daughter away, so pleased Kitty had joined the ranch, had a job she loved, had met Ken who he liked a lot, and got married. Bring on the grandchildren, he thought. Pauline drove them down to the church and acted like a best man. She thought how proud Bill would have been of Ken, his son, and his lovely bride Kitty. Helen gave Ellis away. She was so proud of her, following in her mum's foot steps as a nurse, helping to deliver all of the babies including her own. Now she's getting married to a man she loves, has a new home to move into and hopefully grandchildren to follow. Steve gave Lucy away. Brad was best man to Jack and James. Brad was sad their biological dads were not here to see their sons and daughters get married.

The children did not miss out as so much fuss was made of them all on the day, reception was laid on for them all at the house, lots of food, music. As it got late in the evening, people started to disappear, Lucy, Ellis, James, Jack were hugging and thanking everyone.

Ma said, 'And finally you can move into your new homes.' Big cheer. Ken and Kitty were just happy to go back to the orphanage with Pauline.

The ranch kept up with all the traditions they had established, the children from the orphanage had their annual birthday party. All the new babies had their first birthdays, there were the first year anniversaries, the rowing races became a yearly event. Steve finally won a race, they had a log chopping competition, one to re-stock the pile, but it was a great way to all bond together. Ken and George were miles ahead of everybody, with Ken coming out as the winner, Kitty and Pauline were so proud of him.

The children and adults had a sports day: three-legged race, egg and spoon race, treasure hunt, pass the parcel and musical chairs.

A few more children joined the ranch, sent by Mr Pullman, who now everybody called Paul. Some children in particular stood out, a little Chinese boy named Chang which Ching-Ching took to straight away. He took him under his wing, helped him with his English and sums, read books to him, showed him how to grind flour. It was like the son he never had, he even added Chang to his name so they had Ching-Ching and Chang-Chang, almost the same happened to Mr Matsuda. Two Japanese children arrived at the orphanage, they had an a American mother but a Japanese father. They were quite bullied by the step father, their mother had to give them up or lose her marriage. She thought they would be better off out of a violent house. She never visited them, father's whereabouts unknown, the boy was given an American name, after his mother's father Matt. The little girl was named Sue. So Mr Matsuda now he took care of Matt and Sue. He taught them all about sums, percentages, banking, interests, invoice, tax etc. Mr Matsuda and Ching-Ching said this is more than a coincidence, Mr Pullman, had particularly selected these children knowing how much they would be loved, and how much they would mean to the two men. Like a reward, he's also given us the next generation to take over from us, and everything we own or have can be left to these children. It's a miracle, both agreed.

The first year's trading accounts had come in and been calculated by Mr Matsuda and Suzie. They called a meeting of everyone. Mr Matsuda stood up. 'First good news,' he said, 'profit, profit, profit.' Big cheer and clapping. 'What with things going in and things going out, the annual interest from the bank, the railways, paying the orphanage money up front, the commission on the crops and trees, plus our profits from all of your hard work, cattle, chickens, eggs, fish, crops and vegetables, railway contracts for supplies, we have increased our initial investments by fifty per cent. Meaning that if we have another good year next year, we will all have doubled our initial investments.' Standing ovation, cheering, clapping.

Pa stood up. 'Thank you Mr Matsuda and Suzie for all your efforts in putting this all together for us. People we have a growing industry, and reputation built on quality, reliability, and we're on course to double our investments within two years! I congratulate you all.' Big clapping. 'Which means we still have 51,000 dollars to invest in this year, as we don't have so much outgoings this year. We still have your 49,000 dollars, plus our annual 50,000 dollars profit, and the additional, 33,000 dollars for this year, that adds up to a grand total next year of 183,000 dollars. If we only spend 33,000 dollars over the next period, next year we will have 150,000 dollars in our bank account. Amazing everybody, well done.' Lots of clapping and cheering. 'Now Suzie has drawn up the paperwork, you all have an option: you can withdraw your initial stake money, which has now doubled, you can leave your money where it is and watch it grow, or you can sell shares, or like myself and Ma, we are going to write our wills out: twenty-five per cent to Brad, Alan, Molly and Steve, and they in turn can write their wills out for their own families, and you all in turn can write out your wills for your own families. Saying what you want to do with your share of the money.' Steve and Helen were blown away with Ma and Pa including them as their own family.

'You deserve it,' said Ma, Pa, Brad, Alan and Molly. 'You are family.'

Cliff asked, 'What if we have one child now, but at a later date we have another child?'

'That's OK,' said Suzie, 'just put on the form "all monies, property and processions to be shared equally among my family".'

'Thank you,' said Cliff.

Brad, Alan, Molly, Steve, George, Jack, James, Juan, Gonzalez, Ken, Jimmy, all did the same, Pauline left everything to Ken, Mr Matsuda everything to Matt and Sue, and Ching-Ching to Chang-Chang, Daniel assigned half to the school fund and half to the orphanage, Father assigned half to the upkeep of the church and half to the orphanage.

Over the coming years all the retirement homes were finished with outdoor seating areas, eight in total, over a period of time, people moved in. This was Pa's plan and vision of the future, all subject to change, he also planned to remove the shack's and have new home's built in there place, one shack would not be removed to remind everybody where they all started from, it would be a museum, built with all little mementos, and Daniel's sketches of the group also the canteen, bell, way house and clinic would be untouched. The clinic would have sketches and names one for every baby born here.

Pa's vision extended way beyond the ranch. His intention was to purchase more land, down by the corral, more grazing land, a massive chicken farm, pig pens, increase the sheep. He'd also spoken to Graham. Kitty's father, to purchase the land between the two ranches, half would be to increase their crop growing capabilities, half would be for rental, to new homesteaders. People who wanted to work the land, with families a new generation to the area, expanding their capabilities. He told all the

Daniel ☐

Mr Matsuda ☐

Ching Ching ☐

Father ☐ Alan Sarah

Ma and Pa ☐ Molly Andy

Bob ☐ Brad Suzie

Pauline ☐ Steve Helen

Ted ☐

Guest Spare ☐

George/Free ☐

Robert/Joe ☐

Brandon/Peter ☐

Johnny/Michael ☐

Theresa/Cindy ☐

Virginia/Mary Jimmy/Ginny ☐ Mary, Ginny

Gonzalez, Julia & Kids ☐ Kids

Juan, Julie & Kids ☐ Kids

Maria, George & Kids ☐ Kids

Ken, Kitty ☐ Katy

Mr Pullman & Family ☐

Play Area | Tree House

ORPHANAGE

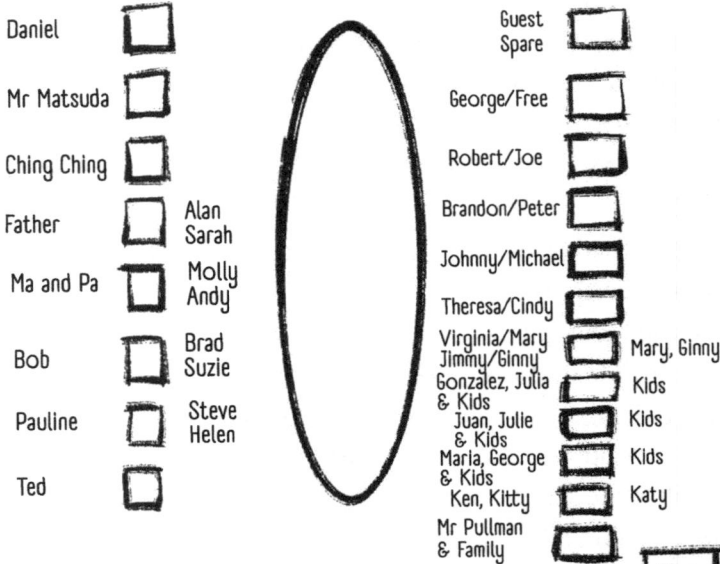

family, 'We must keep expanding, growing, investing, multiplying, if we fail to plan, we plan to fail, what we've started here must continue to grow and expand. If you stay comfortable, others will seize the opportunities and we will be left in their dust. Our children's children must have a future to look forward to, we owe it to them to carry on being successful, and not sit back and be complacent, contented, lazy with no foresight, look at our structure at this moment in time.'

'The older generation Father, Pauline, Mr Matsuda, Ching-Ching, Bob, Ted. Next the young blood I call it, the backbone of the ranch, Brad, Alan, Molly, Steve, Jimmy, Ken, Juan, Gonzalez, Maria, Kellee, Suzie, Dianna, Andy, Helen, Virginia, Kitty, Julie, Julia, George, Cliff followed by Daniel, Jack Ellis, James-Lucy, Brenda, Too, Paul, Christopher. Then we have the children, our replacement work force, George, Free, Robert, Joe, Brandon, Peter, Johnny, Michael, Theresa, Cindy, Mary, plus all of Mr

Pullman's orphans. Then we have the babies, Bradley, Stevie, Janet, Ann, Mandy, Ginny, Tyler, Jay, Jay, Julian, plus all those not born yet! Look at the relationships that will develop. We will have a wonderful balance of boy, girl, mixture, there's bound to be a closeness, even love developing. That's why we must develop and expand for these futures. That's why eventually the shacks will come down for their future housing and homes, the mound with homes one and two will be come three, four, five, six, seven, eight, the big house will be for baby Ma and Pa. Andy and Molly, Dianna and Alan, to retirement homes. Molly and Andy's family will occupy the two new homes. Any questions?' said Pa.

Steve said, 'So you Ma and Pa are the acorns, and we are the roots of the big oak tree?'

'Sort of,' said Pa, 'think of it as a family tree. In years to come, future generations will be able to trace their roots back to the very beginning.'

Steve said, 'What about people like Father and Daniel?'

'They will live on through us, Daniel's drawings and words will give an insight into our world, our way of living, what we did, what we achieved, our sacrifices, losses, achievements, all in picture form. As for Father, he will never be forgotten, the sketch of Father Daniel did which is hanging in the church will be there for a very long time. When your children ask: who married you? Father. Who christened me? Father. Who taught me the way of the Lord? Who taught me how to read and write? You will always remember him, he will be in our hearts and souls forever.'

'How lovely,' they all said.

'Look what a success the orphanage has been, every child has been a tremendous addition to our families, the children are so happy and contented, with many new skills and hobbies already learned. They will need all of our love and support for the future, each child already has a selected career path, a job waiting for them, houses already marked out for them, an amazing community around them, love, activities, so many opportunities for them all. Once the children have grown and moved out to their homes, we must refill the orphanage, and keep bring in new blood, new personalities, new ideas, imagination, these building blocks are the future of the ranch, without new growth, all we have worked for will shrivel and die, we must not let that happen. The seeds have been sown. It's up to your generation, to nurture and grow our future. Me and Ma are passing the baton over to you guys, the future of everyone is in your hands, and we know you are made of the right stuff and ambition to succeed.'

'I thought birds were meant to succeed (suck seed),' said Steve. Everybody roared with laughter.

Ma and Pa said together, 'Now is as good a time as any, ever since the marriages and our grandchildren being born, and our additional grandchildren being added me and Pa have been secretly plotting and planning a surprise for you all, with the help of Daniel and Pa's old jeweller friend. We have been working on something we think and hope you like. It will always remind you of us. What an amazing family we have been, so many good memories, so much happiness so much love, me and Pa, want you to know how proud of you we are, how much we love you. We know we can't live forever, so we want to give you a little something to hold when we've gone, and you want to talk to us for advice, guidance or a general chit-chat, just hold it in your hand, talk and we will hear you. Even if you just want to say goodnight we will hear you.'

The room was already in floods of tears, but everybody understood why they were saying this now. They produced ten gold pocket watches and ten gold necklaces, each pocket watch was engraved to 'whoever, we love you, Ma and Pa', inside was a sketch done by Daniel of Ma and Pa one side, and a sketch of each of their families. The necklaces had 'Love you' one side and 'Ma and Pa' on the other side. When you opened it, again you had a tiny sketch of Ma one side, and Pa the other. Pa said, 'There's one for every member of our family, including Steve, Suzie, and

Steve and extra ones for any new additions.' Tears, hugs and kisses flowed.

Steve said, 'Just to break up the emotion and tension in the room, do I get a necklace or a watch?' It worked. Everybody exploded with laughter.

Pa said, 'It's going to take a little more time, but every person on the ranch will receive a pocket watch, and necklaces, and spares will be made for any additional babies, and last but not least, just in case you have a rainy day or get into any trouble and need quick money, we've left with the bank four gold bars, one for each of our family including and Steve. Family gold can only go up in price, considering how hard it is to find it, be happy and multiply,' said Pa.

'We love you all,' said Ma.

Ma and Pa did eventually move into the retirement homes. They had Father, Ching-Ching, Mr Matsuda, Daniel, Pauline, Ted and Bob for neighbours, they were all excellent company, they would all sit out each night around the tables, talk about the old days and how the world was changing. Jokes, stories, people would come and join them, Brad and his family, Steve and his family, Alan and his family, Mr and Mrs Pullman, George and family, Clara and family, Jimmy and family. He would play lovely relaxing melodies, and sometimes upbeat they all could get up and dance to. It was a lovely atmosphere. They star gazed, had snacks, cool drinks.

Ma and Pa had ten lovely, relaxing, but enjoyable years in the retirement home, they said to each other how lucky they had been in life, with a good family and friends, a thriving business, a good future for everyone. They felt as though they'd given everyone a helping hand in life, a start, and hoped everyone would be as happy in life as they had been.

'I love you, Ma.'

'I love you more,' and they kissed. Ma and Pa lived well into their eighties. Ma passed away first, the doctor was sent for. Before he even arrived Pa, passed away. They say Pa died of a broken heart, he just couldn't live on without his devoted loving wife. The whole ranch was shattered by the sad news. There wasn't a dry eye anywhere. They all owed them so much, giving up their homes, land, making such a success and future for everyone. Andy made a special coffin for them so they could be together forever lying in one coffin, Father coupled their hands together for eternity, George made an amazing metal cross for them, it simple said 'Ma and Pa together forever, from a small a corn grows a oak tree'. Brad, Molly, Alan, Steve and their families were shattered and in mourning for years to come, how would they cope without their beloved Ma and Pa?

Father said, 'Close your eyes, can you still see them, at the house, around the table they haven't left you, they will always be in your heart's and mind's if you want to talk to them hold the watch or necklace they will here you they were truly wonderful people, God bless them and may they rest in peace.'

Ma and Pa's funeral was such a sad day for everyone. Farmers, town folk, old friends all came, it was impossible for everyone to get into the church. Father said it just shows how much they were loved and people wanted to pay their last respects to them. Those that could speak got up on the pulpit, they either read psalms from the Bible, or gave a personal account of their memories of Ma and Pa. Brad, Alan, Molly and Steve's words were so moving, they kept to their word and every night they said goodnight Ma and Pa, or sometimes just held the pocket watches or necklace and just talked to them as though they were still there, Steve was also torn apart with grief.

'In honour of Ma I shall never eat another piece of apple pie for the rest of my life.'

'Oh yes you will,' said Molly, 'Ma insisted we keep making her apple pies and you must eat it to keep your strength up. Plus we need more babies. Me, Janet and Ann were taught by Ma to her own recipe exactly how to make the perfect pie, to make sure you never run out.'

Steve couldn't see through the tears in his eyes. 'Thank you,' he said, 'I miss Ma and Pa so much.'

Ching-Ching was devastated. 'I'd never had a friend like him, he never judged me, he was a true gentleman, honest, loyal, upstanding, a pillar of the society, he took me into his home, where others turned their backs on me, he made me part of his family. I'll never forget the hospitality and friendship Ma and Pa showed to me. I have a gold pocket watch that I will pass onto Chang-Chang and tell him all about Ma and Pa. Their memories will live on forever.'

Daniel had placed in the church an exact copy of the painting in the house of Ma and Pa. Father put forward an idea of a statue of Ma and Pa holding hands at the entrance to the ranch, everybody thought it was an excellent idea.

'I don't think the ranch will ever be the same again,' said Brad, 'but Ma and Pa exceeded all their goals in life, business wise, grandchildren, a legacy, a dynasty that will never be surpassed, now we are all left to make sure all of their dreams will be fulfilled, and we won't let you down Ma and Pa, we all love you so much, and thank you for everything.'

Pauline, Bob, Ted, Mr Matsuda, Ching-Ching and Father all lived well into their seventies. Brad summarised it so well, it was like the changing of the old guard, their senior citizens had passed, the new generations were coming through to take their places. Ching-Ching again was devastated when his best friend Mr Matsuda passed. He was allowed to let off fireworks in his honour.

Brad and Steve said, 'One day, buddy, we will know exactly how Ching-Ching feels when one of us goes first.'

'Don't,' said Steve, 'I can't bear the thought of it.'

Ken had how lost his beloved father and mother, when they did have children one was named Billy Graham, and the girl Paula.

Matt and Sue really missed their father Mr Matsuda but continue in his role at the ranch, Father was the last to be buried, his only wish was to be around to bury his dearest family members and friends. He achieved all of this. Christopher, Mr Pullman's son had been taught everything by Father, and continued in his role as father of the ranch and church. Daniel put on the church walls a sketch of each that had passed, Pauline, Mr Matsuda, Ching-Ching, Bob, Ted, and Father. Placed in the coffin with him was the Bible he purchased when the church first opened, like Pa always said, nobody can live forever, it's the way of life, you're born, you pay taxes, then you must die, so that others can take your place.

Brad said, 'But why does it hurt so much? It's like somebody has reached inside my body and pulled my heart out.'

'It's the circle of life,' said Steve, 'that's why when you can enjoy life to the full. Live every day as though it was your last, as one day it will be, and make sure all those around you and close to you, tell them how much you love them daily.'

Brad said, 'Have I ever told you I love you buddy? You show me love everybody, and I hope you know how much I love you and your family.' They hugged together.

The ranch had amazing growth years, everything Pa had set up flourished. The home traders flocked to the area, which meant trade went up, supplies, meat, poultry, those that were just getting started, deals were struck where they couldn't afford rent to start with, their rents were suspended, until there crops matured. Some would pay with their products, crops, loans were agreed to help them get started, tools were rented, seeds, wood, food, could all be put on a rental basis, repaid over a period of time, which increased the ranch's output. There was always a great demand for food and crops, cattle, sharp, chickens, wood, clothing, everything that could be generated had a price, with an added mark-up price which always gave a profit, over the years to come the rentals started to be paid back with interest.

As the orphanage children grew, they selected their own career path. Ching-Ching taught Chang-Chang everything he knew about the flour mill, so much so that Ching-Ching did retire to the retirement home, and Chang-Chang carried on the good work for years to come.

Matt and Sue were very busy keeping good book work on all rentals, producing yearly accounts on the business. Mr Matsuda instilled in them, write everything down, that way you never forget anything.

Maria and George went on to have another set of twins, this time a boy and a girl. Maria put her foot down. 'The boy,' she said, 'will be called George Blacksmith, after his father so that your name will live on through your children. The girl will be called Georgia, part George part Maria.'

'Yes dear,' said George. Boy George from the orphanage, took an interest in the furnace and metal work. They were kept busy, making tools, hoes, shoes, hammers, sickles, chains. As boy George grew, and George's own sons became apprentices, George could finally ease back a bit. They took one of the new homes near the lake, which they made a sign for and hung outside the front door. It simply said 'Hallelujah!' The girls continued with the flower stall.

Eventually Maria and George moved to one of the retirement homes, they left the children to it. George said at times it was a mad house. They were far enough away for peace and quiet, but near enough to keep an eye on them all. Every day Maria and George thanked the Lord, Brad, Steve, Helen, and counted their blessings. Boy George and Free took one of the houses opposite.

Virginia and Jimmy took one of the new houses. Mary from the orphanage worked alongside Virginia in the clothes making, sewing, repairs as baby Ginny grew she also got involved in dress making. Ginny saw Mary as her elder sister, so Mary moved into the family home, eventually Virginia and Jimmy moved into the retirement home, and Mary and Ginny stayed in the house they also adopted a boy named Jim from the orphanage who had the love of music in him. Jimmy loved teaching him all the knew about music and instruments.

Juan and Julia also took a new house. Too lived with Brenda but visited often, Free moved in with boy George, which just left Jay Jay at home. Moving in next door was Julie and Gonzalez, and baby Juan. They also had another baby a girl named Fortuna. They all continued to help out at the orphanage and carried on doing the cooking for those who needed it. Kellee and Cliff had lots of help, Robert and Joe from the orphanage became cow hands. As they got older they shared one of the new houses, Kellee and Cliff went on to have two more children, a boy named Clifton after Cliff and a girl named Kelsey after Kellee. They never moved out of the corral house. After their deaths the children took over the running of the cattle and horse helped by Robert and Joe.

Kitty and Ken had three children. A girl named Paula after Pauline and two boys, one called Billy after Bill, the other named Graham after Kitty's father. They carried on at the orphanage, with help from Theresa and Cindy, who also lived together in one of the new houses near the lake.

Ellis and Jack carried on with the fishing and nursing, Ellis delivered a lot more children over the years to come. Helen was so proud of her, they went on to have three children of their own. The first born was a boy they named Jackson after Jack his son, then a girl named Jessie, being part J for Jack and Essie for Ellis. Their last child a girl they named Helen after Ellis's mum, Helen was cheered., They carried on helping everybody out, including at the orphanage, then passing their skills on to their children. Jackson into fishing, Jessie and Helen into nursing.

Living next door were James and Lucy, they had three children, the first boy born was named after James and Wayne, the second a boy named Jamie after James, then a little girl they nearly lost at birth. Thanks to the quick thinking of Ellis and Helen the baby's life was saved. They named her Lucky, which was part of what she went through at birth, but also was part of Lucy with a K added. They also carried on helping where it was needed, and with the orphanage, the children, pigs, sheep, the boys followed in their dad's footsteps, and always loved collecting eggs, especially Lucky.

Peter from the orphanage had the gift of drawing and writing. Peter and Daniel spent many a day writing, drawing, teaching all the children their A, B, C, one, two, three. Brandon from the orphanage got into photography, new inventions and better equipment was being invented all the time. He learned how to take photos, how to develop photos. He was encouraged by everybody to get involved. They even set up a fund to buy the best equipment available and to keep buying anything new available. Everybody loved to have their photographs taken, it would capture everything for the future, Brandon and Peter moved into one of the new homes on the lake together. It was full of drawings and photos all over the walls.

Mr Pullman, his wife and children, were so happy with their decision to move to the ranch, they couldn't think of a better place to be, a beautiful house, his wife loved working at the orphanage with the children, they had good neighbours, good friends, a wonderful environment. The children were the happiest they'd ever been. Young Paul wanted to follow his dad into the railways, which pleased Paul senior immensely, he could pass all his knowledge onto his son. He wanted him to work hard and climb the ladder of success, and eventually take over from him, he'd make sure his name was dropped in to the right people, for any forthcoming promotions. He would introduce him to all of his contacts he'd made over the years, over the next ten years father and son made a massive impression on the powers that be. The railway expanded at an incredible rate, zig-zagging across the states, one of the last things he did was to extend the ranch and surrounding area contracts well into the future. 'Well,' he said, 'I've got to look after my one share.' And with Paul Jr next to take over would also ensure the ranch was never overlooked, and guaranteed future contracts. His elder son he was also so proud of, he'd found the one thing in life that meant so much to him, his calling to God, to have Father to guide him and show him the ropes Christopher found his true vocation, to have his own church, congregation, weddings, christening, and unfortunately funerals was such a blessing and he'd always be near his mum and dad. The boys stayed in the family home. Paul would come home whenever his job allowed him to, Christopher would one day take over the family home as his parents got older and eventually moved into one or the retirement homes. Father watched Christopher grow as a father, becoming very popular with everyone. Father said well it's all down to his name he's already got Christ in him, Christopher. Father also knew that one day Christopher would be the father that one day would attend to his own funeral and many others to follow.

Alan and Dianna were so happy with their family life, they loved the way their children were called little Ma, and little Pa. They had so many children to play with, all their cousins, new babies, the future looked so rosy. They eventually moved back into Ma and Pa's house, finally, Alan and Dianna occupied one of the retirement home, which allowed little Ma and Pa to grow up find their sweethearts, marry them, move them in and start some more little mas and pas. Both children grew up nurturing plants of all sorts, cabbage, carrots, runner beans, tomatoes, potatoes, lettuce, spring onions, a whole multitude of different varieties. As they grew older, Brenda and Too helped out. Mandy, Janet and Ann, also helped, at planting time most of the ranch turned out to help, Andy and George invented a system rather than carry the water to the plants you simply filled a water tank. He had pipes with holes in, and taps to turn off and on depending what area needed watering. It made the watering job so much easier. Molly, Janet, Ann, Mandy, little Ma all loved going to Virginia's, doing dress making, knitting, sewing, designing clothes, Molly and Andy occupied the two new houses at the back. They all lived in one, but the second one would be for the girls' futures. Whoever got married first would move into that one. Eventually Andy and Molly moved into a retirement home. The one Ma and Pa lived in. She loved the sense of Ma and Pa's spirits around her, when the girls went to Virginia's for the sewing, Andy started a wood sculpture glasses. It was very popular, most of the men got involved, it got them out of the house and some male company, jokes and laughter. Andy had them working on his new idea, of a wooden carved statue, of Ma, Pa, Alan, Molly, Brad, Steve, it would be done in sections, one person at a time, but when linked together showed that each person had their arms linked and around each other. That way Andy could pin them together from each and nobody would notice.

When it was finished, it was an amazing piece of artwork. They'd captured their minor details, in their faces, in their hair, eyes, expressions, their heart, souls and smiles. To save time Virginia and the ladies said, rather than sculpturing their bodies, legs and arms, just do the heads, neck, and hands although we could make clothes for the hands. Yes and we can get wigs for their hair colouring, and original clothes that each one had worn.

Steve said it seemed a bit spooky, but gave an old pair of boots he used to wear, a pair of denim jeans and a top. Brad, Alan, Molly did the same, they even found Ma and Pa's best dress suits, the ones in the sketch that Daniel did, Andy and the group made a structure for all the dummies to stand in. You entered by a door to the left and exited through the door to the right. Once the dummies were in place, the ladies dressed the dummies, put on makeup, jewellery, rings. Ma was left holding a wooden apple pie, which Steve thought was an excellent idea, once dressed than Andy pinned the hands to the next body. It looked amazing, you could visit any time, to talk to whoever, and with its weather-proof shelter should survive for years. It had a simple sign (The Family). It was visited so often by everybody. Flowers were left on anniversary dates, birthdays, Christmas, hand-written notes were left in pockets later when all family members had passed. It became like a shrine, where people visited, even kissed the dummies, or just talked to them like they were still here. This family plus Steve started this whole adventure, and nobody ever forgot who they were, what they all meant to them, how they developed a community, a company, profits, futures, new generations, and everybody knew none of this would have been possible without this family, none of this would have existed without this family, none of the marriages, children, food, housing, wealth, health, without this family.

One night sitting outside their houses were Brad, Suzie, Steve, Helen. The children were playing or sleeping, Brad and Suzie's family had increased to another five children. The first Bradley, followed by Steven, Suzanne, Molly and finally Alan. Steve and Helen's family increased by four more children. First there was Stevie, followed by Brad, Suzie, and finally Helena. Brad would always rub it in that he was more of a man than Steve, as he'd had five children to his four. Steve would remind him that Helen already had two other children, Ellis and James, so technically he had won, plus he told Brad that he was already a grandparent.

'Let's call it a draw,' Brad said.

'OK,' said Steve, 'but I still won. Do you think any of our children will marry each other?'

Brad said, 'I don't know, but I hope they all inherit my good looks and brains.'

Steve smiled. 'If they like apple pie, they're more me than you.'

'But seriously, buddy,' said Brad, 'we've all been on such a journey, just look around you, at the lives that have come alive all around us. I think we have fulfilled Ma and Pa's expectations, their dreams their desires, their hopes, and the next generation and generation after that. It's been awesome, they all agreed. Just look at the mound with our houses and below our next generation of houses just waiting for them to move into, and have their own families. Pa thought of everything, the shacks have come down bar one, there's housing for all of our children's children. He thought of everybody well in advance, then one day we will move into the retirement homes and our children will take over the houses and the running of the ranch. Your Stevie and our Bradley remind me so much of you and I. The way they play together, the bond they have formed.'

'I think they will be buddies for life, and support each other forever, I hope they don't get married to each other,' said Steve

'But our time and day will come when we move into the retirement home and put our feet up, just like the seniors that passed, Mr Matsuda, Ching-Ching Father, Ma and Pa, Bob, Pauline, Ted, Bill, Baby Virginia. We will fill their places, Daniel will still be up at the top, followed by Mr Pullman (Paul and his wife) Virginia, Jimmy, next to Maria and Georgia, Molly and Andy will take Ma and Pa's old home. Next to them will be Dianna and Alan, then me and Suzie, next to us Helen and Steve, just like it's always been. Hopefully we can all just grow old together, and have great times ahead just like the seniors before us, as we will become the new seniors, watching the new generation take over. We will steer them in the right direction just like Ma and Pa did for us.'

'Yep then we just die,' said Steve.

'Shut up,' the group told him. 'We don't ever want to think about that.'

'Why not?' said Steve. 'It's a fact of life, we are all going to die one day. Who do you think will be first out of us four?'

'You,' Brad said, 'if you don't shut up.'

'Like all life time ticked away. People got older, the kids grew up. Just like Pa predicted, relationships between the children started to form, love started to blossom, when you think of the possibilities, Matt, Sue Chang-Chang, Little Ma and Pa, Janet, Ann, Mandy, Bradley, Steven, Suzanne, Molly, Alan, Steve, Helena, Suzie, Brad, Jackson, Helen, Jessie, Wayne,

Jamie, Lucky, Brenda, Too, Ginny, Jim, Tyler, Clifton, Kelsey, Jay, Jay, Free, Fortuna, Juan, Paul Isaac, Archie Isaiah, George, and George, Georgia, Peter, Paula, Billy, Graham, Cindy, Johnny, Michael, Brandon, Robert, Mary, Joe, Theresa, Julian, Paul, Christopher, Isabelle, I'm sure I've missed some, plus all the new children coming to the orphanage, I think that takes care of the next generation's generation, I just wish I could be here to see who ends up with who.'

'Me too.'

They say life is like a roller coaster, so many ups and downs, twists and turns, highs and lows. The ranch experienced it's fair share, none more so on the night Steve passed away. He'd been feeling a bit weak the last couple of days, tired, loss of appetite. Helen was very concerned, and ran a few tests. Doctor was called, he ran a few tests prescribed some pills for him, called Helen to one side and said, 'I think it maybe his heart, it's racing. I recommend bed rest and I'll come back and see him tomorrow.'

Steve kept saying, 'I'm fine, a goodnight kip and I'll be back to my old self tomorrow. Don't fuss.'

But Helen was worried. She sent for Brad.

'How you doing, buddy, Brad said.

'Just a bit off colour,' Steve said, 'a slice of apple pie will put me right well.'

'I want you to take it easy,' said Brad, plenty of rest.

'OK, buddy,' said Steve. Steve slept most of the day. Helen and Brad never left his side, late afternoon, Steve awoke and seemed a bit more perky. Helen made him some soup.

'I'm only eating this if I can have a slice of apple pie for pudding.'

'I'll get it arranged,' said Helen, and left to get it arranged.

'Well, buddy,' said Brad, 'you and I have been on quite a journey.'

'Yeah and now we're goddamned old,' said Steve.

'But look at our achievements,' said Brad. 'We went through a war together, travelled across the country.'

'Yeah,' said Steve. 'Wagons roll.'

'Wagons roll,' said Brad.

'We both found love with two exceptional women, have amazing children and families, please tell Helen I love her.'

'She knows, buddy, she knows. Any case you tell her yourself.'

'I will,' said Steve, 'I will as soon as she gets back.'

'Good,' said Brad, 'I think you and I have had an amazing life together. You're the best buddy a man could ever have had.'

'You too, buddy. I wouldn't have wanted to miss this journey for the world, you've been more than a buddy to me, a friend, family, neighbour, confidant, adviser. I love you buddy and thank you for being my best buddy.'

'I love you too, buddy, this journey would not have been the same without you.'

Just then Helen returned.

Helen put the soup and pie on the table. Steve said, 'Get into bed with me, darling, i want to hold you.'

Brad said, 'Do you want me to leave?'

'No,' said Steve, 'get in the other side. I want you next to me.'

They both got into the bed and each one held his hand. 'I've told Brad how much I love him, now I need to tell you, Helen, how much I love you. You my darling have been my heart, my soul, my everything. I've loved you from the moment I saw you in the water, every day and in every way my love for you has grown stronger and stronger. You've given me the most wonderful children. I'm so proud of our children, and love you and them very much. If I have to leave you I'm so sorry I couldn't stay around any longer. Promise, Brad, always look after Helen and my family.'

Brad squeezed his hand, 'I promise, buddy, it goes without saying.'

'And Helen, promise me you'll look after Brad.'

Helen squeezed his hand. 'I promise,' she said, 'now let's have a bite of that pie.'

Steve took a bit. 'Mmmm!' he said, 'absolutely delicious.' He swallowed it down, he took a second bite, then his body went completely rigid and stiff, then collapsed down onto the bed. They both knew without saying a word to each other that Steve had passed away. Helen kissed his forehead and so did Brad, as the tears rolled down.

Their just stayed in bed with Steve, holding each of his hands, after a while Brad spoke first, fighting back the tears. He said, 'Do you remember the first time we met, buddy, we'd just come off the battlefield together you sat next to me on a log, with our cans of tucker. I couldn't eat all of mine, and you asked me if you could have my leftovers. Well buddy I'd give anything to have you back.'

Helen spoke, 'Do you remember, Steve, our very first dance and kiss? I knew from that moment you were the man for me, someone I wanted to spend the rest of my life with. Every day, you made me smile and we always told each other every day how much we loved each other. I'm going to miss you so much, so will so many and your children, and friends, your smile and sense of humour light the place up and made people's day.'

Helen and Brad lay there for hours just holding Steve's hand and talking to him about their lives together, funny stories, how he fainted when Helen gave birth, and how he was loved by so many, and would never be forgotten. The hours just ticked by. Eventually they got out of the bed, pulled the white sheet over Steve's head and kissed it for the very last time. Brad and Helen hugged and cried together. Brad said, 'I'll get Father in the morning. Let him stay one last night in his home. We'll gather up all of the children, you can all stay with us tonight or for however long you want to.'

They did just that, they all went into Brad's house. He sat everybody around including his own children and Suzie, and relayed the sad news about their father, and uncle to his own children, after the initial outbreak of emotion and shock, tears and hysteria, Brad and Helen began to tell Steve's life story, hoping that everybody in that room would never forget Steve. The families stayed up all night talking and crying, Father came in the morning, with his blessings, and arranged for Steve to be put into an open-top coffin. The families wanted to say their last goodbyes to their father, uncle and friend. Word soon spread around the ranch, bouquets, single flowers were left outside the house, a horse-drawn carriage was arranged to collect the coffin and take it down to the church. The road to the church and inside the church was packed. Steve was a very loved man and respected in his lifetime. He'd helped so many others. Now they all wanted to pay their last respects to a great man. Daniel had placed an amazing sketch of Steve inside the church along with all the others they'd lost over the years. Brad and Helen spoke the final words in the church before he was buried in the church yard. People wore black armbands for a whole week of mourning. Brad, Helen and the children and the community knew that life without Steve on the ranch would never be the same.

The First World War broke out in Europe. Brad worried about his children and the younger men on the ranch going to war, but they were all seen as essential key workers to the war effort, as well as the country needing guns, weapons, bullets, they also needed food and supplies. It pleased Brad that some of the food the ranch supplied reached the troops far away in a different country. Pa's old business premises were converted and added to, as an ammunition factory producing weapons and machinery for war. The security was very strict. Those working there were not allowed to talk to anyone about what went on there, many of the people at the ranch did shifts there for the war effort. It also increased sales to the ranch.

The men and women on the ranch kept their hobbies going. One day Brad was called to the orphanage garden. They had taken the original wagons Brad and Steve had travelled across America in and arrived at the ranch. They had repaired the wood, weatherised it, fixed it to the floor. There was a wooden statue of Brad in the front wagon holding the reins, and behind was Steve's statue sitting holding the reins. It was a play area for the children, also a history lesson for the children to know who and where it all started. There was an empty seat alongside each statue, where you could sit, and pretend you were riding along with Brad or Steve on their journey to the ranch. On each side of each wagon was printed 'wagons roll'. Brad couldn't resist getting up alongside himself, after pictures were taken he stood up and shouted 'Wagons roll.' They all shouted back 'wagons roll.' He then did the same to the second wagon putting his arm around the statue of Steve.

He kissed it and said, 'I miss you so much, buddy.' Then he stood up and shouted wagons roll for the very last time in his life. Back came wagons roll. He congratulated everybody involved in the masterpiece. He said, 'It's a great tribute to our past and present.' Huge clap and cheering.

Again the years ticked by, marriages took place, new children were born, christenings and unfortunately funerals, more statues appeared on the site, which always made Brad laugh and smile and brought back so many memories of the past. A few stood out for him, the one of himself leaning on a post holding a sign saying welcome to Bradville, the wooden statue of Father in the church, the one of Helen and Ellis in the clinic, Cliff on a horse, George with a hammer in his hand hammering the anvil, Andy sitting with a saw. His favourite was Mr Matsuda and Ching-Ching, sitting at a round table, playing one of their board games, you could sit either side of them, which Brad often did. They had a massive celebration on the ranch when Brad reached his ninetieth birthday, born 7 August 1853 at 7.30 PM. it was now 1943, the Second World War had broken out in Europe. Brad thought to himself would man never learn war is not the way to settle disputes? So many good men and women were lost too early in life. Again, there was more demand on the ranch for food and supplies, more hours were spent working at the ammunitions factory,

One afternoon he asked his son Bradley and Steve's son Stevie – who also became best of buddies, it reminded Brad so much of his friendship with Steve, they had the same banter he and Steve had – would they join him with a walk around the ranch. They were both only too pleased to. Brad used a walking stick, the same one Pa had used later in life, they first went to Bradville, which now was a thriving town, with more shops added over the years, the old jail house, the restaurant, they went across to the school, looked at all the sketches on the wall. 'Close your eyes,' Brad said, 'and listen. Can you here the laughter in the children? Saying their A, B, C, one, two, three.'

'Yes, Pa, we can.'

They went into the church, looked at the sketches on the walls, Chief, Baby Virginia, Bill, Ma, Pa, Steve. So many good good people.

'Close your eyes, can you hear the singing voices? This is where I married your mother, and your parents were married here, Stevie. This is where you were both christened.'

They went out of the back door. 'Look at so many crosses a passing of time, that is why you must live for this moment in time.' Brad, Bradley and Stevie knelt at the crosses and said prayers. On the way out they all kissed and patted the Father statue. They stood and looked at all the cattle, horses, sheep chicken pens. 'We've come such a long way,' said Brad, 'over to this clinic, you were both born here. This is where Steve and I fainted, and cried for joy at our first born.'

They went up to the last remaining shack and went in. 'So many memories,' Brad said, 'this is where our path and journey of life started.' They walked past Chief's wood pile the tables outside the canteen. Brad did a little twirl of dancing around with his eyes closed. 'Can you hear the laughter, the music, the dancing? I can, as though it was only yesterday. The meals, food time, orders of the day, the announcements, parties, barbecues, the meat cooking, the smell of the food coming out of the canteen.'

They went past Bill's bell and Brad gave it one big last clang. They went up through the orchard, allotment', George's blacksmith, Andy's wood saw mill, the big house, past the new houses behind, past the three lake houses. They stopped at the lake, and told them all about the boat races, the three-legged race, egg and spoon race. He pointed to the orphanage that had been filled and refilled over the years. Mr Pullman and his family and the contributions they had made over the years and still do. The retirement shacks that have had the senior citizens retire to over the years sitting outside laughing and talking. 'Close your eyes. I can hear Mr Matsuda, Ching-Ching, Ma, Pa, Steve all laughing and enjoying themselves, plus a piece of Ma's apple pie.'

'Are you alright, Pa,' said Bradley.

'I'm fine, son,' he said, 'just reliving what wonderful people lived here and made this place what it is to this day. We've all steered the ship to this point. Now we're all handing it over to you two, to guide the ship in your lifetime and beyond. Do you know how proud of you I am, and your brothers and sisters and how much we all love you? And know you will always do the right thing for everyone. If in doubt hold grandfather's pocket watch, talk to him. He'll always guide you right. He was a lovely, kind man, supported always by lovely Ma. Well thank you boys for your time, I've really enjoyed your company. Take care, God bless. I love you both,' and he hugged them both. 'I'm a bit tired now after our long walk. I might go and have a nap.'

'Thank you, Pa,' said Bradley. 'We love you too. We'll never forget our family past, nor will our future generations. Our stories will be passed on for generations to come.'

'Yeah,' said Stevie, 'Just like planting an acorn and watching it grow into an oak tree.'

'Just like your pa,' laughed Brad. 'Just out of interest do you like apple pie?'

'Yeah,' said Stevie, 'I love it. It's my favourite.'

'Thought so,' said Brad. 'Goodnight boys, love you.'

'Goodnight, Pa,' said Bradley. 'I'll come and see you first thing tomorrow morning and we'll go fishing.'

'Alright, son,' said Brad. 'Goodnight.'

'Goodnight, Pa.'

'Goodnight, Uncle,' said Stevie.

'Goodnight, God bless you,' said Brad.

They waved to each other as they went their separate ways. Brad entered the retirement hut, put the stick on the table. In his left hand he held Pa's gold watch, in his right hand one of Ma's golden necklaces. He lay on the bed, and drifted into sleep, but he could hear voices talking to him, Alan and Molly calling him from the old tree house.

He heard Ma's and Pa's voice saying come on son we've been waiting for you to join us. Molly, Alan, Father, Mr Matsuda, Ching-Ching and many other voices of the past all mixed up. Pauline and Bill together, Baby Virginia, then he saw Steve's face very clearly, holding his hand out, saying come on buddy, let me give you a hand, I've missed you.

'I'm ready, Lord,' Brad shouted out. 'I'm ready, thank you for a wonderful life, if you want me to go around again I will. It's been amazing, God bless you all, amen.' Brad slipped away.

Bradley found his Pa the next morning still holding the watch and necklace in his hands. Over a thousand people attended Brad's funeral. They lowered the flag on the orphanage to half mast. Wherever there was a statue of Brad flowers appeared, at his home, in the church. Brad had touched so many people's lives, he was the most kind, honest, loyal, fair man they had ever met, and probably would ever meet, a real gentleman. His story would be told over and over again for years to come, and finally he was laid next to his beloved family, friends and Steve.

Bradley and Stevie were talking. 'Our mas and pas and families have an incredible history. They helped and touched so many lives, changed their lives for the better, put this place on the map, and the surrounding area around the ranch. They brought happiness, wealth, prosperity. They started a dynasty, that has grown and prospered to this day, with the future secured. All the different children they helped and gave a future to, love, new families, children, babies, christenings, and eventually a resting place in the church they had all built. A school that educated so many, drawing, sketches, statues we can all look at. Words written down of their lives that we can all read and repeat to others. They truly were an amazing group of people, and I think on this day every year we should have a 'Brad's family day', a bit like a thanksgiving day, and remember them and celebrate their lives.'

'Awesome idea,' said Stevie. 'Shall we go and get some apple pie?'

'Good idea,' said Bradley, and they walked away with their arms around each other, just like their pas did.

The End